ORIENTAL VAGABONDS

A Tale of a Far East Tramp

Richard Regan

A catalogue record for this
book is available from the
National Library of Australia

NATIONAL
LIBRARY
OF AUSTRALIA

ISBN: 9781980845720

orientalvagabonds@ozemail.com.au

CHAPTER ONE

A large fly landed on my forearm. I watched it pick its way through the dense thicket of dark hairs sprouting through the blue tattooed anchor. There was a rooster on the other forearm. Occasionally I was asked about that, why a sailor would have a rooster tattooed on his right forearm. They had obviously never heard the old saying, "Cock on the right, never lost a fight." There were some had to learn the hard way.

The fly paused its crawling to suck at the beads of sweat oozing from my skin. I could feel them trickling down my chest, and there were damp patches under the armpits of my blue singlet. I flicked the fly away. It was only nine a.m., but already the scorching heat of the late summer Sydney day had penetrated the tiny steel box of the ship's office; the bulkhead mounted fan merely stirring the already hot and humid air, ruffling the stack of papers on the desk. The Customs Declaration, Crew List, Health Declaration, and other bureaucratic bumf, with the ink scarcely dry from the assorted stamps and signatures of the Australian port officials.

Whisking aside the curtain that separated the office from the passageway, the steward bustled in bearing a tea tray. He was a compact, dark brown man, with grizzled hair and a piratical leather patch covering his left eye. His white steward's jacket, grey from frequent washing in coal dust tainted water, almost matched his checkered trousers. Worn leather sandals encased his feet.

"Coffee, sahib?" He placed a battered silver coffee pot on the desk together with two cups.

"Thank you, Da Silva."

A native of the Portuguese colony of Goa in southern India, he nodded in acknowledgment and slipped out through the curtain. I filled the cup with the hot, strong coffee; pure Javanese grown arabica, dark roasted the way I liked it, and took an appreciative sip, feeling the reviving effects of the caffeine despite the stifling heat. The fly settled on the desk and I flicked it away with my hand. It rose lazily, buzzing in disturbed irritation, before landing on a silver framed photograph of a young couple. The man was tall and slim, wearing the uniform of a Royal Navy Commander, cap jammed onto his head at a jaunty angle, medal ribbons on his chest, a broad smile on his tanned face which was half turned towards the woman at his side. Almost as tall, with ash-blonde wavy hair, her pale linen dress accentuating her lithe, athletic body, she was holding the commander's hand and gazing lovingly up at him. Together they made the image of the perfect, happy couple. For a fleeting moment I felt a pang of jealousy.

Apart from the whirring of the electric fan and the rustling paperwork, the office was quiet, but I knew that was unlikely to last. And, sure enough, I had only managed a second mouthful of coffee before another hand whisked the curtain aside to admit the distinguished looking Peter Lowther, my chief mate, a complicated man to whom life had already delivered more than his fair share of fortune and disaster. He was in uniform whites with three gold stripes on the shoulder straps, making an odd contrast with my blue singlet and dungarees. But there were dark circles under his eyes, and I could smell the gin on his breath.

"Well, Peter, has the surveyor finished his inspection of the holds, are we ready to load?"

"Coal dust!" snorted Lowther. "He says there's coal dust in number four hold. He's very kindly given us a couple of hours to clean it up before he comes back for a second inspection."

I waved him to towards a chair and nodded in the direction of the coffee pot. There was no coal dust in the hold, or at least there shouldn't have been after our last cargo of jute bales. It was hard enough at the best of times to keep a coal burning tramp steamer free of coal dust, but the holds had been sealed since the crew had last swept them clean. I wouldn't have breakfasted off their floor plates, but they were more than acceptable for the wheat we were to load. The Glebe Island grain terminal was only waiting for the surveyor's clearance before starting up its conveyors, and now we were holding them up. I could order the crew back down into the hold for another sweep, but Lowther and I were not new to this game.

"You've told the watchman where to find you?"

"Yes. I saw the surveyor go down the gangway. There were a couple of shady looking characters lurking about on the quay that he had a word with before he disappeared."

"Shouldn't have too long to wait then." I drained my coffee and pushed back my chair. Lowther also stood, and we exchanged places. I was about to sit in his vacated seat in front of the desk, when there was another sharp rap of hard knuckles on the door frame. I remained standing.

"Come in," said Lowther.

The two men who pushed their way past the curtain and crowded into the office looked like dock workers, wharfies as they were called in Sydney. They were similarly dressed in worn, stained trousers and jackets that might have originally been dark blue or black, or even brown, but were now a dusty faded mottle. Sweat stained, battered fedoras were jammed rakishly down on their heads, shading their eyes. The smaller of the two, with a swarthy, weasel shaped face, was obviously the leader. He sat down uninvited and grinned, revealing a crenelation of stained, broken teeth.

"G'day Mister Chief Mate, mind if we have a word?"

The minder, burly and beetle browed with a squashed nose and cauliflower ears, took station behind him. With my tattoos, blue singlet and dungarees, I was just another seaman, and neither paid me any attention. Which was fine by me as it gave me time to relish their appearance, which reminded me of a couple of low life thugs from one of the Dashiell Hammett crime thrillers on my bookshelf. Lowther stared at them impassively.

"What do you want?"

"Now don't be like that Chief," replied Weasel Face. "We're 'ere to 'elp ya."

"And what help do I need from you?"

"Seems you've a spot of cleaning to do. Some coal dust in number four 'old, as the surveyor has found. You can't start loading until the terminal is 'appy the 'olds is spotless. And cleaning ships' 'olds is the p'erogative of me members, the Painters and Dockers."

"And you just happened to be come board, without my permission I note, having heard the result of the surveyor's inspection. Tell me why I shouldn't have you thrown down the gangway for trespassing?"

"Wouldn't do that if I was you, Chief. You might upset our members. Sensitive they are to threats of violence. We don't want no trouble, and you want to get your ship loaded and away again as soon as possible. You don't want a bit of coal dust holding things up, and we can have that cleaned away in a jiffy. Just say the word and I'll get a gang aboard."

Lowther reached for the coffee pot and slowly topped up his cup. Same old Sydney waterfront, I thought. Always some shoreside chancers trying to pull the wool over the eyes of the unwary ship's mate. There was nothing to oblige us to take this offer seriously, our own crew could do the work, but the Painters and Dockers were notorious as a law unto themselves, and a refusal could sometimes have very unpleasant consequences. Fortunately, we were no strangers to Sydney, and these two jokers were in for a surprise. They might have thought they had come aboard unnoticed, but the crew were used to the possibility of unwelcome visitors, and even an unattended gangway didn't mean that vigilant eyes were not on watch. The two men were starting to fidget, waiting for an answer. It was time to intervene.

"Any trouble, Mister Mate?"

Weasel Face glanced round, surprised to find me still standing in the corner. The minder turned on his heel and took a menacing step towards me, until our chests were almost touching.

"Suggest you call your dog off Chief," said Weasel Face, and then, turning his rat-like eyes in my direction, "This is a private conversation chum, so why don't you 'op it. I'm sure Tiny would be 'appy to assist you through the door if you can't find it on your own."

I was almost hoping that Tiny would take a swing at me. I was conceding height and weight, but I could see he would be slow and clumsy.

"There are no private conversations in MY ship," I thundered. "And while you're aboard you'll call me Captain. And you," I jabbed a finger into Tiny's chest, "if you want to start something go right ahead. But I'll guarantee you I'll finish it. A couple of trespassers frogmarched down the gangway. Who are the police going to believe? The captain of the ship that threw them off, or a couple of bums like you."

Weasel Face held up a pacifying hand. "Keep your shirt on, Captain. I didn't mean no offence. You don't look like no captain I've ever seen. We was only 'aving a quiet word with your chief mate about a small cleaning job for our members."

"Trying to threaten us more like, into paying you to do something we're perfectly able to do ourselves. And I expect you stood over the surveyor in order to force him to say that one of our holds isn't clean enough for grain. I wasn't born yesterday, mister. I know every dirty trick in the book. Hell, I wrote some of them." I hoped the raised voice and the wild-eyed glare were sufficiently convincing. "No one, and I mean NO ONE, comes aboard my ship and threatens ME. What do you think Peter? Shall I call the crew? Wicked bunch of Chinese cutthroats they are. You two would be lucky to get ashore with your skins intact."

The loud, angry words reverberated off the steel bulkheads. Weasel Face had paled beneath his tan, and Tiny stood rooted to the spot, but I was secretly impressed that neither flinched, nor made to leave. These were still dangerous men, it was best not to push them too far. It was Lowther's turn.

"I'm sure we can come to a reasonable compromise, Captain," he said, intervening smoothly. "The surveyor says we've some coal dust to sweep up. The crew have more than enough to do, but I'm sure any self-respecting gang of cleaners would feel embarrassed being dragged down here for such a small job. Gentlemen, what if I was to suggest a donation to your widows and orphans' fund, and in return you let our crew clean-up for the surveyor." Lowther leaned over to Weasel Face and whispered a number into his ear.

Ten minutes later, with the two union men safely ashore, their stomachs warmed by several large drams and their pockets bulging with bottles of aged scotch and cartons of cigarettes, we sat down to enjoy the last of the coffee, into which Lowther poured a fortifying nip of gin.

"Works every time, Peter," I said. "The crazy captain puts the fear of God into them, and the cool headed chief mate suggests a deal that keeps everyone happy. But the Painters and Dockers are no joke, they're tied up in every scam and piece of skulduggery that goes down in this port. It goes against the grain, if you'll excuse the pun, but it's a small price to pay to know we won't find dead cats and dogs, or worse, buried in the cargo, or get a call from the police to identify one of our crew at the local morgue. Now I suggest you call that surveyor back, the news will have reached him by now. Let me know if anything else happens to delay loading."

I was sure nothing would, but I was going to be disappointed if I expected the rest of our stay in Sydney to be trouble free.

* * *

"It's short notice, Captain Rowden, and the wages you tramp steamers pay are hardly likely to attract good men. What happened to your third mate anyway?"

It was a good question, and one to which I did not have much of an answer. "Jumped ship," I replied, frowning with irritation. "Probably ran off with a girl, or gone up country to make his fortune digging for gold."

Or just looking for a better future than the underpaid, overworked, and insecure life of the junior tramp steamer mate. Personally, I was not sorry to see the back of the barely competent, dour and surly Scot who had cleared out during our first night alongside. But if we were not to sail short-handed, I had just over twelve hours to find a replacement. Which is why I was sitting in the office of the Sydney branch secretary of the Merchant Service Guild, the union that looked after the interests of ships' officers, hoping he might have the names of some men looking for a third mate's berth. There were usually more qualified men available than there were berths to fill, and I had sailed in ships where all the officers and half the seamen had master's tickets. But times had changed, and if I drew a blank here I was faced with the prospect of trudging the length of Sussex and Kent Streets, trying the pubs and flea-pit haunts of unemployed seamen.

The Guild secretary laughed. He looked harassed and tired, but sympathetic. "He'll be lucky, not much gold left now. But there's always one ready to listen to any old cock and bull about a lost reef. He'll probably end up in some abandoned working, robbed of his life savings." He glanced at the wall clock. "Listen Captain, it's coming up to noon, the sun's well over the yardarm. Why don't I shout you a beer at the Royal George. There's usually one or two fellows there from the ships in Darling Harbour. Perhaps they'll know of a third mate looking for a berth."

It was cooler under the fans in the bar of the hotel. It was only a short walk along Sussex Street from the Guild's office, but in my shore-going suit I was suffering in the fiery noonday heat. I gratefully removed my hat and mopped my brow with a large checkered handkerchief. It was lunchtime, and as a refuge for hot, thirsty men, the pub was doing a brisk trade. The Guild secretary slid some coins onto the zinc counter and returned with two large, frosted glasses of ice-cold beer.

My thirst slaked by the cooling liquid, I scanned the crowd thronging the bar. The majority were office workers with soft hands and soft bodies, unsuited to the unending grind of hard work and sparse food that was the lot of the merchant seaman. Sydney was a major port, its quays and piers lined with ships. But it was also a magnet for the disgruntled looking for the chance of an easier life ashore. The only sure way to fill a vacant berth was to slip a few pounds to the crimps, unscrupulous owners of shady drinking dens from where a drunken seaman, blowing his wages on beer and women, was likely to wake up at sea with a hangover, empty pockets and the prospect of a long voyage. It was illegal, but I had used them myself more than once in the boisterous, lawless ports of the American west coast. But in Sydney? Unlikely.

The arrival of a freshly charged glass seized my attention, and I was savouring its hoppy bite when the Guild secretary nudged me with his elbow. "Do you see that young fellow seated in the corner, the one with the ginger hair and freckles?"

"And the black eye, if I'm not mistaken. Looks like he's been dragged out of a barroom brawl."

"He probably has. His name's McGrath, James McGrath. Youngest son of a sheep station owner from New England. Fancies himself as a fighter. A makeshift ring in an empty warehouse, or a circle of rope in a quiet back street. Plenty of hotheads keen to pay a couple of bob to watch a stoush, and stake their beer money on the outcome.

"Takes on all comers?" I said.

"Yeah, backs himself and wins, mostly. But he'll come a cropper one day. Sooner or later he'll pick on someone who really does know how to fight, that'll wipe the cheeky grin off his face."

I studied the young man who sat at a corner table engaged in conversation with several other youths. Or rather, the other men talked while McGrath sipped at a small beer. Under the thatch of hair was a pair of wide set, pale blue eyes, a snub nose, freckled face and a red lipped mouth that periodically creased into a puckish grin. A shining black eye spoiled the impish nature of the face, and closer inspection revealed reddened swelling around the cheekbones and nose. His face had certainly taken a hammering. I lowered my gaze towards the hands resting on the table. They were large and powerful, the knuckles cut and bruised.

"He looks like he can handle himself in a fight, and do a hard day's work, but a farmer's son is no use to me. If I needed an ordinary seaman, maybe. But it's a man with a second mate's ticket I need."

"Well it might be your lucky day, Captain. McGrath does have a second mate's ticket, hardly used though. Signed on for his first trip as third mate with the ink barely dry on it, fortunate to get a berth with a local company. And earned himself a D.R. for fighting. No one's taken him on since then. So, if you're desperate?"

"Declined to report, eh? Well he wouldn't be the first. Where'd he serve his time?"

"In square-riggers. Seems they taught him how to hand, reef and steer, but not much else, other than how to use his fists."

"He'd be a rarity these days," I said. "An officer who served his apprenticeship in sail. Call him over, I'd like to hear what he has to say for himself."

The Guild secretary slipped off his stool and picked his way between the drinkers. McGrath's face lit up with interest at the news that a captain wished to speak with him, and as he followed the Guild secretary to our table I noted the broad shouldered, muscular frame, and the intelligent blue eyes that quizzically regarded me as he took the seat opposite. But there was wariness in those eyes too. I nodded in the direction of the bar, and the branch secretary obliged, returning with a glass of beer that he placed in front of the young man.

"I'll have to slip him a few bob to square things away," I thought, before turning to McGrath. "Your Guild secretary tells me you've a second mate's ticket and no berth. Why is that?"

I watched McGrath's pale blue eyes sizing me up, as if wondering how much he could, or should, embroider the truth.

"Last Captain I served with didn't approve of fighting. Signed me off with a D.R. Did me a lousy turn, no one will sign me on as third mate."

"From what I hear you seem to enjoy fighting. Perhaps your captain had a point?"

"Yeah, he was probably right. Officers and gentlemen, that's what he expected us to be. But there weren't any gentlemen in the forecastle, and little discipline any-where in that ship. I put up with the lip as long as I could. When one of the ringleaders pushed his luck too far, I dragged him up onto a hatch lid in full view of the crowd and beat the shit out him. He had it coming. But the old man — sorry, the captain — saw it and the man lodged a complaint. I thought the mate would back me up, but he was scared of the crowd. Paid me off as soon as we got back to Sydney. And here I am. If I can't get a third mate's berth soon I'll have to ship out as a seaman."

I contemplated the battered face and the rebellious tone. "Don't you normally address a senior officer as sir?"

A red flush spread upward from McGrath's neck, and his lips compressed into a hard, white line. I glanced down at the tabletop and saw his fists clenched tight, straining the bruised and split skin. Then the hands relaxed, the blue eyes twinkled and the mouth creased into a sheepish grin. "Sorry, Captain, sir. I was forgetting my manners there. And thanks for the beer, after last night I've a mouth like a dead emu's ... well, you know what I mean."

"I hear you served your apprenticeship in sail. Tell me about it?"

"That's right, sir. In the *Garthpool*, owned by Marine Navigation."

I'd heard of her, one of the last square-riggers sailing under the Red Ensign, eking out a living in the grain trade between Australia and Europe. "Four masted barque, steel hulled, Captain Thompson?"

"Yes, sir. He was very good with the apprentices, taught us all to navigate. I doubt if I'd have passed my ticket without him."

"There's few, these days, would envy your apprenticeship in square-riggers. But there was something unusual about *Garthpool*. Jubilee rigged if I recall?"

"That's right, sir." I was pleased to hear the surprise in McGrath's voice. He was not the only one who had seen service in sail. "No royals or skysails above the t'gallants."

"Designed to be sailed with fewer hands. Harder work for you apprentices though. I take it Captain Thompson didn't give you a D.R.?"

"No, sir. Not much trouble aboard either. If two men had a beef about something then the outcome of a fair fight, one of the mates acting as timekeeper, watch in one hand, belaying pin in the other, usually settled it. But woe betide the man who couldn't stand his watch afterwards."

Despite his last captain's D.R., and the evidence of his hot temper, I was warming to young McGrath. Any man who could thrive on four years in a square-rigger, beating around Cape Horn in winter and competing with the likes of *Passat* and *Pamir* for the fastest passage of the year, had to know something about seamanship and hard work. I was also unlikely to find anyone else. And if I was wrong? Well Singapore was only three weeks away and I'd gladly throw him ashore myself.

"Well then, Mr McGrath. My last third mate jumped ship yesterday and I'm sailing just after midnight. If you can join this afternoon ... well I'm prepared to overlook your D.R. But if you step out of line your backside won't touch the gangway. So, can you be ready to sign on by then?"

McGrath's eyes lit up with unfeigned surprise, and there was gratitude in his voice. "Too right I can ... I mean, yes of course, sir."

"Good, well I can't promise you a crack liner, she's only a coal burning tramp from the war years, but she's seaworthy and the food's better than you'll have eaten in your square riggers."

"Thank you, sir. I won't let you down."

"See that you don't. Now, go and round up your dunnage. If you need anything, leave it for Singapore where you can pick it up cheaper than here. The ship's called *Oriental Venture* and she's alongside at Glebe Island. Report on board before eight p.m. The chief mate's name is Mr Lowther, I'll tell him to expect you. Strictly speaking, you should call him 'My Lord' as he's the son of an Earl, but Mr Lowther is quite sufficient. Any questions?"

"No, sir. And thank you, sir. I'll be on board as soon as I can." He stuck out a hand and I shook it, enjoying the grimace as I squeezed his bruised knuckles. Then he reached for the glass, drained the last of the beer, and headed towards the door.

"I hope you don't come to regret that, Captain," said the Guild secretary.

"I thought that's what you wanted?" I said, smiling. "I'll bet he's been pestering you for days to find him a berth."

He grinned ruefully. "You're right, Captain, he has. And you've done me a favour by getting him off my books. I just hope he won't cause you any trouble."

My smile hardened. "We're not long on officers and gentlemen in *Oriental Venture*. Apart from the mate, that is. And I like a man who knows how to handle himself in a tight corner. It's a tough part of the world, the China coast. He won't have any trouble from the crew. Bunch of Chinese cutthroats they are. But they do what the mate and I tell them. Some of the stokers are a bit rowdy, but, well we have our ways. No, all young McGrath has to worry about is me. If he obeys orders and does his job then he'll be fine. If not? We'll a D.R. will be the least of his worries." I reached into my pocket for some coins.

The Guild secretary held up his hand. "No, Captain, it's on me. You did me a favour." He held out his hand. "Good luck and have a safe voyage."

* * *

So far, so normal.

I had dealt with the petty extortion of the Painters and Dockers, and found what I hoped would turn out to be a useful replacement third mate. Loading was almost complete and, despite the lure of Sydney's fleshpots, there had been little trouble. Most of the Chinese seamen were too careful of their wages to waste them in pubs and brothels. The Somali stokers, being Muslims, did not touch alcohol, but few ventured ashore as Australia was not exactly welcoming towards coloured men. A couple of the younger engineers had returned visibly worse for wear after an evening at The Rocks, although I suspected some of the scrapes and bruises had been inflicted by the local coppers instead of pressing charges. Lowther had divided his time, as usual, between working hours of exemplary efficiency, and, the admittedly few, off duty hours in which he sought gin-tinctured solace from the demons that continued to haunt him.

But it was the second mate, David Griffith, who nearly came to grief.

I liked Griffith and we went back aways, but he was not everyone's pint of ale. The son of a coal miner from the Rhonda Valley, he had the physique of a rugby player and the dark, brooding good looks of a matinée idol. Which meant that he should have had more than his fair share of the ladies.

But not Griffith, his preferences lay in the other direction. Which was not entirely unusual among seamen, most ships had one or two. But in a close knit mining community? Griffith would never have been accepted, and had persuaded his father to put up the surety for an apprenticeship with a Welsh shipowner. Brave decision for a lad who'd grown up amongst the slag heaps and mountains of South Wales; but a good one as he'd done well, and was a good officer, most of the time.

It was hard enough at the best of times, to live for months on end cooped up in a small steamer with a bunch of men to whom, in other circumstances, he wouldn't give the time of day. But to have to hide the truth about himself. I guess we all did that to one extent or another, but it was especially hard for Griffith to suffer the crude jokes and insults from men for whom homosexuality was as much a threat, as a source of humour. And so, sometimes, the pressure valve burst. If a man was picked on often enough he either went down, or learned how to fight. In grimy lanes between the rows of miners' cottages, behind dingy dockside pubs and in smoky, rum drinking dens in Asia, David Griffith had learned to fight. And to fight dirty when he had to. He never went ashore without a knife, usually some sort of switch-blade. But the less I knew about that the better.

As I had said to the Guild secretary in the Royal George, I liked a man who knew how to take care of himself. The China coast was not exactly the most law abiding tidewater. Although, officially, the authorities frowned upon some of the business that came our way, there was many a customs' officer as crooked as a dog's hind leg, happy to have his palm greased in exchange for the turn of a blind eye. And if you thought piracy had gone out of fashion after the likes of Morgan and Blackbeard got their final discharges, well you hadn't seen service in the China Sea. We'd had to repel boarders more than once. Sea Dyaks for example, who had swarmed up the side while we were anchored off a trading settlement in Borneo, ready to slit our throats if we didn't hand over money and valuables. They left empty handed, and no, they hadn't slit our throats! Men who could handle themselves were assets in my eyes, provided they didn't cause any trouble on board.

So, having just managed to find a replacement third mate, I was unlikely to take kindly to the prospect of losing my second mate.

The late afternoon of that baking hot summer's day had seen the arrival of a southerly buster, which offered welcome relief to the crew, and to the tired, sweaty, dockworkers streaming away from the White Bay wharves at the end of their shift. Lowther had given Griffith permission for a run ashore after his watch finished at four p.m., provided he was back by ten. Six hours should have been more than enough to enjoy a few beers before the pubs closed, and perhaps grab a bite at one of the local cafes — or get the muddy water off his chest if he could find another homosexual willing to dispense with extended foreplay — and be back aboard to help get the ship ready for sea.

Should have been! If I had a dollar for every time something "should have been."

It was close to eleven when Lowther caught him sneaking aboard, the right hand cuffs of his jacket and shirt soaked in blood. I should have gone to the dock gate and telephoned the police, wasn't that what any law-abiding ship's captain was expected to do? Except that in those days, out East, the law was often what you made of it with your fists, or whatever assistance came to hand; and after listening to Griffith's gabbled explanation I told him to clap a stopper over his mouth and get cleaned up. If the police arrived before we sailed then he'd have to take his chances. If not, well time and distance had a habit of putting a different perspective on things.

Still, I was keen to get underway, and at thirty minutes after midnight, our scheduled departure time, but with no sign of the pilot, I was impatiently pacing the deck of the darkened wheelhouse. The cool of the night was in sharp contrast to the heat of the previous day, and the Chinese helmsman, standing patiently at the wheel, had donned a patched and faded denim jacket in order to ward off the chill. A match flared on the bridge wing, briefly illuminating Lowther's face, and I could smell the pungent reek of his Javanese cheroot. I was about to light a cigarette of my own when I caught the welcome sound of feet climbing the ladder from the boat deck, and a Chinese seaman lead a uniformed figure into the wheelhouse.

"Sorry I'm a few minutes late, Captain, but I see the tug's here and you're already to go."

"Good morning, Mr Pilot." I tried to keep the impatience out of my voice. "Yes, we're singled up fore and aft and the tug's attached on the starboard bow."

"Very well, Captain, let go all."

"Let go all," Lowther repeated, ringing the docking telegraphs, and I followed the pilot out onto the bridge wing.

The telegraphs rang again to confirm the mooring lines had been hauled inboard, the pilot ordered the engine to slow ahead, and there was a blast of sulphury breath as the engineers opened the firebox dampers, the sudden rush of air blowing thick grey smoke from the funnel, in which red-hot sparks danced like fireflies. Through the soles of my feet, I felt the deck tremble as the giant cylinders of the reciprocating engine beat to life, and the propeller began to churn the dark, murky dock water.

Slowly, as if initially reluctant to shake herself free of the land, *Oriental Venture* nosed cautiously out of White Bay and eased past the Pyrmont finger jetties, each lined with the darkened shape of a slumbering ship. A long blast of the pilot's whistle signalled the tug's skipper to cast off the towline, and as the tug dropped astern we curved our way around Miller's Point and under the recently completed Sydney Harbour Bridge, its coat-hanger arch and massive roadway looming above us in the darkness.

As the bridge dropped astern, we slipped past the squat mid-harbour gun-battery of Fort Dennison, its sinister battlements profiled against the twinkling backdrop of the lights of Sydney Cove, while further over to starboard the reassuringly powerful silhouette of a battleship towered over the Garden Island naval base.

Increasing speed as we crossed Rose Bay, the pilot conned the ship around the darkly wooded cliffs of Bradley's Head, her wake carving a perfect white-flecked arc onto the unruffled, ink-black water, before he steadied her to cross the entrance to Middle Harbour. Then, approaching the ocean, between the ancient guardians of the narrow entrance to Port Jackson, she raised her bows to the low swell like a horse lifting its head in anticipation of the hunt. The massive black crags of North Head glided silently past to port, and to starboard Hornby Lighthouse flashed brightly at the tip of South Head.

There was a single toot from the whistle of a boat approaching from aft, and the pilot gathered up his belongings. "I think you can see your way out from here, Captain."

"Pilot cutter approaching," called Lowther from the bridge wing.

I held out my hand. "Thank you, Mr Pilot, I'll take her now. The seaman will take you down to the ladder. See you next time."

"Good night, Captain, have a pleasant voyage."

I leaned over the bridge wing, and watched until the pilot had climbed down the ladder and was safely aboard the cutter. "Steady as she goes, full ahead." I could feel the quickening beat of the propeller thrusting the ship forward into the easterly swell, and hear the tumbling rush of water, cleaved apart by the bow and foaming past her sides. It felt good to be back at sea again with a full cargo and the wind in my hair, away from the overheated, crowded streets of Sydney's dockland. I turned, hearing footsteps on the ladder from the boat deck. It was Griffith come to take over the watch.

"All secure aft, sir."

"Thank you, Second. My night orders are in the chartroom. Once we're two miles clear of the Heads the course is nor-east. Revolutions for 10 knots. The watch is yours."

"Good night, sir."

"Not quite such a good night though, is it mister?" I said, having no intention of going below until I heard his full explanation for arriving back covered in blood. "You might be in the clear for now. But there's nothing to stop the Sydney police cabling the authorities in Singapore, if they know who to look for." I pulled a packet of Senior Service out of my pocket and held it out to him. I didn't normally play the part of father confessor, but if I was going to shelter a possible killer I needed to know what risk I was running. "It sounds like a damned, hot-headed, stupid thing to have done, what were you thinking?"

He took a cigarette and lit it. In the flare of the match, his face looked pale, and the eyes were red rimmed with strain and fatigue.

"It's like I said, Captain. It was self-defence. I met someone in a pub in Rozelle, just up the hill from the docks, and we went somewhere private, for a drink."

I'd seen enough of life, and the shady fringes of society, to be able to imagine the sort of place that provided men like Griffith with a temporary refuge in which to enjoy like-minded company. He said they had left the place just before ten, Griffith to return to the ship, and the other man to his lodgings. Their way had taken them down a narrow lane. There was a street lamp on the corner, but its pale, yellow light penetrated only a few yards into the darkness. They had stopped beneath the lamp to light cigarettes. And that was when a harsh, nasal voice had called out from the shadows, "Looks like a couple of faggots if you ask me," and a grinning young tough had emerged. Griffith noted the tight fitting jacket and trousers, the bowler hat and, despite the warm evening, the choker knotted around his neck. The dark forms of two more toughs materialised out of the shadows, blocking the lane.

"We 'ate queers," the leader had snarled. "We'll teach ya to come round 'ere, ya stinking perverts."

Homosexual bashing appeared to be something of a sport in the less salubrious parts of Sydney, but odds of two to three were not bad, and I imagined Griffith felt pretty confident, until his new friend turned tail and fled into the darkness. After that, he would have been flexing his muscles in readiness, and reaching for the knife in his pocket as the three men circled their remaining prey. When the leader lunged at him, his response was instinctive. He avoided the thrust and struck back, the wicked switchblade snapping out of the handle and slicing into the man's stomach, spurting hot blood over his hand. Seeing their leader doubled over and screaming the other two shrank back. Griffith seized his chance and bolted down the narrow lane into the concealing darkness. Rounding a corner, he ducked behind a wall to listen for pursuit, but there had been nothing. And so, forcing himself to walk calmly, he continued on down the hill and back to the ship, mopping off the blood with his handkerchief, and tossing the knife into the harbour as he approached the dock. The watchman on duty at the gate paying little attention to him.

I wondered what the police were doing. Were they searching for a suspect? Had they any idea of Griffith's involvement? Or would they even conduct a search? A bunch of young hoodlums out looking for trouble, one of whom got stabbed in a brawl. The police might think he had it coming to him. But what if he was dead? Perhaps Griffith hadn't intended to kill him, but a switchblade in the guts? At best the man would need a good doctor. At worst, well it was self-defence, wasn't it? And what choice did he have against three of them, I wondered? But there were no other witnesses. That was a problem. If the remaining two swore that Griffith started it.

The lights of the northern beachside suburbs of Sydney were fading as we drew away from the coast. Griffith had finished his explanation and was leaning against the rail, a hunched, melancholy, shape merging into the darkness. I took a final drag of the cigarette and stubbed it in the sand box.

"All right," I said. "We'll say no more about it. Unless ... well, let's see what happens when we get to Singapore." I turned towards the ladder. "I'm going below. As soon as you come off watch lash that bloodstained jacket and shirt to an old shackle and chuck them over the side."

"Aye aye, sir," he mumbled, nodding his head.

I climbed down to the boat deck. I didn't feel like sleeping, and leaned against the rail listening to the water sluice past the hull, watching the wave crests paint pale highlights onto the inky darkness of the sea. It was hardly a good start to the voyage, but the old ship had known worse. Sometimes we just needed to be thankful for small mercies. It was a quiet, calm night and *Oriental Venture* was gently rolling and pitching in the long, low Pacific swell. Making a steady 10 knots, ploughing a straight nor-easterly furrow, and leaving a trail of sparkling phosphorescence in her wake.

CHAPTER TWO

Ahot and steamy morning in Singapore. The Chinese coolies were hard at work discharging the wheat, until a torrential downpour sent them scurrying for cover while the crew raced to rig tents over the open hatches. I was on deck escaping the Turkish bath conditions of my office, and saw McGrath sheltering under an awning, leaning against the bulwark and peering through the thick curtain of rain towards the godowns, only ten yards away across the wharf, but barely visible. The raindrops were like big silver shillings shattering on the concrete, their glittering shards splashing as high as a man's knees, with the roaring, rushing sound of a waterfall in spate.

The nineteen days steaming from Sydney had passed uneventfully. McGrath had proved competent. His navigation was adequate and would improve with practice. But his seamanship, the benefit of that four year apprenticeship in sail, was proving a godsend. The crew readily accepting his instruction, and the standard of rope, canvas and bright work had improved dramatically, at least as far as the limited budget of a tramp ship would allow. And, of course, there had been no reason for him to demonstrate his pugilistic skills, the scars of which had long since vanished.

I had been quite truthful telling the Guild secretary that my Chinese crew was a bunch of cutthroats. Many of them had belonged to the pirate gangs whose armed junks, operating from bases in Bias Bay to the north of Hong Kong, had preyed upon ships trading the China coast. Their blatant daylight seizure of the *Irene* back in 1927, had forced the navy to clamp down. And the Chinese trading houses, having also had enough, had offered them Hobson's choice between lawful — perhaps semi-lawful would be more accurate — employment as seamen, or being turned over to the less than tender mercy of the authorities. There were also clan ties to consider. *Oriental Venture's* owners were Chinese with, I strongly suspected, clan connections to those of the ex-pirates who now sailed under my command. Some of the things the owners expected of us were not exactly legal or safe, but as the Chinese said, once a tiger always a tiger, and having sharp and reliable claws aboard was good insurance. That was a two edged sword though. As long as I had the owners' confidence the crew would obey my orders, but if I lost it the claws might be unsheathed against me. Not that I lost sleep worrying about it, even the dragon fears the snake on its own turf, and I knew where some of the bodies were buried.

The torrential rain continued, providing some relief from the oppressive heat. I decided to join McGrath at the bulwark and take advantage of the interruption to ask how he was settling down.

"Well, Third, what do you think of steam after those four years of sail. Must seem like a picnic, eh?"

In truth, I already knew the answer. It was vastly different sailing as third mate in a steamship compared to being an apprentice in a square-rigger. There he would have endured the bone wearying routine of watch on and watch off which, even with the daily rotation of the afternoon dog-watch, meant that it was impossible to get more than four or five hours sleep a night. And even that frequently broken by calls for all hands to change sail. Now, after his four-hour watch ended at midnight, he had the luxury of a full night in his bunk until called to start again at eight the following morning. There were no dizzying climbs up swaying masts in the howling wind and freezing rain of a Cape Horn winter storm. No edging out along heaving yards a hundred feet above the sea, feet desperately pushing back against the foot rope, stomach pressed against the yard, wrestling heavy wet canvas into submission with chapped hands from which the fingernails had been ripped off. The food was also better. Despite the owners' penny pinching, our Goanese cook managed to turn out meals that were an improvement on the boiled salt meat, dried peas, and rock hard, weevil infested ship's biscuit that was the unvarying diet of the sailing ship.

"I always thought blokes in steam ships had it easy, sir," replied McGrath, with a grin that could easily be taken for insolence, but which I hoped was just his native Australian irreverence.

"Be careful what you wish for, mister," I growled. "You might not feel so cocky when it's all hands to load coal, and everything smells and tastes of coal dust. It gets in the food, in the water, in the pores of your skin until you think you're sweating and chitting coal dust. And the South China Sea's no place for the faint hearted. Uncharted reefs that'll rip the bottom open, typhoons that swallow up ships within sight of safety, and junks swarming with pirates just waiting for an unwary mate keeping a poor lookout to let them get close enough to slit our throats."

"Sorry, sir," said McGrath, the grin fading, "I didn't mean ..."

"That's okay, son, no offence taken. But take it from me, life in a tramp steamer, and especially this one, is not all beer and skittles. As you'll find out, if you can hack it." I thought about letting him in on some of the less legitimate things

16

that crossed our track, but decided against it. He'd find out soon enough, and he didn't look like the type who scared easily.

"How come you served your time in sailing ships, Third?" I continued. "I didn't think Australians had any leanings towards seafaring."

"My family owns a cattle station in northern New South Wales," he replied. "Always thought I'd be perfectly content to muster stock, marry one of the local girls, and settle down on a property of my own. But after a few rough seasons, Dad suggested I think about seeking a living elsewhere than on the land. Perhaps he thought I'd get away to university. But after a trip to Sydney, and seeing all the ships in the harbour, well maybe it was a reaction against spending my whole life in the outback, but I just wanted to see something of the world. So I told him I wanted to go to sea. He was shocked, but when he saw I was serious he took me round the offices of the shipping lines, and put up the surety when I was offered an apprenticeship."

"Some of those old sailing ship men were right hard bastards," I said. I'd sailed with a few myself, and still had the scars to prove it.

"Right enough, sir." McGrath grinned. "But they taught me to hand, reef and steer, and how to stand up for myself."

"So I've heard." It was time to explain some of the rules. "But if anyone raises a fist on board without my permission, then they'll answer to me. Is that clear, Third?"

In my version of tramp steaming there was a time and a place for fighting. Men were always going to settle grievances with their fists. I'd used mine many a time. But knife-happy Chinese, and heathen tribesman from Somalia were a volatile mix. When their blood was up I wanted them on my side.

McGrath nodded. "Yes, sir." He paused, frowning, rubbing his chin with his fingers. "Er, the chippy, says you spent a bit of time in sail yourself, sir. Is that right?"

"Is that how the shipwright spends his time?" I snapped. "Gossiping about his captain with the junior mates?"

McGrath's face flushed.

"Well, for your information, mister, I sailed in the forecastle when I was a boy. In home trade barques and schooners, just after the war."

McGrath's eyebrows jumped. "I wondered how you knew what a jubilee rig was, sir. Have you sailed with the shipwright before, then?"

He was plucky. I had to hand it to him. Not many second trip third mates would dare question their captain. Lowther thought he was too cocky, but then he had a jaundiced view of anyone who hadn't learned their trade at Dartmouth. Truth to tell, McGrath reminded me of myself at his age, except that I was a much bigger gobshite, and a troublemaker. And I had indeed sailed with Cramp, the shipwright, before; when I was chief mate in the old *Portneath*. Pig of a ship she was, built well before the war. The seamen were all crowded into the forecastle, just like in a square-rigger. A mixed crowd of Scousers and Geordies, and hard to handle. And the hardest was a Scouser called Begley, who thought he ruled the forecastle. I grinned at the memory. He only crossed me once, and learned a hard and painful lesson, that my bite's a damned sight worse than my bark. Speak loudly, and carry a large belaying pin, my first captain used to say. Advice I'd long since come to appreciate.

"Yes, Mr McGrath," I replied, putting some menace into my voice. "The chippy and I are old shipmates. And seeing as you're on such familiar terms, ask him to tell you about the *Portneath* and a seaman called Begley. And remember this, if you do the right thing by me then we'll get on just fine. If not, well Cramp can tell you what happens to those who cut across my hawse." I glared at him for effect, and was pleased to see a slight shiver ripple through his sturdy frame. "Now, the rain appears to have stopped, so I'd be grateful if you'd get the hatch tents off, and chase the dockers back to work."

I left him to it and went back to my office where the paperwork had not completed itself, and where there was a note from Lowther informing me that we would shortly be blessed by a visit from the owners' Singapore manager, with news of our next voyage.

* * *

"If you can call at Wewak, Captain, I can get cargo of mining and drilling equipment," said Poh Ling Sing, the manager of Anglo Oriental's Singapore office. Short, plump and with a moon shaped face, he was impeccably dressed in a light grey, tropical weight suit with a white shirt and a grey silk tie, held in place by a gold pin encrusted with a large pearl. His feet were clad in white buckskin shoes, and his Panama hat lay on the sideboard. He was sitting in one of the battered armchairs in my day cabin, behind the chartroom. I sat opposite him in the other, while Lowther sat on the couch between us. The electric bulkhead-mounted fan stirred the humid breeze wafting in through the open porthole, carrying with it the stench of the Singapore docks, a combination of hot wet vegetation, rotting seaweed, and the ordure washed down by the drains.

"In addition to mining equipment," continued Poh, in his Singapore accented English, "I have booked big mixed cargo for good friend in Port Moresby. Can also get you full load copra for return trip Hong Kong." He rubbed his hands together, appreciatively. "Should make plenty profit this voyage, Captain."

That was music to my ears. The wheat loaded in Sydney was almost completely discharged and Poh, and his network of agents, had been making the rounds of the local traders looking for new cargoes. As a tramp steamer, *Oriental Venture* worked no fixed route or timetable. She went wherever and whenever cargoes were available, competing against hundreds of other tramp steamers across the trade routes of the Far East. Whether she made a profit or loss on those cargoes depended upon Poh's negotiating the best freight rate, and on my running the ship as economically as possible, while avoiding all the man-made and God-sent perils of the China Sea.

Poh was good at his job and I liked him. Despite his sleek, dandified appearance, he was shrewd and hardworking, and was what was known in the Straits Settlements as a Lobang King. In other words, he knew all the right people and quite a few of the wrong ones too. And I trusted him, which is to say I trusted him to behave in a predictable fashion. In whatever freight he brought our way — the legal as well as the contraband — the terms he negotiated served his own interests first and the owners second, leaving the ship, and me, to pick up the crumbs. Fortunately, those crumbs usually provided satisfying pickings, sufficient to pay the occasional bonus to the crew, and to allow me to build the tidy beginnings of what I hoped would eventually buy me my own tramp steamer.

"Not much of a place, Wewak," I said, wondering what angle Poh was working. "Who's the shipper?"

"Mr Eberhardt, Wolfgang Eberhardt," replied Poh, struggling with the German consonants. "Family business in New Guinea since when it was German colony, and still doing well."

With a name like that, it was hardly surprising he was a German colonist from before the war. But I'd never heard much good said about the way the Germans treated the natives in New Guinea. Nor, for that matter, anything about prospecting or mining around Wewak. "What's this Eberhardt looking for?" I asked.

"I believe him looking for gold somewhere up the Sepik River," replied Poh. "And also drilling for oil. Don't know if any success, but he pay good price for fast, very quiet, delivery of his equipment, if you understand me, leh?" Poh tapped his nose.

"Is he now? What do you think of that, Peter?"

Lowther had been gazing at the bottle rack, drumming the tips of his fingers. It was late morning and Da Silva had brought a pot of strong Javanese coffee for the three of us, which had gone down well, despite the muggy heat of the cabin. But I imagined Lowther was now looking forward to a large gin aperitif before the curry lunch the Goanese cook invariably prepared. My question snapped him back to the present.

"I'm always a bit suspicious when I hear someone is prepared to pay well to have something delivered fast and in secret. What's the catch, I wonder?" he said, echoing my sentiments exactly.

"No catch, Captain," said Poh, a little too smoothly. "You know what happen when story leak of gold or oil strike. I'm sure Mr Eberhardt just protecting investment against loose tongues. Anyway, can ask yourself, he come with you, also bring wife. I'm sure will be nice trip for them," he paused, smiling conspiratorially, "and he plenty generous, if look after well."

"You hear that, Peter?" I said. "We're having the gentleman's company for the ten days it will take to Wewak. You'll have to get the suite aired and dusted, and perhaps lay in some deck chairs and deck tennis quoits." Unusually for a tramp, the ship had accommodation for twelve passengers, but we hardly ever carried any, and I couldn't keep the sarcasm out of my voice.

"We've got the accommodation right enough," said Lowther, frowning, "but it's rare we have the pleasure of passengers of the Eberhardt's calibre. Do they have any special needs?" He addressed the question to Poh.

"People used to living New Guinea jungle will find even this, humble oriental vagabond quite acceptable."

"Humble!" I snorted. Oriental vagabond was a joke we shared. It referred to the homeless nature of the tramp, and could as easily be applied to me as to the ship. "If I didn't know you better I'd think you were teasing me, Mr Poh. This humble ship has done pretty well for the owners these past few years."

"Forgive little joke, Captain Rowden. I also hear Mr Eberhardt likes a peg or two in the evening, but freight rate plenty cover cost of whatever he drinks." Poh stood up and reached for his hat. "Now, if excuse me, I must return to office and draw up departure documents. Thank you for coffee, and I see you again before you leave." He held up a hand. "No, no need show me down, I know humble ship nearly as well as you." His leather soles tapped their way across the timber sheathed boat deck and down the stairway, before fading as he walked aft to the gangway.

I was suspicious, but not overly scrupulous. In the tramping business you took what you could get, and quite often it was don't ask and don't tell, but something about Eberhardt and his cargo smelled fishy. An ex-German colonist in a former German colony, with a cargo of mining equipment he didn't want anyone to know about, and so sensitive he felt the need to babysit it? What was he really looking for, I wondered. There was gold aplenty further south around Lae. If he was prospecting, surely that was the place to look.

"We'll have to keep a careful eye on this Eberhardt and his cargo," I said. "And you'd better find out what he likes to drink. No doubt he'll want someone to keep him company. We can't have him thinking he's on a temperance cruise."

It was meant as a joke, but Lowther's narrowed eyes and compressed lips indicated that he didn't share it. Well he would just have to lump it! I made it my business to know everything that went on in my ship. I knew Lowther's history, of his bouts of the black dog and what caused them, and I knew that he drank to forget.

Something I was prepared to tolerate for as long as he did his job, and ran the ship to my satisfaction.

"We're no passenger ship, that's for sure," he replied in level tones. "But the suite's comfortable enough. I'll have a word with the chief steward and the cook. No doubt the opportunity to extract some baksheesh will motivate them to look after him and his wife."

Left alone, I continued to mull over Poh's visit. Something about what he had said about Eberhardt and his mining equipment did not quite add up. And my fingertips were tingling. Perhaps it was just poor circulation as the doctors claimed, but I had found it a pretty reliable indicator when someone was feeding me bullshit. It was true, we rarely carried passengers, and when we did they were usually more trouble than they were worth. But a German colonist looking for gold in an unexplored part of New Guinea? It promised to be an interesting trip.

* * *

It was close to midnight as I pushed my way through the seething mass of life crowding the night market in Bugis Street. People of all races and colours thronged the pavements and spilled into the road. Chinese compradors in traditional robes and tasselled skullcaps, their wives in bright, ornately decorated cheongsams. Coolies in baggy blue trousers and grubby smocks. Indians in starched white shirts and dhotis, their wives in colourful saris, arms jangling with multi-coloured bangles. Turbaned Sikh policemen in khaki shirts and shorts carrying long lathis, which they could wield wickedly if required to keep order. And, sprinkled among them, pink faced Europeans sweating in the heat and humidity that had dropped only slightly since sunset.

Many of the shops were still open, displaying spices, silks, clothes, household goods, red roasted ducks and strips of pork, sweetmeats, and all manner of oriental products and potions that I couldn't identify. All lit by the garish light of hurricane lamps or strings of coloured electric light bulbs. Some of the shop fronts had been transformed into open-air kitchens with large charcoal braziers, from which smoke and sparks spiralled into the night air. Sweating cooks worked over enormous woks, throwing noodles, chopped meats, vegetables and ladles full of sauces into them. The steam of the cooking mingled with the smoke, and every now and then a splash of oil into a red hot wok would erupt in hellish gouts of yellow flame. I inhaled the enticing smell of the exotic foods mixed with the acrid smell of the charcoal smoke, the pungent odour of the open drains and the exotic perfumes worn by the women. I had been there many times, but still felt something of the exhilaration and bewilderment I had experienced as a young man, fresh out from England, seeing it all for the first time.

The street had been closed to cars, and filled with wooden tables and chairs that were crowded with people eating and drinking. Boys circulated among the tables serving the dishes, and offering Tiger beer and other, less easily identifiable, but more potent, beverages.

I had gone there with Brian Cramp, the shipwright. There were those who would have thought it odd for a ship's captain to take a run ashore in the company of his shipwright. But I rarely worried what people thought of me, and Cramp and I had much in common. We had both been born on the shores of the Thames estuary. Cramp, from the Essex side, was part gypsy and had a golden ring in his ear. A black raven was tattooed on his right bicep, a grinning skull on the back of his right hand, and an anchor on the back of the left. I was from the Kentish side, born into a long line of smugglers and fishermen. One of my ancestors had ridden with Dick Turpin, and had come to a predictably gruesome end. We had both been orphaned because of the Great War, and raised in institutions where boys learned to be callous and brutal in order to survive. But I had been luckier than Cramp. An uncle found me a berth in the forecastle of a coastal schooner, and then bullied me into studying to become an officer.

After leaving the boys' home, Cramp, on the other hand, had drifted into a life of violence and crime. By day he worked as a lighterman on the Thames, plying the unwieldy cargo barges up and down the river, with only the tide and heavy steering oars to propel them. By night he ran with the tier-rangers, the gangs of thieves that robbed the lines of ships moored in London's Docks. A botched attempt to rob a P&O liner had seen him serve time in Wandsworth gaol. Released, he had managed to scrape his way into a seaman's berth in the miserable old *Portneath*, where, as I had told McGrath, we had previously sailed together. Her captain was as weak and as a miserable as his command, and the ship had been run by the chief engineer and a bunch of cronies, who cheated and stole from the owners and the rest of the crew. Begley had been one of the ringleaders, and thought the new chief mate needed to be shown who was in charge. It was a tough fight but Begley was out of condition and slow, and when I knocked him down I made damned sure with my boots that he stayed there. I had to watch my back after that, and nearly came to grief when I was jumped by several of the engineer's pals. It was Cramp who saved me from a severe beating, or worse, with a flurry of well-aimed blows from a wooden fid. I was glad to pay off at the end of the trip, and when I was offered command of *Oriental Venture* I got word to Cramp who was happy to sign on. I wouldn't say he was much reformed, but we understood each other, and he was a good man to have at my back when things got sticky, which they still did on occasion.

We sat down at an empty table, and moments later were enjoying plates of freshly cooked fried rice, noodles, meats and vegetables, washed down by ice cold Tiger beer.

"It's McGrath's first time in Singapore," said Cramp, between mouthfuls. "His kettle finished at midnight, and I told him I'd be here if he wanted to join me for jellied eels and porter."

"He'll be lucky to find those here," I replied, chuckling. "The jellied eels at any rate." It was funny how little things like that brought back such painful memories. Jellied eels were an East End staple when I was a boy. Everyone ate them, including me when I was hungry, but I hated them. Hard lumps of rubbery, boiled eel set in gelatine that smelled as if it had been made from rendered down cows hooves with the dung still between the claws. Cramp was still a typical East-Ender, though, proud of his origins and the cockney dialect he spoke, spiced with thieves cant and rhyming slang. "Kettle" was short for kettle and hob, which rhymed with fob which was short for fob watch, which ... well sometimes you just had to be born there.

I knew I shouldn't have been ashamed of my origins. It wasn't my fault that my father had been killed in the war. Nor that my mother, left destitute, had turned to the prostitution and drink that combined to kill her. I couldn't have done anything about that. But my Kentish accent, which my Industrial School teacher informed me, while sarcastically holding his nose, carried more than a whiff of the sewage of pronunciation washed down river from Wapping, was something else. I thrashed middle-class boys who taunted me about it, until I realised it was easier to mimic their rounded vowels and crisp consonants. It hadn't made me anymore of a gentleman, but it did make me sound like a man who might be afforded the benefit of the doubt. At least until his actions spoke for themselves. But even now, when I got angry, I had to guard against dropped tees and aitches.

We were still eating when Cramp spotted McGrath, and waved him over to join us. The young man's face wore a wide eyed, expectant smile when he saw Cramp, but which faded to an abashed grin as he caught sight of me sharing the table, and he slid warily into the empty seat.

"Relax, Third," I said, signalling one of the boys to bring an extra bottle and a plate. "You're off duty, so enjoy the evening."

"What do you fink, James?" asked Cramp, waving a hand at the bustling night market. "Bet you've seen nuffink like this in Sydney, or wherever in Australia you come from."

"No, it's only sheep, cattle, wheat and farmers where I'm from," replied McGrath. "There are Chinese in Sydney, but I've never had anything to do with them."

A bowl and bottle of beer were slapped down in front of McGrath, and the boy handed him a spoon. He looked down apprehensively at the concoctions of meat and vegetables, all chopped up and floating in steaming, pungent sauces. Cramp laughed at the perplexed look on his face.

"Yeah, I guess it does look all a bit messed up if you're used to meat and taters. But forget what it looks like, just put some of the rice or noodles into the bowl, spoon some of the meat and sauce over it, and eat 'em togever."

McGrath delved gingerly in with his spoon, and then watched wide-eyed as Cramp picked up his own bowl and used chopsticks to transfer food to his mouth.

"Chopsticks," explained Cramp, waving them in front of his face. "The Chinese use nuffink else. Don't worry, they provide spoons for the Gwailos."

"Gwailos?" questioned McGrath.

"That's the name they give us white men, it means 'round eyes'."

McGrath lifted a portion of the food into his mouth, and tentatively started to chew. I could well imagine the taste was like nothing he had ever experienced, a mouth filling medley of flavours and textures; sweet, salty and sour all at once with the crunch of freshly cooked, still crisp vegetables combining with the silky softness of tender meat. Then his lips pursed with a sharp intake of breath, and he grabbed for the beer bottle.

Cramp laughed again. "Sorry, forgot to warn you about the chilli, it burns a bit at first but you get used to it. 'Ave another Pig's Ear, it'll help put out the Jeremiah."

McGrath cooled his mouth with another swig of beer and resumed eating. With the resilience of youth, a filling belly and a second bottle of beer underway, he visibly relaxed, and we sat back and watched the swirling, racial, noisy kaleidoscope of Chinese, Indians, Malays and Europeans.

Circulating among the tables were Chinese entertainers. Aged musicians playing strange tunes on single stringed fiddles. Boys offering to play the shell game, their quick hands shuffling them on the table before inviting the unwary to bet under which shell the ball would be found. Boys with battered packs of playing cards, offering to perform magic tricks. Other boys challenging the less than sober to play noughts and crosses for a wager of a few coppers. Win or draw meant the boys kept the cash, and they never seemed to lose.

And, at the edge of the crowded lanes, elegantly dressed figures in colourful, sparkling, hip-hugging cheongsams, hovered discretely. Their hair exotically combed, their cheeks rouged, and their eyes heavily highlighted, they exchanged glances and whispers with the single men, sometimes being invited to sit down and offered a drink. McGrath's attention wavered from his plate, and his eyes swivelled, as if on stalks.

Cramp winked at me. "If you fancy a bit've skirt we can arrange that later," he nudged McGrath. "But, unless I'm mistaken, I don't fink the Kai Tais are your cup of Rosie Lee."

"They look pretty enough," replied McGrath. "But what does Kai Tai mean, is that the Chinese name for hookers?"

"No James," laughed Cramp. "Those 'ookers ain't women, they're lady-boys, pretty boys dressed up as women. There's some men who like that sort of fing. But there's plenty ain't noticed the difference 'til they've put an 'and between their legs and felt somefing they wasn't expecting."

McGrath's mouth gaped. I didn't suppose he was so naive as not to know about hookers. Any seaman who sailed to the grain ports of South Australia, or the nitrate ports of Chile, would have at least a passing acquaintance with the brothels, and the girls who offered their services there. But from the horrified look on his face it had obviously never occurred to him that boys would dress up as girls in order to attract men.

Cramp saw that look and decided to have a little fun. "I can call one over if you like, she can sit on your lap while you get acquainted."

He went to raise a hand, but McGrath reached over and jerked it down hissing, "Don't do that, what d'you think I am?"

"Easy, James," said Cramp. "Just my little joke, no offence meant. Eat the rest of your supper and watch the passing parade. Then we'll 'ead back to the ship."

McGrath grinned sheepishly. "Sorry, Brian, bit outside my experience these ... Kai Tais. Glad you warned me though, some look absolute crackers. Look at that one over there with the ..."

His shocked voice trailed off, and I followed his glance towards the tall, dark and good-looking figure of my second mate whose arm was draped possessively around the shoulders of an especially attractive Kai Tai.

"Oh, it's Mr Griffith. Well he does have an eye for the *ladies* — if you know what I mean," said Cramp, chuckling.

Griffith's face was flushed, and his animated eyes were focused on the lady-boy at his side. He seemed oblivious to everything around him, including his captain and shipmates whose table he was about to pass. I would have been happy to let him go by. Not for my sake, I'd seen too much to be offended by a homosexual and his lady-boy lover. But Griffith would probably have preferred to keep a discrete distance between his venereal preferences, and the professional relationships with his colleagues.

And all would have been fine, expect that McGrath, his face flaming almost the colour of his hair, was staring at Griffith, his nose and eyes wrinkled with disgust.

"Easy, James," said Cramp, placing a hand on his arm trying to reassure him. "Mr Griffith's okay. He's queer, but he's okay. He won't bother you."

"Too right he won't bother me," snapped McGrath, snatching his arm back. "If he so much as lays a finger on me I'll kill him."

I should have intervened then. It would have been the right thing to do, especially after my warnings about fighting. But I was curious. Perhaps it was that same primeval curiosity that drives men to seek entertainment watching men, dogs or cockerels fighting. McGrath was a fighter; I'd seen the evidence of it in Sydney. And I knew that Griffith would stand up for himself. Two dogs snarling and snapping at each other. Which would back down, I wondered.

McGrath's outburst penetrated Griffith's absorption in the lady-boy. Whether he noticed Cramp and me at the same table I don't know, but he saw McGrath's agitated face and stopped, swaying slightly.

"Well if it isn't young McGrath out enjoying an evening in Bugis Street." He provocatively pushed the giggling Kai Tai forward to give McGrath a better look. "I hope the scenery's to your liking, James? What do you think of my young friend here? Isn't she lovely?"

McGrath shrank back. "Get away from me you filthy—"

"Queer?" finished Griffith, his voice turning menacing. "Who do you think you are to judge, just a boy still wet behind the ears? I suggest you get back to the ship, it's well past your bed time."

Crimson faced, McGrath squeezed his fists into balls and stepped in front of Griffith. "Don't talk to me like that, I'm not a boy, but you, you're not a man, you're something else, you're disgusting."

Hatred blazed in Griffith's eyes. "I don't want any trouble McGrath, but if you want to start something I'm happy to finish it for you." His hand reached for the knife that I knew would be in his pocket, and then checked as if he thought better of it. It was too public a place. Fists would have to suffice.

McGrath's face betrayed indecision, and for a moment I thought he was going to back down. Then his temper got the better of him and he lashed out, a vicious right hook aimed squarely into Griffith's face.

The fist slammed into something solid, but it was not Griffith. Cramp had stepped between them, and caught the blow in his hard, calloused fist, his fingers clamping over McGrath's hand like a vice.

"Now then, gentlemen, this ain't the time or place for brawling." Cramp pulled McGrath away and shot me a questioning glance. I nodded, and he guided him away from the table. "Come on, James," he said. "Let it be, you're on watch in a few hours, time to go." He shepherded McGrath through the crowd towards a short line of battered black and yellow taxis, and I heard his penetrating Cockney voice instructing the driver to take them to the Keppel docks.

Griffith's shoulders slumped, the colour draining from his face as his anger subsided, and at the dawning realisation I had witnessed the near fight with McGrath. He snatched his arm back from around the shoulders of the Kai Tai, as if she had suddenly turned to hot coals.

"I'm sorry, Captain," he mumbled. "I didn't see you there."

Rejected and embarrassed, the young Kai Tai edged away. No matter, I thought, one foreigner's money was as good as any others, and she was pretty enough to find another John before the night was through.

I jerked a thumb at Griffith. "You'd better get back to the ship too, mister," I snarled, the captain re-asserting himself. "You know what I've said about fighting?" I jabbed a finger on the table for emphasis. "Be in my office at 10 a.m., on the dot. You hear me?" I didn't wait for a reply. "Now get away."

Griffith turned on his heel and disappeared into the thinning crowd. I checked my watch. It was past one, but I didn't feel sleepy, nor like going back to the monastic confines of my cabin. But I knew a place where the rum was plentiful and the women were welcoming, whatever the hour. I waved to the boy, left some notes and a handful of coins on the table, and walked around the corner into Malay Street.

* * *

"What makes you think it acceptable to assault a senior officer?"

I was seated at my desk with McGrath standing in front of me, looking decidedly nervous and unhappy. I had summoned him at nine a.m., suffering from a self-inflicted headache and the pangs of hypocrisy. Firstly, I had enjoyed several hours of convivial, albeit it pecuniary, company in a well-known bawdy house in Malay Street. It was not exactly discrete or exclusive, anyone with sufficient funds was welcome, and the police occasionally raided it, if only to keep up appearances. But I had helped the proprietor with the undocumented shipment of some valuable items to her relatives in China, the proceeds of immoral earnings mealy mouthed do-gooders would have called them, for which I earned her undying thanks, free drinks and the pick of the girls. Secondly, I knew I should have prevented the angry con-frontation. A word from their captain would have pinched out the shoot before it poisonously flowered. So now, I had two angry and resentful young men on my hands.

I adopted my cold, hard, judgmental face and glared at him. "Well McGrath, what do you have to say for yourself. You took offence at something the second mate was doing during his time ashore, and felt that gave you the right to assault him. Is that correct?" My tone was ominous, and McGrath shivered.

"No sir. But Mr Griffith had his arm around that ... young man." His Adam's apple wobbled as he tried to keep his voice level. "He was flaunting it, and I—"

"What gives you the right to pass judgment," I thundered sanctimoniously. "What the second mate does in his private time is no concern of mine as long as he does his job. And if it's no concern of mine it's no concern of yours ... if you want to stay in this ship." I paused, fixing McGrath in a steely glare. "Well, mister?"

McGrath swallowed. Perhaps he was genuinely shocked by the thought of a man having sexual relations with another man, no matter how expertly made up to look like a woman. I wasn't all that comfortable with it myself, although whether it was a sin against God, or deserved a life sentence, I sincerely doubted. And Griffith was a good seaman and had served me well. I didn't want to lose him. On the other hand, McGrath had promise too, if he could learn to control his feelings and his temper. He had lost his last berth through fighting, and he could hardly afford a second D.R. I tapped my fingers on my desk, waiting for his reply.

"I'm sorry sir, I think I acted rashly, it won't happen again."

"It had better not. You cannot raise your fist to a superior officer, and you will apologise to the second mate when he relieves you at noon. Well?"

McGrath hesitated, perhaps he had expected a rocket, or even dismissal, but not being asked to apologise.

"Well ... Mister McGrath?" I growled, leaning forward, pressing my hands onto the desk as if preparing to propel myself over it and leap at him. I could be a right nasty bastard if crossed, and I hoped Cramp had made that clear in the taxi ride back to the ship.

"Yes sir. I'm sorry sir, but ..." my eyes flashed a warning, but McGrath doggedly continued, "will the second mate accept it?"

I felt my face flush with anger, but a part of me had to admire his guts, and I managed to keep my voice level. "You just apologise, mister. Now get back to work."

"Yes, sir." He turned, head drooping and shuffled towards the door.

Was it relief on his face that the carpeting was over, or was it resentment? Normally with red headed, fiery types it was easy to tell. But for once I wasn't sure. Not that it should have mattered. I could have swatted him down with my fists, thrown him down the gangway, and the shipping master wouldn't have given his protests the time of day. Rebellious young men did not get far in China Sea tramps. But something in McGrath's face demanded more by way of explanation, and now was as good a time as any to open his eyes to the nature of what he had signed on to.

"Wait!" I beckoned him back with a finger. "Listen carefully, McGrath. I'm not going to comment on what Mr Griffith does in his private life, but he's a good officer and he causes no trouble on board. You might not like homosexuals, but in this profession you have to learn to live and let live."

"I'm sorry sir, I guess I was just taken by surprise, seeing him and that ... Kai Tai together."

"It takes all sorts McGrath, as you'll find out if you stay in this ship long enough. I suspect you've already heard stories about the types of cargoes we sometimes carry. Not everything that comes over the rail is entirely in accordance with the manifest. Strictly, that's not your concern, it's me and the chief mate whose balls are on the line. But a man who knows how to keep his mouth shut, and who's not afraid of a spot of trouble. A man who can handle himself in a tight corner and keep a clear head, well I can use a man like that. I've got one in Griffith. Question is, have I got one in you? Now as I see it you have a choice. You can sign off now and I'll stamp your discharge book with a Very Good for conduct and sobriety. It shouldn't be hard to find another berth among all the ships here. Or you can apologise to the second, and he and I will say no more about it. Oh, and if it makes your decision any easier, the shippers of these — unusual — cargoes can sometimes be quite gener-ous."

I had said more than enough, it was up to McGrath, but I was pleased to see a feral grin spread across his face.

"I'm no piker, sir. I signed on for the duration. I'll speak to Mr Griffith at noon."

"Don't let me have to talk to you again," I glared at him for emphasis. "Now, the chief mate tells me that the crew are rigging the derricks in order to swing in the cases of mining equipment. They're to go into the tween deck in number four hold. See to it please."

"Aye aye, sir."

Later that morning Griffith reported to my office. I got straight to the point.

"I don't know what game you're playing mister. There are eyes and ears every-where, and someone always ready to report trouble between Europeans in a place like this. Your preferences are your own business just as long as they don't affect what happens on my ship. But last night they became my business. The third mate was wrong to throw a punch at you, and I've spoken to him about it. But your behav-iour and your attitude were completely out of line."

"Sir, in my defence—"

"Don't interrupt me, mister," I cut him off angrily. "Let me warn you, that even here in the East, where some things are more tolerated than they might be in Britain, it's not wise to make yourself too obvious. If you can't be discrete then maybe you're in the wrong line of work. Am I making myself clear?" My voice was hard and I spoke slowly to make certain he got the message.

"Yes, sir." His voice was strained, as if there was a painful lump in his throat, and I could see he was fighting to contain his anger.

"Whatever you think of young McGrath, he has the makings of a good officer, and you'll have to work with him for as long as you both remain in this ship. He'll apologise to you, and you'll accept it, is that clear?"

My tone brooked no argument, and I waited, stony faced, until Griffith had mumbled his assent. "After what happened in Sydney I'd have thought you wanted to keep your head below the parapet," I continued in a milder tone. "Look, you're a good officer David, and you've sailed with me for a while, but don't think I won't hesitate to pay you off if you cause me any more trouble."

It was a hard fact of life for men like Griffith, being hated and feared for something they were born with. Tramp steamers were no place for the faint hearted, having to gain the respect of the rough and hard as nails men who made their meagre living in them. And Griffith had won their respect, with his fists when necessary. But pity and sentiment were not luxuries I could afford in this business. Which was difficult and dangerous enough, without having to play nursemaid.

"Well, what's it to be."

"I'm sorry, sir. There won't be any more trouble."

I dismissed him and pressed the bell for Da Silva. My head still ached, and I needed a good strong cup of his coffee.

CHAPTER THREE

Midway through McGrath's forenoon watch, and I had taken my coffee onto the bridge wing to escape the paperwork in my office. There was no wind and the sea was a deep cobalt blue, its glassy smooth surface gently undulating in a long, low swell. Every so often flying fish burst into the air and skimmed above the surface for a hundred feet or so, their wings sparkling in the sunlight, trailing water droplets like strings of pearls, before diving back into their normal element. The sun, while only half way to its zenith, was already beating down upon the exposed steel decks and fittings, making them burning hot to the touch. I stood in the shade of the canvas awning stretched over the port bridge wing, and enjoyed what little breeze was created by the ship's ten knot passage. Away to port an unfolding panorama of the remote south coast of Borneo slid slowly astern. The coastal plains and low hills covered in lush, dark green vegetation, with here and there a plume of smoke curling upwards into the still air, indicating a Dyak settlement. And in the distance, the pale, grey-blue outline of the mountainous, mysterious, interior.

So far it had been an uneventful passage.

Wolfgang Eberhardt and his wife Amelie had come aboard on the day of departure and occupied the main passenger suite, from which they had since only emerged to take short strolls around the boat deck in the early morning before the sun got too hot, or in the cool of the evening after sunset. Their meals were carried up by Da Silva, and served in their cabin. From what I had seen of him, Eberhardt appeared to be about fifty years of age, tall, but turning to fat with blonde hair, fair skin and blue eyes. His face bore the evidence of many years of exposure to the tropical sun, coupled with overindulgence. His wife, on the other hand, was short and petite with silvery grey hair. She always wore a hat or carried a parasol to protect her complexion from the sun, and her pale, almost porcelain, skin made a striking contrast with the reddened, toughened hide, with its sunspots and blotches, of Eberhardt's face.

Despite my suspicions, Eberhardt appeared to be just as Poh had described him. There was nothing obviously suspicious about his cargo of mining equipment, and all the paperwork appeared to be perfectly in order. Still, it was unusual for a well-heeled merchant to take passage in an old tramp steamer, even the one carrying his own cargo. The liner service operated by Burns Philp was a much more comfortable and quicker way of traveling home to New Guinea. Now, though, I had the opportunity to study him more closely. Because a note penned by Eberhardt had been delivered by Da Silva to my office that morning, requesting the pleasure of joining my officers and me for dinner.

Oriental Venture's dining saloon was, as a rule, sparsely attended. I normally took my meals there, as did Lowther and the junior mates although with one of them always on watch, in something of a relay. The radio officer kept watch according to the Marconi timetable of radio transmission and silence periods. He ate in the saloon or the radio shack depending on the timetable. The chief steward, being responsible for all of the ship's catering arrangements, also normally ate there. The chief engineer and his assistants, while entitled to it, saw themselves as a breed apart, and preferred the relaxed atmosphere of their own duty mess, where they could eat in their overalls.

I grinned, thinking of the traditions and ceremonies of the naval wardrooms Lowther would have experienced. With their bullshit rituals, uniforms, polished silverware, immaculate white jacketed stewards and mediocre food, compensated for by copious amounts of alcohol. Ours would be a rough and ready dinner, even by comparison. Hong Kong tramp steamers were famous for neither the quality nor quantity of the food their owners were prepared to pay for. Fortunately, the chief steward and I were familiar with all the little wrinkles that could supplement the ship's victualing allowance, and the crew usually ate pretty well, provided they were not too fussy.

Nevertheless, a request from the Eberhardts to join the officers at dinner meant we needed to put on a special effort.

In answer to Eberhardt's note, I had penned a formal invitation to him and his wife, and sent an instruction to all the officers to join us in the saloon, with clean hands and white shirts. I then had a word with the chief steward about the menu. He seemed to take Eberhardt's request as a challenge to his capabilities, and hurried off to consult the cook. Then there was the matter of drink. The ship's fresh water, often loaded from untrustworthy sources, and stored in infrequently cleaned iron tanks into which disinfectant was poured, tasted of mud, chlorine and coal dust. True to his word, Poh had supplied us with several cases of beer, which were taking up valuable space in our meagre cold store, and the Scotch whisky that Eberhardt preferred.

I watched McGrath emerge from the wheelhouse and climb the steps to the compass platform to take bearings of the nearest headlands, which he would plot on the chart to establish our position. As far as I could tell, McGrath and Griffith had made peace with one another. There was no overt sign of ill feeling, although little hint of cordiality either. Well, you didn't have to like a man in order to sail with him. I'd sailed with men I wouldn't have given the time of day to in other circumstances. Board of Trade acquaintances they were called, men you sailed with for as long as you signed on, and never saw, nor wanted to see, again. And there were plenty of drunken, lead swinging, violent misfits masquerading as seamen in the ports of the Far East. Having their wages docked and threatened with a report to the authorities was like pouring water onto a duck's back to some of the hard cases I had come across. But, despite the four gold rings on my sleeve, I'd come up through the hawse pipe, and knew all the forecastle's dodges. A man only ever crossed me once. If he learned his lesson well and good, if not, the second was much harder. He paid the fine in bruises and blood, and the authorities were likely to find him sprawled in a dockside alley.

I believed I ran a taut ship and a contented one for the most part. The pay was fair, the food gave little cause for complaint, and the ship, though old, was seaworthy, and more comfortable than the average wartime built tramp. The work was hard, but so it was on any ship struggling to earn a living on the irregular and low paying cargoes of the East, where the competition was cutthroat, and rules and regulations more honoured in the breach than the observance. In that lay opportunity though. As I had told McGrath, the Rowdens were a Kentish family with a long pedigree in seafaring and smuggling; traits I had inherited in full measure. I had also developed something of a reputation as a captain who knew every secluded anchorage, and every dishonest official between Calcutta and Vladivostok. Whether it was justified or not I left others to judge. There never seemed to be any shortage of lucrative requests from Poh, and others, to deliver items about which no questions were to be asked, and on which the attention of the customs' authorities and their import taxes were to be avoided.

It was this that made me suspicious. The fact that Poh had emphasized Eberhardt's desire to have his cargo delivered discretely and trouble free, while babysitting it. Was it to be landed in some remote cove away from prying eyes, or were the authorities in Wewak to be induced to turn a blind eye? But if so to what? There was nothing illicit about a shipment of picks, shovels, drills and water pumps. Poh had mentioned nothing specific. But then why mention anything at all? Was it a hint that I should expect further instructions from Eberhardt himself? Which might explain his desire to meet me formally first, so that he had an excuse to be seen talking to me privately afterwards. Or was Poh hinting at something else, warning me to be on my guard perhaps. Well, I wasn't going to solve the puzzle out there on the bridge wing, watching the pristine, jungle clad, coast of Borneo gliding mysteriously astern.

A flying fish burst from the glassy heave of a nearby swell and glided away. I could almost imagine it trying to beat its elongated fins in order to put further distance between itself and its pursuer. Which was a dolphin, erupting through the surface just astern of the fish, leaping bodily into the air, water cascading from its flanks and tail, its gaping snout revealing its wicked row of teeth. It was a perfectly timed leap, the dolphin's jaw snapping shut on the unfortunate fish just as it splashed back into the ocean. The hunter and the hunted, demonstrating life at its most basic. I thought myself more hunter than hunted, but through the thin veneer of civilisation that cloaked most of our actions, it was not always possible to tell the difference.

It was pleasant in the breeze on the bridge wing, but I had work to do. There was paperwork waiting for me in the hot, cramped office. I drained the last of the coffee and headed back inside. I needed to check the chief steward's arrangements for the evening's dinner, and make sure Da Silva could find me a clean white shirt.

* * *

Standing in the centre of the anteroom to the saloon, I cast a critical eye over my officers as they made their entrance. Lowther, tall and thin, almost elegant in his worn but freshly laundered and starched white shirt with its three gold shoulder stripes and row of medal ribbons, including the Distinguished Service Cross. Normally he would have been on the bridge as it was his watch, but Griffith was relieving him and would join us later. McGrath, looking very young in his new white shirt with a single gold stripe on each shoulder. The chief engineer, Fraser, a florid, rotund, grey haired Scotsman from Leith, with a quick wit and an equally quick temper, was already grasping a large glass of his favourite whisky. Several of the junior engineers clustered around the small servery, draining glasses of the chilled beer the chief steward had brought up from the cool room. With their rough manners, and their meaty, oil stained hands, they looked out of place in their white shirts, some of which they were clearly wearing for the first time.

Promptly, at seven p.m., Wolfgang Eberhardt and his wife stepped arm in arm into the anteroom. Despite the tropical heat, and *Oriental Venture's* worn and workmanlike appearance, they had dressed for dinner. I had to admire Eberhardt's tailored white dinner jacket — not something I would have been comfortable wearing — and his wife's long black cocktail gown, which complemented her pale complexion and luxuriant grey hair.

"Good evening, Captain Rowden," he said, grasping my hand and firmly shaking it. "I trust we have not kept you and your officers waiting. Gentlemen, may I present myself, Wolfgang Eberhardt." He drew himself erect and made a slight, formal bow. "And this is my wife, Mrs Amelie Eberhardt. Thank you for allowing us to accompany you on this voyage to our home in Wewak." He spoke in a strong, clear voice with the clipped accent and precision that indicated his north German origins.

"Not at all, Mr Eberhardt," I replied. "The pleasure is all ours. Please let me present my officers to you." I named each of them in turn, conscious that some of the younger men, for whom passengers were outside their normal seagoing experience, had little idea of social graces and stared at the couple as if they were beings from another planet. It was a relief to turn to Lowther; he at least was the genuine article, an officer and a gentleman. "And may I present Commander, the Honourable, Lord Peter Lowther, my chief mate."

"You are a Lord, Commander Lowther?" The raised inflexion clearly conveyed Eberhardt's surprise at finding an aristocrat amongst the crew of a battered old tramp steamer. Then, quickly recovering his poise, "Should we address you as My Lord?" His wife dropped a modest curtsey at her husband's emphasis on the title.

Embarrassed by the use of a title I knew he would rather forget, Lowther forced a smile. "That won't be necessary, Mr Eberhardt. Mr Lowther or even Peter will be fine. There is no need for formality in these professional surroundings."

Eberhardt was looking intently at the medal ribbons on Lowther's chest. "If I am not mistaken, Mr Lowther, zat is the Distinguished Service Cross you are wearing. This means you have been in the Navy, and have performed some especially gallant service?"

"I had the privilege of serving in the Royal Navy," Lowther replied, stiffly. "And the medal was awarded after the Battle of Jutland."

"*Ach*, Jutland," said Eberhardt, his face lighting up with interest. "I should very much like to hear your views on zat battle, if you are willing and time permits. But, Captain," he turned back to me, "we are delaying you and your officers from your dinner. May I suggest we sit down?"

Grim faced and with tightly clenched fists, Lowther muttered something to Da Silva, and the piratical old steward darted into the pantry and returned with a large glass of pink gin. I led our guests to the centre table in the mahogany-panelled, but well-worn, dining saloon, held the chair for Mrs Eberhardt, and then waved for Lowther and Fraser to join us, noting that Lowther had already drained half his glass, and was signalling for Da Silva to replenish it.

The saloon tables were laid with crisp, white tablecloths, and an unfamiliar array of silver and chinaware. Goodness knows where the chief steward had managed to source it all, or where he had hidden it. I caught some of the younger men perplexedly staring at the array of cutlery, clearly wondering in what order to use them. God forbid their mothers should have taught them any table manners. Not that mine were any better at their age, despite the efforts of the Industrial School to drill them into me.

"Please don't expect too much of us, Mrs Eberhardt," I said, hoping she was enough of a lady not to notice forks being used as shovels, by coal dust ingrained hands that looked as if they had not seen soap in weeks. "We're a tramp ship, we spend our days chasing cargoes in the less salubrious parts of the Far East. It's rare we have the pleasure of passengers. But we'll do our best to look after you until we reach Wewak."

"Please don't vorry on my account, Captain," she replied. "Both Volfgang and I have lived and vorked in remote parts of New Guinea vithout any of ze comforts of civilisation. Compared to that I am sure your ship will be fine."

Da Silva, wearing a clean and pressed white jacket for the occasion, and a shiny new eye patch, served them with a soup the chief steward informed us was mulligatawny. I wondered whether the peppery, tamarind-sour soup would be to the Eberhardts' taste, but they emptied their bowls without comment. Grilled spiced chicken accompanied by plates of fried rice and steamed oriental vegetables followed the soup. The chickens had come aboard in Singapore in wicker coops, and the cook had wrung their necks and plucked them that morning.

Eberhardt continued to eat with simple appreciation before finally putting down his knife and fork.

"Thank you, Captain Rowden," he said. "One hears stories of the seaman's diet, salt beef, biscuits and weevils. After a lifetime of living among Orientals I find this food much more to my taste."

"I've eaten my share of salt junk and hard tack," I replied, to accompanying nods and grins from the officers. "But I'm happy to say that this is not one of those 'pint and pound' ships. Our owners are a little more, generous."

"Pint and pound?" queried Mrs Eberhardt.

"The seaman's name for the minimum scale of rations permitted by the Board of Trade. Water by the pint, and meat and bread by the pound, to make up a weekly allowance. Some ships are still run that way, but not this one, even when we don't have the pleasure of guests." I turned towards Eberhardt, keen, now that the conversation had relaxed, to satisfy my curiosity about the man. "I understand your family settled in New Guinea in the last century?"

"Ya, indeed," he replied. "My father vas one of the founders of the German New Guinea Company. He and my mother arrived there in '84, and I was born the year after. I have lived there all of my life. Of course, things have changed a great deal in zat time. The German New Guinea company is no more, but our family has adapted, and we have built a business that has survived," he smiled wistfully, "how shall we say, changing circumstances."

"I've spent most of my life at sea, Mr Eberhardt," I said. "And history was never my strong point at school. But am I right that Germany possessed part of New Guinea and the islands."

"You are quite correct, Captain," replied Eberhardt. "There have been German settlers in the western Pacific for over seventy years. The northern half of New Guinea, and the Bismarck Archipelago were part of Germany until the outbreak of the World War. I was a young officer in the militia when Australian troops landed at Neu Pommern, New Britain as you would call it. We held out for a while, until resistance was pointless. After the war, the League of Nations placed New Guinea under Australian administration. So now I am not sure if we are Germans, New Guineans or Australians." He laughed. "But in many ways life has not changed. We have learned to speak English. We trade with the natives and the Chinese, and do some exploration for gold and oil, traces of which have been found. One day New Guinea will be a rich country, Captain Rowden, and perhaps there is still time for me to be part of it."

"Aye, but what of the natives, sir?" said Fraser, the chief engineer, who had been listening in silence, but now broke in with his broad Scottish brogue. "What place for them in your new land of riches?"

It was not exactly the turn of conversation I would have encouraged. Fraser had a strong streak of the Jacobin in him, and a Jacobite opinion of the English, but then so did all the best tramp ship engineers. *Oriental Venture's* boilers and engines had been built at Kirkaldy on the Firth of Forth, and had proven especially reliable, so perhaps they responded better to Gaelic imprecations than to Anglo-Saxon profanity.

"Cannibals, head-hunters, thieves," snorted Eberhardt. "Completely unfit for ze modern world."

"Or like children who need to be brought to God," said Mrs Eberhardt. "The missionaries try very hard to turn them from their evil vays. There are still occasional reports of cannibalism from up in the highlands."

"But they don't work, *ya?*" continued Eberhardt. "We found zat out in the days of the Company. Reward or punishment, neither seemed to make any difference. In the end we had to import labour from elsewhere. I believe you British did the same for your sugar plantations in Fiji and Australia."

"Right enough, Mr Eberhardt," said Fraser. "But it's their land, surely they deserve a share in its riches?"

"They have done nothing to deserve it. Whatever wealth is in the islands we Germans created. If the natives want to share zat wealth they must contribute, they must work, they must abide by civilised laws." He stopped, conscious that his voice had risen and the saloon was silent.

I was probably failing in my duty as host to keep the conversation away from controversial topics, although the passage money, plus the freight he was paying for his cargo, entitled him to leap onto his soapbox if he wished. I caught Fraser's eye, and he nodded in acknowledgment.

"But, gentlemen, you know what I mean," Eberhardt continued in a calmer, conciliatory tone. "We are all living under the benefit of the British Empire on which the sun never sets, *ya*? Good, strong government benefits all who live by the rules."

"Aye, right enough, Mr Eberhardt," said Fraser, his round face splitting into a grin. "Even us heathen Scots."

"And yet your Scottish soldiers have been some of the Empire's best warriors, as we Germans have learned to our cost."

"Aye, there's many have taken the King's shilling right enough. If you can't beat 'em, as they say," replied Fraser.

It was time to change the subject. Mrs Eberhardt didn't look the type of woman to engage on the topic of sex, my views on religion were highly unconventional, and I knew nothing about sport. Which left politics, which should also have been taboo, but Eberhardt's defence of the German colonisation of New Guinea had piqued my interest.

"What do you think of the situation in Spain, Mr Eberhardt," I said, wondering how much attention he paid to events in Europe. "Germany and Russia supporting opposing sides in the civil war. The British papers talk of that conflict spreading, but from out here in the East, that seems remote."

"We are a long way from Europe, and I read only what news I see in those rare newspapers that find their way to Wewak," said Eberhardt, dismissively. "But what I hear of Comrade Stalin and the communists makes me fear for the future. If what is happening in Spain is not to spread, then someone has to stand up to him."

"And your chancellor, Mr Hitler? Do you think he's the right man for that?" From the little I'd read he didn't sound a pleasant character, but then I wasn't German.

"There are some fanatics among the National Socialists who spout a lot of racial nonsense," said Eberhardt, the narrowed eyes and furrowed borrow indicating he was choosing his words carefully, "but I can assure you, gentlemen, zat there are many good, sensible Germans in the government, and its armed services, who have worked hard to rebuild our country. They don't want another war with Britain and its Empire. Take my word for it."

"But what of the talk of rearmament? New aircraft, submarines, battleships," interjected Lowther. "Surely we all saw enough of war during the last one."

"Europe must stand up against the communists, Mr Lowther. We must be prepared to defend ourselves. I can assure you zat Germany does not want war, but you

British are complacent. You do not understand the threat of Russia, nor the threat to your interests in the East."

"The Russians are hardly any threat to us out here, and the Japanese and Chinese are busy arguing with each other," said Lowther, "they're hardly likely to take on the British Empire at the same time."

We were reaching the boundary of polite conversation, but before I could change the subject Eberhardt held up his hands. "Captain Rowden, gentlemen, I must apologise. Politics is not a fit subject for discussion among friends at the dinner table. I will say only this, zat the world is becoming more dangerous, and it is best to be prepared, as Germany is preparing. Now, I propose we change the subject and talk about history. You were present at the Battle of Jutland, Mr Lowther. My brother also saw action there. The High Seas Fleet did very well against the Grand Fleet, I'm sure you will agree?"

"I believe I could challenge that assumption," replied Lowther, rising from his chair. "However, with your permission, Captain, and with apologies Mrs Eberhardt, but I must relieve the second mate who's standing part of my watch so I could join you for dinner. Perhaps we can have that discussion another time. Now, if you will please excuse me."

"I shall look forward to zat," said Eberhardt, as Lowther disappeared up the stairs in the direction of the bridge.

With Lowther gone, I steered the conversation into calmer waters. Fraser asked Mrs Eberhardt about her life in New Guinea, and she obliged with a description of the missionary work she hoped would encourage the natives to abandon their wicked practises of head hunting and cannibalism. Eberhardt, his tongue loosened by several glasses of whisky, confined himself to ironical interjections, suggesting he had little faith in her ability to convert them into good Lutherans. Therefore I was relieved when, the meal long since over, Eberhardt announced that he and his wife intended to take a walk around the boat deck while he smoked a cigar, and then retire to their cabin.

Leaving me free to climb to the bridge, hoping that Lowther was still there after handing over the watch to McGrath. Eberhardt's attitude over dinner had only fuelled my suspicion, and I had thought of a way of satisfying my curiosity.

* * *

McGrath and Lowther were studying the chart of the Bismarck Sea when I pushed open the chartroom door. McGrath excused himself and moved towards the curtained entrance to the wheelhouse, assuming I wanted a private word with the chief mate.

"It's okay, Third, this concerns you, too," I beckoned him back. "We'll talk here where it's more private, but keep your voices down, Eberhardt might still be wandering about on the boat deck." I turned towards Lowther. "So, what do you make of him, Peter?"

"He seems highly opinionated, and very well informed for a man claiming to rarely see a newspaper," said Lowther.

I nodded in agreement. "His idea of a peace loving Germany seems to include bombing defenceless Spanish towns and seizing the Rhineland. Then there's that business about being in the militia, and having a brother in the German Navy. Perhaps he's still got connections with German military authorities?" I said, the germ of an idea forming at the back of my mind. "I've never heard of anyone mining for gold or drilling for oil around Wewak, but mining equipment is a pretty loose description that could cover all sorts of things, including explosives, that would be very useful in the event of war. So what's he up to and what's really in those boxes?"

"I don't know, he seemed harmless enough to me. A bit old fashioned in his views, nostalgic for the Germany of the past, maybe," replied Lowther. "But even if the Nazis are preparing for war, what's that got to do with us?"

"Call it a sixth sense if you like, Peter," I said, "but I get a feeling in my bones when something isn't right, and right now they tell me to be wary of friend Eberhardt. There's something about him makes me think he's up to no good." I paused and lit a cigarette, pensively turning the battered petrol lighter between my tingling fingertips. Then I reached a decision and tapped on the chart table.

"We need to take a look at those boxes of his. If there's anything there that's not supposed to be, I want to know about it before we arrive in Wewak, and the authorities start crawling all over this ship." I turned to McGrath. "Listen, Third, rustle up a torch, a hammer and a jemmy and meet me outside the engineers' duty mess. We'll go down into number four hold and have a good look at Eberhardt's boxes. Open one or two and have a look inside. Check the contents against any markings. The chief mate will take over here until we get back."

"Aye aye, sir," replied a grinning McGrath, obviously keen to hasten the end of his watch by clambering around a hold in the dark. He turned to go.

"And Third, Eberhardt was on the boat deck earlier, we don't want him to suspect anything, so go quietly and put on a dark shirt, we'll need to keep in the shadows in case he's still about."

"Will do, sir."

McGrath left the wheelhouse, and I went back to my cabin where I pulled off the white shirt I had worn for dinner and slipped into old blue overalls.

Quietly closing the cabin door, I padded softly down the stairs, and aft along the passage to the duty mess where McGrath was waiting. He handed me the torch, I opened the door onto the main deck, and we stepped out. Apart from the glow of the steaming light high up on the mainmast, there was no deck lighting and it took several minutes for my eyes to adjust to the near total darkness. It was not that I was afraid of my footing. I knew every derrick post, ringbolt, ventilator, cargo winch and hatch lid on the main deck, and could find them blindfolded, but I wanted to be able to see in case Eberhardt was snooping about outside.

There was a partial moon, but only a few stars faintly visible. Just before sunset a bank of high cloud had rolled over from the north-east, and far away on the beam lightening flickered along the horizon. The increasing cloud cover had heralded a stiffening breeze that drove the funnel smoke aft in a ragged stream, ghostly illuminated by the mainmast light. As my eyes adjusted, I could see white capped wave crests looming out of the darkness before breaking against the ship's side. I ducked as a larger burst of spray swept the deck, tapped McGrath on the arm and we slipped quietly aft to the deeper shadows beside the derrick post, lifted the hatch access lid, and climbed down the ladder to the tween deck, the intermediate level between the main deck and the bottom of the cargo hold.

The hold was a black, noisy, humid cavern smelling of dusty jute, wood, oil and rancid bilge water. Below us, running along the centre line at the bottom of the hold, inside its steel cased tunnel, the propeller shaft rotated in its bearings, filling the space with a low pitched, repetitive, rumbling. Eberhardt's crates were stowed on the tween deck close to the main hatch opening, so that we could get to them easily in Wewak. Which also made our job that much easier. I flicked on the torch and swept the beam around the deck, the soft yellow light seemingly absorbed into the pitch darkness. I shivered, imagining rats lurking in the shadows, and then grinned, reminding myself that a rat was no match for a man armed with a jemmy.

We worked our way around the tween deck examining the crates in turn, me holding the torch, and McGrath reading the labels and tapping the sides for anything out of the ordinary. He loosened the lids with the jemmy, levering them high enough for me to shine the torch through the gap. I saw nothing suspicious, the contents were exactly what they were supposed to be.

It was hot and airless in the hold, and I was soon sweating like a pig. After McGrath had hammered the nails back into the lid of the crate we had just examined, I motioned him to sit down and take a breather. Checking my watch I realised we had been down there for over an hour, and that Lowther would be wondering where we were. Perhaps I had been wrong about Eberhardt, and his cargo really was just a shipment of mining equipment. But we had still not checked all the crates, and I was not going to admit defeat.

The hold was loud with the rumbling of the propeller shaft, the creaking of the hull and the fretting of the close packed wooden crates as the ship rolled in the seaway, but our ears had accustomed to the noise and we both heard the scrape of leather soles on the steel rungs of the ladder. McGrath's eyes widened in surprise and I switched off the torch. The darkness, held at bay by the yellow beam, leaped back and engulfed us. It was so total I could not see my hand in front of my face, until I turned it over and the faintly glowing dial of my watch floated disembodied before my eyes.

From the direction of the ladder, there was the heavier tread of leather on the steel deck and the forced breathing of someone out of condition, then the darkness was rent by a powerful torch sweeping around the hold like a searchlight. Hidden by the crate we were crouched behind, there was just enough reflected light for me to signal McGrath. He nodded, grabbing the torch. Lowther might have sent someone to look for us. If not, I hoped he was a quick thinker.

"Hello?" he called, switching on the torch and standing up, his voice unnaturally high. Then in a deeper, gruffer tone, "Who's there?"

The other torch beam swept towards him, and I wriggled around and managed to squint along the gap between two crates.

To where McGrath had stopped, transfixed by the light, and staring down the barrel of a large pistol pointed menacingly towards his stomach.

"Who is that?" The voice behind the torch was loud and commanding. "Identify yourself."

Temporarily blinded by the light in his eyes, McGrath would not have been able to identity the gunman, but he recognized the German accent, as did I.

"Mr Eberhardt, isn't it?" He sounded more confident than he must have felt with a pistol pointed at his midriff. "I'm the third mate, McGrath. What are you doing down here in the middle of the night, sir?"

"I came down to check on my cargo, and I might ask you the same question, Mr McGrath. I did not expect to find anyone snooping about amongst it." The pistol remained levelled at McGrath's waist.

"There's no question of snooping, sir," said McGrath, his voice strengthening in protest. "And I'd be grateful if you'd put that away," nodding in the direction of the gun. "I'm down here on captain's orders. There's a possibility of foul weather, so he ordered me to look round the holds and check the lashings. No problems so far, but we don't want heavy crates sliding about and damaging themselves." It was a plausible lie, and I uttered a silent prayer of thanks to Saint Woolos, the patron saint of pirates and smugglers, as Eberhardt lowered the barrel, and slid the big pistol into his coat pocket.

"I had difficulty getting to sleep, Mr McGrath. Not wanting to disturb my wife, I decided to take a turn about the deck. I saw the access was open, and wondered if someone was interfering with my cargo. So I decided to check for myself."

"But really, sir," said McGrath. "You shouldn't be down here, it's dangerous. If you need to check your cargo you should ask Mr Lowther, and he'll send someone with you during the day, when there's more light."

"In my business I find one cannot be too careful. There is valuable equipment in those boxes, and I would not like anything to be damaged, or misplaced."

"There's no question of that, sir. Everything is fine, but you're welcome to check. And then we must return to the deck so I can continue my inspection."

Eberhardt swept the torch beam over his boxes. I thought for a moment he was going to take McGrath up on his offer and check them all himself. So I was relieved to hear him respond, "I'll take your word for it, Mr McGrath."

McGrath waited while Eberhardt climbed the ladder ahead of him. Then he followed, climbing slowly but noisily and waving the torch about. I took the hint and moved as close as I dared to the foot of the ladder. Once he reached the top, he switched off the torch. I heard him say good night to Eberhardt and their footsteps faded, leaving me blindly groping in total darkness. I froze, afraid that stumbling over a crate or a lashing would result in a twisted or broken ankle, which would make Eberhardt even more suspicious. We had not checked all the crates, but the fact that Eberhardt had been snooping about, armed with a pistol, only reinforced my determination to find out what was in them. It would have to wait though, until I could be sure he would not come looking.

As I considered the problem, and my eyes adjusted, I realised that McGrath had left the access open. A faint hint of light, just a slightly paler patch of darkness, showed the direction of the ladder. My gratitude was tinged with suspicion that Eberhardt might have hung around to see if anyone else had been in the hold. But the deck was empty when I cautiously eased my head clear of the coaming, and I silently lowered the lid and screwed on the securing lugs.

From the privacy of my cabin, I blew into the speaking tube to the wheelhouse and asked Lowther to join me before he turned in for his watch below. He wouldn't like it, but I had thought of a way to keep Eberhardt entertained while I had the chance for a proper look at his cargo.

* * *

It was Eberhardt's suggestion of re-fighting the Battle of Jutland with my chief mate, that presented me the opportunity to finish checking the contents of his cargo. The Eberhardts had resumed their earlier practise of having meals sent to their cabin, but I intercepted them during their afternoon stroll around the boat deck, and invited them to join Lowther and me for dinner in the saloon. The prospect of discussing the battle with Lowther brought a roguish twinkle into Eberhardt's blue eyes, and he thanked me profusely. I hid the mischievous twinkle in my own eyes behind a frown. "I should, perhaps, warn you Mr Eberhardt that Lowther's memories of that time are not happy ones. He may need some encouragement to loosen his tongue."

"*Ach*, I believe I understand you perfectly," said Eberhardt, tipping me a theatrical wink. "May I trouble you to provide some bottles of that excellent whisky that your Mr Poh so obligingly placed on board for us?"

"Of course, Mr Eberhardt. Lowther might prefer gin, but we have some of that too. I'll instruct Da Silva to see to it."

In truth, I knew that Lowther hoped the voyage would end before the opportunity for any such discussion arose. It was not that he was an especially modest man. He had the natural reserve that was more common among the aristocratic classes, at least among those few I had met, than the silly ass buffoonery of the Wodehouse novels I secretly enjoyed reading. But discussing Jutland, especially with a German, would inevitably bring back memories I knew he preferred to forget. Not just because of the outcome, with the survivors blamed for not destroying the enemy fleet, but also because of the subsequent ignominious end to his career.

The angry scowl on his face betrayed his feelings when I told him my plan. "I need to see what's inside those crates," I reminded him. "We know from what happened the other night that he's suspicious. So the only way to give me enough time to have a really good look, is to keep him occupied for an entire evening, and send him off to bed to sleep it off."

"If I must, sir." The tone of his voice was flat.

"I'm afraid you must, mister mate," I replied. "I've told Da Silva to lay on a supply of Eberhardt's favourite whisky, and you need to keep him occupied drinking it. I appreciate it might be a long night, so Griffith and young McGrath can split your morning watch between them. It'll do them good to be reminded of what watch and watch was like."

"Very kind of you, sir," responded Lowther, with barely concealed sarcasm. "It's rare to be expected to overindulge to the point where I can't be expected to stand a watch. I do hope I'm up to it."

"Oh, I'm sure your liver's well used to it, Peter. And if anyone can lubricate Eberhardt's tongue, and make him forget about his precious cargo for a few hours, it's you."

He might have found the order distasteful, but he was too professional to show it, and the Lowther that appeared in the saloon later that evening, freshly shaved and in a clean drill shirt bedecked with medal ribbons, would almost have passed muster in a battleship's wardroom. I also asked Fraser to join us, and as we sat down to the meal the conversation ranged between his Gaelic accented, and piercingly witty descriptions of some of the more exotic ports we visited, and Eberhardt's reminiscences of life in New Guinea. Once the meal was over, Mrs Eberhardt excused herself, kissed her husband on the cheek, bade us all a pleasant evening, and retired to their suite. The prospect of grown men re-fighting over the saloon table, part of the war that was supposed to have ended all wars, no doubt offended her Christian sensibilities. Fraser, on the other hand, seemed to relish the prospect, and produced a bottle of his own that contained a dark oily substance smelling of peat smoke, which he pronounced to be malt whisky from Loch Laphroaig on the Inner Hebridean island of Islay. He poured four generous measures, and watched while Eberhardt took a mouthful of the opaque liquid and swirled it around appreciatively.

"An excellent drink, Mr Fraser, we don't see whisky of this quality very often in New Guinea."

"Aye, well it's rare we have guests in this old tub, so this is something of a special occasion. Let me top up your glass," replied Fraser, adding a measure to the remaining half.

"Thank you!" Eberhardt raised his glass. "*Prost.*"

"*Slainte mhath!*"

"So, Mr Lowther," said Eberhardt, his face beaming with anticipation. "I have been looking forward to this discussion. Did I tell you zat my younger brother, Dieter, also fought at Jutland?"

"Yes, sir, I do recall you mentioning it."

"Well gentlemen, he had the honour to be a gunnery officer in the battle cruiser *Derfflinger*, a relatively new ship, commissioned in 1914, under the command of Captain Hartog."

He picked up the saltshaker and placed it on the tablecloth.

"Here she is, in Admiral Hipper's scouting squadron leading the High Seas Fleet into action. The battle began at about 4 p.m. when they ran into your Admiral Beatty's battlecruisers." He placed the peppershaker close to the saltshaker.

"The main German fleet is to the south." He placed the mustard pot to denote them. "While your main fleet is to the north-west." He placed a glass in position.

It was a familiar story, although not one I had heard from Lowther himself. Fraser, who had been an engineering artificer at Jutland, had related his version to me one evening in Hong Kong, where the sight of a fleet review of British, French and American battleships had prompted him to reminisce. He had a surprisingly wide-ranging appreciation of the battle, considering he had spent most of it confined to the engine room of a destroyer.

Unsurprisingly, Eberhardt's description of events was heavily slanted in favour of the German High Seas Fleet, as witnessed by his brother from a front row seat in the *Derfflinger*. He wove the items on the white tablecloth into intricate patterns as he described the course of the fleets as they converged, fought, feinted and converged again. Finally, he slid a glass away from the other fleets.

"And so, gentlemen," he concluded, "during the night Jellicoe withdrew to avoid any further action, and the following day Admiral Scheer led his fleet back to

Germany having sunk three of your British battlecruisers for the loss of only one German battlecruiser and one obsolete battleship. British casualties were nearly 7,000 while German were only 3,000. Surely, then, you will allow me to say that the Battle of Jutland, or the Battle of the Skagerrak as we call it, was a German victory?"

Eberhardt drained the last of his whisky and sat back in his chair with an air of triumph. Fraser topped up their glasses. Lowther sat quietly, gathering his thoughts, before replying.

"There's many in Britain share your opinion, Mr Eberhardt. They expected another Trafalgar. But you know what Mr Churchill has said in defence of Admiral Jellicoe?" He stared doggedly at Eberhardt, waiting for him to reply.

"No, Mr Lowther, I don't believe I do."

"He said that Jellicoe was the only man on either side who could have lost the war in an afternoon. Had he lost, had the High Seas Fleet been freed to control the seas around Britain, it would have been the end for us. So in examining his tactics at Jutland we have to keep that in mind."

"Well then, I am looking forward to your analysis, Commander Lowther," said Eberhardt. "But first, may I be so impolite as to ask you to tell me something of your own role in the battle?"

"It seems your brother had a ringside seat for the majority of the action. I'm afraid mine was a much more limited horizon."

"I am sure you are too modest," replied Eberhardt. "The Distinguished Service Cross is not won lightly."

"I did my duty, Mr Eberhardt," said Lowther, quietly, "and was lucky to survive. There were many that deserved a medal who did not live to see Rosyth ... or Wilhelmshaven."

"Well said, Commander, there were brave men on both sides. Now let us drink to their memory, and then please tell me your opinion of the battle."

They raised their glasses.

"Well," said Lowther, reaching for the items that Eberhardt had used to illustrate his description. "As I said, the strategic importance of the battle was somewhat different for Britain than it was for Germany. Admiral Jellicoe had a number of difficult decisions to make, and in my view got most of them right. And he perhaps misjudged Admiral Scheer, in assuming he would remain at sea to resume the engagement on the following day."

He started to re-arrange the items on the tabletop. "Now, if we go back to the afternoon of the 31st May."

They talked far into the night, Eberhardt's face turning from flushed to florid as he became argumentative, unwilling to accept any criticism of Admiral Scheer. Around midnight I made my apologies, with the excuse that I was required on the bridge to witness a change of course. Eberhardt hardly noticed my departure.

Together he and Lowther had consumed enough whisky to inebriate a forecastle of seamen, but the argument showed no sign of ending, and their drunken voices followed me up the stairs, fading only when I closed the door to the chartroom.

Cramp, the boatswain and a couple of seamen were waiting for me in the darkness of the wheelhouse, almost invisible in dark overalls with rags tied piratically around their heads, and their faces smeared with burnt cork. The darkness hid my smile at their romantic enthusiasm. It was going to be a long night, but by the end of it I would know what was in Eberhardt's crates.

* * *

Eight hours later, I was sitting behind the desk in my day cabin, with the door and portholes open to catch the breeze. I was tired and there were dark circles under my eyes, but I was freshly shaved and dressed in clean shirt and trousers. Lowther sat in an armchair sipping strong black coffee. He looked, and no doubt felt, a darned sight worse than I did. His head must have been aching from the effects of the previous evening, and he was grim faced as he recounted the conversation with Eberhardt.

"It's quite clear the Nazis are rearming for another war," he said, rubbing his temples as if that would reduce the pounding. "Despite his protestations, Eberhardt seems to know quite a bit about what's going on in Germany. How their Navy understates the tonnage of new battleships, and secretly built submarines in Holland and Sweden. Very well informed for a man living in New Guinea, under Australian administration." He paused to light a cheroot, and inhaled a deep lungful of its soothing smoke. "Oh, and he also revealed that when the German Navy was cut back after the war, his brother was transferred to the merchant marine, where he's now a senior captain."

"I knew there was something odd about this from the start," I replied. "I've sailed these waters for years and never come across anyone wanting to explore for gold or oil in that part of New Guinea. Maybe he is going to do some exploration. But that's not all he's doing, and now I've the evidence to prove it. While you were busy entertaining him I had a good look at his cargo. And guess what I found?"

Lowther opened his mouth to reply, but I held up my hand. "Don't worry, Peter, I'll spare your sore head the guessing games. Several of the crates have false bottoms, and there were enough guns in them for a small army. Rifles and machine guns to be exact, with ammunition for both. Oh, and several boxes of hand grenades. Something more than just a businessman is our Mr Eberhardt.

"I wonder what he was going to do with his arsenal?" said Lowther. "Declare independence and hand New Guinea to Hitler's new German Reich?"

"Come on, Peter, you were in the Navy during the war. Their commerce raiders lead you a merry dance, hiding out in remote islands and sinking merchant ships all over the place. If they did it once they could do it again."

"And they would need caches of stores and ammunition," mused Lowther, glancing down at the chart "If there is going to be a war then the Nazis will be looking for friendly places to supply the U-boats and cruisers that Eberhardt seems to know so much about. Where better than remote islands in the western Pacific, which also just happen to lie close to the trade routes between India, China and Australia. I wonder if that's what Eberhardt is doing. Establishing a supply base for his friends in Germany."

It did seem a logical explanation, and I couldn't think of any legitimate reason why Eberhardt would smuggle a small arsenal into New Guinea. Unless someone else had the false bottoms built into the crates without his knowledge. Was that why Poh had dropped a hint about the sensitive nature of the shipment? Had he expected me to search and find the weapons? But if so, what did he expect me to do with them?

"Are you going to inform the authorities and let them deal with it?" asked Lowther, voicing the question I had already wrestled with. "Surely we can't let that stuff be landed."

"Oh, they won't be landed, Peter, but neither will I tell the authorities. Not in Wewak anyway. Whatever he is, Eberhardt will have a lot of influence there. If we hand the guns over to the local customs' boys, Eberhardt will deny all knowledge of them, but I wouldn't put it past him to talk, or buy, or shoot his way out of trouble and seize them back. No, they're safer where I've put them." I sat back in my chair, and lit a cigarette.

"And where have you put them?" inquired Lowther, warily.

"In the cofferdam at the forward end of the bunker hold. It took us most of the night, chippy and me, with the help of the boatswain and a couple of the more trustworthy seamen. It's no wonder that space is called a smuggler's hold. With the coal piled high over the manhole, I'd defy anyone to find it who didn't know the ship. In fact I didn't know about it myself until that rogue Jim Coffin of the *Nimrod* told me, the old pirate."

I lapsed into a broad grin as I recalled the lantern jawed Bostonian, master of *Oriental Venture's* sister ship. They had been consecutive deliveries from Thompson's slipway on grimy Sunderland's, River Wear.

"But surely we can't keep a load of undeclared guns and grenades aboard?" said Lowther, shaking his head in disbelief.

I was a little surprised by his sudden attack of the scruples. We had carried plenty of contraband before. Admittedly, though, I usually drew the line at guns. "This part of the world is becoming an increasingly dangerous place, Peter. The Japanese seem intent on conquering China, and are stirring up independence movements in the Dutch Indies and French Indochina, even in our own British possessions. A few weapons might prove good insurance."

Whatever way I twisted it, I couldn't find a better solution than the one I had chosen. I would keep those guns for the time being, and see what happened. Life was indeed becoming more dangerous, and perhaps we would need their protection before too much longer.

"Let's hope we're safely out of Wewak before Eberhardt finds out the guns are missing," I said. "Then he can go whistle for them."

CHAPTER FOUR

arly morning, and *Oriental Venture* was anchored in ten fathoms of water, flying the yellow quarantine flag and waiting for the customs' launch to bring us clearance to berth. There was no wind and the surface of the crystal clear sea was glassy smooth. Brightly coloured fish were plainly visible fathoms down, swimming in the shade of the ship, exploring the marine growth on her hull, with others, deeper still, patrolling the bright yellow sand of the bottom. Chief Engineer Fraser and I leaned against the boat deck rail, breathing the hot, jungle scented air.

A mile way across the water was the settlement of Wewak. A few white painted government buildings and weather-beaten wooden structures were clustered around a rickety looking timber jetty. A white sandy beach stretched away on either side, fringed with palm trees amongst which native huts nestled. We watched those natives in their outrigger canoes, paddling around the stern of the ship, offering to trade fruit and coconuts with the Chinese seamen. Both women and men wore little more than loincloths twisted between their thighs; their bare breasts garlanded with necklaces of shells and sharks teeth or, in the case of some of the younger women, brightly coloured tropical flowers. There was excited giggling and pointing from the younger seamen, not used to seeing attractive, semi-naked women unashamed of their natural state.

The door to the passenger suite opened and Eberhardt stepped smartly onto the deck, wearing a crisp, white tropical weight suit that Da Silva must have starched and flat ironed for him, and a white Panama hat. He raised the hat and dabbed his brow with a red handkerchief.

"Good morning, Captain, Mr Fraser." He waved the handkerchief towards the settlement. "It might not look much from here, but it's home to me and Amelie, and we like it."

"It's been a pleasure having you aboard, Mr Eberhardt," I said, not entirely untruthfully. If I was right, we had thrown a little grit into the gears of one of Herr Hitler's schemes. And if I decided to dispose of the weapons, there were always customers willing to ask no questions. I could hardly resist a smile. "But I expect you'll be glad to get home."

"The pleasure was entirely ours, Captain Rowden," he replied. "And I especially enjoyed discussing the Battle of Jutland with Commander Lowther. We have agreed to disagree over the outcome, but," he paused, and his brows knitted, "he said little about his own part there. To be awarded such a medal, surely it must have been significant. *Ach*, but perhaps he is too modest, an example of your British stiff upper lip, *ya*?"

"Aye, he's a modest man, right enough," said Fraser, beside me. "Fact is, though, the man's a bloody hero, and there's many wouldn't be here today, myself included, but for what he did that night."

Eberhardt raised an eyebrow. "I had not realised zat you and Commander Lowther were old shipmates."

"Aye, we served together. Back then I was just an engine room artificer, and we didn't have much to do with the officers."

"And this was in one of the ships at Jutland?"

"In the destroyer *Falcon*. It's no secret, but Mr Lowther wouldn't thank me for running tales behind his back, so if I tell you I'd ask you to keep it to yourself, until your away ashore."

"On the word of a gentleman, I assure you, Mr Fraser."

"Aye, well, Mr Lowther was the navigating lieutenant in the *Falcon*. During the night, in those madcap skirmishes that followed the main battle, we sighted the German battleship *Danzig*. The captain ran in for a torpedo attack, weaving at full speed to put the *Danzig's* gunners off their aim, but she hit us several times. The bridge was destroyed, killing the captain, and another shell killed the first lieutenant. Mr. Lowther was the senior officer still alive, and took command."

Fraser paused, his pale blue eyes retreating beneath the tangled, ginger overhang of their eyebrows, as he recalled the events of that terrible night. "Of course, I saw none of this down below. We could only feel the blows of the shells bursting into the ship, and hang on for dear life as she was thrown about like a bone being tossed by a dog. Mr Lowther continued the attack, and took the ship right under the guns of the *Danzig*, so close they couldn't be aimed low enough. But at point blank range the blast alone was enough to blow half the superstructure away. Then he rammed her, ripping a twenty-foot section off the *Danzig's* side plating, leaving a hole big enough to nearly sink her. By this time, *Falcon* was a wreck. Mr Lowther ordered smoke, and in the confusion and the darkness he managed to slip us away. It took twenty-four hours to get back to Rosyth. Pumps barely holding their own, bulkheads shored with every piece of timber we had. When we made the dockyard we still had the *Danzig's* plating lying on deck." He paused, and wiped a hand over his sparse gingery hair. "I told you, the man's a hero and but for him I wouldn't be here."

Eberhardt nodded in admiration, then his brows knotted quizzically. "Excuse me, Captain Rowden, but it strikes me as unusual zat a man of Commander Lowther's age and experience, and with that record, should not be in command of a ship of his own. No doubt he has his reasons?"

"He has his reasons, right enough," I replied. "But it's not my place to pass judgment or to gossip. He's a good chief mate and that's enough for me." And it certainly wasn't my business to explain to Eberhardt how Lowther had been forcibly retired from the Navy after running off with the wife of an admiral. Nor how she had died bearing their child. It was still a doubly hard cross from him to bear.

"I quite understand, Captain," said Eberhardt. "And thank you, Mr Fraser, you have explained much. Now, if you will excuse me I will check if Amelie is ready. I expect we shall be berthing soon."

"Just as soon as the local boys give us clearance to go alongside, you should know what jungle time is like," I said.

We watched Eberhardt's white coated back disappear forward towards his cabin. "Bit different to your brother's experience," Fraser muttered. "Safe in a well armoured battlecruiser. But it was those of us in the small ships who copped hell. And what thanks did we get. Labelled as cowards for letting the High Seas Fleet escape, and then put onto the beach as soon as the war ended. What with that and the death of his woman, can you blame a man for seeking solace in a bottle?"

What thanks indeed! My father had been a fisherman before the war, but had volunteered for the naval reserve. My mother never got over his death. She'd sought solace in a bottle too, until it killed her. I sometimes wondered how things would have turned out for me if he had lived. But it was a pointless question. Things were what they were. I was about to say something to Fraser when McGrath hailed from the bridge wing.

"Customs' launch is just coming alongside, Captain. There's an army chap on board her as well."

"Thank you, Third. Have them shown up to my day cabin, let the chief mate know and send for Da Silva to bring some coffee."

Things were getting more interesting by the minute. What, I wondered, would bring an army officer to a remote port in New Guinea to greet a law-abiding tramp steamer? My mouth split into a piratical grin. No doubt we would find out soon enough.

Up in the day cabin, behind the chartroom, I introduced Lowther and myself to the two uniformed officials who had boarded the ship. The army officer introduced himself as Major Spencer, the Australian Army's attaché for New Guinea. He was accompanied by another Australian called Simpson, who said he was the district officer for Wewak, and responsible for customs and excise. Left in the launch, tied alongside the lowered gangway, were two locals dressed in blue shirts and shorts with government insignia on their shoulders.

Major Spencer accepted a cup of coffee, but politely declined the offer of something stronger. Simpson looked as if he would have been pleased to accept, but upon Spencer's refusal thought better of it. I couldn't resist asking Spencer to whom, or to what, we were obliged for the presence of his company.

"I'll come straight to the point, Captain," said Spencer. "We've had a bit of a tip off from the authorities in Singapore, there might be something on this ship that's not exactly under the description of lawful cargo."

Fortunately, I'd had plenty of practise dealing with unexpected officialdom — or perhaps this time it wasn't so unexpected. I narrowed my eyes and tried to look surprised and offended at the same time. "I hope you are not accusing me, or my crew, of anything illegal?"

"Let's not be too hasty, Captain," replied Spencer. "No one's accusing anyone of anything. The information received was vague, so we don't know what's supposed to be on board, or who put it there or even who it's intended for."

"So there could be nothing at all. This might just be someone trying to make trouble for me, or to see you all sent off on a wild goose chase," I said, maintaining the offended tone.

"I don't think so, Captain. The source was a usually reliable one, and seemed certain that the item or items, whatever they are, are consigned to Wewak. Can you tell me what you're carrying for this port, sir?"

Lowther handed over the cargo manifest, and pointed out Eberhardt's mining and drilling equipment.

"I see," mused Spencer, rubbing his chin. "It shouldn't take too long to have a shuftie through this little lot. I'm told you've a good ear for the jungle drums, Captain. Is there anything else on board you have any suspicion about, any gut feel that something might not be quite kosher, if you know what I mean?"

"I'm not sure how to take that, Major. I make it my business to know what's being carried in my ship. The rest of the cargo is all for Moresby. All for reliable shippers. But if you don't believe me you're welcome to look for yourself." I had rarely spoken truer words. Spencer was in for a surprise if he expected to find anything illegal in Eberhardt's cargo, and I doubted he'd think to start shovelling coal aside looking for a manhole he didn't know existed.

"All in good time, Captain," replied Spencer, coolly. He turned to the district officer. "Simpson, I suggest we have the ship brought alongside, and have this lot unloaded into the shed where we can have a good look at it." He tapped the manifest with his finger.

Simpson nodded his acquiescence. "Right you are sir, I'll just check through the arrival documentation, and then we can give the word to get underway."

Lowther handed Simpson the folder containing the health and customs' declarations.

"What do you know of this man Eberhardt?" said Spencer

"He's a local bigwig," replied Simpson, looking up from the paperwork. "German origins, part of the original colony. Operates a family business with trading posts across New Guinea and the islands. By reputation a shrewd and tough businessman. Other than that, I've never met him."

"He's importing mining equipment. Any mining or exploration being done around here?"

"Not that I know of, sir," replied Simpson. "There's gold to be found around Lae, but that's quite a way south, and I've heard talk of copper and other minerals in the outer islands."

"Of German origin you say, very interesting," mused Spencer. He turned back to me. "As soon as Simpson is satisfied will you place the ship alongside, Captain? And I'd ask you to say nothing to Mr Eberhardt. I'd like to see his face when we have his cargo ashore, and Simpson here tells him we intend to open it."

* * *

"I can assure you, Major Spencer, you will find everything in order. I am a respectable businessman, and have never had any trouble with the import of my goods into Wewak."

Oriental Venture was alongside the jetty — it was old and fragile and I had taken extra care to come alongside gently, easier said than done in the building sea breeze — with her aft hatch covers off and her derricks rigged. Eberhardt's cargo had been discharged under the watchful eyes of Lowther and Simpson, who had checked each crate against the ship's manifest. They were now laid out inside the cargo shed, with Simpson, the packing lists in his hand, ready to order his men to begin opening them. It was baking hot inside the shed, the sun beating down on the galvanised iron roof and turning the interior into a furnace. The sea breeze wafting in through the open doors promised only a hint of coolness. Eberhardt's face was flushed with anger, and he was sweating profusely in his white suit.

"Nevertheless, Mr Eberhardt, we have instructions to open the cases and confirm the contents. Please proceed, Simpson," said Spencer, firmly.

Eberhardt stepped in front of Simpson's men. "I strongly protest, and I can assure you I will be taking this up with the authorities in Moresby. You have absolutely no reason to suspect me of doing anything illegal."

54

"I can assure you the authorities are well aware of our actions, Mr Eberhardt," said Spencer, rather pompously, I thought. "And we are acting on information received."

"Information, what information, and from whom?" snarled Eberhardt.

"That, I am not at liberty to say," said Spencer, primly. "Now please stand aside."

Eberhardt snorted with exasperation, but moved aside to let the men pass. They inserted small crowbars under the rims of the crates and stated to lever the lids off, accompanied by the tortured squeaking of the long nails as they wrenched free from the timber.

"Are you responsible for this, Captain Rowden?" demanded Eberhardt. "Have you requested these men search and harass me? Because I am German, or have offended you in some way?"

I had been watching impassively from the rear of the shed.

"Not at all, Mr Eberhardt, I know nothing about this," I replied, wondering why he should point the finger at me. I believed Spencer when he said he'd had a tip off from a reliable source, he wouldn't have come all this way otherwise. In which case I clearly wasn't the only one who had doubts about Eberhardt's cargo. "I know only that Major Spencer has orders to search the cargo and, presumably, my ship."

One by one, the crates were opened and their contents unpacked onto the floor of the shed. Eberhardt paced up and down, agitatedly looking at each case, and checking the contents at the same time as Simpson ticked them off against the packing list.

"Shovels, pickaxes, winches, pulleys, washboxes, handrills, sledgehammers. Exactly as listed," he declaimed, angrily. "What are you hoping to find?"

"We will know if and when we find it," replied Spencer, enigmatically.

Eberhardt's eyes blazed, and he raised a clenched fist, threateningly. "You don't know what you are looking for, or why you are looking for it ... because there is nothing to find," he shouted. "I am being harassed for no reason, and I shall be raising a formal complaint. See for yourselves, the boxes are empty. Which of the items in front of you is not on the packing list?"

It was true. The cases were empty and the contents all accounted for. Simpson stared questioningly at Spencer, presumably thankful he had been under instructions to follow the major's orders. No blame should attach to him if Eberhardt made good on his threat to lodge a complaint.

Major Spencer walked slowly around each crate, examining them one by one. Those containing the smaller items of equipment were rectangular, and of roughly the same dimensions. He started at them, eyes darting from one to the other, grim-faced, looking for any obvious signs of difference. Then his eyes narrowed, and the corner of his mouth twitched. He bent down to examine the bottom of one of the crates, and then turned to check the one next to it.

"Ah!" he stuck out a hand. "Jemmy?"

Snatching the offered crowbar, he rapped the bottom of the crate. There was a dull, hollow thud.

"That's interesting," said Spencer, his mouth twisting into a frown. "This one's got a false bottom." He worked his way around the other crates and found two more that made the same hollow sound.

"Open them up and let's see what surprises they have in store for us."

Eberhardt stood transfixed, as Simpson's men used their crowbars to lever open the false bottoms. I kept my eyes on his face and saw his jaw drop, and his eyes widen with astonishment as the bottoms came off to reveal the empty compartments beneath.

"What's this?" snorted Spencer, whom I was happy to see looked as equally surprised as Eberhardt. "Dummy compartments with nothing in them. Is someone trying to play tricks on us? What do you say to this Mr Eberhardt?"

After the initial shock of seeing the empty compartments, Eberhardt had quickly regained his composure.

"I know nothing at all, Major Spencer." He replied. "I did not manufacture the crates. The equipment was delivered to me already packed in them. I merely checked it was all correct as ordered. I saw nothing to suggest they had false bottoms. You must question others as to zat." I had to hand it to him, he sounded convincing, for someone who had just discovered the theft of his arsenal.

"We will sir, don't worry," Spencer replied, fixing me with a steely-eyed glare, which I returned with what I hoped was injured innocence. "However for the time being all appears to be in order. I'll have the crates repacked, Mr Eberhardt, and you can remove them from the shed at your leisure."

"Just before you do that," I interjected, stepping forward with a document folder. "Before I hand the cargo over to you, Mr Eberhardt I need you to sign for the release of the banker's draft for the freight payment." It was hard to keep the knowing smirk off my face. "Please sign here, to confirm your cargo has been delivered in full, and in good order."

Eberhardt's eyes bored into mine, his livid face a mask of suppressed anger. He snatched the document and pulled a fountain pen out of his jacket pocket. "Have I received all of my cargo, Captain Rowden?" he hissed, in a voice at once both soft and menacing, pitched so that it reached my ears only.

"Yes you have, Mr Eberhardt," I replied emphatically, preparing to twist the knife. "As you can see. All according to the packing list."

"According to the packing list!" he repeated through gritted teeth, unscrewing the cap on the pen and jabbing his signature onto the paper. "I won't forget this Rowden."

This time the words carried, and Major Spencer looked up inquiringly.

"Yes indeed, Captain Rowden," continued Eberhardt, smoothly, his voice dripping barely concealed sarcasm. "Thank you for a most pleasant voyage which I will never forget. And now, if you will excuse me, I will claim my goods and continue on my way."

Simpson's men repacked the crates and hammered the lids back on. Major Spencer took my arm and guided me out of earshot.

"What do you make of that, Captain?" he asked. "Eberhardt seemed very agitated when we found the false bottoms, but as astounded as we were to see them empty."

"Perhaps he really had no idea they were there," I replied, wondering if I was digging myself into a hole. "But in that case I can't imagine what they were there for, or who asked for them to be made that way." I paused, and then, still digging, I couldn't resist adding, "Or perhaps someone got there before you did, before the crates were even loaded onto *Oriental Venture*."

"Or while they were on board her," retorted Spencer, clearly jumping to the obvious conclusion.

"Surely you can't think my crew would have opened those cases? But like I said, if you want to search the ship, be my guest."

Spencer stared at me, unblinkingly, and for a moment I thought he was going to rephrase my question. "Somehow, I don't think I'd find anything if I did, do you, Captain?"

I shrugged. "The offer's there. But if I do come across anything suspicious I'll let you know." I held out my hand. Spencer hesitated, then took it and we shook.

"Very well, Captain. Good luck and keep safe."

Was there a hint of warning in his voice, I wondered, and if so against whom was he warning me. I almost had a moment of weakness. If Eberhardt was as guilty as I thought he was, it occurred to me that Spencer might be persuaded to look upon my removal of the weapons as a public service. But old habits die hard, and I signalled to Lowther that we should leave them to it and get back aboard.

* * *

The shade under the bridge awning, cooled by the last of the sea breeze, was a welcome relief to the heat of the cargo shed. Lowther puffed contentedly on a cheroot, and I nursed a Senior Service in a cupped hand. The crew were securing the derricks and hatch covers.

"Have everything squared away so we can sail for Moresby at first light," I said. "And no one's to go ashore. I don't suppose Eberhardt will try anything, but double the watch on deck."

"Aye aye," replied Lowther, pausing as if uncertain whether to pursue the subject. "If you don't mind my asking, skipper. I saw Eberhardt's reaction down there when they opened the false bottoms. Did he say anything when you asked him to sign for acceptance of his cargo?"

"He was furious, but tried to hide it. I think he guessed what must have happened. He threatened me, quietly so no one else would hear. But he signed the release of the banker's draft. What else could he do? All the manifested cargo was delivered exactly as contracted. Who was he going to complain to? Tell Major Spencer he had guns hidden in those compartments, but they'd been stolen? He signed the release, but he knows we've got them."

"What about Major Spencer and Simpson? Have they any idea?" asked Lowther.

"Simpson's just a boy, he'll do what Spencer tells him," I replied. "But Spencer is suspicious. He doesn't buy that the boxes were built with false bottoms, but nothing was put in them. He thinks we're involved, that whatever was hidden in those boxes is now tucked safely away on board. I've told him he's free to search, but he's decided not to. Unless he changes his mind, it looks like we're free to continue the voyage."

"But if the authorities do know about the guns, wouldn't it be safer to hand them over?" asked Lowther, eyeing me cautiously. It was a reasonable question, the same one I had asked of myself, and rejected.

"Like I said, Peter, these waters are becoming increasingly dangerous. There are still pirates working out of the remote islands, and Chinese warlords fighting over control of their ports and rivers. And now Eberhardt. If he is working for the Nazis, things are likely to become more dangerous still. It might be good to have a bit of extra insurance, or at least something to bargain with." I could tell from Lowther's face that I protested too much. It was one thing to have foiled an attempt at gun running. It was quite another to let my pride — offended that someone had tried to put one over on me — leave me open to the same accusation. I turned towards the ladder, not wishing to argue with him. "I'm going below, call me if anything unusual occurs. Other than that we sail at dawn."

Back in my cabin, I locked the signed banker's draft into my safe. I would be glad when I had safely handed it to the owners in Hong Kong. It was irrevocable, and they would get their cash whether Eberhardt liked it or not. The safe also contained a Mark VI Webley pistol and a box of .455 ammunition. Something told me it would be a good thing to give it the once over, so I carried it to the desk and pulled out the cleaning kit. When I had finished, I loaded the chambers, checked the safety catch was on, and locked it in my desk drawer.

Finally, I strolled out onto the forward end of the boat deck, just outside my cabin, an area known as the captain's bridge, where I leaned on the rail, enjoying the last breaths of the sea breeze. The sun was sinking behind the range of hills to the west, the short tropical twilight quickly fading in a soft glow of reds and purples. With the arrival of darkness, the yellow flames of cooking fires flared and guttered among the palm trees as the natives prepared their evening meals. The mingled odours of wood smoke, rotting seaweed and fish tailings, borne on the first whispers of the land breeze, reminding me of the foreshore in Whitstable where I had lived as a boy. In a tiny fisherman's cottage perched on the shingle, its black, tarred canvas sides and roof stretched over wooden beams stained by years of smoke and grime.

I had well and truly taken the boy out of Whistable, but I couldn't take Whitstable out of the boy. Smuggling was in my blood, and despite Lowther's foreboding's, I smiled at the thought of the dozens of rifles, machine guns and grenades safely stowed away in my ship. They were good insurance, and would also be worth a pretty penny in the right quarter. I certainly had no intention of starting a war with them.

CHAPTER FIVE

Oriental Venture lay alongside the government jetty in Port Moresby, the capital of the Australian administered territory of Papua. White painted government and commercial buildings crowded around the end of the jetty, and spilled out on either side along the foreshore. Behind them, clusters of woven palm frond and corrugated iron shacks sprawled amongst the trees, and climbed the lower slopes of the scrubby hills that formed the backdrop to the harbour. Rising in the distance, to the north-west, were the blue hazed mountains of the Owen Stanley Range.

It was a hot and humid morning, the sun beating mercilessly down on the ship. But the big white clouds building up over the hills offered the promise of welcome, if only temporary, relief in the form of an afternoon downpour, during which children would dance and laugh as they splashed about in the puddles, their naked bodies glistening in the rain.

We had already spent a week in Port Moresby, unloading the cargo from Singapore, and then back loading bagged copra, which was slowly filling the tween decks and holds. The dried meat of coconuts, the copra was bagged in rough hessian sacks which were slung aboard by our own derricks, and then stacked in the holds by gangs of natives, the sweat pouring in shining rivulets down their dust caked, ebony skin, grunting and wheezing as they heaved the heavy sacks into position. With freight earned by the ton, the more copra we could squeeze into the ship the better the return, and Lowther drove the mates hard in order to screw as many bags as possible into every available space. I'd heard of ships where they even stowed bags in the alleys and mess rooms of the crew's quarters. Not a pleasant prospect for the men who had to share those spaces, as the copra contained insects and emitted a foul smelling gas.

Of Walter Eberhardt and his missing cargo, we had heard nothing. Major Spencer had returned to Port Moresby and paid me a short visit, only out of courtesy he said; but I had the distinct impression he knew more than he was prepared to let on, and wanted me to know that he had his eye on us. For my part, I remained convinced that Eberhardt was involved in some sort of monkey business connected with Nazi Germany, but I kept those thoughts to myself. I had an ingrained suspicion of government officials, and I saw no advantage in sharing my knowledge of what had become of the weapons. I wasn't even sure that Spencer knew what had been in those false bottoms, and, if not, I wasn't the one to tell him.

Of more immediate concern was the state of the coal bunkers which were already half depleted. We had enough to reach Hong Kong provided the stokers were not too heavy handed, although it would probably eat into our safety margin. Running out of coal was one thing, but I also didn't want to arrive with the manhole to the cofferdam exposed. "We don't want any nosey customs' joker noticing a manhole behind the coal and wondering where it leads," I had remarked to Fraser, as I instructed him to keep the coal trimmed so that the manhole remained buried.

"That we don't, Captain," Fraser had replied, his eyes twinkling in his round pink face. "Wouldn't do for the old girl to get a reputation for hiding things under her skirt."

Further along the foreshore, a second jetty jutted into the emerald bright waters of the harbour. It had been vacant when we arrived, but for the last few days a large German merchant ship named *Dortmund* had occupied it. Her hull was entirely black, but her deckhouses and superstructure were spotless white. Above the engine casing, a squat black funnel bore the owners' markings of broad white and red stripes. She was a large modern ship, and an oil burner by the look of her. Checking the shipping register revealed that she belonged to the German-Australian Line; but she looked too large and too modern to be tramping to the outports of the Pacific. I kept an eye on her, but saw nothing but routine cargo activities and the normal comings and goings of her crew.

Nevertheless, my sixth sense made me wary.

"It seems an amazing coincidence," I remarked to Lowther, as we stood on the bridge watching the coolies busy on the *Dortmund's* deck, "that Eberhardt tries to smuggle in a cargo of weapons, and then days later a big German ship arrives."

"Well it might make sense if you're right about Eberhardt setting up a supply base for commerce raiders," replied Lowther.

I nodded in agreement. "The Nazis wouldn't want the embarrassment of one of their own ships being caught smuggling guns into Australian territory. Much easier to have them shipped in an unsuspecting, harmless looking tramp like us."

We were not exactly harmless, but I hated being taken for a mug, and the thought that Eberhardt had attempted to use my ship to smuggle weapons into Wewak, perhaps even with Poh's knowledge, was like a painful slap in the face. I fully intended that Poh feel the extent of my displeasure next time we were in

Singapore. In the meantime we still had cargoes to carry and owners to satisfy, and it wasn't my job to take on Nazi gun runners, at least not to any greater extent than I already had. Depriving him of a few dozen rifles and machine pistols, had undoubtedly added Eberhardt to the growing list of people who had crossed me off their Christmas card list, but was hardly likely to make much of a dent in Herr Hitler's ambitions.

"Like I said, Peter, these waters are becoming more dangerous, but whatever Eberhardt's up to, best we keep our noses out of it, and leave him to the likes of Major Spencer. We're sailing tomorrow so I'm going ashore this afternoon to meet the agent. I suggest you get Griffith to check over the courses for Hong Kong, and double check we have enough coal to get there."

* * *

Later that afternoon I sat on the veranda of the Papua Hotel, hoping my damp clothes would dry in the hot, sticky conditions. The afternoon downpour had arrived early, and I'd had to run the last hundred yards. I was early for the meeting with the agent, and took a seat to wait for him, signalling to a waiter to bring me a beer. It arrived in a tall frosted glass, ice cold to suit the taste of the Australians that made up the majority of the hotel's patrons, and gratefully refreshing after the hot walk from the port.

As I drank the beer, I listened to the rustling of palm fronds, the chirp of geckos as they hunted insects in the crevices of the ceiling, and the rasp of cicadas in the bushes. The hotel was set back from the edge of the dusty road, behind a coarse grass lawn over which tall palms swayed in the afternoon sea breeze. Dotted among the palms were bushes of scarlet and purple bougainvillea, their sharp thorns a hazard for the unwary, or the tipsy, who stumbled into them. The hotel was a two storied, timber framed building set on metal-capped wooden stumps as a defence against termites. The walls were hardwood planks from which the white paint was peeling, and the roof was clad in red painted corrugated iron. A broad veranda ran around the entire hotel supported by wooden pillars and decorated with wrought iron scrollwork. The lower story contained the bar and a restaurant. There were bedrooms on the floor above, in one of which I had once enjoyed the company of a young native woman. I had managed to smuggle her into the room without the desk clerk noticing. He caught me on the way out, however, and would have raised a sanctimonious row, except for the offer of a few Straits Dollars (almost as many as I'd paid the girl) backed up by the threat of my unholy fist.

Smiling at the memory I checked my watch, and clicked my tongue in annoyance as I realised the agent was late.

Any further thoughts of his tardiness were driven aside by the sight of a ship's officer in a starched white uniform, complete with cap, mounting the steps to the veranda, and striding towards my table. There were four gold stripes on his shoulders, and gold lace embroidering the peak of his cap, on which there was a badge of oak leaves surrounding a small red and white striped flag. The same coloured stripes as on the *Dortmund's* funnel.

My lips pursed in a silent whistle. There was no doubting this man's occupation; he was the German ship's captain.

I watched him approach through narrowed eyes. There were plenty of other vacant tables, but he made a beeline for mine, stopped, stiffened, almost as if to attention, and then spoke in a precise and familiar sounding voice.

"If I am not mistaken you must be Captain Rowden of the *Oriental Venture*." He paused, as if waiting for some acknowledgment, and then continued. "Allow me to introduce myself, Captain Dieter Eberhardt of the *Dortmund*." He held out his hand.

It was as if some particularly well matching pieces of a complex jigsaw had suddenly fallen into place. Wolfgang Eberhardt, a Nazi sympathiser, attempting to smuggle arms into New Guinea, and then the arrival of a smart, modern - and out of place - German cargo ship commanded by his younger brother, a former - or perhaps even still serving - German naval officer. My suspicions were proving well founded, and I wondered, again, about the sixth sense that had, on many occasions, saved my skin. That tingling in my fingertips when I sensed I was being lied to, or the approach of danger. I couldn't explain it, perhaps it was something I had inherited from all those Rowden smuggler ancestors. What was it they called those things, genes? A smugglers' gene perhaps?

I froze my features into a polite smile to mask my surprise, stood and grasped the offered hand. It was a public place and the civilities were expected. Up close, I could see the resemblance. Dieter Eberhardt was a younger, thinner version of his brother. Tall and fair skinned with the same blonde hair and pale blue eyes. But where Wolfgang had the softness of good living, Dieter appeared whip hard, a man used to commanding others, and being obeyed.

"Would you care to sit down, Captain Eberhardt?" My sixth sense told me that Eberhardt was not there to wish me a pleasant voyage, but I kept my tone civil. "I'm waiting for the agent, but he seems to have been detained."

"Thank you, Captain Rowden, I will join you for just a few moments."

I resumed my seat and Eberhardt took the chair opposite. He pulled a slim gold case out of his shirt pocket, flipped it open and offered me a small cigar.

"Sumatran tobacco, the best, I can assure you."

There was no point declining the offer of a good smoke, so I took one. Eberhardt lit us both with an expensive looking sliver lighter engraved with the arms of the

Imperial German Navy. Then he sucked in a lungful of smoke and blew it slowly towards the ceiling.

"I think perhaps you have heard of me, Captain Rowden?" he said, with just a hint of menace. "I have certainly heard about you and your ship from my brother, who had the pleasure of sailing with you to Wewak."

"Indeed, it was a most pleasant voyage." I beamed my best Cheshire cat grin at him. "Is your brother in Port Moresby? I'd be delighted to renew his acquaintance." We both knew I was lying, and I guessed what Eberhardt's answer would be.

"No, no, I saw him when we called at Wewak ourselves, on our way here. We had a most interesting conversation. Wolfgang tells me your chief mate fought at Jutland."

"Yes, he and your brother had a long conversation about it. It seems your ship distinguished herself."

"Wolfgang tends to exaggerate. Perhaps we were a little lucky. However, I understand Commander Lowther was decorated for his action in taking on one of our battleships and surviving. A brave man, I should like to meet him, but, alas, there will be no time as we sail tonight."

I leaned back in my chair, wondering when Eberhardt would get to the point.

He took a long pull on the cigar. "You are, perhaps, wondering why I have encountered you like this?" His smile thinned and hardened.

"I didn't imagine you were here by accident."

"Indeed not." He dropped his voice, and leaned forward over the table as if to share a confidence. "I believe you have some things zat belong to my brother. I think it would be a very good idea if they were returned."

"I have no idea what you are talking about," I replied, almost convincing myself that I sounded innocent.

"Come, come, Captain," said Eberhardt, his voice almost conciliatory. "I think you know the cargo you delivered to Wewak for him was incomplete, and that you know where the rest of it is."

"I saw the customs' officer find false bottoms in some of the crates, if that's what you mean. But they were empty." The truth can be a powerful defence sometimes. "Are you accusing me of stealing something that was supposed to have been inside them?"

"I am merely stating what I believe to be a fact, Captain Rowden. I believe you know what was in those crates, and zat you know where it is now, and I repeat, it would be better it was returned."

"Or what? Are you threatening me?" It was time to display some teeth.

"I know of your reputation, Captain Rowden, you are not a man to be intimidated. But I warn you, you are making powerful enemies." He stubbed out the end of his cigar in the sand filled ashtray and rose to go. "I believe I see your ship's agent approaching. I shall take my leave. I sail at midnight. If you wish to avoid trouble I suggest you send a man to my ship after dark, and we shall arrange a transfer of the ... goods." He touched his fingers to the peak of his cap, turned on his heel and strode from the veranda, leaving me to listen to the mumbled apologies of the agent for his lateness.

The agent, a young Australian called Hicks, his face bathed in sweat from hurrying in the afternoon heat, took the chair just vacated by Eberhardt.

"My apologies for being late, Captain. It's been a busy day and I've been preparing the paperwork for *Dortmund's* departure this evening ... but that's no excuse for keeping you waiting." He wiped his brow with a clean, white handkerchief. "I'm from Perth and I'm used to the heat, but it's the humidity here that does for me. I see you've met Captain Eberhardt. His *Dortmund's* a fine ship, and he runs her very well." He paused, conscious that in praising the German he might have offended me. Although even I would have admitted that *Oriental Venture* paled by comparison.

"Runs it like a warship you mean," I said, smiling to put him at his ease. "Not really surprising considering he used to be in the German Navy. But, actually we were talking about his brother, who travelled down with us to Wewak from Singapore."

"Really, what a coincidence," replied Hicks. "Small world."

"Coincidence by buggered," I thought, and then, out loud. "Yes, and getting smaller all the time. Now what have you got for me?"

He handed over a sheaf of paperwork. "These are the departure papers. And there's been a last minute request for the shipment of some barrels of diesel and petrol to Lorengau, a small settlement on the north coast of Manus Island. Do you know it, Captain?"

I nodded. I had been there several times. A tricky approach through the reef, and there were sand bars and coral heads to the north of the anchorage that needed to be watched for. We were lower on coal than I would have liked, but Manus was more or less on the direct track to Hong Kong.

"They'll have to go on deck though."

"The shipper's already agreed to that," replied Hicks. "It's not much of a load, only a dozen or so barrels of each. Appears they're close to running out of fuel, and need the shipment in a hurry. There's no jetty can accommodate you, but a workboat will meet you and you can sling the barrels into her."

"Who's the shipper?" I asked, a hint of suspicion forming in my mind.

"Mr Leung, one of the local Chinese businessmen. He sells fuel around the islands to the fishermen and small interisland traders. Don't worry, he's good for the freight, you have my word on that," replied Hicks, mistaking the frown that had flashed across my brow. "If you can take them I'll have them delivered as soon as you start closing up after the copra. And I'll be down first thing in the morning for the signed papers."

"I'll let the mate know to expect them," I replied. "Now, if there is nothing more let me buy you a beer. You look as if you could do with one. Then I'll be getting back to my ship."

The sun was well down towards the horizon by the time I was back aboard. I found Lowther in his cramped office, completing the stowage plan, and relayed the conversation with Dieter Eberhardt to him.

"I think it's pretty clear now, where we stand," I said. "The Eberhardt brothers are in this together. They suspect we have the weapons, in fact Dieter Eberhardt has just accused me of stealing them."

"Why not just report it to the authorities, that man Major Spencer?" replied Lowther, the voice of reason, as ever.

"And have to explain why we broached Eberhardt's cargo, stole the guns and concealed them from the customs' inspection at Wewak," I replied. "Those weapons were intended for the *Dortmund.* Heaven knows, Peter, I'm not averse to smuggling. I come from a long line of smuggler's, but if the Eberhardts think they can smuggle something in my ship without telling me, then they can take the consequences!"

Poh, the old devil, had hinted there was something special about Eberhardt's cargo, but I guessed he hadn't wanted to tell me quite how special, and share the benefits with me.

"You don't think they'll try and get them back?" said Lowther.

"Possibly. I don't think Eberhardt will try anything here, but you never know. Who's on watch this evening?"

"I've given young McGrath a couple of hours off, but Griffith's on board." replied Lowther.

"Well, post some extra hands on deck this evening, and tell them to sing out at the first sign of anything suspicious. Tell whoever's on watch to let me know when the *Dortmund* sails, whatever the time."

Lowther nodded, and I rose and picked my way past him towards the door. "I'll be in my cabin. Call me if anything at all happens."

I was probably worrying about nothing, except that the tingling in my fingertips suggested I hadn't seen the last of Dieter Eberhardt.

* * *

I had no doubt that McGrath set out to enjoy his wander around Port Moresby. It would have made a pleasant change to have a few hours to himself. To feel the land firm under his feet, to smell the rich, ripe, scents of the tropical flowers and bushes that grew in profusion in the hothouse climate, and to hear the cheerful laughter of the naked, native children playing amongst the palm trees that fringed the shore.

There was not much chance for exercise as an officer in a steamship. So a couple of hours brisk walking along the foreshore was a chance to keep fit, as well as a break from the ship's routine. And it should even have been possible for him to find somewhere to get a decent steak and some fresh vegetables, if he fancied a change from the ship's fare. But young men being what they were, the lure of cold beer and the possibility of being able to ogle such of the European women who were game enough to walk out in the frontier-like town, inevitably drew him towards one of its pubs. Unsurprisingly, therefore, it was at the Papua Hotel where I found him.

It was shortly after eight, and the start of McGrath's watch, when Lowther knocked on my door and told me he had not returned. Had he just forgotten the time, I wondered? His timekeeping was reliable enough on board, and I had not seen him worse the wear for drink. On the other hand, I remembered the Guild secretary's caution back in Sydney, and had seen the short fuse to his temper when he raised his fists against Griffith in Singapore. Despite being on the frontier of what Europeans thought of as civilisation, however, Port Moresby was a relatively quiet place. There were no crowds of thirsty labourers or dockworkers eager to let off steam after a hard shift. The white men who lived in Papua were mostly government officials, clerks and planters. There were hard drinkers among them certainly, but would they want to pick a fight with a young Australian ship's officer, or he with them. Thirsty seamen, though, that was another thing entirely. The only other ship in Port Moresby was the *Dortmund*. She was due to sail at midnight. Were some of her liber-tymen indulging in a last fling?

"All right, I'm going ashore to investigate." I heaved myself out of my chair and crossed to the clothes' locker. "Give Griffith a shout and tell him to come with me. If we're not back in an hour send word to the police."

I grabbed the shoulder holster from inside the locker and strapped it on under a loose fitting, khaki jacket. From my desk drawer I pulled out the big Webley revolver, span the cylinder to check all the chambers were loaded, and slipped it into the holster, feeling its reassuring bulk in my armpit. I met Griffith at the gangway, there was a wicked gleam in his eyes, and I wondered if he had slipped a knife into his pocket.

I lead the way as we walked up the road into the town, which was not large, so there were not many places a man could go missing, unless McGrath had met an accident out in the scrub, in which case we would have little chance of finding him until daylight. The pubs were obviously the place to start, though. The Papua Hotel was the largest and closest to the waterfront, so I headed towards it.

I heard the commotion before I caught sight of what was causing it. With Griffith at my heels, I plunged down the dark tunnel between the trees and bushes, following the path towards the hotel entrance. Ahead of us the noise resolved into the shouts and cheers of men yelling encouragement. I stopped in the shadows where the path emerged between the bougainvillea bushes. The lawn beyond was illuminated by a pool of light streaming out of the hotel windows, in the centre of which was a circle of shouting, gesticulating onlookers. And in the centre of the circle were two bloodied and bruised men, trying to pound the life out of one other.

One of them was German; there was no mistaking the language in which his backers were cheering on their countryman. He was a big man, much bigger than his opponent in both weight and height.

The rest of the crowd was Australian, and they were enjoying the contest greatly. They would bet on anything, Australians. Even two raindrops sliding down a window pane. I had once heard two men leaving a Melbourne picture house, after a matinée showing of *Captain Blood*, wagering on Olivia de Havilland's bust size. How they were to settle the bet I could hardly imagine. So I was not entirely surprised that, despite his smaller size, there appeared to be a number of Australians prepared to risk their money on the German's opponent. Perhaps they thought they were being fair to the underdog, although in my experience it's not the size of the dog in the fight that matters, as much as the size of the fight in the dog. And in this case the smaller dog was clearly the better fighter.

For all his advantage of height, weight and reach, the German was a brawler; slow and his punches predictable. He was strong, though, and any blow he landed could do real damage. And he was tough. There was blood dripping from his nose, and one eye was starting to close, but he kept doggedly advancing, throwing hay-maker punches and causing the smaller man to backpedal, ducking and weaving furiously.

But the smaller man was a boxer. Fast and light on his feet. For every punch the German threw, he counter punched two. Lightning fast combinations of jabs and crosses, mixed up with hooks and uppercuts. He hadn't dodged all the German's blows, though. There was a cut opening over one eyebrow and both eyes were swollen. He was working furiously to keep out of the German's clutches, just one solid blow from those massive fists and he would be down.

And I might be short of a third mate, again.

Motioning Griffith to stay close I pushed my way into the rear of the circle, edging men aside in order to obtain a better view. An Australian, his sweaty face flushed with exhilaration, turned sharply in response to my elbow shoving him aside; fleetingly considered arguing and then, catching sight of my face, thought better of it.

I watched as the men continued to trade blows. The advancing German launched his fists in another attack, flailing in desperation, trying to knock McGrath down. He missed, dropped his guard momentarily, and McGrath seized the opportunity to step in close and fire a combination — hard left jab, right uppercut and hard left jab again, the blows beating a rapid tattoo on the German's jaw — before dancing clear again. The big German grunted with pain and shook his head, but still he advanced and McGrath backed away, his bloodied fists maintaining his guard, desperate to keep on his feet. The German launched another punch, and there was a collective groan from the Australians as McGrath skipped back to avoid the skull-crushing round-arm and lost his footing. He was up in a moment, trying to twist away out of reach, but there were hands at his back forcing him forward, into the path of the advancing German.

One of the seamen shouted something and the big German grunted a reply. His bloodstained, split lips twisted into a painful grin as he squinted malevolently at McGrath through battered, half-closed eyes. The Germans had grown tired of the fight and wanted to end it. The big German swayed as he stepped forward and spat blood onto the ground.

"Now I finish you," he growled, in English.

McGrath tried to step back out of reach, but the German seamen crowded behind him, preventing him from dodging the blow. The big German drew back his massive fist — there was no escaping it — and buried it into McGrath's midriff, knocking the breath out of him and collapsing him to the ground. German arms dragged him to his feet as the big man prepared to strike another deadly blow.

"Cover my back," I whispered to Griffith, pushing my way through the crush into the centre of the circle. The mood of the crowd was turning ugly. Men with bets on McGrath were howling abuse at the Germans, who were shouting back, urging their man to finish the young Australian. The big man raised his fist.

"Stop!" I thundered, in a voice I knew was loud enough to carry from the quarterdeck to the maintop of a square-rigger in a full gale.

Momentarily, the Germans froze.

"Gentlemen," I continued, in my normal voice of command. "This hardly looks like a fair fight, all of you against one man."

The big German lashed out, his blood-lust obviously unsatisfied by the inconclusive fight, angry and frustrated by the painful, cutting blows McGrath had landed. Through half closed, lash-clotted, eyelids, desperate to hurt someone, he made the mistake of launching a fist at me.

I evaded the blow easily, had expected it, and as the big man's arm flailed the empty air I slammed my right fist into his nose, feeling the bones crumple. The big man dropped to his knees holding his nose and groaning, blood pouring between his fingers. There was an animal growl and the other Germans edged menacingly forward, like wolves encircling their prey. Griffith and I couldn't fight them all, and McGrath was in no state to help. I had to end this quickly. I reached inside my jacket and pulled out the big revolver. The Germans hesitated at the sight of the threateningly large muzzle. The Australians, realising the fun was over, and anxious not to be associated with any shooting, melted rapidly away, settling bets as they went.

"This is the largest calibre version of the Webley," I said, pointing it at the big man's belly. "Just about the most powerful hand gun ever produced. Is there anyone not prepared to take my word for it?" The Germans stood transfixed. They might not have understood all the English, but they knew what a large pistol meant. "No? Well then, please let my third officer go. Come Mr McGrath, I'm disappointed to find you brawling again."

German hands released his arms, and McGrath stumbled forward his lips cracking into a painful looking smile.

Which faded at the sound of a German accented voice behind me.

"Kindly drop your gun, Captain. Zere vill be no further trouble, but I will relieve you of the responsibility of my men." I twisted my head and saw the *Dortmund's* chief mate, three gold stripes on his shoulders, and a Luger pointed into the small of my back. I lowered my gun, wondering where the devil Griffith had disappeared to. I needn't have worried. Like a cat pouncing silently onto its prey, he slipped out from the surrounding shadows and grasped the German chief mate's head, pulling it back with one hand while the other pressed a razor sharp knife against his throat, drawing beads of blood.

"I don't think so boyo," purred Griffith, in his Welsh accented English. "I suggest you drop your toy pistol, or I'll slit your throat from ear to ear." He turned his head towards me. "Sorry, Captain, saw this one lurking amongst the bushes. Thought it would be safer to take him from the rear, so to speak."

The German chief mate dropped the luger, and slowly raised his hands. I rounded on him angrily.

"First your men attack one of my officers, and then when I intervene to break up the fight you threaten me with a gun." I neglected to mention that I had drawn a gun first, and gestured to Griffith to pick up the Luger.

"I'm returning to my ship. I won't hesitate to inform the Australian authorities if there is the slightest hint of any more trouble. Mr Griffith, would you please assist the third mate?"

He handed the Luger to me, and slipped an arm underneath McGrath's shoulder.

"Come on, James," he said, gently.

I waited until they were well concealed by the shadows, and then backed away, the Webley prominent in my fist in case any of the Germans had fight left in them.

Angry words from the German chief mate followed me into the darkness. I couldn't understand the language, but the tone was clear and I guessed the crew were in hot water. Despite the warning he had delivered to me, Captain Eberhardt would not have wanted unnecessary attention drawn to his ship. His crew brawling with a British officer in a public place in Port Moresby, was exactly the sort of trouble he would not want. If the *Dortmund* sailed under orders of the German Navy, then her crew would be subject to naval discipline. I had no doubt that Eberhardt was a hard man, and there would be additional scores to settle if ever they came across *Oriental Venture* again.

CHAPTER SIX

pproaching noon in the forenoon watch, and I was relaxing in my day cabin listening to McGrath bustling about in the chartroom, and then to his brisk footsteps as he strode out onto the bridge wing. I glanced through the porthole, open to admit as much of the breeze as possible, and saw him swing a sextant up to his eye, and press the button of a stopwatch in order to record the exact time of the sun sight.

The swelling on his face had started to go down, but he still had a shiner of a black eye, and his lacerated knuckles were spotted with purple blotches of iodine. The cut over his eye had been deep, and I had put a couple of stitches in it. A shot of rum had provided the only comfort; not for McGrath, who winced as I shoved the needle through the ragged edges of the cut and dragged them together, but for me, to steady my hand.

I had listened to McGrath's explanation of the brawl, and had given him the benefit of the doubt. At first, the German seamen had seemed friendly enough, and had bought him a beer. Things had turned ugly, though, when they realised he was a junior mate in a British ship. Several of them, including the big man called Kurt, were determined to provoke a fight. Against a bigger man, backed by a hostile crowd baying for blood, I would not have blamed him if he had turned and run. But from what I'd seen of McGrath, that was never a possibility. Would I have backed down in similar circumstances? Not likely. And McGrath had more than held his own. Left alone he could well have beaten the big German. I asked him how he had learned to fight. He told me the painfully familiar story of a first trip apprentice bullied by the forecastle hard men. The *Garthpool's* sail maker had taken him aside and offered boxing lessons. "Always fight fair Jimmy, always fight fair," he had said as they squared up for sparring. Then, with a wry grin, had added, "Unless you're getting beat. Never let yourself be beat." Then he had shown McGrath some tricks that would never have been allowed by the Marquess of Queensbury.

It sounded, too, as if the German seaman Kurt was more than just a hot bloodied bully. Stories of brown shirted Nazi thugs beating up political opponents had been widely reported in the pro-British newspapers in Singapore and Sydney. Perhaps Kurt was one of them, a Nazi fanatic who believed Hitler's lies, and was ready to stamp a jackboot into the face of anyone who stood in his way. And where there was one fanatic there were likely to be more. If Eberhardt and his officers were cut from the same sailcloth, then *Dortmund* might prove a dangerous opponent to anyone who crossed her path.

As if there were already not enough dangers in the Far East, with its triads, pirates, bootleggers, drug smugglers, pimps and crooked officials. Its ports and waters were not for the faint hearted, and a man could lose his life as easily as his wallet. The Chinese and the Japanese were at each other's throats, and now it looked as if the Nazis were going to provoke another war in Europe. It painted a grim picture. But I smiled, recalling something an old Australian rogue had said to me. "It's a grand life William, just as long as you don't weaken." Well I had a good little nest egg tucked away in a place where few questions were asked and fewer answers given. A few years more and perhaps I could find a quiet place to drop anchor for a while, and smell the moonflowers on a deserted beach with a beautiful wahine. Meanwhile it was as well to be prepared for the unexpected, and to keep a sharp lookout.

In the few days it had taken us to work our way around the south coast of Papua, and then north-west across the Solomon Sea, we had seen no sign of the *Dortmund,* or any other shipping apart from the dugout canoes of the islanders fishing close to the reefs. The previous evening we had passed New Britain. It had been a clear night with a partial moon, and the volcanic cone on nearby Umboi Island, looming black against the starry backcloth, had guided us through the narrow channel into the Bismarck Sea. Now, half way across, McGrath was shooting the sun to establish a position from which we would set course to avoid the outlying shoals guarding the eastern approaches to Manus Island. A chain of reefs also guarded its northern coast, and I intended to wait until daylight before picking my way into the lagoon, at the bottom of which lay the tiny settlement of Lorengau.

Thinking about Lorengau, and the cargo we were carrying there, brought back the unwelcome image of Dieter Eberhardt on the veranda of the Papua Hotel. Every inch the naval officer in his spotless, knife-edged, white uniform, I hated his casually arrogant assumption of superiority. I'd had none of the silver spoon advantages of the Eberhardt brothers, and had travelled a long, hard road to become master of my own steamer. In which I now had a small arsenal stowed away.

Why had I done it? And having done it why had I not reported it to Major Spencer. Was it really a matter of injured pride, the suspicion that Eberhardt and Poh were pulling one over on me. Or maybe it was just that old smuggler's gene, seeing an opportunity and seizing it without thinking of the consequences. I grinned, recalling something Bill McFee, an old chief engineer friend of mine, once said, "Doing what's right is no guarantee against misfortune." I'd suffered enough misfortune to learn the truth of that, and of its corollary that doing what's wrong does not necessarily prevent good fortune.

Well, right or wrong I had the guns, and even if I dumped them over the side the Eberhardts would still hold me responsible. But in reality, what could they do. Seize the ship by force and risk drawing attention to what they were doing? I didn't think so. No, I was going to keep them, at least for the time being. As I had said to Lowther, they could prove good insurance, and I could always find a buyer later.

Peter Lowther; now there was another concern. He was an excellent seaman and had learned well the business of chief mate in a merchant ship. He was also a gentleman, a real one, the younger son of an earl, with an honorary lordship. With his cut glass accent, polished manners and well-groomed appearance he was the exact opposite to me, the orphan boy who had fought his way out of reform school, and climbed the grimy ladder to the semi-respectability of the British merchant marine. We got on well enough, but I sometimes had to remind myself that, despite being some years younger, I was his captain and his superior in all things professional, if not otherwise. His drinking bothered me, though. It was not that I objected to drinking, I had done enough of it myself, but I knew what it could do. It had taken my mother, and I'd seen many men broken by it, screaming and thrashing about in the horrors of the D.T.s.

Lowther drank because he blamed himself for the death of the woman he had taken away from an Admiral, and who had died bearing his child. The scandal had forced him out of the navy, and he had run away from all of the things — family, friends and home — that brought back memories of a life he'd rather forget. He still had that picture of her on his desk though, so at least he kept her memory alive, but the alcohol was the crutch that made it all bearable. In other circumstances, he would have made a good captain. I had told him so several times. But he had shrugged his shoulders and said he was happy being chief mate. Commanding a merchant ship, where the men were often unruly and resistant to authority, and where the penalties for breaking the few rules and regulations were limited, took a man secure in his own skin. Perhaps Lowther felt himself lacking, not perhaps in ability, but in his inability to come to terms with the past, except through the bottom of a glass. So preoccupied with his own failings that he couldn't set the example he felt he ought to be. The Old Man, unflappable, master under God, dispenser of justice and wisdom; not an ageing, drunken failure, axed from the Royal Navy.

All nonsense really. I had seen enough of Lowther's style of leadership to know that the man who had rammed a destroyer into a battleship at Jutland, and taken her home again afterwards, was the type of man other men followed instinctively, without the encouragement of fists or belaying pins. And I had known plenty of captains with far less ability than Lowther, and who drank as much or more, and who carried out their duties in a state for which they would dismiss others.

"Sometimes, men think too much," I mused. "It's better just to get on with things and let our fears and inadequacies sort themselves out."

"I beg your pardon, sahib?" said Da Silva. The old pirate entered the cabin bearing a thermos jug of iced water. "Did you require something?"

I looked up surprised, realising I had spoken the thoughts aloud. "No thank you, Da Silva, I was just talking to myself. One of the hazards of command."

"Yes sahib, thank you sahib," he said, wobbling his head, replacing the thermos jug and taking away the empty one, leaving me to wonder what future hazards the voyage might have in store for me.

* * *

The first rays of sunlight flashed across the darkened sea, sweeping the last of the twilight before them. We were about a mile offshore, closing Los Negros, the largest of a chain of small islands and reefs that bounded the northern coast of Manus Island, creating a sheltered lagoon at the bottom of which lay the settlement of Lorengau.

A narrow, palm-fringed beach stretched along the coast of Los Negros. Native huts were dotted amongst the palm trees, and dugout canoes were pulled up on the sand. Smoke rose from cooking fires.

Beyond Los Negros was a mile of coral outcrops and sandy islets, before a break in the reef, and the deep-water channel that gave safe access to the lagoon.

"Reduce to manoeuvring speed and call the anchor party, young McGrath can go forward and take charge."

"Aye aye," affirmed Lowther, ringing the engine room telegraph and relaying the order to a seaman who disappeared below to call McGrath.

"Port fifteen."

"Port fifteen, sir," repeated the helmsman, his hands turning the spokes.

The bow swung towards the gap in the reef.

"Midships." I waited until we were lined up with the centre of the half-mile wide gap. "Steady as she goes, steer south by west."

The helmsman span the wheel half a turn to meet the swing, and then steadied on the new course to take us through the gap and on towards Lorengau.

Which lay on the southern shore of a shallow bay. Opposite the centre of the bay, and about a mile offshore, was a small islet in the middle of a patch of reef. From previous visits, I knew it was safe to anchor between the islet and the eastern arm of the bay. I'd marked the spot on the chart, and calculated the length of chain that would hold us securely, with plenty of room to swing clear of any reef heads.

The water inside the shelter of the lagoon was almost glassy as *Oriental Venture* nosed towards her anchorage. I waited until the islet was fine on the starboard quarter, ordered the helm put hard over, and watched the wake inscribe a white, flecked circle on the shimmering, blue surface. When the bow pointed back towards the islet I ordered the engine to slow astern, and waited until we just started to gather stern way.

"Stop engine, let go forward."

I heard the splash of the anchor hitting the water, and the rumble and rattle of the chain as it ran over the windlass in a thick cloud of red dust. I watched Cramp hauling on the brake to slow the rush of the chain, then screw it on tight once the required length had rumbled into the water.

"Thank you, Peter," I said, in reply to his confirmation that the ship was safely anchored. "You can ring finished with engine."

I reached for my binoculars, and walked out on to the port bridge wing. Lorengau was merely a collection of native huts clustered around the shore of the shallow bay. The huts were thickest on the western headland where the palm trees had been cleared. Behind the line of huts fringing the beach were more substantial structures, one of which, with its white painted walls and rust streaked roof, was the principle trading post. A rickety, narrow wooden trestle jetty jutted into the bay, just long enough to accommodate the coastal trading schooners that plied the tiny out-ports.

Our arrival had aroused interest on the shore, and I watched some of the locals dragging their canoes off the beach and paddling out towards us. Intending, no doubt, to see if the crew had anything to trade. But of the workboat that Hicks had said would meet us, there was no sign.

There was still no sign of it by mid-morning, and I climbed up to the bridge and examined the settlement though binoculars, searching for signs of a reception com-mittee. Time was rather a fluid concept in the islands, where life was regulated by the cycling of the sun, the ebb and flow of the tide and the turn of the trade winds. I could have had one of our boats hoisted out and gone ashore to see if I could find Mr Leung, but I reassured myself with the thought that if he was as short of fuel as Hicks had suggested, he would eventually come out and get it.

Towards noon the sea breeze began to kick in, and *Oriental Venture* swung slowly round at her anchor. I was reading in my cabin when there was a knock on the door, and Lowther's head poked round the privacy curtain informing me that a boat had just pulled away from the shore.

I joined him on the bridge and through the binoculars made out a small, motor launch bobbing its way towards us, rolling uncomfortably in the waves kicked up by the sea breeze. There were two men in it. One, a bare chested native in a loincloth, squatted in the bow. The other, a young Chinese, in white shirt and trousers sat in the stern sheets, one hand working the tiller.

Half an hour later the young man, who informed me he was Mr Leung's son, was sitting in my day cabin.

"I very sorry for delay Captain, and for my father unable greet you in person." He spoke surprisingly good English for one who spent most of his time communicating with the natives in pidgin. "You make good time and we not expect you so soon. Boat make delivery to Yin. Not expected back until tomorrow."

"Yin? Where is that?" I asked.

"It about forty miles to the west. We have small trading post there. My father gone with boat. Also be here tomorrow."

"Very well, I look forward to meeting him then," I said, annoyed, and wondering why it had taken so long for Leung to come out and tell me. "But I'm short of coal, and can't afford any more delay."

"I assure you that boat, and my father, be here in morning," he replied. "You will be on way Hong Kong by evening."

My mood was somewhat improved by the arrival of Da Silva with a large pot of coffee. I poured a cup for Leung, and offered him one of my Senior Service.

"I hope you not mind," he said. "But I prefer cigar." He pulled a box of small cigars out of a pocket and accepted a light from Lowther.

"Do many ships call here?" I asked.

"Very few," he replied. "You first we see in months. Most business done with trading schooners from Rabual or Moresby. We fortunate you passing on way Hong Kong, Captain. Otherwise have long wait for fuel." He drew on the cigar and contentedly exhaled a thick stream of blue smoke.

"There was a large German ship in Port Moresby," I said. "Black with white superstructure. I thought she might also be on her way to Hong Kong. But you haven't seen her pass by?"

"No, Captain, we no would see, unless come into lagoon. You only ship to visit."

"Very well," I said, seeing little point in continuing the interview. "If there is nothing further, we'll rig the derricks ready for the morning. We'll look forward to seeing you then, and to meeting your father."

"Pleasure entirely ours, Captain. I wish you pleasant afternoon."

He stubbed the cigar into the ashtray, rose, and offered his hand. I shook it, and Lowther accompanied him down to the gangway. He returned to find me examining the remains of the cigar.

"Not thinking of taking up stogies, are you?"

"You can call me overly suspicious if you wish," I said, holding the stub out to him, "but I don't trust that man. He says he hasn't seen another ship for weeks, but he smokes the same brand of cigars as Dieter Eberhardt."

"He seemed friendly enough to me," said Lowther, turning the stub over in his fingers. "It's a Dutch brand, fairly common in the islands."

"It's just too much of a coincidence," I said, rubbing my fingertips to ease the tingling. "I'll bet the *Dortmund's* been here recently, and he's lying about not having seen her."

"That's a lot to conclude from one cigar stub."

"Maybe, but I thought Leung was desperate for the fuel. So why is he gallivanting off with the workboat when he should be here to collect it?"

"I don't know," replied Lowther, still pensively examining the cigar stub. "But perhaps they really weren't expecting us so soon"

"Look, I know it's just a feeling, but I'd hate to be caught with my pants down. It won't hurt to post extra lookouts tonight," I said.

"Are you sure you're not over reacting," said Lowther, the forbearing tone and wry grin, clearly suggesting that he thought I was. "If you're that concerned, why don't we up anchor and head on to Hong Kong. We can always plead some kind of emergency."

Despite the tingling in my fingertips, I was beginning to wonder whether he was right.

Unless!

Unless the fuel was the start of a supply dump the Eberhardts were setting up, and the *Dortmund* was waiting to collect it. Or was I just seeing Nazi shadows where none existed?

"Perhaps it's the smuggler's blood in me, Peter. Hopefully we'll discharge these drums tomorrow, and be on our way with no harm done. But if the *Dortmund* is sniffing around, and the Chinese are up to no good, then we'll be on our guard. So break out some of the rifles and arm the lookouts." I paused, seeing the bemused grin on Lowther's face, and wondered again if I was just overreacting. "I suppose some of the crowd do know how to handle a rifle?"

"Probably, one of the benefits of having a crew of Chinese ex-pirates. And some of the Somali stokers rode with the Mad Mullah in their youth. I'll find those with the most experience, and the chief engineer and I can probably remember enough of our basic training to set up a quick refresher course. Can't afford any target practise, though, if you want to keep things quiet."

"I should have thought of this earlier," I said, ruefully. "There's not much point acquiring a small arsenal, but having no one trained to use it. We'll chuck some old dunnage over the side when we're back at sea, and they can practise on that."

"There's not just rifles though," replied Lowther. "There are machine pistols and grenades too, and they're all German. The rifles are bolt action Mausers of war-time vintage, but anyone who's familiar with a Lee Enfield can work out how to use them. The machine pistols are an updated version of the Bergmann MP 18s used in the Great War. The grenades are the standard German infantry stick type, known by our troops as 'potato mashers'."

"For a Royal Navy type, you seem to know a surprising amount about German infantry weapons."

"The Navy contributed several Brigades of troops during the war," replied Lowther. "At one point I considered volunteering. Went so far as to do some basic infantry training. That put the idea right out of my head. But we did a fair amount of rifle shooting and grenade throwing. Surprising how that's coming in handy now!"

"Well, if you and the chief can teach some of the men how to use them, without shooting or blowing themselves up, that would be very useful."

"Aye aye, skipper. Seeing as how you appear to know how to handle a Webley, would you like to be included?"

I could see from his smirk that Lowther thought my precautions were well over the top, and I had no wish to tempt fate. "We'll see, Peter, we'll see."

* * *

I woke to the sound of knuckles rapping on my cabin door. The handle rattled and Griffith's head appeared round the edge, his face dimly backlit from the pale light of the passage.

"Just after four a.m., Captain. Mr Lowther's on the bridge and I'm away to my watch below."

It had all been quiet when I turned in, but I had left orders to be called at the start of the morning watch.

"Thank you, Second," I said, shaking my head to clear it, before throwing off the thin sheet that covered my naked body. The land breeze wafting in through the open porthole had done little to dispel the heat. I padded over the linoleum-clad deck to the light switch and flicked it on. By the dim light of the bulb I examined my face in the washstand mirror, admiring the two-day growth of beard in which there was not a hint of grey, before splashing it with water. Having pulled on khaki trousers and shirt, I grabbed my cap from the hook behind the door and climbed up to the bridge.

"Good morning, skipper," I heard Lowther call softly from the port wing.

"Morning, Peter," I replied, making my way out to join him. The land breeze had strengthened overnight, swinging *Oriental Venture* around so that her stern was pointing seawards. Lowther was facing forward, examining the shore through a pair of night glasses.

"All seems quiet. Nothing reported by the lookouts. I sent a man round to check everyone was alert."

The moon had set, and high up, above the land breeze, a thin layer of cirrus cloud was sliding in from the north, obscuring the brilliance of the stars. It was possible to make out the line of the shore with the naked eye, though, where the lighter streak of sand gave way to the darker backdrop of the jungle. Cooking fires twinkled among the palm trees, and the steadier light of paraffin lamps shone from the windows of some of the larger structures.

Raising my own night glasses, I slowly scanned the horizon, but there was nothing visible on the inky surface of the water to suggest the approach of any kind of craft. I was tempted to go back to bed. Perhaps it was just a coincidence that Leung smoked the same brand of Dutch cigars as Dieter Eberhardt, and I had built a castle of suspicion on the foundation of one stub? If something was going to happen, though, then it would probably be just before dawn, when those asleep were sleeping their soundest, and those on watch were supposedly at their least wakeful.

I rubbed my fingertips together to ease the tingling, and raised the glasses for another sweep of the horizon. Was it starting to lighten towards the east or was I just imagining it? There were more lights on the shore now, and I caught the scent of wood smoke from the early morning fires, carried out on the land breeze.

There was no sound from the land, we were anchored too far off to be able to hear the calls of the native birds and other jungle dwellers, but I could hear the breeze riffling about the masts and rigging, and the gentle lap of the waves against the hull.

And something else.

Something I had been barely conscious of for the last few minutes. A faint, low-pitched rumbling. I tried to focus on where it was coming from. It seemed to be from out on the starboard beam, and I swung the glasses in that direction, but saw nothing.

"Can you hear that, Peter," I called.

There was no answer, and I thought for a moment that Lowther had not heard. Then he was beside me.

"What do you think it is?" he said.

"I think it's a boat approaching from the west. I can't see it yet, but I can hear the engine."

Lowther raised his glasses again and scanned the darkness, before focussing on a point directly abeam. "Ah, there it is. Very faint lights, red and green, coming straight at us. Single steaming light, almost directly abeam, two miles away perhaps. It must be the workboat coming back from Yin."

"Probably, but why come so early?"

"Daylight's not far off, and perhaps they want an early start, having kept us waiting since yesterday," said Lowther.

He was likely right, in which case we would be on our way to Hong Kong by mid-morning.

"If it is their boat, tie it up alongside number five hatch, and we'll start unloading as soon as it's light enough to see. Put the crew on the shake, and get McGrath up. He can relieve you here, and you can standby aft to deal with the boat."

"Aye aye," said Lowther.

I touched his arm as he turned away. "I know you think I'm being overly cautious, Peter, but at the back of my head there's still a voice telling me that there are just too many coincidences. Keep the armed lookouts handy, but out of sight. You can laugh at me later if I'm wrong."

Lowther nodded, the corner of his mouth turning up in a sardonic grin, prepared to humour me, if not quite ready to laugh. "Aye, skipper, don't worry, if there's any trouble we'll be ready for it."

Then he was gone, and I was alone with my doubts until McGrath thrust the chartroom curtain aside, rubbing the sleep from his eyes.

By the time the boat was within hailing distance a pale rosy flush had spread across the eastern sky, although to the west the darkness of the night still held sway. I could now see that the approaching craft was, in all likelihood, the awaited workboat, and I studied it through the night glasses. The foredeck was occupied by a squat cabin, atop which sat the wheelhouse. Aft of the cabin was the engine casing with a tall, thin funnel, and abaft that a flat open deck for the carriage of cargo, empty now, in readiness to receive the fuel drums. The workboat slowed as it approached, and Leung appeared at the wheelhouse door, he cupped his hands around his mouth and hailed.

"*Oriental Venture*, good morning. Permission come aboard?"

"Port side aft, pilot ladder," I heard Lowther call back from the main deck.

The boat slid around our stern, nosed alongside to allow Leung to scramble up the ladder, then backed away to stand off, drifting with its engine idling. Lowther lead the young man up to the bridge.

"Good morning, Captain Rowden," Leung said, sticking out his hand. "I apologise for very early start, but boat just return from Yin, and as you kept waiting yesterday we not waste time today."

"Good morning, Mr Leung," He was on his own, and I glanced towards the workboat. "Your father is with you?"

"Sadly, no. He very tired after voyage from Yin. He go ashore and ask me convey humble apologies."

"Very well," I replied, wondering whether I should read anything into that news. The boat was here and ready to take the drums, so what did it matter if I didn't meet the man who had paid for them. "I'm sorry not to have met him. We'll be ready to start as soon as there is enough daylight. I suggest you bring the boat back alongside, and have your men ready to receive the drums when we swing them out."

"Thank you, Captain." He strode to the rail and hailed the workboat in a flurry of Cantonese. There was an answering hail, and the boat nudged back alongside and was secured, gently nestling against the fenders. Leung climbed down to the main deck, swung himself over the rail, and disappeared into the cabin.

It was not long to dawn, the eastern horizon was distinctly lighter, and the dark undersides of the fair weather clouds were flecked with gold, promising another hot day. The workboat was secure alongside and all was perfectly normal. I was about to concede that I had been worrying over nothing, when McGrath bounded out of the wheelhouse.

"Sir, I think I can see smoke over to starboard," he said, the raised pitch of his voice alerting me to his urgency. "It's still dark over there, and the horizon's hard to make out, but there looks to be a smudge of smoke, or something."

I strode quickly to the other side with McGrath scampering behind, and raised the night glasses.

"Where away, mister," I snapped.

"Just abaft the beam, sir."

I followed his outstretched arm, searching the western horizon for signs of smoke.

And then I saw it, a tell-tale dark trail against the paling sky. I searched below the smoke but there were no lights, just a pale flash of white water that might have been a bow wave reflecting the dawn. If it was a ship then it was approaching from the western end of the lagoon, where the reef ended, leaving a wide, easily navigated entrance. But, as Leung had said, few ships came this way. Unless!

Unless it was the *Dortmund*, and she had been anchored further along the coast, out of sight and waiting for our arrival.

"Well done, Third," I said. "I'll lay odds she's the *Dortmund*, approaching from the west under cover of darkness. You were lucky to see that smoke, otherwise she might have been upon us before we noticed her. Get down aft and warn the chief mate. Tell him to cast that workboat off and be ready to get underway. Call the second mate to go forward with the chippy and stand by to heave the anchor. Then get back up here quick smart, we don't have much time."

"Aye aye, sir," said McGrath, before sliding down the ladder, and darting aft along the boat deck. I blew into the engine room voice pipe, and when Fraser answered told him we needed to be ready to move, and that when I rang for full speed I wanted every available revolution.

The light was improving rapidly, and I could see the approaching ship clearly in my night glasses. There was no doubting now that she was the *Dortmund*, I recognised the graceful sheer of her black hull, and the white superstructure. She was at full speed, her bows cleaving the sea apart in a white capped furrow. In their desire to get every last half knot, her engineers had carelessly pumped too much fuel into the engine, the unburnt residue resulting in the oily plume of smoke. I wondered if Eberhardt was aware of it, and was venting his anger at the engineers, while hoping our lookout was distracted by the sunrise or thoughts of relief. I darted back into the wheelhouse to check the chart, and ran back to the bridge wing. The *Dortmund* was coming up fast, I didn't need glasses to see her now, and I hoped we had enough time to get clear of the workboat.

I swivelled my gaze to the poop, looking for Lowther, and saw him standing beside the bulwark, just forward of the deckhouse. McGrath had delivered his message, and was making his way back along the deck. I saw Lowther wave an arm, and several seamen ran forward to where the workboat's mooring lines were secured. They were about to let them go when there was a long blast on a ship's whistle.

I jerked my head round in time to see the small cloud of white steam from the *Dortmund's* funnel as her whistle blast died away. For a moment I wondered what Eberhardt intended, the blast from his whistle being bound to alert us to his arrival.

And then it struck me. If we had not seen him in the darkness, then the whistle blast and his sudden appearance would distract our attention.

Away from the workboat, for which it was also a signal.

I muttered a quick prayer to St Woolos, and called to the helmsman to stand by the wheel.

The sainted Welshman must have been awake because, down aft, Lowther had arrived at the same conclusion and I saw him dash to the bulwark, yelling to the seamen to cast the boat adrift. They leaped to comply, just as grappling hooks clattered onto the deck, and a head appeared over the bulwark.

Lowther roared a warning, and I saw him jump to where a large German seaman was attempting to scramble over the bulwark. There was a Bergmann in Lowther's hand, but with no time to aim it he smashed the butt down hard onto the fingers grasping the rail, and then swung it into the man's face. He grunted, and dropped back to the workboat, blood spurting from a mashed eyebrow, but there more Germans on its deck, hauling themselves up our side with the grappling hooks' lines.

Lowther shouted again, armed Chinese and Somalis scrambled out of the deckhouse and aimed rifles over the bulwark. Before they had a chance to fire, the door of the workboat's wheelhouse was yanked open, a German petty officer thrust a machine gun through the opening and jerked the trigger. Bullets burst and zinged off the ship's steel plating, causing Lowther's men to duck for cover. The petty officer barked an order, and the German seamen continued to swarm up the grappling lines.

"Slow ahead," I yelled at McGrath, who had burst back into the wheelhouse, gasping after his sprint along the deck. The telegraph jangled, and I hoped Fraser was alert in the engine room.

From aft I heard Lowther yelling at the Germans to halt. To assist their hearing he sent a stream of bullets in the direction of the petty officer, who ducked back inside the workboat's wheelhouse.

"Fire," he yelled at his men, who had poked their heads back up over the bulwark. For a moment they hesitated, and then a ragged volley of rifle shots splattered into the workboat's deck. None struck home, but the German seamen dropped and ducked for cover. Lowther kept his Bergmann pointed at them, shouting for his men to cut the boat free. I saw their knives flash, and as the cut lines dropped away I felt our propeller start to bite.

With nothing securing it, the launch began to slide away from the side. The German petty officer, seeing the chance to board slipping away, darted back out of the wheelhouse, raised his machine gun and sent a stream of lead towards the bridge. I dropped to the deck, hearing the bullets smash into the wooden railings, sending splinters whistling past my ears. There was another burst of firing, and when I poked my head up Lowther was lowering his Bergmann, and the German petty officer was being dragged to shelter.

The workboat slipped further astern as our speed increased. I thought she would try and pursue, but a threatening rank of rifles pointing over the stern rail must have deterred whoever was in charge. Telling McGrath to keep an eye on her, I turned my attention back to the *Dortmund*, which was still approaching at full speed.

It was almost full daylight now, and any moment the sun would heave itself over the eastern horizon. Footsteps clattered on the boat deck ladder, and Lowther appeared in the doorway.

"For someone who turned down the chance to fight with the Naval Brigade, you look pretty handy with a machine gun," I snapped.

"I said I didn't like the infantry training, not that I didn't take the lessons seriously," retorted Lowther, his eyes blazing with excitement.

"Well done, anyway, Peter. Now get back aft with your troops, and keep that boat away. I think Eberhardt's aiming to trap us in the lagoon. I'm going to try and get ahead of him. When I do, get as many of those barrels into the water as possible. Shoot holes in them. Take a Verey Pistol with you. When the *Dortmund* gets close to the barrels shoot the flare among them. Hopefully it will set fire to the oil and distract him."

"Aye, aye, sir," he replied, grabbing the Verey pistol from the signals' locker, and turning to run aft again.

Oriental Venture had been pointing towards the shore when I ordered the engine to slow ahead. The anchor was still down, and I hoped to use it to clubhaul her, swinging her around as quickly as possible. It was a dangerous manoeuvre, but I had little time and little choice.

With the ship's speed increasing, I ordered the wheel hard over to port, causing the anchor cable to veer to starboard.

I waited until the cable was leading at right angles.

"Hard a starboard! Half ahead!"

With the effect of the rudder, and the bar taut cable straining against the anchor, the ship began to swing rapidly to starboard. I grabbed the speaking trumpet, and shouted at Griffith on the forecastle.

"As soon as she comes right round start hauling in the anchor, it will break out as we pass over it."

"Aye, aye," there was an answering shout from the forecastle.

But would it break out? Or would the flukes lodge behind a lump of rock or old coral, pinning the anchor, and us, as securely as a moth pinned to a board, unless the cable parted.

I glanced down at my fists, realising I had clenched them tight, the tingling in my fingers gone, now that I could see who the enemy was. But the *Dortmund* was almost upon us, and even if I did get the ship clear of the anchorage, she would still be able to overhaul us with her superior speed.

And then we were round, the bow pointing just to the west of the reef behind which we had been anchored. From the forecastle I could hear the sluggish clank, clank of the windlass fighting to heave in the anchor as it dragged along the bottom. I prayed it would keep coming, almost jumping with relief when the docking telegraph rang anchor aweigh.

"Full ahead, steady as goes," I shouted.

The *Dortmund* was coming up fast on the port bow now, Eberhardt probably sensing that I intended to make a run for the entrance to the lagoon, and aiming to cut me off. I had put us on a collision course, and if I knew anything at all about him, I did not expect him to blink first.

The gap between the two ships was shrinking rapidly; I took one last calculating glance, then yelled, "Hard a starboard."

Raising the speaking trumpet I bellowed to Lowther down aft. "Now! Get those drums in the water."

Oriental Venture was turning directly into the path of the *Dortmund*, but she was faster and would catch up in minutes.

"Steady," I shouted to the helmsman, watching as the compass needle swung onto a heading that would put the *Dortmund* directly astern.

From the bridge wing, my hands gripping the rail so tightly that my knuckles ached, I watched the boatswain and his men manhandling the drums over the side as fast as they could. Half were already bobbing in the wake, blue for diesel and red for petrol, looking like gaily-coloured flowers floating in the white foaming wash. Lowther was at the stern rail aiming the Bergmann. I could hear the crackle as a stream of bullets punctured the drums.

I clenched my jaw to stop shouting in desperation, afraid I had left the turn too late, and that the drums would not catch fire.

Most of them had now gone over the side, and Lowther was still shooting holes in them.

"Now, Peter, now," I yelled, knowing he could not hear me over the noise of the gunfire.

Lowther dropped the Bergmann, and raised the Verey pistol. He cocked it, pointed it into the middle of the flotilla of drums and fired. The flare rocketed out of the barrel and straight onto the oil-slicked surface of the sea, where it continued to burn. Nothing happened, and I banged my fist onto the rail in frustration.

Then there was a flicker of blue flame as the petrol caught alight, the flames spreading rapidly across the surface, enveloping the floating drums from which petrol and oil continued to gush.

I held my breath, and said a quick prayer to St Warna, the patron saint of Cornish wreckers.

There was a deafening bang as one of the petrol drums exploded, and then the flames began to turn yellow as the furiously burning petrol heated the mingled diesel to flash point.

And ignited an inferno. Turning what had been a rapidly narrowing gap of water between the stern of *Oriental Venture* and the bow of the *Dortmund* into a spreading lake of leaping flame and black smoke.

The *Dortmund* was aimed right at the centre of the inferno, and I watched in grim fascination to see if Eberhardt would risk steaming straight through in order to head us off, or turn away.

I had no idea how much attention Eberhardt had paid to the water depth before he set his ship charging down on us. Just before getting underway I had snatched a glance at the chart to see how close I could pass without grounding on the reef. The *Dortmund* was a larger ship, and drew several feet more, and I hoped the burning oil was a distraction, obscuring the fact that he was chasing me into water that was perilously shallow.

I could feel the increased vibration as the propeller struggled in the shoaling water. If I had misjudged the turn, and was even slightly too far to the north, *Oriental Venture* would, herself, plough onto the reef. I could see the coral heads in the shallows off to port, and gritted my teeth in anticipation, but still the ship raced on. Astern the bows of the *Dortmund* were entering the leaping flames, the men on her forecastle shrinking back from the heat and smoke.

Finally, Eberhardt blinked, and I watched as the *Dortmund's* bow edged away from the flames. Had he realised the danger of following me over the edge of the reef, or was he just trying to avoid the worst of the blazing sea?

Then the *Dortmund* seemed to stagger, her bow rose, she hesitated, and then rolled to starboard, as if shrugging off a grasping hand.

"She's struck," I heard myself yell.

It was a glancing blow, the *Dortmund* sliding across the reef and back into deeper water. Had the hard, cement like coral ripped a gash in her bow? With water pouring in Eberhardt would surely have to stop and inspect the damage.

I watched the islet in the centre of the reef slide astern until it was almost right aft, and then ordered the helm hard over to port. "Steer north by east," I ordered the helmsman, a course that would take us directly through the gap in the outer reef, and into the open expanse of the Western Pacific.

Glancing astern, I watched the *Dortmund* slow to a stop, and saw the splash of her anchor. I reached for the engine room voice pipe, hoping Fraser would not hear the elation in my voice.

"We've given them the slip, you can reduce to normal revolutions."

"Aye, aye," came the Scotsman's unflappable brogue, almost drowned by the thump and clank of the steam reciprocating engine.

I turned to the wide-eyed McGrath, who was staring in open-mouthed disbelief at the dying flames and the anchored *Dortmund*. Despite my warning in Singapore, this was probably the last thing he had expected. But he would just have to get used to it.

"It's your watch, Third," I snapped harshly, in order to focus his attention. "You can see the gap in the reef right ahead. Take her straight out, and then set course for Hong Kong. I'll be in my day cabin if you need me."

CHAPTER SEVEN

It seemed I had been right in my suspicions about the Eberhardts, but there was little comfort in that. Dieter Eberhardt had bared his teeth, and although we had bettered him this time, I imagined that would not be the end of it. He had to find us though, the China Sea was a big place, and I was pretty sure he didn't know it as well as I did.

And if he did find us, well he knew now what we were capable of.

It wasn't the first time we had been obliged to fight our way out of an attempted boarding, and some of the Chinese crew, in their previous life as Bias Bay pirates, had taken part in ship seizures that resulted in cut throats and men thrown overboard into the bloodied jaws of circling sharks. So they took such things in their stride, and it was only a matter of a few watches after giving the *Dortmund* the slip that the excitement of being shot at faded, and they slipped cheerfully back into the never ending tasks of chipping and painting.

I was left with a dilemma though. Should I report the attack, and, if so, what exactly should I report?

Lowther suggested I report it, arguing that we should behave as if we were the outraged victim of an unprovoked and unexpected attempt at piracy, and radio the authorities immediately.

It was a valid point, except for one thing. "How could we report it without explaining the bit about the *Dortmund*," I said. "And the weapons we stole from Eberhardt?"

"We could dump them overboard, explain they were missing from the shipment, and that Eberhardt thinks we took them. But there would be no proof," said Lowther.

But I was sure there was more to this than just a missing cargo of rifles and machine guns, otherwise why go to the trouble of attacking us. To get them back, or to shut us up so that no one would learn what they were up to, setting up caches of fuel and weapons to replenish Nazi commerce raiders.

I mulled this over for a few days while keeping a wary eye astern, half expecting to see a smudge of smoke, and then, assuming the damage had not crippled her, *Dortmund's* bow heaving over the horizon, using her superior speed to overhaul us. We sighted nothing, but were still very much aware of her presence.

On a hunch, Sayce, the radio officer, had been scanning the less well-used radio frequencies, and had picked up messages in Morse code, in a language he could not identify. They consisted of random groups of letters and numbers that made no sense to him, or to Lowther or me as we pored over the transcripts, wondering if they were from the *Dortmund*.

Lowther observed that they reminded him of coded naval messages. "But we don't know Eberhardt sent them, they could have come from anywhere," he said.

"That's true," replied Sayce. "But if these messages did come from the *Dortmund* I might be able to prove it."

Lowther and I looked at him quizzically.

"It's the handwriting, or signature, as we Marconi men say. Every radio operator has a slightly different way of sending his Morse code messages. It's all in the spacing and rhythm of the way he taps the Morse key. After a while you can work out who the operators are, without even hearing their call signs."

"So if you listened to *Dortmund's* transmissions you might be able to tell if these messages had also been transmitted by her?" I said.

"Not yet exactly, sir, I wasn't thinking along those lines when I recorded them. I'd have to listen to her normal transmissions for a while, and then listen out for more of the coded ones, and see if there are any similarities," replied Sayce.

It didn't take him long to discover *Dortmund's* regular wireless timetable. After listening for several days, he established there were two radio operators transmitting from the ship, each with a distinct signature. After that, he spent every possible hour hunched over his radio, earphones clamped over his head, tuning and retuning the receiver, searching the airwaves for more coded transmissions.

Until he found them.

And banged excitedly on my cabin door, well after midnight, muttering "Got him," and thrusting a message into my hand.

"It's him, sir," he continued, his voice raised with excitement. "I'm sure of it. One of *Dortmund's* radio men is faster than the other. He transmitted the coded messages and that," he pointed to the slip of paper in my hand, "is one he's just sent."

I glanced down at the unintelligible groups of letter and numbers. "Good work, Sparks. We now know Eberhardt's sending coded messages, but we don't know to whom or what they are about. They might be important, or we could be just wasting our time. Anyway, keep an ear out for more. Perhaps we can find someone in Hong Kong who would be interested in trying to decode them."

Although I was by no means sure whom, if anyone, would. They might just be a private code that Eberhardt used to communicate with his owners. He might even have radioed a complaint against us for trying to set fire to his ship. In which case it might be wise to file my own report of the attempted piracy. I decided it could wait though, until we reached Hong Kong. Any radio message we sent now might be picked up by the wrong ears.

In the meantime, we continued steaming north-west, following the line on the chart that ran straight from Manus Island to Cape Engano, on the north-eastern tip of Luzon, where we would turn west towards Hong Kong. For almost three weeks we followed this imaginary line on the featureless surface of the deep blue water of the Western Pacific, checking our progress with noon sun sights and morning and evening star sights. We had the ocean to ourselves for the most part. We sighted few ships, and were too far offshore for the fisherman of the East Indies or the Philippines. We we did sight a large hammerhead shark, though. It swam up from the depths one forenoon and circled lazily around the ship several times, possibly attracted by the daily dumping of the ship's rubbish from the galley. Meagre pickings, since I discouraged waste.

So far, the weather had remained perfect. The daytime sky an immense arc of blue above the deeper cobalt of the ocean, and at night a blaze of stars. So bright that even on nights with no moon there was almost starlight enough to read by. We were making good progress, and it looked as if my earlier worries about running out of coal were unfounded. Fraser had kept a close eye on consumption since leaving Port Moresby. *Oriental Venture* burnt about 30 tons a day at her normal cruising speed of 10 knots. Three weeks since leaving Manus, and with three days to Hong Kong, we had a shade over 100 tonnes remaining. Eating into our safety margin, but enough to avoid the severe embarrassment and expense of running out of coal, and having to call a tug to tow us the last few miles into Hong Kong.

But then all that changed.

* * *

I was sleeping fitfully, tossing and turning in my stuffy cabin, when Lowther woke me to tell me he had reduced engine revolutions.

It was almost a relief to be awake. With no breeze to cool its hot, stale atmosphere, which the little electric fan only seemed to make worse, my cabin was a sweatbox. I pushed the damp sheet aside and padded naked to the bathroom. Splashing my body with lukewarm water from the cold tap provided only temporary relief.

By the time I had towelled dry and dressed, I could feel beads of sweat running down my chest, and when I reached the bridge I could have wrung my shirt out. There was no wind and the surface of the sea had a viscous, oily appearance, while overhead the stars seemed unnaturally large, the major ones appearing to glow like large, silvery fruit that I could almost reach up and touch. There was a moderate swell from the north-east in which *Oriental Venture* was rolling comfortably, and a glance astern revealed her arrow straight wake lit with phosphorescent highlights.

"Second engineer reports the sea temperature has risen, and he's having trouble maintaining steam pressure," Lowther reported as I joined him in the chartroom. "It's over 110 degrees down below, hotter in the boiler room, so I've told him to reduce revs."

I nodded my assent, and together we checked the chart and the dead reckoning position Griffith had plotted for 4 a.m. The coast of Luzon lay over 100 miles to the west, and on our present north-westerly course we would converge later in the day. I measured the distance to Cape Engano. We had 90 miles to run and would round it during the afternoon, using it to fix our position before safely turning west for Hong Kong.

The eastern sky was brightening as I strolled onto the bridge wing to light a cigarette, and watch Lowther aim his sextant. It was normally a good place to stand on a hot day, enjoying what little breeze the ship's speed created, but this morning the air itself felt oppressive, bathing us in a hot, humid blanket. The oily surface of the sea was veiled by a thin mist, and instead of a sharp dividing line between the night-dark sea and the paler sky, the horizon was an indistinct smudge. So although there were plenty of stars for position fixing, I could see that Lowther would have difficulty accurately measuring their altitude.

While I was waiting for him to finish his calculations, I went into the chartroom to check the barograph, a barometer fitted with an arm at the end of which was a pen. The nib pressed against a sheet of graph paper fixed around a drum that rotated once every seven days, tracing the daily variation in atmospheric pressure. In the tropics, the pressure normally rose and fell in a regular pattern called diurnal variation, with lower pressure during the heat of the day, and higher pressure in the relative cool of the night. Earlier, the trace had been following its familiar pattern, but now it was erratic, the smooth, synodal curve replaced by a jerky descent. It probably meant bad weather, and I was considering whether it was likely to be close enough to bother us, when Da Silva appeared with a pot of coffee and two cups.

The old pirate must have had second sight to know I was already on the bridge, but the coffee was hot and strong, and tasted good despite the Turkish bath conditions in the chartroom. I didn't know why I always thought of Da Silva as a pirate. The black eye patch must have had a lot to do with it. The rumour was he had lost the eye in a knife fight over a woman in Chittagong. It seemed unlikely to me, as Da

Silva was a Goanese catholic, whereas the Bengali port of Chittagong was mostly Muslim. But there was no accounting for the course of love, and with his large hooked nose, deeply etched wrinkles and grizzled, wiry hair, it was hard to imagine him ever having been the subject of someone's adoration, apart from his mother maybe. I had also never seen him carry a knife, or even lose his temper, although he could be heard savagely muttering under his breath, in a blend of Portuguese and Hindustani, whenever a request struck him as beyond his definition of reasonable. But there was a flinty glint in his remaining eye, and a stealthy, cat like quality to his tread, that hinted at untamed passions still lurking beneath his white jacketed breast.

By the time Lowther had finished his calculations the night had been banished by the short tropical twilight, and the sun was shouldering its way over the horizon. The observation, if it was accurate, placed us several miles to the west of the intended track, and Lowther made a quick calculation to allow for the drift, ordering the helmsman to steer half a point to starboard. I nodded to confirm my agreement.

Stepping out of the chartroom, I was surprised to see the swell had increased markedly over the last half hour, rolling in regular ranks from the north-east, already approaching eighteen feet. *Oriental Venture* was taking them almost beam on, and was starting to roll more heavily, although not uncomfortably. And in place of its familiar blue, the sky had taken on a coppery tinge. The sun, instead of its usual golden brilliance, had a reddish glow and was surrounded by a misty halo. It was still calm though, and the agitated surface of the sea heaved and shimmered like dull mercury.

I strode back into the chartroom to check the barograph, and was not surprised to see it had continued its erratic fall. What did surprise me, though, was the speed with which it was now dropping. Judging by the fall, and the direction of the swell, we were probably feeling the outer effects of a severe storm somewhere in the Pacific, which I hoped wasn't headed in our direction. I told Lowther to keep an eye on conditions, and went down to my cabin where Da Silva had laid out toast and the last of the bacon for breakfast.

At the eight a.m. change of watch, I went back up to the bridge to check the barograph. The conditions were starting to cause me concern; the trace was still falling steeply, and although there was still no wind, the swell was ominous. Ranks of large, heavy rollers were bearing down from the north-east, throwing *Oriental Venture* from side to side, their crests breaking against the rail and cascading green and white water over her decks. It was oppressively hot, and the humid air seemed thick and hard to breathe.

"Looks like there's some dirty weather coming our way," I said to Lowther, who was waiting for McGrath to relieve him.

"Judging by that swell, and the barometer's fall there could be a typhoon to the north of us," replied Lowther, putting voice to the conclusion I had already reached.

The door to the chartroom opened, and McGrath joined us.

"Morning, Third," I greeted him. "We could be heading into a storm, a nasty one by all the signs. We're running in towards Luzon so we don't have a lot of sea room. I want to know the moment the wind kicks in, it will give us some idea as to the storm's direction."

"Aye, sir," replied McGrath, moving over to check the chart.

I had already checked Lowther's dead reckoning position for 8 a.m., and had measured the distance to Cape Engano at just over 70 miles. Seven hours at normal speed, but with the heavy rolling, and the reduced engine revolutions we would be making little more than seven or eight knots. The east coast of Luzon was still 80 miles away, but our course was taking us closer. I remembered what it was like to be in a sailing ship, driven downwind towards a lee shore. Struggling to keep as much canvas aloft as she would bear, fighting for every cable of sea room, while praying for a wind shift or change of tide. In theory it was different in a steamer, provided the engines did not let us down, but there were plenty of stories of ships, hove to against typhoons, being driven backwards and cast helplessly ashore like so much driftwood. I shivered, despite the heat.

In the wheelhouse, I watched as the helmsman was relieved. Steering had become a struggle, and he was bathed in sweat from the heat, and the effort of fighting to keep the ship on course against the increasingly heavy swell.

Having been relieved by McGrath, I sent Lowther below for breakfast, with instructions to make sure everything was battened down. If we were in for a blow, then the ship needed to be properly prepared. Lifelines rigged, ventilator cowls removed and their openings plugged, hatch covers checked and their wedges banged as tight as possible. Deadlights fitted over all portholes. Lifeboats and derrick booms double lashed.

After that, there was little McGrath or I could do apart from brace ourselves against the motion, and watch the deteriorating conditions. The swells had coloured to a deeper, more threatening blue-green, and their surface was confused and opaque, ruffled by fitful and confused gusts of wind. To the west, the sky was still relatively clear, but to the east, an ominous bank of heavy, dark cloud was slowly filling the horizon. The ship was beginning to struggle in the unending line of swells, her rivets creaking as her aging ribs and plates strained with every roll. As she dipped her starboard rail under each successive wave, the crest would cascade across the deck and burst around hatches and deck fittings in an explosion of white water, before pouring in torrents over the port side. Not all the water could escape before the ship righted herself, so from the wheelhouse it seemed as if she was almost permanently underwater.

Richard Regan

"Can you imagine this in your square rigger, Third?" I asked McGrath. "No wind, so you'd be rolling your guts out with all the top hamper of the masts."

He grinned at me with the exuberance of youth. "And wondering which way the first gust will hit us. And what it'll carry away when it does."

"Aye, what direction will the wind come from? That's the rub," I said. "The storm's somewhere over there." I waved an arm in the direction of the oncoming swells. "But how far away and where it's headed we don't know." The barograph was still falling which meant the storm was closing on us, but until the wind picked up I wouldn't be able to tell whether we were in its path or behind it. It was June, and at that time of year typhoons generally tracked north-west and then turned north, but would it, that was the question?

"Tricky situation, eh, Third? Luzon over there," I said, pointing west to where the coast was less than 80 miles away. "We don't want to run towards a lee shore, but then we don't want to turn into the swell in case that's putting us more into the storm's path. And not enough coal to turn back. So we just have to press on, and hope that when the wind does come, that we're not in the danger zone. Still, it's better than being in your square-rigger, at least we have a chance of running ahead of it."

"That it is, sir," replied McGrath, with a puzzled look on his face. "But what did you mean about the danger zone. Isn't it all dangerous, a typhoon I mean?"

"Think of the storm as a small circle tracking north-west," I said. "It's most likely to turn north at some point, so the northern side is the danger zone if you're on that side of it. Question is, are you ahead or behind it? If you're behind then it's moving away. But if you're ahead of it, then you're in the dangerous quadrant, and look out, it's going to roll right over you."

"But how can you tell if you're ahead of it?" asked McGrath.

"By the direction of the wind," I replied. "The wind blows towards the low pressure at the heart of the storm, but is skewed by the earth's rotation. You must have heard your square rig officers talking about using wind direction to gauge where the centre of a storm is?"

McGrath scratched his head for a moment, and then his face lit up in recollection. "Ah yes, face the wind, and the storm's on your right."

"In the northern hemisphere yes, but I like to remember it the other way round," I replied. "Wind up your arse, storm's on the left, so if the wind was coming from the north, where would the storm centre be?"

McGrath pointed to the east.

"Behind us yes. And if we maintained course and the wind stayed in the north?"

McGrath thought for a moment. "We'd be right in its path?"

"Aye, we would, and the correct procedure would be to put the wind on the starboard quarter, and keep altering course as the wind backed to take us clear of it. But that would steer us towards the coast, and cost us valuable sea room and coal."

That was the dilemma all right. All I could do was wait for the wind to tell me where the centre of the storm was. While all the time the conditions worsened, the cloud bank continuing to roll threateningly towards us, swallowing the sun and creating a sinister looking gloom. The temperature dropped several degrees, but the heat was still oppressive, and a curtain of funnel smoke trailed slowly astern, softly raining soot onto the decks, the sulphury smell prickling the eyes and nostrils.

With the increasing gloom the swell grew in size, the faces of the waves becoming steeper and higher, the tops starting to curl and tumble as the crests advanced towards us, picking the ship up and throwing her onto her side, her masts inscribing sickening arcs against the clouds, the main deck awash in green water and white breaking spray. Even with the lifelines rigged, it would be a hazardous journey for anyone venturing out of the crew accommodation in the poop to make their way forward. There was another way though, by climbing down a vertical ladder in the narrow, dimly lit escape shaft that lead to the crew's quarters from the propeller shaft tunnel at the bottom of ship. It was possible, in calm weather, to safely walk all the way forward to the engine room. But not in these conditions. One slip on the oil-slick deck plates and the rotating bronze shaft would hurl a man against the bulkhead. It was dangerous, and only marginally better than the risk of being washed overboard by the rollers sweeping across the decks.

If it was uncomfortable and dangerous for those above decks, it was even more so for the men down below. On the floor plates of the stoke hold, surrounded by tons of coal that might slide and bury them. Or in the boiler room, struggling to keep their feet while shovelling coal through the fire doors, with the violent rolling threatening to break bones or burn them. I waited until the ship was momentarily level, let go of the grab rail and staggered over to the engine room voice pipe, struggling uphill for the last couple of strides as the deck canted alarmingly.

"Chief here." The answering voice was reassuringly strong against the background thump of the engine, the whistle of steam and the boom of waves crashing against the hull.

"How's it going, Chief?" I had to shout to make sure he could hear me.

"Not so bad, Captain. Steam pressure's down and the lads are struggling to keep the coal up to the fires. We've got a few burns and bruises, but we're managing."

"I'm afraid it's going to get worse before it gets better, the storm hasn't hit us yet. Tell the men from me they're doing a good job."

"Aye, skipper, we do our best."

I replaced the cover over the polished brass tube. Looking ahead, I saw that the cloud bank had filled the northern horizon, and was now curving a thick, black, seemingly impenetrable wall across our track. Lightning flashes lit the inside of the clouds with a hellish flickering. The ship was struggling beam on to the monstrous swell. I gritted my teeth.

"Bring her a point or two to starboard, Third. Put those waves on the shoulder. The Mackems built her well, but she won't take too much more of this rolling. And tell the chief to come down a few more revs. We'll see how she rides with that."

The storm was closing on us, and I might just have made matters worse by altering course towards it. But there was nowhere to run. It might track north-west towards the tip of Luzon, and from there go on to batter Hong Kong. Or it might veer north and vent its fury on Formosa, and the Japanese islands.

And right in its path, steamed *Oriental Venture*.

* * *

The wind, when it hit, was both a shock and a relief.

Shocking in its sudden fury. McGrath and I watched the outriding gusts leaping from wave top to wave top, slicing off the crests and sending them flying towards us in white clouds of spume. Then the full force of the gale fell upon us like a howling clawing banshee, screaming through the rigging and heeling the ship with the fury of its blast. We clung to the grab rails inside the wheelhouse and prayed the bowing windows would hold against the wind, and the hurtling spray bursting like shrapnel against the glass. It would have been impossible to stand outside and not be blinded by the flying water, or to breathe against the lung bursting pressure of the gale.

The sudden assault on the ship momentarily set my senses reeling, and I could only hang on and wait for my survival instincts to kick in. Which, once the initial shock of the assault wore off, they thankfully did, and I was able to assess the situation. The very sudden onset of storm force winds suggested that the typhoon was intense, very intense, but hopefully small in size.

The relief, if it could be called that, was that the wind was from almost right ahead, which meant that the storm centre was to the north, and might pass in front or even veer away from us. If it did move away then we might, just possibly, avoid the worst of it, but with the coast of Luzon now only 70 miles away, we had very little sea room.

With the monstrous northerly swell now combining with huge north-westerly seas whipped up by the storm force winds, *Oriental Venture* was pitching and rolling like a cornered animal desperate to throw off an attacker. Burying her bows under tons of cascading green and white water, shaking herself free and clawing her way up each oncoming mountain with its viciously curling crest, sliding sickeningly over the top, screw racing madly as the stern left the water, and then plunging back into the trough to start the cycle again.

Rain followed the wind, pouring in thick torrents out of the doomsday clouds, merging with the spray whipped from the wave crests and hurled horizontally by the gale, flaying the ship's steelwork and instantly shredding the canvas awnings. The sky so thick with water at times, that it seemed as if we were under the surface of the sea rather than clinging precariously to it. And with visibility reduced to only a handful of yards, the grey, spume streaked crests of the waves reared viciously up out of the gloom like giant claws from hell.

I had learned from bitter experience the truth of the old saying that things could be worse at sea; and sometimes much worse. I was not sure how much worse things could get, but, for the moment, all we could do was hang on, ride the storm as best we could, hope that nothing vital carried away and wait to see how the wind shifted. And how the barometer moved. As long as it continued to fall the storm was closing on us, but when it steadied, or better still rose, then it was stationary or moving away. With the ship being hurled onto her beam-ends one minute and then bodily thrown over an oncoming cliff the next, I was grimly clinging onto the grab rail in self preservation, and it was only by timing my dash for the momentary lull at the bottom of a trough that I was able to scramble from the wheelhouse into the chartroom. Wedging myself into the corner, I checked the barograph. Despite all of my years of experience, I felt my sphincter twinge when I the saw the extent of its fall, the needle having dropped almost vertically over the course of the watch, and now hovering under 980 millibars. The rapidity of the drop meant that the storm centre could be as little as 60 miles away, or even less!

"Captain!" The urgency in that shout was unmistakable and I lunged back into the wheelhouse, stumbling hard against the bulkhead as the ship took another stomach-churning dive into the trough of an oncoming wave. As I dragged myself to my feet and peered through the streaming window, I felt a cold dagger of fear pierce my chest. Out of the gloom reared an approaching wall of water. For a moment the ship lay upright in the trough between two longer than usual swells. The oncoming wave was almost double the height of the ones preceding it, higher than the level of the wheelhouse, higher even, it seemed, than the top of the foremast. Although I realised, or hoped rather, that this was probably just an illusion. I sprang for the engine room telegraph, yanked the handle back to half ahead and yelled to the helmsman to meet the wave head on, to avoid, at all costs, the ship's head slewing round so that she would broach to, slide sideways down the face of the wave, roll underneath, and plunge straight to the bottom.

"Hang on!" I yelled at a wide-eyed, white-faced McGrath, a corner of my mind already pitying those below decks who couldn't see, and wouldn't be able to brace themselves against what was coming.

Then the monster wave was upon us. At first the bow rose to meet it, lifting higher and higher until the ship appeared to be climbing the oncoming wall. Above the bow, the towering crest was already curling and cascading down towards us. For a moment the propeller held us on the impossibly steep face, I could imagine it beating at the water like the paws of a terrified animal.

Until it lost its grip.

And the ship shuddered, starting to slide back down. I had a sudden image of her plunging stern first into the trough and cartwheeling to her doom. But, just when it seemed that all was over, and she had lost her battle to remain on the wave, the crest passed under the bow, which emerged shaking and shedding tons of water.

For a sickening moment, she balanced on the wave crest, half in and half out, every rivet screaming as the unsupported bow threatened to break off.

Then she reached tipping point and the bow plunged down and down, burying itself into the gaping trough behind, while above, the next wave, almost as big as the first, thundered down. The ship staggered as hundreds of tons of water forced her bodily downwards, submerging the entire forecastle and foredeck. The advancing wave crest broke against the front of the accommodation block with sledgehammer blows, smashing one of the toughened panes and flooding the wheelhouse.

"She can't survive this," I thought, surprised I was even able to think, in the face of such terrifying fury.

But, somehow, amazingly, the ship continued to swim.

Slowly, it seemed to take an age, the bow rose, shedding the hundreds of tons of water that had been holding her down. I gripped the grab rail, knuckles turning white, willing her to survive. Almost miraculously, the helmsman was still at the wheel. Up to his knees in water, cap dislodged by the gale, head bowed to keep the water driven in through the open window from blinding him. Still the ship answered her helm, and she began her climb up the next wave. Once again, the foredeck disappeared under raging white water, burying winches, hatch tops and deck fittings, and it seemed to me, in the relative safety of the wheelhouse from where I viewed her suffering, that the ship's centre island was all that remained of a submerged reef, pounded and battered by the waves.

Staggering under that fearful assault, somehow, *Oriental Venture* struggled on, rising unsteadily, groggily, to face each wave with what I wanted to believe was growing confidence. As if the ship herself had sensed she could survive the worst that could be thrown at her.

In the aftermath of the freak wave, the sea seemed to settle down a little. The waves, while still enormous, were more regular and *Oriental Venture* rode them a little easier, although she still pounded and lurched and corkscrewed and groaned as she battled each one. I glanced across at McGrath who was gripping the grab rail and staring out at the apocalyptic scene around us. I noticed him shivering with wet and cold, and had to yell to make myself heard against the painful shrieking and howling of the wind.

"Nip down below, Third, and put on dry clothes and your oilskins, quick as you can."

McGrath waited for the roll and then bolted nimbly to the door.

He returned together with Lowther who scrambled his way into the wheelhouse holding a bath towel and my oilskin. He was hatless, wearing an oilskin coat, wet hair plastered over his scalp, and blood ran down from a cut over his right eye.

"Bit of a mess down there," he yelled, jerking a thumb in the direction of the staircase. "Bit of a mess topsides too, both the starboard life boats have been carried away and we might have lost some of the foredeck gear. Hatch covers appear to be holding, so far, but I can't risk sending anyone forward to check."

I nodded, released one hand from the rail to grab the offered towel, and rubbed myself down as best I could. Then I reached for the oilskin and struggled into it.

"How are the crew taking it, any casualties," I shouted back.

"A few cuts and bruises but nothing serious, thank God. I've accounted for everyone, and those not in the engine room are mustered in the saloon or the engineers' mess," yelled Lowther.

I nodded again, grateful for his foresight, and stared through the streaming windows, edging sideways so I could glance through the hole left by the shattered glass, shielding my eyes from the driving rain and seawater.

"I think the wind's backing, could be the storm's moving away."

I let go of the rail, and lurched and stumbled across the violently heaving deck into the chartroom. The barograph had stopped its headlong descent and had levelled off. I stared closely at the blue trace. Perhaps it was wishful thinking, but the more I peered at the nib, the more certain I became that the trace had begun to curl upwards. I transferred my attention to the chart, trying to estimate our position. The log still streamed astern, and normally the lookout would go aft every hour to read the number of miles clicked off by its rotations. That was now impossible; but I knew that heading directly into the monstrous seas and the typhoon strength winds, *Oriental Venture* would barely be making headway.

"I think the typhoon's slowly pulling ahead of us," I shouted, putting my mouth close to Lowther's ear. "We'll just have to keep plugging on, hope that it continues to draw ahead, and that we're not so far off track that we don't pick up Cape Engano lighthouse."

The wheelhouse door bust open as the ship made another violent lurch, and Griffith was hurled into the chartroom, stumbling against me and managing to break his fall by grasping the edge of the chart table. He was dressed in oilskins and sou'wester, and grinned apologetically.

"Relieving the third, sir," he bellowed over the noise of the gale, "and the chippy's brought a board to plug the window."

With the board nailed over the broken window, and with wind and water no longer forced howling through the opening, conditions in the wheelhouse were more manageable. The broken glass was swept up, the helmsman relieved, and I turned my attention back to the problem of our position. With the wind backing into the west, we would be making leeway east, away from the coast of Luzon. Better than being wrecked on a lee shore, but placing more distance between us and our destination, while our coal stocks continued to fall. If we were driven too far off course, and failed to see the lighthouse on the tip of Cape Engano, we would miss the entrance to the Babuyan Channel, and have to run north to clear the outlying islands. But by then we would be burning our reserves, and still have over two days steaming to go.

With the ship clawing its way slowly north-west, the best we could hope for would be to sight the lighthouse sometime before midnight, if the visibility had lifted sufficiently and if we had not been blown too far to the east. The chart stated that the light had a nominal range of nearly 30 miles, but in thick weather, with the clouds almost down to sea level and the air full of whipped spray and blasting rain, it might not be visible at five miles or even less.

The appearance of Griffith on the bridge reminded me that the watch had changed, noon had come and gone and, despite the conditions, I was hungry. I glanced at Lowther.

"Has the crew eaten?"

"The galley's flooded and the range is useless. The cook's got biscuit and tinned bully beef for those that can stomach it," he replied.

"God help us, emergency rations, and a tot of rum to wash them down with I suppose? You naval types don't change." I managed to grin at him.

"Got to keep morale up," he replied.

"And lead by example," I said silently, having already smelled the rum on Lowther's breath when he entered the wheelhouse. "Right, well I'm going below for a few minutes to get into some dry clothes and grab some of those emergency rations. I'll be back shortly. And Peter, I suggest you get some rest before the dog watch, it's going to be a difficult night."

If the typhoon was drawing ahead, it was doing so slowly. As the afternoon wore on the barograph made hesitant and frustratingly small upward steps. The wind continued to shriek and tear at the ship, slicing the tops off the waves and hurling them downwind, flaying every exposed surface. From the relative safety of the wheelhouse, I could see the paint on the windward side of the masts and derricks blasted away by the force of the water. In the strongest gusts, the windowpanes bowed inwards and Griffith gingerly backed away from the glass. Looking astern, I could see the empty davits where the lifeboats had been ripped away, their falls and blocks wildly swinging and twisting in the gale.

The ship continued to battle the monstrous seas, sometimes thrown onto her beam-ends, so that we had to cling to the grab rails to avoid tumbling down the almost vertically inclined deck and breaking bones against the opposite bulkhead. At other times, she climbed over waves so high that her bow appeared to disappear into the ragged underside of the dark storm clouds racing overhead, before plunging over the crest and burying her forecastle under the oncoming wave. But her engine continued to beat, and, despite the groaning and creaking of her hull, she continued to swim. As the hours wore on, I felt a grudging respect for the Mackems who had built her, and for the old ship herself which, despite her worn, rust streaked and antiquated appearance, was weathering the battering like an ageing prize fighter, dodging and weaving, and riding out the worst of the blows.

As the afternoon faded into evening, and Lowther relieved Griffith, the rain eased, but the sky remained a wrack of dark scudding cloud, which trailed skirts of torrential showers. Sunset was about six pm, but by five the light was fading, and the spray chilled wind penetrating the cracks in the wheelhouse doors and windows had us shivering, despite being well inside the tropics.

Sunset brought total darkness, and the world closed in around us until it seemed we were the entire focus of the storm's violence and anger. The wind continued to howl and shriek, and out of the pitch-black darkness monster waves reared suddenly up in front of us, their white, breaking crests visible in the dimly reflected glow of the navigation lights. I left Lowther in charge on the bridge and made my way around the accommodation, offering words of encouragement to the seamen sitting or lying in the alleyways or the mess room. Those gathered in the saloon were silently clinging to chairs, or sprawled on cushions on the floor. It was still impossible to light the galley range and the cook was offering round cold tins of Maconachies beef and vegetables. The rusty tins with their torn, faded labels looked old enough to have come from a job lot of army surplus disposed of after the Great War, and I was not surprised that few could face eating. I exchanged a few words with those that felt like talking, and then made my way down the succession of ladders into the depths of the engine room. As I climbed down, I was struck by the contrast between this hot cavernous space, lit by incandescent light bulbs, filled with the regular, reassuring thump of the steam engine, and the cold, wet, shrieking, blackness of the wheelhouse. Despite the gut wrenching rolling and heaving, which even down here had me clinging for my life to the railings, there was a sense of normalcy. The regular thump of the engine was like the ship's heartbeat, as long as it continued its reassuring rhythm there was a promise of salvation.

Fraser greeted me on the floor plates beside the great triple expansion engine, bending his head close to my ear in order to make himself heard over the noise.

"It must be serious if you feel the need to pay us a visit," he said, his flushed and sweating face breaking into a grin. I had discarded the oilskin before entering the engine room, and was clad only in damp shirt and shorts, but already I could feel the sweat breaking out on my brow, and see wisps of evaporation rising from my shirt.

"We're through the worst of it," I shouted. "I wanted to see how you were getting on, and say thank you for keeping us going. If we'd lost power or steerage way it would have been the end."

"Aye, thanks Captain, I'll see the men are told. Some of them stokers are a nasty, violent bunch that you wouldn't trust within a mile of your aunty, but they know how to work when they have to."

"I think the storm's passed ahead of us and might have veered to the north, so conditions should ease tonight. If we can pick up the lighthouse on the tip of Luzon we can safely turn towards Hong Kong. How much coal have we got left?"

"We're already burning our reserves, Captain. We've enough left for another two days, if we're careful."

"It's 450 miles from Cape Engano to Hong Kong, that's over 45 hours steaming and we're still some way short of the Cape. How far I can only guess, as we haven't had a fix for over 12 hours. I don't want to have to radio for a tow."

"Sure, there's always the hatch boards. You can chop them up and they'll burn right enough," replied the chief. Then, turning serious, he put his hand on my arm.

"We'll do our best, skipper. I'm already shutting down as much of the electrical power as I can to save steam. There won't be any ice for the cold rooms, and you should turn off as many lights and fans as you can."

"Thanks, Chief, let me know if there's any change."

By the change of watch, the wind had backed well into the west but was still blowing fiercely, and I instructed McGrath to alter course to port to counteract the leeway. With no position since Lowther's morning star sights, and only guesswork to estimate our position, I hoped we would sight the lighthouse before midnight. If not, then as Julius Ceaser said of the Rubicon, we would cross that river when we got there. But the thought of missing Cape Engano in the darkness, and running aground among the reefs and shoals to the north continued to play on my mind.

With the typhoon drawing away the seas started to ease and the wind, while still gale force, lost its terrifying, shrieking edge. The torrential showers persisted in the storm's wake, though, and even had it been daylight we would have seen very little. The easing of the sea meant it was possible, barely, to read the ship's log. McGrath volunteered to go aft, and I had several anxious minutes wondering whether he had been washed over the stern rail, before his streaming, grinning figure reappeared, like a large, wet, friendly terrier.

The log revealed we had managed only 40 miles since the last reading over 12 hours ago. Subsequent readings showed we were slowly picking up speed and making five knots through the water, reasonable considering the conditions, but wasteful of our precious, diminishing coal stocks.

As the wheelhouse clock ticked off the hours towards midnight, I anxiously scanned the horizon with my night glasses, looking for the faintest loom of Cape Engano light. The night was as black as the depths of a tomb, and I wondered whether the typhoon had battered the lighthouse badly enough to extinguish its lamps. In which case the only warning we could expect would be the sight of the breakers on the cliffs before our bottom was torn open. For a second I was tempted to turn the ship around, and steam directly out to sea away from the danger. In other conditions I would have ordered the deep sea lead line used to sound the water depth, but it was far too dangerous with waves still breaking heavily over the ship.

"Is that lightening flashing behind the clouds?" My thoughts jerked back to the horizon at the sound of McGrath's voice.

"Where away, mister?" I called, swinging the night glasses up.

"Three points to port," came McGrath's reply. "It's too regular for lightening." His voice had risen with excitement. "I'm counting the flashes. One ... two ... three ... four ... five. Yes, it's Cape Engano, sir." His yell was almost triumphant.

"Well spotted, Third. Take a bearing as soon as you can and start plotting a running fix."

"Thank you," I whispered, hoping that whatever deity had taken pity on *Oriental Venture* was still listening. I was sure I had seen worse storms, although I would have struggled at that moment to recall exactly when. But having survived the typhoon, it would have been too much of a cruel joke to miss the lighthouse and run the ship aground.

So it was with a profound sense of relief that I watched McGrath busy at the chart, plotting our position. I could almost envy him. It had been a dreadful day and I wondered if he had any idea how close we had come to being overwhelmed by the typhoon. If the storm centre had been even a little way further south. If it had not veered off to the north. If, If!

But it hadn't, and I had no doubt that McGrath, with the resilience of youth, would be looking forward to getting his head down as soon as Griffith relieved him.

I scanned the horizon again; the flash of the lighthouse was more distinct now. "Time for another bearing, Third?"

No rest for me yet, though. I ran my fingers through my salt encrusted hair. My eyes burned, and I knew they were red rimmed with big black circles beneath them. We still had several hours before clearing the Cape and reaching the safety of open waters. And with every passing minute our last few tons of coal were disappearing into the boiler, shovelful by shovelful.

CHAPTER EIGHT

Two days later *Oriental Venture* wearily picked her way between the islands at the western entrance to Hong Kong harbour. The typhoon had swept the China Sea clear of the sampans and junks that normally plied their trade along the coast. No doubt, there were many who had read the warning signs and taken refuge in the typhoon anchorages. There would have been others, though, with less foresight or too far from shelter, overwhelmed by the storm and drowned in the pitiless waters, leaving grieving families to count the cost. It was the same wherever men left the safety of the shore in search of fish or other ocean-borne riches, and the Rowdens had seen plenty of their own sons sacrificed in the service of the sea.

But not this time. The ship made a battered, but defiant spectacle as I conned her slowly up the Tathong Channel, the stokers heaving the last shovelfuls of coal dust into her boiler fires. Her upperworks bore the scars of battle with the typhoon. Two lifeboat davits hung twisted and empty, and the mangled or missing deck fittings made her look as if she had grappled with the Kraken. Great swathes of paint had been flayed away by the force of storm driven water, leaving dull patches of bare steel that were already bleeding rust.

In contrast with the limping, tattered ship, the morning was bright and beautiful. The sun had not yet risen high enough for its heat to draw the moisture from the green, forest clad slopes of the mountains that ringed the harbour. The craggy summits of Pottinger Peak and Mount Parker stood out so crisp and clean against the washed blue of the morning sky, that it seemed as if it were possible to reach out and touch them.

As we rounded the headland and turned towards the narrow entrance to Lyemoon Passage, I saw the pilot cutter slicing its way down the channel towards us. I slowed the ship as the cutter curved alongside, and watched as a perspiring, ruddy faced Englishman in white Bombay bloomer shorts and a starched, but already wilting, white shirt, clambered up the pilot ladder and the stairs to the bridge.

"Good morning, Captain," he said, offering a pudgy hand, and gathering his breath from the brisk climb. "It seems you had a pretty torrid time of it judging by the look of you."

I grasped the hand, feeling the man's moist, soft grip, and shook it briefly.

"Aye, we had a few hours there where it seemed touch and go." I affectionately patted the teak capped rail. "But she came through it pretty well."

"Think you were lucky, Captain, there's reports from Formosa of a number of ships beached or sunk." He paused as if waiting for a reply, but when I merely nodded acknowledgment of our own good fortune, continued. "I've orders to put you alongside at Kowloon Point."

"Okay, Pilot, she's all yours. We're burning dust and slack now so I'm not sure how much longer the steam pressure will last. But you've a tug ordered?"

"Yes, Captain, it's following me down."

As we emerged from Lyemoon Passage, the expanse of Kowloon Bay opened out in front of us, revealing a sturdy tug bustling its way past North Point. I turned towards Lowther who was beside me on the bridge wing.

"Almost feels like home, Peter. Are we ready to pass muster with the owners?"

Lowther grimaced at the rhetorical question. As soon as it had been safe to work on deck he had turned the crew to, tidying up the havoc wrought by the storm; and I had dispatched a wireless message to the owners advising our condition and needs, but I was sure the ship's appearance would still raise a few eyebrows.

Not that of the crew, though. I never failed to marvel at the resilience of seamen, and their ability to push aside the terrors of the storm. Of the bone chilling hours soaked by rain and spray, deafened by the shrieking wind, exhausted by the heaving and plunging of a ship fighting for her life. Clustered on the foredeck, with the bright sun on their backs, and the majestic vision of the steep, luxuriant peaks tumbling down to the sheltered waters of the harbour, the typhoon was already a fading memory. I could hear their excited Cantonese chatter as they pointed to their native villages, and to the junks and sampans ghosting among the islands. Not for nothing did Hong Kong mean fragrant harbour in Cantonese. The dew-fresh, verdant smell of the jungle, the wood smoke from countless cooking fires, the smell of the racks of drying fish, and the coal smoke from the ships at anchor were deeply evocative. I drew in a lungful of the warm, heavy air, savouring the multitude of scents and feeling the Orient being absorbed into my fibres.

Ahead of us, I could see the cluster of ships anchored in the roads between Tsim Sha Tsui and Victoria, with the Star Ferries picking their way between them. Clustered along the water's edge to port were the naval base and the commercial heart of the waterside city, with its honeyed sandstone government buildings and white painted banks and trading houses. Over to starboard, the drydocks and engineering works of Hong Ham Bay hosted a rank of tramp ships, moored side-by-side undergoing repairs. As we rounded Kowloon Point, with its neo-Gothic railway station and clock tower overlooking the timber landing stages of the ferry terminal, the tug nestled alongside, exhaling hot, sulphury breath. Then we were nudging against the finger jetty, heaving lines snaked through the air and were caught by the Chinese dockhands, who heaved the heavy manila mooring warps onto the wharf, and dropped their eyes over the bollards. As soon as we were all secure, I rang the telegraph to finished with engine. Not a moment too soon for Fraser, I was certain, as the boilers must have been burning air by then.

Finally, with the gangway lowered, a waiting procession of officials clambered up the steep steps. All of them, I knew, bound for my cabin. There would be no peace for the wicked.

* * *

"And you have no idea why you were attacked at Manus Island? Pirates you say?" said Captain Fairclough, director and Hong Kong port manager for the Anglo Oriental Steamship Company.

The initial rush of officialdom had subsided, and Fairclough sat back in the chair in my day cabin and puffed on the battered stem of a yellowing Meerschaum pipe. A thick moustache covered his upper lip. It would have been grey to match the short stubble on his head, except that it was heavily nicotine stained.

"None at all. Like I said it was a routine call at Manus to deliver drums of fuel, until the attempt to board us."

"Most odd, most odd. I can't believe that old Mr Leung would have been party to such a thing. Our agent in Moresby speaks most highly of him. Must have been a sneak attack by a rival to get his hands on the fuel." Ash dropped from the pipe bowl onto the trousers of the dark grey suit he habitually wore, even in the heat and humidity of a Hong Kong summer. He brushed it away irritably. "But why wait until you reached Hong Kong to report it, Captain Rowden? You could have reported by radio. Then there might have been a chance to catch them."

"There was no harm done, Captain Fairclough, apart from the skulls we cracked, and whoever did it would have been long gone by the time the Australian authorities could have got someone up there."

"S'pose your right, Rowden," growled Fairclough. "Damned strange, though, damned strange, all for a few drums of diesel. Have to let the insurers know though. Bound to be a claim from old Leung. Beats me why we haven't heard from him already."

I was sure I knew the answer to that, but decided not to make Fairclough's life any more complicated. "The chief mate will you give you all the details from the log-book and the cargo manifest," I replied, nodding towards Lowther.

"You seem to have had an interesting voyage in more ways than one, Captain," continued Fairclough. "Attacked by pirates, then a typhoon. But what am I to make of these?" He held up two buff telegram forms. "One's a request from the local police to interview you in connection with the death of a man in Sydney. What do you say to that, Captain?"

It had been nearly three months since we had left Sydney, so the wheels of justice had certainly ground slowly. But how fine, I wondered?

"A murder in Sydney?" I surprised myself by the indignation I managed to put into my voice. "What could it possibly have to do with me?"

"Keep your shirt on, Rowden," replied Fairclough. "No one said anything about a murder. They just want to check the details of when you departed from Sydney, and whether any of your crew were ashore at the time of the death. I'm sure it's just routine."

"What's the second telegram about?" I snapped, enjoying keeping him on the back foot.

"It's from a Major Spencer who claims to be the Australian Army's attaché for New Guinea. Bit mysterious that one, says he has information that needs to be delivered face to face."

Lowther shot me a quizzical glance. I had a fair idea what it was Spencer wanted to talk to me about, but I kept my face straight as I replied.

"I've no more idea what that's about than I do about any death in Sydney. When can I expect them?"

"The police will be here this afternoon, as soon as I confirm you're ready to accept visitors. Major Spencer's cable says he's arriving on the Imperial Airways flight from Darwin, so he should be here in the next day or so. I've replied that there's no urgency as you'll be here for several weeks with cargo, and while we patch you up. Imperial Airways, eh?" Fairclough chewed on the stem of his pipe. "Must think himself a pretty important Nabob, if he has to fly up to see the master of *Oriental Vagabond*. Not exactly the Navy are we?"

I managed to ignore the sarcasm, while Fairclough took a long satisfying suck on his pipe and puffed clouds of pungent blue smoke.

"Would you care for another gin, Captain Fairclough?" Lowther asked, his voice neutrally polite, despite the implied criticism of the ship's appearance, and the unflattering joke.

It was strange how the jovial and canny Poh could make the pun on the ship's name sound almost like a compliment, while from the mouth of the stuffy, priggish Fairclough it felt deeply insulting. Thankfully it was approaching noon, and Lowther had already helped Fairclough to two large pink gins as well as mixing the same himself. I had accepted one, but it remained half-drunk and warming on the coffee table.

"No thank you, Lowther." Fairclough pulled a silver fob watch out of his waist-coat pocket and consulted it. "Promised the memsahib I'd be home for tiffin. I'll be back this afternoon to check on progress."

He gathered up his papers from the coffee table, stuffed them into a slim leather briefcase, and rose to go.

"Oh, I almost forgot. You can also expect a visit from the chairman. Not sure when he'll come down but I'll try and send word first." He held out his hand. "It's good to see you safe Captain, these are difficult times."

I stood and shook the proffered hand before Lowther escorted him down to the gangway. I had refreshed my glass by the time he returned.

"Go on, Peter, pour yourself another," I encouraged him. "I'm sure you need it after the last few days. Griffith's on watch this afternoon and the wharfies know what to do. Everything else can wait until tomorrow."

Lowther picked up his glass and reached for the gin bottle. "There's a load of coal to get in, enough for the galley range and to maintain steam for the generator until we can bunker."

"Griffith and the chief can look after that. Take advantage of an evening off, blow off a bit of steam. It'll all be still here tomorrow."

Lowther took a swallow of gin and smiled ruefully. "It's a while since I had a run ashore here. Let's see how the afternoon pans out. I want to hear what the police have to say about Sydney. And what do you think old Fairclough meant about diffi-cult times?"

"I've been thinking on that myself, Peter. The Japs taking on the Chinese again? The Nazis threatening Europe? And on top of all that we have Major Spencer to look forward to. I had a feeling we hadn't seen the last of him."

I picked up my glass and drained it.

"Slosh a bit more gin in here will you, Peter?" I held it out while Lowther tipped the bottle. "Aye, life's tough enough tramping around these waters. But it'll get harder, much harder, if General Tojo and Herr Hitler get their way."

* * *

"Inspector Jardine of the Hong Kong Police, good of you to see me, Captain."

The inspector held out his hand and I shook it, feeling the man's firm grip, his palm surprisingly dry in the stuffy heat of the cabin. I cast an envious eye over Jardine's crisp uniform with its freshly starched, knife-edged creases. I felt very workman-like in comparison, with my crumpled and faded drill, tinged grey after countless washings. Even Lowther, in his naval style whites looked unfavourably scruffy, compared to the neat and efficient appearance of the inspector.

Jardine appeared unfazed by the scrutiny, and offered his hand to Lowther.

"Is that the DSC, sir?" his nasally vowels betraying his Midland origins, "from the war?"

"Yes, inspector. I'm Lowther, chief mate. Please sit down." He waved in the direction of the chairs.

Jardine flipped off his cap, laid it on the coffee table and sat down.

"Now, how can Captain Rowden and I help you? Something about a death in Sydney we understand."

"That's right, sir. Committed on the night of the 20th of March, three months ago that is. Man found knifed, stabbed to death in a place called Rozelle. Local police haven't turned up much, but witness reports suggest the perpetrator might have been dressed like a seaman. So they've been checking on the ships that were in Sydney around that time. Your ship was one of those, Captain, so our colleagues in Sydney asked if I could talk to you."

"We were in Sydney then," I replied. "I'd have to check the log, but my recollection is that we sailed that evening, Peter?"

"We sailed at about half past midnight, I think it was on the morning of the 21st," replied Lowther. "What time exactly was the death, inspector?"

"I'm afraid the Sydney boys are a bit vague on that. The body was found by a cleaner on her way to work early on the 21st. Nasty fright she must have had. The coroner put the time of death between ten p.m. the previous evening and two a.m. Initially no one came forward to report it, but inquiries turned up a couple of lads who confessed to being in the victim's company the previous evening. Said there was a scuffle with two men, one of whom ran away before they got a good look at him, and the other looked like a seaman. They thought he might have had a knife, but scampered when the scuffle broke out. They weren't sure of the time, thought it was just before midnight."

"So they left their mate, who might have been stabbed, and ran away?" I said.

"Appears that way. Truth is that these lads were probably up to no good. The dead man was reported to be the leader of the local push."

"Push?"

"Gang," replied Jardine. "There's also a report from the dock watchman at White Bay. He said there were a number of seamen who passed through the gate that evening, mostly in twos and threes, but there was one chap walked in on his own. But again he can't be sure of the time, around midnight was the closest he could put it."

"So what do you want from us? Do you want to interview the crew?" I asked.

"I don't have the power to do that, Captain," replied Jardine. "New South Wales is not in my jurisdiction. All I can do is ask if you know if any of your men were ashore that night, and if they were acting suspiciously when they returned."

"I don't know if anyone did go ashore that evening, as we were due to sail around midnight." The lie came easily after years of dealing with the unwelcome attention of inquisitive officials. "We could check though. You know inspector, we've a pretty good crowd. They're not angels, they get into their share of trouble, but I've never had to deal with anything more than black eyes and sore heads. What would happen if one of the men did turn out to have been ashore that night?"

"I could question him, with your permission of course, and send a report to Sydney. I've no authority to arrest anyone if that's what you're asking."

"Easy, inspector," I said, hearing the bristling tone in his voice. "We're happy to cooperate. The chief mate will check and see if anyone went ashore that evening. Where can we get hold of you if we need to?"

Jardine extracted a metal calling card case from his breast pocket, flipped it open and handed one to me.

"You can telephone me on that number. Don't get me wrong, Captain. I've no desire to make life difficult. This isn't a murder inquiry, not yet anyway. My impression is the Sydney police are not sorry to see the back of the dead man, and would probably look upon what happened as self-defence. So, if you think there's anyone in your crew I should talk to, well it's up to you, unless I hear otherwise from Sydney."

He rose. "Thank you for your time, Captain, Mr Lowther. I'll see my way out." He picked up his cap, placed it squarely on his head, and pushed aside the privacy curtain. We listened until his footsteps faded down the stairway.

"I don't think we need to check, do we Peter?" I said. "We know who was ashore that night."

"It was self-defence though, surely?" he replied. "The inspector implied as much. Although he might think it suspicious that we didn't report it at the time."

"True enough, but I don't feel like giving Inspector Jardine the pleasure of jumping to any conclusions. The Sydney police obviously have no idea who they're looking for, and I intend to leave it that way. It sounds as if the man who was stabbed had a thing for beating up homosexuals, so maybe he had it coming to him." I saw the look on Lowther's face.

"All right, Peter. I'll have a word with Griffith. I'm happy to sin by omission, but if the police can produce the evidence to arrest him, then he'll have to take his chances. Ask him to come up, will you?"

Lowther went to fetch Griffith, leaving me with a few minutes to think about what to say to him. From what he had told me the night we left Sydney, and with Jardine's assertion that the Sydney police were not looking to pin a murder charge, I felt certain that Griffith had acted in self-defence. But he had killed the man, and I was equally certain that a judge would not look too kindly on a sailor who stuck a knife in people, whatever the provocation. And the fact I had not reported it earlier was probably a crime in itself, if they could prove I had known. But as I had said to Lowther, it was up to the police to make whatever case they thought would stick. Or not, depending on what evidence they could turn up.

"Shut the door," I said as Griffith appeared in the entrance.

He stood tight lipped, with narrowed eyes, as I related the conversation with the inspector. I held my hand up when I had finished, not wanting him to ask the obvious question.

"Listen carefully, Griffith. The chief mate and I told the inspector we didn't believe anyone went ashore that night. I think he's inclined to leave it at that, unless the Sydney police provide any firm evidence to the contrary. Of course, we'd be party to the offence if it turned out we'd withheld information, but I didn't see or talk to anyone who came back late that night, and neither did the chief mate." I emphasised the final words, paused to let them sink in, and then, to be certain, "Have I made myself clear?"

Griffith raised his eyebrows, and the ghost of a smile crossed his lips. "Perfectly, sir."

"You can wipe that grin of your face, mister." I snapped. I wasn't going to let him think he'd got away with it that easily. "There's always the piper to pay. Just make damned sure that neither the chief mate nor I have any reason to question our memories. And pray that the Sydney police don't turn up any other witnesses."

I dismissed him. I had no intention of contacting Inspector Jardine, and I doubted he expected me to. And if he got further word from Sydney? Well, we could be who knows where by then, and there was no point worrying about things that might never happen.

On the other hand, we had good reason to be worried. We just didn't know it.

CHAPTER NINE

A week had passed since our arrival, and *Oriental Venture* continued to lie alongside the Kowloon finger jetty discharging her cargo of copra. I had taken a break from the paperwork in my office and was trying to enjoy a smoke on the bridge wing. Watching rope nets bulging with copra bags being hoisted out of the holds by the small army of stevedores, who swarmed over the decks shouting to each other in Cantonese. Their singsong voices accompanied by the rattle and clank of the derricks, and the squealing and hissing of the steam winches. Half the bags were being swung onto the quayside, where they were manhandled onto barrows and pushed into the godowns at the end of the jetty. The other half were going straight into the holds of the fleet of lighters moored on the opposite side. Each shaped like a small junk with curved prow and square stern, its bow decorated with Chinese symbols; stylised flowers, eyes, animals, dragons and characters. A small deckhouse aft was home to the owner and his family, all of whom took part in the operation, unslinging the nets, heaving the copra bags into the hold, and urging the stevedores to work faster. When one was filled, its owner disappeared below to start the engine, and then took the helm in the primitive wheelhouse, his wife and children handling ropes and fending off other craft, as it bumped and jostled away from the ship's side and chugged slowly off, belching black smoke.

Despite the muggy heat of a Hong Kong summer's day, I might have enjoyed watching this bustle of activity, but quickly decided otherwise. In addition to discharging the cargo, gangs of coolies were also hard at work chipping, scraping and painting where the force of the typhoon had blasted the paint away. All of them working in a choking brown cloud of rust and flaked paint, combined with copra dust and steam escaping from the winches. The deafening noise of their chipping hammers added to the din, so it was a relief to finish my cigarette and return to the relative quiet of my cabin.

With the porthole closed against the dust, and the electric fan struggling to circulate the hot, damp air, my cabin felt as hot as Calcutta's Black Hole, made worse by the need to wear my uniform. A note from Captain Fairclough, delivered by Da Silva after breakfast, had warned that Mr Khoo, the chairman of Anglo Oriental, would be paying me a visit that morning. My starched whites were wilting in the heat, and I poured myself a glass of water from the rapidly warming water jug, adjusted the fan for maximum airflow over my sweating face, and mopped my brow with a limp handkerchief. I was about to sit down at my desk when there was a sharp rap on the door frame, Da Silva's brown hand whisked aside the curtain, and the elderly, but dapper figure of the chairman stepped into the office.

"Good morning, Mr Khoo," I said, beaming at him and extending my hand, hoping that an effusive welcome would make up for my failure to meet him at the gangway in person. "I apologise you had to find your way up here on your own, and for the state of the ship."

"No matter, Captain Rowden," replied Mr Khoo, shaking my hand with his firm, bony grip. "I am early, and your third mate, McGrath is it, met me at the gangway." He waved towards a chair. "Please let us sit down, but if you don't mind, it is a warm day and I shall remove my coat."

He slipped out of the jacket of his expensive and immaculate cream linen suit, hung it on a peg behind the door, and sat down in the armchair. I asked Da Silva to bring us a pot of coffee, and took the other chair. In his shirt sleeves, with a pair of braces holding up his trousers, and with soft brown eyes and modest smile, Khoo looked anything other than he was, a man who had worked his way up from tally clerk on the Shanghai waterfront, to tenacious and successful owner of a fleet of tramp steamers.

"Captain Fairclough informed me of the details of your voyage, the typhoon, the pirate attack in Lorengau," he said, in his deceptively soft voice. "Most unfortunate, but the insurance will cover any damage and the voyage was profitable. You are to be congratulated Captain, the typhoon was a bad one. Some ships were lost, and we were worried about you. It's good to see you, and the ship safe."

I had sailed on ships whose owners could hardly have cared less for their safety, or that of the men who manned them, as long as they made a profit or the insurance covered the cost of their loss. Mr Khoo was not one of them. Which is not to say he was soft hearted. He could be ruthless, and was a dangerous man to cross, but he was a good judge of men and he was loyal, even a friend, to those he trusted with command of his vessels, as long as they repaid that trust. It was the ships he really loved, though. He chose his purchases personally and his judgment was usually flawless. Age and appearance made little impact on his selection. He studied the Lloyd's reports to gauge a ship's reliability. He knew which builders took the most pride in their work. He talked to the captains and the mates about the feel of a ship in which he was interested. Sometimes the superintendents shook their heads at the ugly, slab sided, filthy, aged craft that Mr Khoo proudly presented them with. But once cleaned up and refurbished to his satisfaction, the costs almost always matching to the cent the budget set by Mr Khoo himself, the result was a workable vessel. Still ugly, still old, but tight, staunch and strong, and well capable of repaying the usually modest sums he paid for them.

"We came through the typhoon well enough," I replied. "Couple of boats ripped out of their davits, some bent or broken fittings. But the hatch covers survived and she swam pretty well. A tribute to the Mackems."

"Mackems? I am not familiar with that term."

"It's what the Geordies, the men of Tyneside, call those from Sunderland. Comes from the saying, 'In Newcastle we build ships, but in Sunderland they mackem'."

Mr Khoo gazed at me inquiringly, before his mouth creased into a smile of understanding. "Ah, it is a jest, based on all those strange dialects you English speak. In Sunderland they don't build ships, they make them." He chuckled as he repeated the words.

"I was never very good at mimicking accents, I have enough trouble with my own," I said.

"It is just the same in China," said Mr Khoo. "You are fortunate that English is the language of business. Now, tell me what you think about the matter in Lorengau. I do not know Leung personally, but others speak quite well of him. He has a son too, I believe. Did you meet either of them?"

Concealing some or all of the truth was part and parcel of a ship-master's life in the China Sea in those days, and I prided myself on being able to maintain a neutral facial expression every bit as inscrutable as the Chinese were supposed to possess. It went against the lay to lie to Mr Khoo though, so I stuck to the truth as closely as I could, without mentioning the *Dortmund*, but speculating whether pirates, seeing an opportunity to lay their hands on a shipment of fuel, had seized Leung's launch. Fuel was a valuable commodity in the remote islands, and Mr Khoo nodded gravely as I finished my explanation, but the piercing glint in his eyes suggested he wasn't entirely convinced.

"There have been reports of boats from the southern Philippines attacking small ships among the islands," he said, stroking his chin. "So perhaps you are right."

"Where are we heading next, sir?" I said breezily, trying the change the subject.

"Shanghai," he replied, the eyes softening into a smile. "I almost wish I could accompany you. My doctor says a sea voyage would be good for my health. Get me away from the stress and grime of Hong Kong. And it would be good to see my old home town again."

I had heard whispered stories about Mr Khoo's days as a young clerk on the Bund in Shanghai, working for British and French liner companies. Saving his salary and taking advantage of every opportunity to supplement it with small, and then increasingly larger trading activities on his own account. Buying and selling condemned ships' stores, the paper work carefully arranged to conceal the reason for the disposal. Privately shipping items that never appeared on official manifests. Finally putting together enough to invest in a ship of his own, the start of a small shipping company in Shanghai that had grown into the Anglo Oriental, now based in Hong Kong.

The smile died as Mr Khoo's eyes narrowed and hardened.

"It was a wrench, the day I decided to move to Hong Kong. People said I was mad to leave Shanghai, the Paris of the east, for this British outpost. But times are changing, Captain Rowden. My poor country is in turmoil. The Communists threaten from Sian, the Japanese occupy Manchuria and the Nationalists are little better than warlords and gangsters. This cannot last and I fear the worst. Shanghai is a valuable prize, and as you British know, who controls it controls access to the heart of China. But can you hold onto it if the Japanese invade? Maybe, maybe not, but safer here in Hong Kong under the guns of the British Navy." The twinkle in his eyes returned and he laughed, opening his mouth wide and revealing the gold fillings in his teeth.

"And now I want you to take this ship there. Trouble is good for business, yes? Freight rates are high. I have advertised the voyage in the paper. There are many people wishing to ship things to Shanghai, and some already thinking of things they should be shipping out. I think it will be a good voyage."

"When would you like us to depart?" I asked.

"When can you be ready, Captain?" Mr Khoo replied, sharply.

"The repairs to the storm damage are well in hand. The superintendent has sourced two replacement lifeboats. Discharge and cleaning will take another week. We then need to move to the coaling berth. After that loading should take ten days." I made a mental calculation. "I should say three weeks from today."

"I would prefer you were ready in two weeks."

I was about to protest when Mr Khoo held up his hand. "I know you will tell me it is impossible, Captain Rowden, but I must push you to do your best. Events are currently in our favour, but that might change. You will ask Captain Fairclough for anything you need to expedite things." He paused, and a sly grin slid over his face. "Now, there is another matter of some importance. You will be carrying a consignment of tea."

"Tea!" I echoed, unable to contain my surprise. "Tea ... to China?"

"Ah yes, Captain. The finest Darjeeling tea, grown on the slopes of the Himalayas. The preferred beverage of your English ladies in Shanghai. I am sending it personally to one of my oldest friends there, who has been guaranteed a very good price from the hotels and department stores on Nanjing Road."

"Darjeeling tea!" I flushed as I realised I was echoing him like a parrot. "Yes, of course, Mr Khoo, but you said it was important?"

"I want you to deliver it personally into the hands of my friend. His name is Tung, but that is common enough in Shanghai. To be certain I will provide you a photograph from which you will be able to identify him. Tea is so very common in China that some might think a few chests of Indian tea to be worthless stuff, and treat them accordingly. Mr Tung is relying on me, and I on you, to see they are delivered in perfect condition."

"I'll take good care of it, and I apologise for appearing so surprised. I'm no expert on tea, prefer Typhoo myself, strong with a couple of sugars."

"I shall have to educate you." A roguish twinkle appeared in his eyes, and I wondered what else he had in store for me. "And one last thing, Captain. I have advertised that you have berths available for passengers."

"Pass ...." I checked myself. "Very good Mr Khoo, I'll need—"

He held up a hand. "All taken care of. Extra food and drink are being sent down, and we have engaged two additional stewards who will be here shortly to clean and air the staterooms. So far, you have two guests, a Lady Ashworth and her maid. I hope there will be more. She is no Cunarder our little *Oriental Venture*, but I've always found her most comfortable. I can rely on you and your officers, Captain?" It was an instruction rather than a question.

Apart from the Eberhardts, I could hardly remember the last time we had carried passengers. With the exception of Peter Lowther, none of the officers in *Oriental Venture*, including myself, could have remotely been considered a gentleman acceptable to the likes of a Lady Ashworth. And as for the polyglot mix of seamen and stokers, they were another species as far as English ladies were concerned. I sighed inwardly, then reassured myself with the knowledge that it would only be for four days. "It will be a pleasure Mr Khoo."

He rose from his chair, reached for his jacket and took my arm, smiling but not fooled by my less than effusive reply. "Come, Captain, help an old man down to the gangway, then you'll be free to get on and get this ship ready for sea."

I escorted him down the stairs and along the alleyway. He stopped at the bulwark gate, and held out his hand.

"Goodbye, Captain Rowden. Remember, if there is anything you need to hasten your departure please tell Captain Fairclough, and if I don't see you again before you leave, have a safe and profitable voyage."

"Thank you, sir," I replied, gently grasping the old man's bony hand and shaking it. "And thank you for taking the time to visit."

"Always a pleasure to see one of my ships, and her captain."

A uniformed Chinese driver assisted him down the gangway, and into the black limousine parked at the bottom. I raised a hand to my cap. I was genuinely fond of Mr Khoo, whose trust had led to my command of *Oriental Venture*. I saw a hand raised in acknowledgment. Then the door closed, and the car weaved its way among the piles of cargo on the jetty, leaving me to ponder on the matters of Darjeeling tea and English lady passengers.

* * *

Discharge had finished and the holds had been swept swept clean, but before loading could commence I moved *Oriental Venture* to the coaling berth to re-fill her bunkers. It was a filthy task. The chute from the loading tower shot the Welsh anthracite straight down the coaling hatch, much quicker than the old-fashioned chain of coolies passing baskets from hand to hand, but no less dusty and dirty. Dust blew off the conveyors on the tower. It blew out of the gaps in the loading chute, and a cloud of it hung around the coaling hatch, despite the efforts of the engineers to seal the opening with canvas. All the vents and portholes were screwed tight, but even so the dust penetrated the accommodation, settling in a grimy film on every surface. It was a miserable day, and I was thoroughly glad when Chief Engineer Fraser announced that every inch of the bunker spaces were crammed full. The crew were glad to turn to with shovels and brooms before hosing the decks down. Meanwhile the stewards set to work to thoroughly dust and clean the passenger suites. I doubted Lady Ashworth would appreciate having her fine linen and lace soiled by grimy coal dust.

Back alongside the cargo jetty, I sent word to Captain Fairclough that we were ready to receive cargo. Although that was hardly necessary, the waterfront telegraph having already alerted the stevedores to our return. Gangs of coolies were assembling, and piles of crates, bales and drums were already heaped up on the jetty. Picking his way among them, followed by a porter balancing a well-travelled holdall on his head, was the uniformed figure of Major Spencer. He raised his arm in an ironic salute when he saw me on the bridge wing, waited until the gangway had been lowered, and skipped briskly up it.

Ten minutes later he was relaxing on the couch in the privacy of my cabin, enjoying coffee freshly brewed by Da Silva, balancing a cup and saucer in one hand while smoking a cigarette with the other. He inhaled a lungful of smoke, and blew it out in a long blue stream towards the ceiling where it was caught up in the fan's draught and dispersed.

"Have a nice trip, up?" I asked, observing the pleasantries.

"Bloody long way by plane from Darwin. And it was a bit bumpy on the last leg from Saigon. Prefer having my feet on solid ground." He glanced around and grinned. "Present surroundings excepted, of course."

"You look pretty comfortable there to me," I replied, not returning his smile. "Mind telling me why you've flown all this way to see us?"

He placed the cup down on the coffee table and took another long, slow drag on his cigarette, eyeing me almost as if he was a cat contemplating a mouse.

"Heard you had a spot of bother on the way up here," he said, almost too casually, exhaling another lungful of smoke. There was the slight crease of a smile on his lips, but his eyes were deadly serious, and he fixed me with them, waiting to see how I'd react. I returned his gaze. He wasn't dealing with a mouse, and I'd played this game a long time. It was too early to start laying any cards on the table.

"Nothing we couldn't handle."

"Heard you made a call at Lorengau, and there was some shooting."

"Just a boat load of pirates, Sea Dyaks probably, trying to get at the deck cargo. We saw them off. It's all in my official report."

"Some of those Dyaks spoke German, and came from a ship called the *Dortmund*." He continued to gaze at me. "That wasn't in your report."

"You seem very well informed, Major."

I wondered who could have told him. It seemed unlikely that Dieter Eberhardt, or the Leungs, would have reported to the Australian authorities what happened. Spencer was obviously no fool, but I was still wary. "If you know what happened, then what do you want with me, why aren't you out chasing German pirates?"

Spencer leaned forward, stubbed his cigarette out in the brass ashtray and sat back, his eyes narrowed, his military moustache making a neat line above compressed lips. We glared at each other for a few moments, like two buck deer about to battle over a doe, then the corners of his mouth curled upwards, and he snorted softly.

"Okay, Captain Rowden, it's time for some straight talking. As you've probably gathered from what happened in Wewak, we've had an eye on Walter Eberhardt for some time. And now his brother's arrived, in command of a big, modern, German ship called the *Dortmund*, which you just happened to run foul of at Lorengau." He paused to let the information sink in. "So why don't you tell me what happened, from the beginning."

I sat in silence, thinking about the question and wondering how far I should trust him. In my experience the authorities, especially those in the Far East, were rarely to be trusted. I could count on the fingers of one hand the policemen and customs' officials whose honesty I would have bet my life on. "Trust no one" had become something of watchword, and it had served pretty well over the years.

"When you say 'we', who exactly do you mean?" I asked.

"Officially, I'm a major in the Australian Army, based in Port Moresby and keeping an eye on military matters there and in the islands. But unofficially, or perhaps that's also officially, sometimes I don't think even my lords and masters know which, I also report to army intelligence in London." He pulled out his silver cigarette case, offered me one and then lit us both. "You're wondering if you can trust me, is that it Captain?" he asked, inhaling a lungful of smoke. "Somehow, you've managed to tangle yourself up with the Eberhardt brothers. That's brought you to our attention. Probably best for both of us if you tell me what happened."

I sensed a veiled threat in the words, and felt myself bristle at the seeming assumption he exercised some sort of authority over me. I'd heard similar claims from officials up and down the China coast. Generally, their self-aggrandisement faded under the influence of vintage brandy and the flickering aura of gold. That, or the painful warning of an unfortunate accident. But this was different, we were in British Hong Kong, and Spencer appeared very well connected. It might be dangerous to make an enemy of him. I counted slowly to ten before replying, and then, starting with the encounter at the Papua Hotel with Dieter Eberhardt, related the events that lead us to Lorengau, the Germans' attempt to board from the workboat, the arrival of the *Dortmund* and our subsequent escape.

Spencer pursed his lips and emitted a low whistle as I finished. "That's quite a story, Captain. Piracy and daring do in a remote Pacific lagoon. Sounds almost romantic, but for one thing, my sources say you fought the attackers off with automatic weapons. Forgive me, but I didn't think machine guns were issued to merchant ships."

I clenched my fists, the knuckles turning white, and glared at him, tempted to smash the calm, smug grin off his face.

"Calm down, Captain." He held up a pacifying hand. "We're on the same side here. You defended yourself well, and I am not going to say anything to cast doubt on your official report. Listen man, despite what I told you in Wewak, I know what was hidden in the false bottoms of Eberhardt's crates. My sources are impeccable. The weapons were there when the crates came aboard your ship, and were not there when they went off again. Ergo, they were removed while on board. I've made some inquiries about you, Captain. You're not a man to take things at face value. My guess is you were suspicious of Eberhardt and decided to take a look at his cargo. You found the weapons and removed them. You used them to fight off the Germans in Lorengau, and they're still on board. You're too shrewd to throw away something that can give you an advantage. But one thing I know for sure. If I searched the ship from top to bottom I wouldn't find them. You are as much a pirate as the Eberhardts." He paused, smiling and drew breath. "So, how am I doing ... close to the mark?"

"Aye, Major, close enough," I conceded. "And there's more to the story. After leaving Lorengau my radio officer intercepted some coded messages he assures me were sent from the *Dortmund*." I opened the desk drawer and pulled out the sheaf of telegrams. "They mean nothing to me, but perhaps you have people that can make sense of them." Spencer glanced at the indecipherable groups of letters and numbers, folded the pages and stowed them into a pocket of his tunic.

"That's good work, Captain, I'm sure we have some bright young code breakers itching to have a try at reading those. They might reveal what the Eberhardts are really up to."

"Any theories, Major?"

"War! The Nazis seem hell bent on provoking one, and if it comes it won't be confined to Europe. There's valuable pickings out here. Rubber, oil, tin. The Nazis will be wondering how they can get their hands on them, and deny them to Britain at the same time. My guess is the Eberhardts are both working for the Nazis, with orders to find ways to cause trouble if, or rather when, the time comes. But they're not the only problem right now."

"As if I didn't have enough to worry about already," I chuckled. "Now I've got Nazi sympathizers after my blood."

"It's the Japs who are a bigger concern just at the moment," continued Spencer, with a touching lack of sympathy. "Things were reasonably quiet after the fighting stopped in Manchuria, despite the Chinese arguing amongst themselves, and the country divided between the Nationalists, the Communists and a few Warlords. But there are signs the Nationalists are forging some alliances in order to expel the Japs. They won't take that lying down. I've been tasked with assessing the potential strength of any Chinese alliance, and the likely reaction from the Japanese if they form one."

"And that's why you're here in Hong Kong? Not just to give me a hard time over some stolen Nazi weapons."

"No, that's why I'm going to Shanghai. With you as it happens." He waited while I absorbed the unwelcome news. "So you'll have the pleasure of my company for a few days, if you can tear yourself away from the lovely Lady Ashworth," he finished, laughing at a joke I didn't share.

Which is when I should have realised that he really was a spy.

* * *

The jangling, as McGrath tested the telegraphs were ready for our imminent departure from Hong Kong, interrupted my reverie. I was out on the bridge wing, waiting for the pilot, and had been gazing up at the Peak, the highest of the mountains on Hong Kong Island that framed the southern shore of the fragrant harbour. It had been several years since I had last taken the Star Ferry across to Central, and caught the funicular Peak Tram that clattered and rattled its dizzyingly steep way to the summit, the tracks laid perilously close to the near vertical drops of the upper slopes. On a clear day the view was magnificent, the expanse of the harbour stretching away east and west, its surface dotted with a myriad of ships, junks and sampans, all looking tiny from the 1,500 foot elevation. If I had time, I also liked to enjoy a walk around the gardens, before retiring to the terrace of the Peak Hotel for a refreshing glass of beer and a peaceful cigarette.

Not this time, however, we had been far too busy. The chairman's instructions that the ship be loaded and made ready for sea as quickly as possible, had translated into long hours with little time for shore leave. There had been some grumbling from the younger men, who usually spent their spare time in Hong Kong drinking in the cheapest dockside bars, before blowing the rest of their sub in the equally cheap and dirty brothels. The older men just took it in their stride. If we had to get back to sea in a hurry then that was that. Hong Kong would still be there next time and, anyway, there was Shanghai to look forward to. Such was Cramp's opinion at any rate.

"Don't worry about not seeing much of 'Ong Kong," I heard him reassure McGrath, as the two of them enjoyed a cigarette on the bridge wing while we continued to wait for the pilot. "Shanghai's much better. You can get anyfing you want there, anyfing!" he emphasized. "There's a night club called the Great World that's owned by a bent copper named Wang. Six floors seeving wiv people and noise, and crammed wiv every form of entertainment the Chinese 'ave been able to fink of."

McGrath's face betrayed his amazement.

"Don't look so surprised," Cramp continued. "Like I said, you can get anyfing in Shanghai, for a price. Wang bribed 'is way to being 'ead of the Chinese Police in the French Concession, and from there to 'aving a finger in every dodgy racket in the city. And you can find all of 'em at the Great World. On the first floor there are mahjong tables, sing-song girls and slot machines."

"Sing-song girls?" questioned McGrath.

"'Ores," replied Cramp. "Comes from the Chinese 'shi shong'. They will sing for you, if that's all you want." He laughed, and then continued. "But that's not all. On the second floor the girls wears gowns split right up their thighs, and there's a café, barbers, and men who'll remove the wax from your ears. On the next floor there's a cabaret with a jazz band and more girls, this time with their high-collared gowns slit to reveal their hips, in case you wasn't satisfied with looking at the thighs of the ones downstairs. On the fourth floor, there's a shooting gallery, fan-tan tables and massage benches. On the fifth floor the girls wear their dresses slit right to the armpits, and there's peep shows and a Chinese temple filled with 'orrible looking Gods and joss sticks. And on the roof there's tight-rope walkers, seesaws, and even a small open space where dozens of Chinese who've lost their last cent, can regain their honour by throwing themselves off, and dashing out their brains on the pavement below."

"That sounds like some place. There's a Chinatown in Sydney, but it's nothing like that," McGrath replied.

"I wouldn't be too sure," said Cramp. "Maybe you gwailos don't know it, but I'll bet the celestials 'ave their gambling and their opium dens there, just the same as they do in 'Ong Kong and Shanghai."

"But what did you mean about the French Concession?" McGrath asked. "I thought Shanghai was part of China?"

I lit a cigarette, and continued to listen to Cramp's surprisingly evocative description.

"So it is, but the old Emperor was forced to 'and some of it over to international control and grant trading rights. So there's a bit known as the International Settlement, which is under British control. The French, as always, wanted some of their own, so they 'ave a Concession on the south side of the British bit. The International Settlement is where we're going, but just because you'll see British uniforms, it don't mean the law's got a long arm. It can be a dangerous place."

"You seem to know your history, Chippy," McGrath said. "I didn't pay that much attention to China when I was at school."

"School!" snorted Cramp. "Never went to no school. Learned to read and write in me first ship, the storekeeper taught me. And everything I've learned since about our so called Empire on which the sun don't set, I've picked up first 'and. A bobby's boots 'urts just as much in Shanghai as they does in London, but they comes more easily out 'ere. But don't you worry," he continued, seeing the concerned look on McGrath's face. "I knows me way around. You stick close by, and we can 'ave as good a run ashore in Shanghai as anywhere."

I grinned at Cramp's description of the Great World. It was, more or less, as he had described it to McGrath. A place that catered for almost any vice, and despite its sleazy reputation, or perhaps because of it, was a favourite haunt of the bohemian European community of the International Settlement, Shanghailanders as they were known.

I had spent some very pleasant, well-lubricated and anticipatory hours in the Great World, prior to negotiating the price of a night's entertainment with one of the Sing Song girls. Any further reminiscences would have to wait, though, as the clatter of feet mounting the boat deck ladder announced the arrival of the pilot, and a smoke-belching tug bustled up alongside the bow and blew its whistle. I watched the seamen lower a thick manila towline, while the tug's skipper expertly swung its stern in close enough for his crew to grab it, and drag it over the towing hook. The tug eased slowly away from the ship's side, my crew paying out the towline as it went, until the skipper raised two fists and crossed them in the universal signal to "make fast".

"Let go all," called the pilot, and then, as the mooring lines were hauled inboard, "dead slow ahead."

The telegraph jangled again, the pilot blew a loud blast on his whistle, and the tow rope stretched and creaked as the tug took the strain, its screw churning the dirty harbour water, sending a foaming brown tide containing smashed timber, soggy paper, rotting vegetable matter and fish frames, swirling back around *Oriental Venture's* bow. I could feel the vibration as the propeller bit into the water, and she slid away from the quay, the tug pulling her clear as she nosed into the roads. As soon as we drew abreast of Kowloon Point, another blast of the pilot's whistle ordered the tug to slacken and release the towline.

As the crew heaved the line inboard, *Oriental Venture* began her turn to port, rounding Tsim Sha Tsui point, and heading across Kowloon Bay towards Lyemoon Passage. With all the mooring lines retrieved and safely stowed away, I sent word forward for McGrath to rejoin me on the bridge, leaving Cramp to standby the anchors until we cleared the harbour.

Lyemoon Passage made a pretty spectacle as the channel narrowed, the land rising steeply on either side, the upper slopes of its jungle-clad terraces giving way to weathered basalt that glowed warmly red in the afternoon sunlight. Beyond the passage I could see the equally rocky High Junk Peak, and, at its foot, Junk Town, a collection of rough wooden huts. Clustered off the town, anchored just clear of the shoreline in the shelter of the Peak, were dozens of junks. Each with its elegantly curved prow and square stern, some with a single mast for one large sail, others with two or even three masts. One of the larger junks was making ready to put to sea, and I pointed her out to McGrath. The crew were hoisting the mainsail, rectangles of old canvas or burlap lashed between supporting battens, the peak splayed like a fan, and I could hear them chanting a Cantonese version of a hauling shanty.

I watched McGrath studying the rig, his seaman's eye assessing its sailing qualities. "Missing the square-riggers are you, Third?" I chuckled.

"No fear, sir," McGrath snapped back. "But at least those poor devils don't have to climb the masts when they need to shorten sail. They can reef using those battens, do you see?" He pointed at the mainsail, which was now being sheeted home. "They only hoist as much or as little as they need. But even so, I'd rather be here, with my watch below spent in a warm bunk, not sleeping with one ear listening for the call for all hands to change sail in the middle of the night."

Oriental Venture ploughed on, and the junks disappeared behind the shoulder of High Junk Peak. I dropped our speed as the pilot's cutter sliced alongside, watched as he climbed down the ladder, and then rang full ahead as soon as its whistle confirmed he was safely aboard. The cutter sheered away, and then accelerated down the channel ahead of us. Approaching from seaward was a large P&O liner, its smart black hull and buff superstructure looking clean and freshly painted compared to the shabby, rust streaked appearance of *Oriental Venture*. A yellow and blue striped flag streamed from her signal halyard, requesting a pilot to guide her into Hong Kong. I ordered the helmsman to hold a steady course, and watched as the liner slowed to embark the pilot. A busy afternoon for him, I thought. One ship leaving and another arriving, departures and arrivals, the life of the seaman.

Once clear of the inbound liner, I ordered the helm to port to take us around Tamtoo Island, and then set course north-east towards the Formosa Strait. With the sun sinking behind the peaks of Hong Kong, the burning heat went out of the day, and it was pleasant on the bridge, cooled by the breeze and feeling the bow lift as the ship met the gentle swell rolling in from the South China Sea. The surface was a deep, rippled blue, and flying fish were already fleeing the ship's advancing shadow.

"Looking forward to dinner tonight, Third?" I heard Lowther ask McGrath inside the wheelhouse, where they were checking the courses for the evening watch. "All those passengers to entertain, including that Australian major we met in Wewak, and the lovely Lady Ashworth."

"She's out of my league, sir," replied McGrath, chuckling.

"You'll have to mind your Ps and Qs, and wear that fancy dinner jacket and bow tie the owners have kindly supplied."

"Feels strange enough just having to wear a uniform," replied McGrath. "We rarely bothered with it in sailing ships, but to wear a special rig just for dinner. Well, I suppose it's good practice for when I join a liner company, like that big P&O boat we saw coming in."

"You need to be a gentleman to work there. Too good for the likes of us, eh Third?"

"Speak for yourself, sir. I know which knife and fork to use, thank you very much."

"Cheeky sod," replied Lowther, grinning.

I smiled at the irreverent exchange, doubting that Lowther would have tolerated such backchat from a junior lieutenant in the Navy. But then none of them would have sailed around Cape Horn in winter in a square-rigger. I also tried to remember when I had last seen him smile like that, with genuine pleasure.

And realised I couldn't.

CHAPTER TEN

The evening was calm and clear as I left Lowther in charge of the watch, with the ship swinging easily in a long, low easterly swell. After the short tropical twilight, darkness fell swiftly and I enjoyed a quiet smoke on the boat deck, watching the masts inscribe slow, lazy arcs against a backdrop of stars that seemed to hang in the sky like diamonds pinned to black velvet. Stubbing the butt into the sandbox on the rail, I returned to my cabin to change for dinner. Da Silva had already laid out fresh clothes, and closed the curtains so that light from the porthole would not affect the night vision of those on the bridge.

I was still dressing when there was a knock on the door, and Major Spencer answered my invitation to enter. He accepted my offer of a drink, mixed it himself and dropped into an armchair.

"Thoughtful of Mr Khoo to arrange dinner jackets," I said, standing in front of the small mirror over the bathroom sink, struggling to knot the unaccustomed bow tie. That was for Spencer's benefit. In reality, I was far from happy at how well Mr Khoo was expecting us to look after the passengers. After all, it was only a four day journey, and *Oriental Venture* — perhaps in this case *Oriental Vagabond* really was more appropriate — was hardly a crack liner suited to the ways of gentry and their ladies. It had been bad enough entertaining Eberhardt and his wife on the way to Wewak, but at least we had not been expected to dress up.

"I can see you're not used to wearing a dinner jacket, Captain, but I'm sure the passengers will be impressed." He watched me continuing to wrestle with the tie, and then sprang out of the chair. "For God's sake, let me do it for you, or we'll be here for hours."

I strode out of the bathroom, and Spencer stood in front of me, his hands expertly knotting the black silk, and pulling it tight between the wings of the stiff collar.

"That looks better," he said. "Good of you to invite me for a drink before dinner, but I didn't expect to be called on to play Jeeves to your Bertie Wooster."

I growled softly in protest then sat down on the couch, waved at Spencer to resume his seat, and asked whether his cabin was to his liking.

"No complaints, Captain, especially seeing as you've berthed me next to the lovely Lady Ashworth. She's originally Russian you know?"

"Yes, I had gathered that," I replied, wondering where the conversation was headed. Fairclough had mentioned that to me when we were discussing the passenger berthing arrangements. But from the few, brief glimpses I'd had of her she looked every inch the English lady, with a cut-glass accent that was, perhaps, a shade too perfect. Leading me to wonder what had induced her to take passage in a battered old tramp steamer, instead of one of the regular liner services.

"She speaks a number of languages, all of them fluently," continued Spencer. "Accomplished woman, as well as being something of an actress."

"You seem to know a lot about her."

"No more than you read in the papers. Daughter of a White Russian, General Kovtoun, whose family fled to Paris during the Civil War. The general was shot by the Bolsheviks, but left a bit of money that provided just enough for his widow to raise their two children, Helena and her younger brother Tomas. She was a stunner was young Helena, with a wide circle of admirers. Her mother wanted her to work as a dressmaker in one of the Paris fashion houses, but Helena was having none of that. She was offered a part as a chorus girl in a review, and was soon something of a star. It was rumoured she wasn't averse to appearing in racy French cabarets, or accepting gifts from admirers, if you take my meaning?"

All of this was news to me. "So how ..."

"Don't look so surprised man. How did she become a Lady?"

"Yes, sorry, I'm not used to discussing the affairs of female passengers." Lusting after them perhaps, but not speculating about them with another passenger. Spencer was not just another passenger, though. So presumably, there was a purpose behind his revelations.

"The sea's your mistress eh?" Spencer said, laughing. "Well, Helena Kovtoun had aspirations to be more than just a cabaret star, and so she moved into the theatre. With her flair for languages she managed to pick up roles in Berlin and London. In the latter she met Bobby Ashworth. Inheritor of some old, but minor title, and an equally minor fortune that the good lord was doing his best to gamble and drink away. Helena didn't know that of course. Ashworth was a good looking man, charming, affable. She saw the chance of a title and a path to security, so she took it. Didn't turn out too badly. Ashworth hadn't lost all the money, when some scandal over a gambling debt forced him to quit England. They moved to Shanghai where they lived reasonably comfortably, until Ashworth died. Heart attack apparently, but his body was found in an opium den, so there might have been more to it. I don't think he left Helena very much, and she went back on the stage. For the love of it she claimed, but I imagine it's to help make ends meet. Then she was invited to appear in Hong Kong. You know how these snobby colonial women like to fawn over the nobs."

"And you read all this in the newspapers? I'd have thought you had better things to do than pore over the society pages," I replied, wondering why on earth he thought I would be interested in all this.

"Port Moresby's not the most entertaining of places you know. I have to find some way to pass what spare time I have."

"Reading about the love lives of society ladies. Well Mr Khoo, the owner, is obviously smitten with her too," I replied, chuckling at the thought of Spencer reading the society columns in between polo chukkas, or whatever it was the Australian Army did for amusement in Papua. "He invited her to travel home to Shanghai in this ship," I continued. "Told me it would attract other well-heeled types to make the passage with us. And it worked. All the cabins are booked. Not something I normally look forward to."

"I can see that by the way you look so uncomfortable in that jacket and bow tie," replied Spencer, laughing again. "Who are the other passengers, by the way?"

I reached over to the desk and shuffled through the papers strewn across it. Finally, I found what I was looking for.

"I've a list here," I said, consulting the paper. "There's Mr Wilson and his wife. He's something with the Hong Kong and Shanghai Bank, traveling back to his office there. Mr Evans, who's a merchant travelling there on business. There's Mr Hill-Davis who's a schoolmaster. He and his wife have been on leave. And finally, Mr Trimble. Says nothing else about him here."

I'd met each of them briefly, and was not exactly looking forward to four days of small talk and bourgeois etiquette.

"Any friends amongst them?" I asked, wondering why he wanted to know. Despite the gossipy nature of his disclosures about Lady Ashworth, I suspected he was not one for idle curiosity.

"Just like to know what I'm up against by way of competition."

"You'll see for yourself, shortly," I replied, pointing at the empty glass in Spencer's hand. "Fancy a refresher before we head down?"

"A burra peg of courage before facing the fray. Don't mind if I do, as long as you're going to join me."

I poured a stiff measure into both glasses and topped them off with iced water from the thermos jug.

"Bottoms up, old boy," said Spencer taking a large swig and swirling it round his mouth.

I took a more measured swallow, put down the glass and checked the bulkhead clock. The hands had ticked up to the hour. "I've sent word to Lady Ashworth that we'll escort her to dinner, so if you'd be so kind as to lead on, Major."

* * *

Lady Ashworth was sitting in an armchair when Lucy, her Chinese maid, admitted us, having first gone through the rigmarole of checking whether her mistress was ready to receive visitors. I would have been the first to admit that I didn't know much about women, not the titled, expensive types anyway, but I knew what I liked to look at, and Lady Ashworth was certainly worth looking at. I had greeted her when she first came aboard, but then she had been dressed in a loose fitting pantsuit, with a broad brimmed hat and a veil to protect her complexion from the sun, and from the prying eyes of the seamen who had watched her tantalisingly glide up the gangway.

The face that now looked up at me from the armchair was breathtaking, with mesmerizingly green, almond shaped eyes above finely sculpted cheekbones that betrayed a hint of Tartar ancestry. Her pale, creamy skin was free of the ravages of time and exposure to the tropical sun, apart from the beginnings of some finely etched experience lines around the corners of her eyes, which looked as if they had been drawn there by an artist, to add a touch of humanity to an otherwise perfect complexion. And as if all that was not enough to turn a man into an acolyte, her head was framed by luxuriant waves of auburn hair that tumbled onto her creamy shoulders.

She had selected a figure hugging, green, ankle length gown that set off both her green eyes and auburn hair, and did little to disguise the lithe limbs and shapely curves beneath; although the modestly high neckline was obviously intended to deter love starved seamen from paying too close attention to her bosom. She smiled coolly as she patiently submitted to my appraisal, as if this was just one more performance. Which it was. I was just one more audience to be entertained, teased and then forgotten. Between the fingers of her manicured right hand, she held a pink Sobranie Cocktail cigarette. She lifted it to her lips, careful to avoid smudging her red lipstick, inhaled delicately, and let the smoke trickle out of her elegant nostrils.

"Good evening, Captain Rowden," she said, remaining seated, but politely offering her hand.

"Good evening, Lady Ashworth," I replied, gingerly reaching for the delicate object and wrapping my horny fist around it, careful not to crush her fingers.

I held onto her hand for longer than was strictly necessary, as her green eyes critically scanned my appearance, and a hint of a smile played across the crimson lips.

"You seem far more comfortable in that dinner jacket than I expected," she said, fixing me with a gaze that was as much challenge as payback for my earlier staring. "It suits you."

In truth, I would have felt far more comfortable in a well-worn working uniform, than dolled up in the unaccustomed dinner jacket. It was made of lightweight, cream cashmere, but cut close, so that my chest and arm muscles seemed to be straining against the fabric.

She held my gaze for a moment longer, her deep, emerald eyes, appearing to generate interior sparkles of light, and then tugged at her hand.

"I should like to retrieve my hand, before there is any danger to my fingers. And perhaps you would introduce me to the other gentleman?"

I was surprised to find that I was still holding her hand and released it, hoping the self-conscious grin did not look too doltish. "May I present Major Spencer," I said.

"Your servant, ma'am," said Spencer bowing, taking the recently released hand and raising it to his lips. Despite the evening hour, he had chosen to remain in his daytime khaki uniform. But it was neatly pressed, and with his hair cut short in the military fashion, and with a groomed moustache, he looked every inch the dashing soldier.

There was an unexpected peal of laughter. "That's very gallant, Major. Good to see the British Army still maintains some traditions."

"Australian Army, Lady Ashworth," replied Spencer, straightening up. "We don't often get the pleasure of a lady's company in New Guinea, so you'll forgive me if my manners are a bit rusty."

"Ah! New Guinea. Head hunters and cannibals, how romantic," the slight rolling of the R and the drawn out O betraying her Russian origins. "You must tell me something of the interesting things you've seen there." She delicately stubbed the cigarette into the ashtray, and, flicking spots of ash from her scarlet nail polish, rose from the chair in a gentle rustle of green silk. "Come, let us descend."

Preceding us down the staircase, she paused at the bottom and offered me her arm. Then, with Major Spencer in tow behind us, she made her entrance, sweeping the dining saloon and its occupants with an imperious glance.

"Ladies and Gentlemen," I said, in my best voice of command. "May I present Lady Helen Ashworth." I escorted her around the table and made the introductions, assisted by the discreet name cards the chief steward had left at each place.

"Mr and Mrs Wilson." I presented the banker, a stout, balding man wearing a black dinner suit with a wing collar and black tie. His wife was solid and plain, her straight, mousy hair drawn back in a tight bun, her dress an old fashioned mid-calf length brown, with a double layered skirt and tassels at the neckline.

"Mr Wilson is head clerk at the Hong Kong and Shanghai bank." Wilson bowed and his wife curtsied in a depressingly middle class display of outmoded respect for the widow of a minor member of the aristocracy. Lady Ashworth shook their hands and greeted them breezily.

"Mr and Mrs Wilson, how do you do? The Hong Kong and Shanghai Bank is such a grand building, don't you think? Right in the heart of the Bund."

I guided her on to the next couple before the Wilsons had a chance to reply.

"Mr and Mrs Hill-Davis. Mr Hill-Davis is a House Master at the Cathedral School in Shanghai."

Dressed in a white dinner jacket, Hill-Davis was a tall, severe looking man with a beaked nose and greying hairline. His younger looking wife was blonde, with tightly curled hair, freckles and a slight gap between her front teeth. Her gown was full length grey silk, sufficiently low cut to present an inviting vista, compared to Lady Ashworth's more modest neckline.

She reached for their hands before they had any opportunity to follow the Wilsons' obsequious example, and flashed a knowing smile at Mrs Hill-Davis. "I expect those boys can be a handful. All those high spirits?"

"Yes, I do have to look out for roving eyes when we invite them for tea," replied Mrs Hill-Davis with a girlish peal of laughter, masking her mouth behind a gloved hand.

Mr Evans, the merchant, was a prosperous looking gentleman. Tall and well fed, with a pink face and close-cropped brown hair.

"Mr Evans, a pleasure to meet you," said Lady Ashworth, accepting his offered hand with a sly grin, her eyes trailing over the quality of his black dinner suit, the large gold cuff links and the gold, diamond encrusted rings. I fancied she could almost smell the wealth he was flaunting. "Your wife must be very trusting to allow you to visit our wicked city on your own."

"What happens in Shanghai stays in Shanghai," he said, returning her quip with a leering wink, ignoring the discomfited Wilson's embarrassed cough.

The final passenger was something of a puzzle. Dressed in a Harris Tweed jacket and brown Oxford bags he looked like a student, save that he was well past undergraduate age. Unkempt wavy black hair and a false boyish grin were signs he was trying to preserve his youth, but the deep creases around his eyes and the dark half circles below them suggested it was becoming a struggle.

"Mr Trimble," I said, as the Bohemian figure extended a hand, and flashed a bashful, almost furtive grin.

"Lady Ashworth," he greeted her, effusively shaking her hand. "I'm thrilled to meet you. I saw you at the Queen's Theatre last week. I must confess that I attended five times."

"Five times!" she replied, looking startled. "You must really enjoy *The Barretts of Wimpole Street*."

"Only because of your performance, Lady Ashworth," replied Trimble, with embarrassingly pitiful, puppy-dog devotion in his eyes.

"Oh, I don't think I do the role half as much justice as Katharine Cornell," said Lady Ashworth, with discouraging firmness. "But it's very kind of you to say so." She retrieved her hand, and, as I lead her over to meet the officers, she bent her head towards me and whispered, "Thankfully, I don't have to sit next to him."

Grouped around a second, smaller, table were those officers I had asked to join us at dinner, all freshly scrubbed but looking uncomfortable in their new white dinner jackets. Lady Ashworth shook each of their hands and graciously exchanged a few words with them. The white haired Chief Engineer Fraser beamed paternally at her. Sayce, the radio officer, shook her hand nervously, and I expected that by midnight he would be tapping out the news to his air-wave friends that he had dined with a famous actress.

Freshly shaved, and clearly overawed by Lady Ashworth's beauty, McGrath looked very young, and giggled when she exclaimed, "Does your mother know you've run away to sea, Mr McGrath?"

"Don't be deceived," I said, anxious that McGrath not feel he was being made fun of. "Mr McGrath is the only man aboard, who's entitled to put both feet on the table. And you should have seen the mess he made of the last man who challenged him to a fight."

"Then I certainly shan't provoke him," she chuckled. "But what do you mean about feet on the table?"

"It's a sailors' tradition that only a man who's been round both Cape Horn and the Cape of Good Hope under sail, can put both feet on the table while he eats," I explained.

"Goodness! Is this done at every meal? Shall we see you do it this evening Mr McGrath?"

"No ma'am," said McGrath, beaming at her attention. "If we were eating salt horse in the forecastle, perhaps. But not in polite company."

"Salt horse? Ah, another of your sailors' traditions. I do believe Mr Khoo promised us better fare than that." She smiled wistfully. "However there were times in Russia when I have eaten worse."

Griffith was the last to be introduced, and as she took his hand I saw her gaze at him thoughtfully, looking very much the matinée idol in his dinner jacket, with his brooding, chiselled features.

"Good evening, Mr Griffith. I do hope we'll have a chance to become better acquainted."

There was nothing coquettish in her statement, and they could have made a very attractive couple, apart from the fact of the obvious disparity in their backgrounds, and Griffith's, less obvious, sexual preferences. The look he returned was coolly appreciative, as if admiring the perfection of an artwork.

"I hope you enjoy the voyage Lady Ashworth," he said, turning to take his seat.

I ushered her back to the centre table, took the seat at its head, beneath a photographic portrait of the King, and placed Lady Ashworth on my right. Once the ladies were shown to their seats, the gentlemen sat down, leaving one place empty at the far end of the table.

"Mr Lowther, the chief officer, is on watch and will be joining us shortly, as soon as he's relieved by the third officer," I explained.

"I'm glad to know there's someone in charge up there," said Evans, the ensuing laughter breaking the ice, prompting the conversation to ebb and flow around the table.

I had placed Major Spencer to the right of Lady Ashworth, and opposite them, to my left had placed Mrs Wilson and her husband. Much to my relief it proved an inspired choice, as the major possessed a surprisingly deep lode of small talk, and saved me the embarrassment of displaying the limit of my own social graces. I might have learned to speak something approximating the King's English, and to use the cutlery in the correct order, but I was far from being a gentleman. And while I didn't feel uneasy in the company of my, supposed, betters - the four gold stripes on my sleeve were sufficient to command their respect - I didn't relish the prospect of making conversation with people who might as well have lived on another planet, as far as the lives of most seamen were concerned.

Under Major Spencer's gentle prompting, however, and the tongue lubricating effect of cocktails, the passengers shared anecdotes about their lives in Hong Kong or Shanghai. He even managed to persuade Lady Ashworth to display the theatrical flair that had taken her to Hong Kong, and recite passages from some of her favourite roles, much to the delight of Trimble, who clapped his hands and called bravo after each stanza.

Though Lady Ashworth's appetite was meagre, it was not the fault of the food, which was surprisingly better than I had expected, even with Mr Khoo's generous supplement to the provisions. There was a light soup, a portion of steamed fresh fish and then a choice of grilled chicken or a mild goat curry. Half way through the meal, all the heads turned to greet the arrival of a new face in the saloon. I noticed Lady Ashworth gazing intently, with what appeared to be recognition, at the tall, distinguished figure of my chief mate, dressed in a white naval mess jacket with his row of service ribbons.

"Lady Ashworth, Ladies and Gentlemen, may I introduce Mr Peter Lowther, my chief officer," I said. I could have used his title, but he wouldn't have thanked me, and it would probably only have produced more fawning from the Wilsons.

Lowther moved around the table shaking each of their hands, and then took his seat at the far end where the steward had placed a bowl of soup. Lady Ashworth offered her hand as he introduced himself, but if she did recognise him, she betrayed no further sign of it, although her eyes followed him while he took his seat between Trimble and Evans.

Evans seemed to have taken on the role of court jester, and had just finished a mildly risqué anecdote, which set the table laughing, including grim Mrs Wilson, whose ample bosom heaved beneath her brown dress. Trimble, too, was laughing, and I watched Lady Ashworth's eyes flicker back and forth between him and Evans. In his tweed jacket and bags, Trimble reminded me of a scruffy spaniel, desperate for attention, with the careworn eyes of a man always on the lookout for a friend to borrow from, an enemy to run from, or a bottle to hide in.

"Penny for your thoughts?" asked Spencer, leaning towards Lady Ashworth, and pitching his voice low so that those at the far end could not hear him.

"Oh, I was just wondering about Mr Evans and Mr Trimble there," she said, adopting the same conspiratorial tone. "Both traveling to Shanghai alone. One with money who is hoping to make more. And one, I would say, who would like to have money, and thinks he will find it there."

"No prize for guessing which is which, Lady Ashworth?"

"None at all. But tell me, Major, what takes you to Shanghai? Or would you rather tell me about the misfortunes that can befall devotional women brave enough to take the Gospel to the natives of New Guinea?"

"I should hardly think such things suitable for polite company," he chuckled. "Or at least not after such an enjoyable dinner."

"A pity. Although I should quail to hear of missionaries boiled and eaten, their heads shrunken and worn on a necklace."

"I can see the safer course, Lady Ashworth," replied Spencer, grinning broadly. "You are determined to find me out."

From the other end of the table, the booming voice of Evans interrupted their conversation.

"My you do eat well," he said, pushing back his chair to give his stomach more room. "You hear terrible stories about food aboard ship, salt beef and hardtack with weevils. But you've done us proud, Captain." There was general assent from the others, but I held up my hand apologetically.

"It's the owners you have to thank," I said. "They like us to run a tight ship normally. But this is something of a special voyage with some distinguished company," I nodded to right and left, "so they told us to push the boat out, if you'll pardon the pun."

Evans slapped his knee and roared, his laughter infecting the others, the noise signalling to the steward that it was time to clear away the remains of the meal. Touching her husband on the arm, Mrs Wilson said something to him and he pushed back his chair. The men rose and the Wilsons said goodnight, before walking the few steps down the passage to their cabin.

"Best we don't make too much noise," said Evans in a stage whisper, resuming his seat. "We don't want to disturb the lovers." He raised an arm amid the chuckles, and waved to the steward who was still hovering at the rear of the saloon. "Could we have some coffee please? And would you care to join us in a nightcap, Captain Rowden?"

I had intended to leave them to it, but it would have seemed churlish to refuse. So I agreed to take a coffee, and a small brandy from one of the dusty bottles the steward produced from behind the bar. As he placed a glass in front of Lady Ashworth she held up a hand to decline.

"Mrs Hill-Davis, gentlemen, if you'll excuse me, it's been a long day." She started to rise from her chair, and then Major Spencer was behind her and sliding it back.

"Are you sure you won't take a coffee, Lady Ashworth," he said. "I'd be most grateful if we could have a few words before you retire. Perhaps we could sit over there?" He pointed to one of the adjacent tables.

I could see that she was conscious of the others watching them, and I wondered whether Spencer was attempting to stake a claim. Although she didn't look the type of woman to be easily daunted by a clumsy attempt at a pass at her.

"If you insist, Major, I'll take just one cup." There was a note of irritation in her voice, but she accepted the offered seat. Spencer sat down on the opposite side of the table, waited until the coffee had been poured, and then bent towards her in earnest conversation, to which she appeared to respond, but in voices inaudible above the hubbub from the larger group.

Their tête-à-tête continued for several minutes, during which whatever it was that Spencer was saying seemed increasingly to frustrate her. Her head shaking became emphatic, the bright auburn hair swishing angrily across her neck. Finally, there was a pained scraping as she pushed her chair back across the linoleum-clad deck.

"What you say is most interesting, Major Spencer," she said, loudly enough to be heard across the saloon, her green eyes flashing. "But I'm not sure how, or even if, I can be of assistance to you. Anyway it is late, a lady needs her beauty sleep, so if you'll excuse me?"

Spencer jumped to his feet. "Of course Lady Ashworth, I apologise for detaining you. But perhaps we can speak again if you have further thoughts on the matter?"

"Good night, Major Spencer," she said firmly, before composing herself and turning an alluring smile on the remaining company. "I wish you all good night!"

There was a determined swish of green silk as she strode from the saloon, followed closely by Mrs Hill-Davis, who took the departure as her own cue to retire. With the ladies gone, the men pulled cigarette cases out of their pockets and the saloon quickly filled with a blue haze of tobacco smoke.

"You seemed very cosy with Lady Ashworth," said Evans, beckoning Spencer to the vacant chair beside him. "What were you two conspiring about?"

"She asked me what it was like in New Guinea, I was just entertaining her with some awful tales of shrunken heads and dismembered missionaries," said Spencer, lying smoothly. I had read from Lady Ashworth's face that she had asked nothing of the sort.

Care to share them with us, old boy?" asked Trimble. "I like a good story before bedtime."

"It's been a long day, perhaps another night," replied Spencer, stubbing out his cigarette and levering himself out of his chair. "I'm off to bed."

The whisky bottle between Evans and Trimble was already more than half-empty, and it looked as if they were set in for the evening, so I decided to make my own excuses. Which were genuine, we were still in the main shipping lanes close to Hong Kong, and I needed to be alert in case McGrath needed assistance.

"Good night to you," I said, and then with a nod to Hill-Davis. "Don't let these two seasoned travellers lead you astray."

Climbing the stairs to my cabin, I was tempted to call in on the major and ask him what he had said that had annoyed Lady Ashworth. But his door was closed, and I decided it was probably none of my business anyway.

Which was a rare example of how wrong I could be.

* * *

The luminous dial on my watch revealed it was 11.30 p.m., half an hour before Griffith was due to relieve McGrath on the bridge.

After leaving the saloon, I had checked that McGrath was coping with the watch and had written my night orders. I then read for an hour in my cabin. It was a toss-up between Sam Spade, or Bill McFee's story about a second mate called Spokesly, who unexpectedly finds himself in command of a battered coaster, smuggling military stores between Salonika and Smyrna during the war. The latter won and I spent an agreeable hour in Spokesly's ambitious company, chuckling occasionally, and wondering why McFee, whom I regarded as every bit as good as Joseph Conrad, albeit with a better sense of humour, was not more widely known.

I then paid another visit to the bridge to check progress. There was little traffic, just the occasional passing steamer inbound for Hong Kong, and junks ghosting along closer inshore. It was all peaceful enough, but I warned McGrath to keep his eyes peeled nonetheless. We were tracking across the mouth of Bias Bay, from where, only a few years before, pirates had preyed upon passing ships. Their nests had been cleaned out now, but there was still a chance that some of the hard cases had drifted back. I didn't really expect any trouble, but I also didn't want McGrath getting complacent.

Finally, I leaned against the rail at the front of the narrow deck just forward of my cabin, enjoying a cigarette and listening to the tumbling rush of water as the ship forged ahead at a steady 10 knots. I was also thinking about Dieter Eberhardt and his *Dortmund*. I had made some discrete inquiries in Hong Kong, but had turned up nothing. Since leaving Port Moresby she had not been reported by any of the shipping authorities. It was as if she had disappeared into the remote Pacific. Was she still pursuing us? Surely a few dozen rifles, machine pistols and grenades were not worth that amount of trouble. On the other hand, it might be personal. Neither of the Eberhardt brothers was likely to forgive and forget being robbed by the vagabond skipper of a scruffy, British tramp steamer.

I had also expected Major Spencer to show more interest in the *Dortmund*. He had come to Wewak expecting to catch Wolfgang Eberhardt smuggling weapons into New Guinea. Weapons intended for the *Dortmund*, so I thought Spencer would have been keen to track her down. Especially if she was part of a Nazi plot to set up a network of raiders and U-boat supply dumps ready for a surprise attack on British shipping.

And why, I wondered, had Major Spencer chosen my ship, in which to travel to Shanghai on his intelligence gathering mission. Surely there were quicker and more discrete ways of getting there? Lady Ashworth's presence on aboard was bound to attract newspaper gossip. Which was hardly the type of attention I would have thought the major's dealings needed.

And what was I to make of Spencer's rather obvious attempt this evening to draw Lady Ashworth into a private conversation. Why do it in the saloon in front of everyone, if he just wanted to see if the hunting season had re-opened following the end of mourning the dead Lord Ashworth? Or was he just trying to make it appear that way?

Taking a final drag on my cigarette, I stubbed it out on the metal rail and flicked the butt overboard. Stepping away from the rail, I was on the point of returning to my cabin, when a white clad figure caught my eye on the opposite side of the deck. My night vision was sufficient to make out the form of Lady Ashworth, her gossamer gown ruffling in the breeze. I was on the point of crossing over to speak to her when Griffith emerged from the darkness.

"It's Lady Ashworth, isn't it?"

She turned, seemingly surprised at being discovered alone on deck in the middle of the night. The polite thing to do would have been either to declare my presence and join them, or mind my own business and return to my cabin. But I'd learned the hard way that everything that happens in my ship is my business, one way or another. So I stepped back into the shadows and continued to listen.

"I'm sorry, I didn't mean to frighten you. It's Griffith, the second mate, I'm on my way to the bridge to take over the watch. Is everything all right?"

"Yes, thank you, Mr Griffith?"

"Is there anything I can get you, Lady Ashworth? Would you like me to call your maid?"

"I'm perfectly all right ... and please call me Helena. I wasn't born a Lady and sometimes I get tired of always having to act like one."

I wondered for a moment if I had strayed into the pages of a women's popular romance. In my experience, limited as it was, women who had come into money and titles never tired of acting the lady, and made damned sure that everyone knew it.

"You find me attractive, yes?"

That was an unfair question, if ever I'd heard one. Lady Helen Ashworth, or Helena Kovtoun if she preferred, was the type of beauty the ancient Greeks fought the Trojans over. And look how badly that turned out. But of all the men on the ship to pick, I had to smile at the irony of her picking Griffith. Standing close to her in the darkness, so close that he could probably feel the heat of her body through the thin gown, and smell the scent of her perfume. Yet impervious to her obvious attractions.

"But not as a man is normally attracted to a woman?" she continued.

It was statement as much as a question, an extremely intuitive one. I recalled the way she had looked at Griffith when I introduced him in the saloon. She had clearly seen more than just his brooding, Celtic, good looks, which I ought not to have been surprised about. If what Spencer had told me was true, she had much more experience of certain aspects of life than was normally available to men who spent the majority of their time in the absence of female company. Men like Griffith, whose silence indicated his confusion.

"You have no idea what it's like to be able to talk to a man of your own age who doesn't want to go to bed with you. Are you shocked at an English woman talking in this way? You shouldn't be. I was once a dancer in Paris, and I am Russian not English."

"Lady Ashworth, I ..."

"Don't worry, I'm not going to embarrass you, your secret is safe with me."

"Secret?"

"That you are not attracted to women. It's quite common among the males in my profession. But less so, I suspect, in yours, and not something you would want shared with your colleagues."

"Excuse me, Lady Ashworth, but I'm late for my watch."

I could hear the coldness and the anger in his voice, and I could imagine the resentment that a miner's son from South Wales might feel at having his protective shell probed by an expensive, pampered member of the British upper class. I watched as he made to push past her, but she placed a restraining hand on his arm.

"I'm sorry if I've offended you. That was not my intention. But if you knew how tiresome it is to be constantly pursued by men attracted only by my looks. Sometimes I feel as if my beauty is a curse. It would be so pleasant, if only for a few days, to enjoy the company of a man who was not always thinking of ways to get me into bed."

"I'm not offended, Lady Ashworth," I heard Griffith reply, wondering where this conversation was heading. I had once, in a moment of bored desperation, tried to read one of Barbara McCorquodale's romances, but the dialogue was as stilted as the one I was listening to.

"Please, call me Helena. Your name is David, isn't it?"

"Yes."

"Well, David, I think we can be friends, yes? A gentleman with whom a lady who is no lady can feel perfectly safe. It will be our secret. Now, you must go to your watch and I must return to my bed." She bent forward and kissed him on the cheek, like a sister. "Good night David, or perhaps it is now good morning. Or, as we prefer in Russian *dasvedanya*, until we meet."

Then she was gone, slipping back into the shadows and disappearing in the direction of her cabin. Leaving, I imagined, a very confused Griffith to climb the stairs to the bridge.

Leaving me amused at the touchingly sentimental scene between the two most attractive, but romantically incompatible, representatives of their sex, on board.

Confused too. Had she been waiting for him, hoping he would pass by her cabin on his way to the bridge? Or had it been a chance encounter. In either case, what game was she playing? It seemed that Major Spencer was not the only one on board who was something other than he appeared to be.

CHAPTER ELEVEN

L ate morning and *Oriental Venture* was steaming steadily north-east along the coast of the province of Canton. The day was warm and sultry, and I had climbed up to the bridge to enjoy what little breeze blew over the canvas dodger. Abeam lay the city of Swatow, hidden by the sandy islets and low peaks that marked the narrow entrance to the Rong River, beyond which lay the broad expanse of Swatow Harbour.

The route to Shanghai was a busy one, and a steady procession of southbound ships passed us, en-route from Japan and northern China to Hong Kong and Singapore. A fast liner ploughing her way north had overtaken us. Her turbine driven propellers thrusting her powerfully through the long swell, leaving *Oriental Venture* to amble along beside the arrow-straight furrow of her wake. Inshore of us a fleet of junks sailed sedately along, their sails spread to extract the most out of the gentle breeze, looking like a slowly migrating, ragged flock of mottled geese. Satisfied that McGrath was unlikely to hit anything, I retreated to the bridge wing to enjoy the breeze and a cigarette, while pacing back and forth the handful of steps the short space of teak decking afforded.

I had paced the distance a dozen or so times when, turning at the end, I noticed Lady Ashworth step out of the passage leading from her suite. She was dressed in a short sleeved, white, cotton dress that came down to just below her knees. Her bare legs were tanned and she had ankle length white socks under white pumps. Her hair was brushed back in a ponytail, and she wore a broad brimmed sun visor. She looked about, as if disappointed there was no one to accompany her, and turned to walk along the boat deck.

"Good morning, Lady Ashworth, you look as if you're ready for tennis," I heard Lowther greet her, as his lean form appeared at the top of the stairs from the main deck. "I'm afraid there's not much chance of that aboard this ship."

"Thank you, Lord Lowther. I'll just have to make do with a stroll around the boat deck before luncheon. Have you time for a circuit?" Her tone was playful, almost teasing, but I caught sight of Lowther's grimace at the use of his title, as he took stride beside her, and wondered, again, whether they were already acquainted. They walked aft in what looked like earnest conversation, and I turned back to continue my pacing of the bridge wing.

Ten minutes, and another cigarette later, I heard their voices at the foot of the boat deck ladder.

"Thank you for accompanying me, Peter, but I believe I'm holding you up from your duties."

"Time and tide, as they say. Yes, I do have some things to attend to before lunch. But if you'd care to have a look at the bridge I'm sure the third mate, McGrath, would be pleased to explain the intricacies of watch keeping. He's Australian and young, but he served his apprenticeship before the mast, which is a rarity these days."

"Before the mast?"

"In sailing ships, working alongside the seamen. I doubt he's met many ladies, either there or in the outback, so he might be inclined to stare."

"I'm used to that. I should be happy to see the bridge. But I assumed the captain was always there."

"He'll be there night and day if necessary, but in normal conditions the officers can be trusted to keep the ship safe, and to call him if they need help. After you if you please."

Lady Ashworth's auburn-crowned head appeared at the top of the stairs, then the rest of her rose above the timber decking, like a sports-ready Botticelli Venus, with Lowther close behind. She paused when she saw me, and smiled disarmingly.

"Peter — Lord Lowther — said it would acceptable for me to visit the bridge, I do hope I'm not intruding, Captain."

It was bad enough having to carry passengers, without them inviting themselves into my domain, but in deference to Mr Khoo's instructions, and to the inescapable fact that Lady Ashworth was smiling her most beautiful smile, I made a conscious effort to be friendly.

"Not at all," I replied, also wondering about her quickly established familiarity with Lowther. "It's the third mate's watch, and he'll be delighted to show you around." I called McGrath, who came scurrying out of the wheelhouse with a nervous look on his youthful face, to find himself confronting his captain, the chief mate and the beautiful female passenger he had briefly met at dinner the previous evening.

"Lady Ashworth, I'm sure you remember Mr McGrath our third mate." She nodded to him while he stared back as if she were an apparition, and then flushed and lowered his eyes. "Lady Ashworth would like a short tour of the bridge. May we leave her in your capable hands?"

McGrath looked at Lowther and then at me with the eyes of a frightened rabbit, and I smiled inwardly, wondering if he was the same man who had faced down a bunch of hostile German seamen. Lady Ashworth was looking at him expectantly, while Lowther, despite holding his mouth in a firm straight line, seemed to be on the verge of laughing.

Then he pulled himself together. "Of course, sir."

Lowther turned on his heel and climbed back down to the boat deck, while I moved aside to allow Lady Ashworth to follow McGrath into the wheelhouse. By the look on her face I imagined she was still surprised by his youth, and wondering, despite what I had told her about him last evening, whether he really was old enough to be left in charge of the safety of the ship.

"Please don't let me disturb you Mr McGrath, I don't want to get in your way."

"It's no trouble at all, Lady Ashworth," said McGrath, flushing again, no doubt acutely aware of the difference between his broad Australian vowels, and the clipped, plummy pronunciation of the English aristocracy.

I stayed out on the bridge wing, not wanting to embarrass McGrath any further, but watching through the doorway as he explained the functions of the gleaming brass instruments, showed her how the helmsman steered the ship, and pointed out our current position on the chart. By then it was approaching noon, and time for him to fix the ship's position in preparation for handing over the watch, so I ducked my head in through the door, and asked Lady Ashworth if she would join me on the bridge wing.

"Thank you, Captain Rowden, I do hope you don't mind me visiting your domain."

"Not at all. I trust the third mate has acquainted you with the duties of a watch keeping officer."

"He has, Captain, admirably, I had no idea there was so much involved."

"In that case, we have half an hour before lunch, perhaps I could offer you some refreshment."

If my spur of the moment invitation surprised her, there was no sign of it. No doubt, she was well used to men trying to manoeuvre themselves into opportunities to be alone with her, and why should a ship's captain be any different. Why indeed? Despite the fact of her acquired title and exotic looks, she was still a woman, and little different, underneath the fancy clothes and jewels, to those I normally spent my dollars on. As one of the madams I knew had succinctly put it, "All women cost you money, but at least with mine I quote you fixed price." I grinned, wondering if the late Lord Ashworth had got his money's worth. Before inconsiderately dying and leaving her, as Spencer suggested, having to work for a living again. Well, captain's rank had its privileges, and asking a beautiful woman to enhance the decor of his scruffy quarters was definitely one of them.

"That's very kind, Captain," she said, a trifle warily, following me into the day cabin and accepting a seat on the couch. I left the door open but pulled the curtain across for privacy, and then pressed a bell above the desk. Da Silva materialised almost instantly, his grizzled, eye patched face appearing around the curtain, his remaining eye grinning fiercely. He must have been waiting in the pantry, having been warned by the jungle telegraph that Lady Ashworth had appeared on the bridge. I asked him to fetch a jug of iced lemon squash and a bottle of rum, smiling as his aged frame was galvanized into gazelle like action in order to satisfy a pretty lady's request.

"What an interesting looking man, positively piratical."

"He's from Goa, Portuguese territory on the Malabar Coast. He was here when I took command. God knows how old he is. The story is he lost the eye in a fight over a woman. Killed the man, but lost the woman too, and ran away to sea. Part of the fabric of the ship now, never leaves it."

"Oh, how romantic."

Fortunately, Da Silva chose that moment to return bearing a tarnished silver tray with jug, bottle and glasses. He placed the tray on the stained coffee table, offered Lady Ashworth a glass of lemon squash, and then poured a healthy measure of dark, pungent rum into the other glass. Lady Ashworth's nose wrinkled at the sweet, sickly smell of molasses. I reached for the iced water jug and sloshed a measure into the rum.

"Grog," I offered, by way of explanation. "The sailors' drink of rum and water. They used to add lime juice to it in the old days to ward off scurvy. It was the only way they could get them to drink the juice."

"I've heard Americans sometimes refer to the British as 'limeys'," she replied, glancing around the austere day cabin, with its cream painted steel bulkheads, old but well-polished wooden furniture, and the threadbare square of carpet on the deck. With the door and porthole open, and the bulkhead fan turning, there was just enough of a breeze to dispel the worst of the heat.

"British ships were known as 'limejuicers', and the men who sailed in them as 'limeys'. These days the owners usually supply enough fruit and vegetables to avoid scurvy, but even now getting seamen to eat what's good for them is not always easy."

"Oh, I don't think that's just confined to sailors," she countered, with a chuckle. "In my experience men eat and drink too much of all the wrong things."

"Good health," I reached for the glass and then, almost apologetically, as I noticed the faintest elevation of her eyebrows, "just one before lunch, aids the digestion."

"Undoubtedly. But I'm disappointed you think grog's not a drink fit for women. I'm also Russian, remember?"

I apologised half-heartedly, pulled another glass out of the cabinet, poured a tot of rum, and reached for the water jug.

"*Nyet!*" Her perfectly manicured hand reached for the glass.

I handed it over, expecting her to sniff the contents, and attempt a dainty sip.

"*Nastrovje!*" She placed the glass to her lips, threw her head back, drained it and banged it back onto the table.

I watched with amusement as her cheeks flushed, and her green eyes opened wide with surprise.

"Oh, it's awful! That is not a drink for ladies, give me vodka any day." Then her eyes narrowed and her lips pursed. "Ooohh, but it does warm nicely on the way down."

I reached for the bottle, but she laughed and grabbed the glass of lemon squash instead. "Not so fast sailor, you only invited me here to aid the digestion, as I recall."

"I trust you find your cabin to your satisfaction, Lady Ashworth?" I said, injecting a note of formality, prepared to steer the conversation into safer waters. My job was to get the ship and her cargo safely to Shanghai. Deliberately damaging any of it was called barratry, although I doubted what I would have liked to do with Lady Ashworth fell strictly within that definition. But Mr Khoo might have seen it as damaging to his interests, which probably came to the same thing.

Or perhaps I was just flattering myself, and my ship. That she was old was plain to see. Even Lady Ashworth's suite, the best on the ship, was hardly palatial. The stewards had worked hard to make it clean and presentable, but they couldn't do much about the faded and threadbare furnishings. The curtains smelled of damp and coal dust. The mahogany panelled bulkheads were stained dark from years of exposure to salt air and wax polish, and creaked with every heave of the ship. Cockroaches nested behind them and Lucy, the maid, had already squashed several with a well-aimed sandal. Da Silva had enthusiastically pumped the flit gun, but I knew its effect would be minimal. Nevertheless, we had done our best, and from what I heard of conditions in Russia after the revolution, I guessed that Helena Kovtoun, if not Lady Ashworth, had lived in far worse. And cockroaches were a mere irritation in overcrowded, squalid cities such as Shanghai.

"Everything is perfectly satisfactory, Captain," she replied, with her actresses' talent for lying to protect people's feelings. "She seems a very well built ship."

"She's tight and strong right enough. A tribute to the men who built her, even if she has seen more than a few sea miles."

"Not unlike the rest of us," she murmured, before sipping the lemon squash.

"Forgive me for asking," I said, wondering if what I was about to ask was an appropriate question, "but have you met Peter Lowther before?"

Her eyes hardened, and she gazed at me inquiringly. "I see that my conversations with your officers are not entirely my own business," she tossed her head with annoyance. "But to answer your question, no, I had not met Lord Lowther before last evening. But my late husband once introduced me to the Duke of Askrigg. When Bobby told him we were heading east to Shanghai, he mentioned he had a younger brother who had disappeared off to Hong Kong. He talked quite a bit about him, actually. About his naval service at Jutland, quite the hero apparently, before the scandal of adultery ruined his career. When dear old Mr Khoo asked me to take passage in this ship, he told me that one of the officers was a Lord, and when he mentioned the family name I put two and two together." She paused, continuing to hold me with her gaze. "So here he is, the prodigal son."

"I'm sorry, Lady Ashworth, I didn't mean to pry into private conversations. Peter Lowther's a good officer, but I don't think he'd appreciate unpleasant memories being stirred up from his past."

"You mean you wouldn't, if it upset the workings of your ship. Is that what you thought I was doing, stirring up the past?"

She was right of course, and I realised I was treading on dangerous ground, but having seen her cross swords with Major Spencer, and then flirt with Griffith, I thought I had good reasons for wondering what games she might be playing.

"No, but I know him well enough to believe that expressions of sympathy might be unwanted."

"Sympathy?" she flashed back. "He had an affair with the wife of an admiral, and she bore his child. Some would say that was wrong. Yes, I'm sorry he lost them both, but it's not sympathy I was offering, it was some advice."

"Advice!"

"The old Duke of Askrigg was a man of strict principles, he disinherited Peter over the affair. But the current Duke is, I think, more flexible. I told Peter he might find him open to reconciliation."

"You seem very well informed about the affairs of my chief mate's family. But perhaps some wounds cut too deep."

She held up a hand. "Excuse me, Captain Rowden if I've shocked you with my frankness. I'm afraid my Russian temperament sometimes overcomes the reserve expected of an English lady. But life is so short. Let's change the subject by all means. Shall we discuss the weather, or are you a devotee of the theatre, like that strange man Trimble?" The playful tone had returned, accompanied by a coquettish smile.

"I don't get much opportunity for the theatre, so you have the better of me there, Lady Ashworth. We didn't study Besier at the school I went to."

"What school was that, Captain?" she replied, with a raised eyebrow denoting surprise that I knew who had written *The Barretts of Wimpole Street*. I was surprised myself, the lives of Victorian British poets not being my strongest suit.

"The Stanhope Industrial School, at Ashford in Kent."

"That sounds very technical, was that in preparation for your career?"

"You could say that, it was a reform school for boys fallen foul of the law."

"I'm so sorry, Captain, I didn't mean to be inquisitive."

"No more than I was earlier." I gritted my teeth, feeling a sudden flush of anger at the implied suggestion I had anything to be ashamed of. "Since you asked, you may as well hear the rest of the story. My father was a seaman, he was killed during the war. My mother took to drink, and then to men who would buy the drinks for her. I got into trouble for stealing, and the court packed me off to Stanhope. It taught me how to read and write — and how to fight dirty. So, I'm sorry if I'm a bit like my ship, we've both been knocked about, and we're both rough around the edges."

The vehemence in my voice surprised us both, and her face flushed.

"You've nothing to apologise for, Captain," she replied, regaining her composure. "You are what you have made yourself. And we are not so different. Yes, my father was a General in the Tsar's army. But after the Bosheviks shot him and we were exiled to Paris, we had little money and I had to earn a living. I danced, I sang, I acted, not always in the nicest places. I met Bobby Ashworth at a party. He told me he was handsome, he had a title, he loved me, and that he was rich. The first three were true. Then he died. A title doesn't put food on the table. But I'm still an actress, so I can earn enough to get by."

It was a tear jerker of a monologue, and confirmed what Major Spencer had previously told me. But she did have one big advantage over me.

"Ah, but you are ..." I stopped, realising from the look on her face that my less than subtle attempt at flattery was going to be as welcome as a Viking in a nunnery.

"Beautiful, is that what you were going to say? My face is my fortune? God, but men can be so bloody patronising." For a moment, she glared at me with hard, narrowed eyes. I glared back. At least a staring contest didn't leave bruises. Not physical ones anyway.

"It seems we are equally touchy, Captain. I have Slavic fire in my veins and you ..." she paused, and the smile returned to her lips.

"I come from a long line of smugglers and pirates, just honest seamen trying to earn a living."

She laughed, her strong peals filling the cabin. "I'd say there's still plenty of the pirate in you, Captain Rowden. I've met many English gentlemen, and I can assure you most of them are more dangerous than pirates. Pirates I can deal with. Chests of gold and jewels, a bottle of rum, a full belly and a pretty woman to kiss. Treasure and pleasure ... and usually in that order."

"Treasure and pleasure!" I laughed. "Well I haven't seen much of either in the China Sea recently. Perhaps I'll have better luck in Shanghai?"

"Oh, I'm sure you will do very well on either front in Shanghai," she replied, with a downward flutter of her eyelids. "Although perhaps I should warn you to be wary of scheming Russian girls who marry English peers for their titles and money, and live dissipated lives in that most dissipated of all cities, Shanghai, the Paris of the east."

"I'll be on my guard, if you'll point one out to me."

The gaiety of her laughter only served to highlight the drab confines of my cabin.

"Come, let us drink to fiery Slavs and piratical Englishmen," she said.

I poured a small tot of rum into her glass, we chinked them together and drank.

"Next time with vodka. Now, thank you for the rum, but you must excuse me so that I can make myself respectable for luncheon."

I stood, intending to escort her below.

"Please, I will see myself out."

She turned, pushed past the curtain, and disappeared down the stairs to the boat deck. I reached for my glass and drained the contents, wondering how she'd persuaded me to let my guard down and talk about my origins. But I hadn't told her the whole truth, about the anger that still burned deep at the men who had destroyed my mother's life, and at the warders and the older boys who had made a hell of my time at the reform school. I had tamed that anger, but whenever someone or something threatened me, I could fan it back to white heat, tempering my resolve like steel. I knew what it felt like to be despised and hated, humiliated and beaten, and nothing would ever take me back there again.

* * *

"She's awfully thick with that second mate, Griffith. Can't see what she sees in him myself. A young boyo from the valleys, probably still got coal dust under his fingernails."

I heard the tail end of Trimble's remarks as I entered the saloon, seeing him sitting at a table beside the bar clutching a glass of pink gin. Evans, the Hong Kong merchant, was seated opposite him. They looked up as I entered, and Trimble raised a hand in greeting.

"Would you care to join us in a cocktail, Captain?"

Having made the effort to put in an appearance before dinner, it would have been churlish to refuse, so I sat down and asked the steward to bring me a rum and water.

146

"Thought you were in with a chance, did you?" replied a chuckling Evans, keen to get back to their previous conversation. "Because you've seen her five times on stage."

Trimble flushed. "Not a bit. It's just I'd have thought she'd pay more attention to mature, prosperous types like you and me, rather than —" He choked off the rest, suddenly realising he was in danger of criticising one of my officers. I could have taken offence, except there was some truth in Trimble's observation. But in a flash of intuition, surprising as it was unexpected, I recalled the image of Griffith and Lady Ashworth chatting on the boat deck on the first night out, and realised she had latched onto him as a precaution against precisely the intentions now being expressed by Evans.

Who was chuckling again at Trimble's confusion.

It was perfectly clear, now, what Trimble was, a down at heel remittance man, banished by his family to the Far East to make his fortune, or to disappear in the process. I recognised the type, and no doubt Lady Ashworth had too. But he had paid his fare like the rest of them, and the niceties had to be observed.

"Don't worry, Mr Trimble," I said. "We'll soon be in Shanghai and you can pursue the lady without fear of tripping over Mr Griffith."

"You might have some stiff competition old boy," said Evans. "I hear she's pally with a Russian general." The final words were accompanied by the clacking of heels in the passage, and then a girlish laugh as Mrs Hill-Davies swept in, followed by her husband.

"Good evening, Captain," she greeted me, before turning to Evans and Trimble.

"What are you old gossips up to," she giggled, "not ruining my reputation I hope?"

We rose from our chairs, Evans waved for the steward to bring them drinks, and to refresh those of Trimble and himself.

"That would be unthinkable my dear Mrs Hill-Davies," replied Trimble. "No, Evans here was telling us that Lady Ashworth has some odd friends in Shanghai."

"I don't know about odd," said Mrs Hill-Davies. "When we've seen her at the occasional government do, she's usually hob-nobbing with ministers and diplomats, nothing odd about them."

"Her late husband seemed very well connected," affirmed Hill-Davis. "I must say she seems all right to me."

"I'm not saying she's not all right, merely that Evans and I have noticed she spends quite a bit of time chatting with the second officer, and Evans has just told me she's friendly with a Russian General. But each to their own of course," said Trimble.

"Ooh, you are a pair of gossips," giggled Mrs Hill-Davis. "Thank goodness Bertie's with me," squeezing her husband's hand while winking flirtatiously at me, "or you'd have me married off to the captain."

It would have been ungentlemanly to say that, despite her superficial charms, I found Mrs Hill-Davis singularly unattractive, representing as she did all the squalid pretentiousness of so many of the English middle-class. In other circumstances she would not have given me the time of day, it was merely the four gold stripes on my sleeve that attracted her. Not being a gentleman I had, on occasion, resorted to the favours of unattractive women, and I was wondering how Mrs Hill-Davis might compare in that department, when the steward arrived with the drinks. There was a pause in the conversation, as he placed the glasses in front of them, which spared me the need to reply.

"It seems you might have an admirer," said Evans, nudging my arm.

I would happily have risked Mr Khoo's displeasure and punched him. I was not used to being made fun of in my own ship, as far better men than Trimble or Evans had painfully learned to their cost. Instead, I took a large swig of grog, felt the soothing warmth and forced my face into an affable grin. "I can't imagine why. I'm just a battered old sea-dog that's seen better days, just like my ship."

"I think you look quite piratical, if you ask me," replied Mrs Hill-Davis, apparently desperate to remain the centre of attention. "A pair of earrings and a parrot on the shoulder, and I'd be expecting to walk the plank ... or worse." She arched one plucked and pencilled eyebrow in the direction of her husband, who, by the embarrassed look on his face, might have been quite willing to contemplate her walking the plank. Although any pirate worth his pieces of eight would hardly have wasted the opportunity of ravishment, even of such a tiresome woman.

"I hope you don't mind me saying so, but I shouldn't be at all surprised, with that accent," replied Hill-Davis, apparently with more courage than I would have given him credit for.

"Really, I don't hear anything of the West Country. Ah-haarrr," replied Trimble.

"It's his party trick," explained Mrs Hill-Davis, placing a reassuring hand on her husband's arm, as if she thought he might need protection from me. "Bertie can pick where people come from just by listening to their accents."

"Just like Professor Higgins in *Pygmalion*," Trimble laughed.

I tried to keep my expression neutral, but Hill-Davis proved a better judge of character than his wife.

"North Downs, I'd say," he said, diplomatically. "North Kent coast, rife with smugglers in the 19th century."

"'Brandy for the parson, baccy for the clerk'," said Evans. "Learned it at school, forget who wrote it though."

"Kipling," replied Hill-Davis. "He lived in Kent for a while. Probably heard stories about a famous smuggling gang called the Seasalter Company."

"Strange sort of knowledge for a Cathedral School master," observed Trimble.

"Oh, I don't know," said Hill-Davis. "Have to keep the boys amused somehow." He turned to me. "Well, Captain, was I right?"

I was surprised by his precision, and a little relieved that his ear had diplomatically filtered out the overlay of Wapping.

"Quite correct, on all counts. I was born in Whitstable, next to Seasalter, and the Rowdens are a well known family of fishermen, with more than a smattering of smugglers, and even a highwayman who rode with Dick Turpin."

The conversation was interrupted by the heavy tread of shoes on the stairs, and the khaki clad figure of Major Spencer appeared in the doorway.

"Good evening," he greeted us cheerfully. "Enjoying a snifter before tiffin? Mind if I join you?"

"Not at all old boy, pull up a pew," said Evans, waving once again to the steward.

"Major, my husband was just saying he could tell by the captain's accent that he's probably a pirate. You seem to know him rather well. Would you be able to confirm that for us?" Mrs Hill-Davis' words were drowned in a hearty roar of laughter.

Spencer waited until the noise subsided, and then said, "You can tell that by the way he talks? I'll have to watch what I say then ... or rather how I say it."

There was more laughter.

"I merely observed I could detect traces of the North Kent coast in the captain's accent, and mentioned that it was an area once famous — or notorious — for smugglers," said Hill-Davis.

"Ah, I see," replied Spencer. "Well it wouldn't surprise me to learn that Captain Rowden is a pirate. I'd say you'd need to be pretty sharp to deal with the sharks who circle around these waters."

Mrs Hill-Davis gave a theatrical shiver. "Surely, Major, you're not suggesting we're in any danger on a British vessel?"

"You're forgetting ma'am, that some of the most famous pirates in history were British, including Sir Francis Drake and Blackbeard," replied Spencer with a chuckle. "But I'm sure Captain Rowden will see us all to our destination unmolested."

"Oh, I'm almost disappointed," replied Mrs Hill-Davis, who obviously still saw herself in the role of Olivia de Havilland in *Captain Blood*. But she was mistaken if she saw anything of Errol Flynn in me, the unabashed villainy of Basil Rathbone was more my style.

"But, if I may ask about you Major Spencer," she continued, "you don't sound terribly Australian, does he Bertie?" She turned to her husband for support.

"I was born in England, Mrs Hill-Davis," said Spencer. "My father was in the Army, a company commander in the British Expeditionary Force, the Old Contemptibles. He managed to survive the early battles, and when the ANZACS arrived in Europe they were short of experienced officers, so he was offered one of their battalions. Later on he joined the staff of their Australian commander, General Monash. He liked serving with Australians, and when the war ended he moved us all out there, to Melbourne. I was fourteen. I finished my schooling at Melbourne Grammar School, and then followed my father's footsteps and went into the Army."

"Well, does that make you British or Australian?" asked Mrs Hill-Davis.

"I think of myself as a bit of both, really," replied Spencer.

"So what takes you to Shanghai?" asked Trimble.

"Something of a busman's holiday," said Spencer. "I was due a spot of leave. One of my old regimental colleagues is based there, and invited me to come for a bit of a look around, so here I am." I hadn't expected him to tell the truth, but the lie seemed to come as if it was second nature. Which perhaps it was.

"And what about our fellow traveller, Lady Ashworth, are you acquainted with her?" asked Mrs Hill-Davis.

"Ah, you noticed me talking to her after dinner on the night we left Hong Kong. No, we're not acquainted, I simply thought I'd steal a march on you other gentlemen." He waved his hand around the table, and once again there was an outbreak of laughter.

"Well you don't seem to be succeeding old boy," broke in Evans, "the lady seems preoccupied with our Welsh second officer, Mr Griffith."

"Is that so? Well jolly good luck to him."

"He may need it, Mr Evans tells us that you both have a rival — a Russian General," said Mrs Hill-Davis.

"Ah well, rank, even Russian, does have its privileges," replied Spencer grinning and rising from his seat. "Now, here are Mr and Mrs Wilson come to join our happy band. Will you have a drink before tiffin?"

I drained my grog and signalled to the steward to refill the glasses, reflecting on the ability of the middle class to recreate a familiar corner of England in the farthest flung reaches of the globe. Even in my scruffy, ageing tramp steamer, whose stained panelling and creaky riveted hull now echoed with unaccustomed laughter. It made a change from typhoons, German gunrunners and dodgy customs' officials, and I felt my cynical, leathery heart relent sufficiently to suggest that I should enjoy an evening's relaxation.

Sound advice, if I'd known what was to come.

* * *

The morning watch of our last day at sea. We were due to arrive at the entrance to the Yangtze River later that afternoon. The jagged, grey-green hills of the Chusan Islands were visible through my porthole, providing a picturesque backdrop for a small fleet of fishing junks above which a flock of seabirds noisily wheeled.

I was sitting at my desk, checking and re-checking all the bumf that had to be prepared in triplicate for the byzantine layers of the International Settlement's bureaucracy, when there was a loud bang on the open door, and a hand reached round the privacy curtain to whisk it aside. Major Spencer's ruddy face greeted me cheerfully.

"Morning, Captain, mind if I come in for a minute."

"Not at all, Major, makes a break from this damned paperwork. What can I do for you?"

"Would you mind if I closed the door. What I have to say is a bit delicate," said Spencer, tapping his nose conspiratorially. "For your ears only."

I nodded my assent and Spencer closed the door behind him. He took a seat on the couch, and I swivelled round in the chair to face him.

"I'll come straight to the point, Captain. It's about Lady Ashworth. I believe you've had some conversations with her, and she's spent a fair bit of time in the company of your second officer, Griffith isn't it."

"Really, Major," I said, feeling the beginnings of an angry flush rise to my cheeks, at what seemed to be an unnecessary and inconsequential interruption to my work. "If you've come here with some tittle-tattle about Lady Ashworth, then I've got better things to do with my time."

Spencer sat and regarded me with that knowing look I had come to expect, then pulled a cigarette case out of his pocket.

"Do you mind if I smoke?"

He didn't wait for an answer, but flipped the lid of a polished steel lighter, rasped the flint and took a long satisfying draw.

"Well?" I said, irritated by his coolness.

"What do you think of her, Lady Ashworth?"

"I hardly know her, and even if I did, I'm not sure I'd share my thoughts with you," I replied, annoyed at his smug self-assurance. "She's Russian, she was married to Lord Ashworth who drank himself to death, and she lives in Shanghai. All of which you told me yourself, before we left Hong Kong. She seems friendly enough. But I really don't see what all this has to do with you."

"I apologise, Captain, but I'm afraid I've not been entirely honest with you," said Spencer, brushing a speck of ash off the front of his immaculate uniform.

"That seems to be a familiar story," I snapped back.

"Keep your shirt on, old boy. Truth is that the lovely Lady Helen Ashworth, formerly Helena Kovtoun, is not exactly what she seems."

"Oh, for goodness sake. Are you going to tell me she's not Russian either?" Despite my anger at his manner, I was beginning to see some humour in the major's cloak and dagger antics.

"Oh yes, she's Russian all right, and the daughter of a White Russian general executed by the Bolsheviks."

"So? No lies there, then?"

"No, but given that bit of history, don't you think it's a bit strange that she's now the mistress of the Red Army's military attaché in Shanghai, one General Ivan Maslennikov whom, I suspect, also holds the same rank in the NKVD."

"NKVD? What's that," I asked.

"I won't try to pronounce the Russian, but it's their internal security service. They report directly to the Kremlin. Now don't you find it odd that a woman whose family was exiled from Russia, and whose father was executed by the Bolsheviks, should be openly associating with a high ranking party member?"

"I don't pretend to know much about politics, or about women for that matter. But I'm guessing you haven't just come in here to play twenty questions. Get to the point."

"All right," replied Spencer. "Here's what I know. Before she married Bobby Ashworth, Helena Kovtoun was a very beautiful and reasonably successful actress. As well as Russian, she spoke flawless French, German and English, and had a string of high profile lovers. But she kept clear of Russian politics, which was unusual, as most White Russians exiled in Paris formed secret societies, and raised funds to fight the Reds. And then she married Lord Bobby Ashworth." He paused for a draw on his cigarette, and grinned as if he enjoyed wasting my time. "Now, have you heard of the Cliveden Set?"

I raised an eyebrow, and was about to remind him that tramp steamer masters knew little and cared less for the doings of English aristocrats, when he took the hint.

"Cliveden is the name of the country house of Lord and Lady Astor. Lord Astor controls the London *Times*. His brother, Major Astor, owns *The Observer*. Both newspapers have been encouraging the government to come to an accommodation with Nazi Germany. Lady Astor and Major Astor are both members of Parliament. They hold frequent get togethers with a group of powerful, like-minded politicians and businessmen at the Astors' country house, Cliveden. It's not a secret, even our Australian labour rag, *The Worker*, knows the details, and refers to them as the 'Cliveden Set'."

"But what's this all got to do with Lady Ashworth," I interjected, and, more importantly, wondering what it had to do with me. I was beginning to harbour the suspicion the major was drawing me into something I would rather avoid. "Maybe she just fell in love. I hear he was quite handsome."

"Possibly, looks, a title, and the promise of money can do wonders with knicker elastic. But there are two things that suggest she might have had an ulterior motive, or at the very least a strong incentive to fall in love. Firstly, the Nazis are declared enemies of communism. If the British government were persuaded to forge closer ties to Germany, then that would make life more difficult for Stalin, and encourage those seeking to throw him, and the communists, out."

"Ah, the enemy of my enemy is my friend," I said, with growing comprehension.

"Exactly. Although Helena steered clear of politics, she'd have had no love lost for those who killed her father. If her adopted country was working with the Nazis against the Russians, well it might be an opportunity for her."

"Yes, I can see that," I said. "But what's the second thing?"

"Bobby Ashworth was a member of the Cliveden Set. He was a distant cousin of Lady Astor. And now he had a beautiful and exotic wife, so they were frequently invited to Cliveden."

"So if she wanted revenge for the death of her father, and to do some damage to the communists, then she was among people who might be of a similar mind."

"Spot on again," said Spencer, grinning. "I'm beginning to think you're wasted as a ship's captain."

"But what was she going to do, lead a band of counter revolutionaries paid for by the Astors?" I said, ignoring the jibe.

"Nothing so dramatic. But consider, she is famous, she speaks several languages fluently, she is well connected in European capitals where she performed on the stage and ... well let's just say she knows a number of well-placed men. She might be very useful to someone, or to some government, interested in exchanging information that might advantage one side against another."

"As a spy, you mean?" I was beginning to wonder whether anything Lady Ashworth said could be trusted, and why she had chosen to travel home to Shanghai in my ship. I could hardly imagine that Evans or Trimble were Nazi apologists, or Hill-Davis and his empty-headed wife. Perhaps the Wilsons were secretly funnelling the Shanghai Bank's money to a Berlin bank account. It didn't seem likely, though, and I certainly hadn't experienced any of the usual warning signs, but that didn't mean Spencer was wrong.

"I think that's too vulgar for Helena don't you think," he continued. "No, they just needed an alert listener, a discreet channeler of information, someone who could drop a hint into a sympathetic ear. No daggers and pistols."

"And you know she's doing this?"

"Let's just say that Ashworth being invited to join the Cliveden set was looked upon favourably by certain people in Whitehall."

He paused to light another cigarette.

"So, Lord Ashworth was planted to spy on the Astors," I said, as more pieces of the picture fell into place. "And their pro-Nazi friends, which included his own wife?"

"Bobby Ashworth was friends with the Astors, and he had friends in Whitehall. It's good to have friends, even if you don't always appreciate their help. The Astors are well respected as well as powerful, but a good friend might sometimes see what is in their best interests more clearly than they do."

"And what's your connection to these ... friends, in Whitehall?" I asked.

"I'm a solider in the Australian Army, our job is to fight the King's enemies, a friend is someone who helps us do that job."

"British Intelligence?" I mused, recalling what he had told me earlier. "You're just as much a spy as you claim she is."

"I'm not saying any more than that, for your safety ... and mine," he replied, over-dramatically I thought.

"Okay, but you came in here worried about me and my second mate talking to Lady Ashworth. Even if she is a spy, we know nothing of any value to anyone. And anyway, Ashworth is dead and she lives in Shanghai, so she can't be of much interest to the Cliveden Set." Nor much of a threat to me, I thought. It was Spencer I needed to be wary of.

"I'm not sure about that," he replied. "There's plenty of talk in Europe about the possibility of another war. But if you haven't noticed Captain, that war has already started out here. The Nationalist Chinese are fighting the communists who are backed by Stalin. The Japanese control large parts of northern China and, cheered on by the Germans, are itching for more. And not just China, they'd be very happy to control the resources of the East Indies, and even India, more oil, rubber and tin for their war machine. And you're sailing right into the heart of it, Captain. Into a small European enclave surrounded by Nationalists to the south, Communists to the west and the Japs to the north. Shanghai is where it all meets. The city is awash with refugees, spies, conniving diplomats and rumours of Japanese invasion, all stirred up together with money and corruption. And you're sailing into it, loaded with goodness knows what, and carrying the famous Lady Helen Ashworth, who just happens to be the mistress of the Russian military attaché."

He paused to draw breath, took a long drag at the cigarette, and continued. "All I'm saying, is that you and your people need to be careful. It's not what you know or are carrying, it's what others might imagine you know or might be carrying. Just be careful, that's all I'm saying."

I was tempted to laugh, not knowing whether to be amused or angry, then my jaw clenched obstinately. "I thought when you barged in here you were concerned for the moral welfare of Lady Ashworth, slumming it with the likes of us sailors, but now you're suggesting I don't know my way about the waterfronts of the east. I know every dodgy wrinkle between Singapore and Sapporo. I know my way around Shanghai, and I'm damned sure I can take my ship in and bring her safely out again, despite all your war mongering spies and rumours."

"Don't take things the wrong way, Captain, what you do or talk about with Lady Ashworth is your own affair, and I'm not suggesting you aren't a match for all the scoundrels who prey on the honest sailors who ply these waters. But times are delicate, China is on a knife-edge. I'm just asking you, as a friend, to be careful."

"Ah, as a friend." I was about to loosen the sheets on my sarcasm, until it occurred to me that he had no reason to have shared any of this with me. "I've heard about your ideas of friendship," I snorted, a reluctant smile forming on my lips. "But I'll keep my wits about me, and maybe take a bit of extra insurance when I go ashore."

Spencer eyed me questioningly, and I rose and walked over to the desk, opened the drawer and pulled out the big Webley, which glinted dully in the hazy sunlight filtering in through the porthole.

"Ah, the Mark VI. Hell of a kick, I hope you know how to use it."

"I haven't bothered to carve any notches on the grip," I replied, smiling grimly. "But I can shoot straight enough when I have to."

As a last resort, I might have added. Although that wasn't strictly true. But I'd never shot a man in cold blood. And usually not before I'd tried some other means of persuasion.

Spencer also rose. "It looks like you know how to take care of yourself. Thanks for hearing me out, Captain," He stuck out a hand. "I've taken up enough of your time."

He winced slightly as I grabbed his hand and squeezed it in my horny, powerful fist, nodding my head in appreciation. Then he turned, pushed the curtain aside and left me to ponder the question I should have asked.

Which was, what were he and Lady Ashworth really doing in my ship?

CHAPTER TWELVE

Just after eight a.m. and *Oriental Venture* lay snugly berthed at the China Merchants Central Wharf, one of a line of cargo wharves that stretched along the northern bank of the Whangpoo River, downstream of the Bund. Not only was the ship securely moored against the wharf's floating pontoon, but she was also hemmed in against it by ranks of lighters, four or five deep. The nearer ones lashed alongside and the outer ones lashed to each other, with a multitude of ropes of all sizes and materials.

I was standing on the foredeck, the back of my shirt already stained with sweat in the stifling heat of the Shanghai summer's day. Around me, the crew was busy readying the ship for the discharge of her cargo. Stepping to the rail, I glanced down at the raft of lighters, their crews squatting patiently on the narrow decks beside their open holds, their inscrutable eyes watching from beneath the brims of battered, conical, split bamboo hats. When filled, their decks nearly awash, their crews would scull them upstream or down to their destinations.

Despite the fiery morning sunlight, my eyes were stinging with fatigue, and I blinked to clear them. It had been a long night passage up the wide estuary of the Yangtze River, its banks invisible in the darkness, but sensed on either side from the smell of mud and rotting seaweed. After several hours, we had reached the light-house marking the mouth of the Whangpoo River, and the pilot ordered the course alteration to take us up its smaller channel towards Shanghai. On the northern bank, the heavy guns of the Wusong batteries guarded the entrance. In daylight it would have been necessary to dip the ensign in courtesy to the Chinese government's control of the river, although the mark of respect was purely symbolic, the Chinese government being obliged by the force of the Yangtze Patrol of British and American gunboats, to permit access to any ship seeking passage to the International Settlement.

The eastern sky was lightening as we picked our way upstream in the twisting, narrow channel of the Whangpoo River, passing junks and sampans drifting downstream on the current. A couple of hours later, with the sun having already dispersed the early morning mist, we swung around the final bend and sighted the Bund, the row of historic buildings lining the waterfront of the International Settlement. A pair of elderly tugs bustled downstream to meet us, their big wakes shouldering aside any flimsy sampan that impeded their passage. Belching smoke and with a toot of whistles, they took *Oriental Venture's* lines, swung her around against the current, and roughly shoved her alongside the pontoons of Central Wharf. Just astern of us, Hong Kew Creek wound its way northwards into the grimier parts of the International Settlement, its stinking waters filled with refuse and human waste. Its banks crowded with ancient godowns interspersed with narrow tenements, from which the smoke and smells of countless cooking fires drifted skywards in the sultry air, only partially masking the smell of ordure and rotting vegetation.

I had sent Lowther below to grab a couple of hours sleep on the upriver passage, and as soon as the ship was secure alongside, I left him in charge of dealing with the stream of officialdom. Down in my cabin Da Silva produced a pot of his strongest Java coffee, and several cups had partially restored me. But with the heat, and the hot glare from the coppery surface of the river, the tiredness had slid back into my bones, and I decided to take a turn around the deck to try and clear my head. As I cast my weary eye over the preparations for unloading, I caught sight of McGrath directing the hoisting of derricks. He had snatched as little sleep as anyone during the night, but apart from the dark circles under his eyes, his young, fit body showed no signs of tiredness. He crossed the deck when he saw me watching.

"Any orders, sir?"

"Yes, Third. Send the customs-wallahs and all the rest of them up to the chief mate with their infernal paperwork. And you can go round to the passengers, and tell them they're to be in the saloon at ten o'clock for immigration and customs' inspection. After that, the agent has laid on a number of taxis to take them to their destinations. I'll be in my cabin if anyone specifically asks for me. Got all that?"

"Aye aye, sir."

I took a final glance at the river, where a continuous parade of ships, tugs, junks and sampans bustled up and down between the ships moored alongside its wharves, and the midstream file of slender, grey warships. The riverbanks were lined with slipways, dockyards, godowns, factories, offices and the rough tenements of countless Chinese. Further upriver, on the other side of Soochow Creek, began the Bund, with its grand hotels, banks and office buildings. Their solid granite edifices and gabled or turreted roofs, reminding me of the British colonial buildings that grandly imposed themselves on the streets of the other capitals of Empire, such as Bombay or Sydney.

It was no cooler in my cabin, and I turned on the bulkhead mounted fan, wiped the sweat from my face, and poured a glass of water from the thermos jug. I took the glass with me to the couch, wondering if a nap would ease the aching tiredness in my limbs, but I had barely sat down when there was a polite tap on the door, and a suave looking Chinese in an expensive linen suit eased his way past the privacy curtain into my cabin. Removing his light grey homburg to reveal long, black, oil-slicked hair, he adjusted the red carnation in his button hole, pulled a pair spectacles out his pocket and slipped them over an unusually straight nose, the round, gold-rimmed, lenses magnifying his eyes. He introduced himself as Ling, from Mr Tung's office, and I invited him to take a seat while pushing the bell to summon Da Silva, from whom I ordered another pot of coffee.

"I assume you're here to discuss arrangements for delivery of the Darjeeling tea," I said, once the preliminaries were dispensed with.

"Indeed, Captain," replied Ling, his toad like eyes bulging at me through the thick lenses. "And to convey Mr Tung's sincere apology for being unable to meet your esteemed self in person. He is indisposed, and his doctor advises complete rest. However, I am authorised to accept the shipment on his behalf."

I rubbed my fingertips together to relieve the tingling, but I hardly needed their warning this time. If ever a man looked untrustworthy it was the expensively dressed, cologne scented Ling. "That's most unfortunate. Please convey my sympathies to Mr Tung. I expect to be here for several days at least, time for him to recover I hope."

Ling's smooth brow creased into a frown, and there was a hastily concealed flash of annoyance in his eyes.

"I do not understand, Captain, why should you wait for Mr Tung's recovery in order to release his cargo to him?"

"I believe you understand perfectly, Mr Ling," I replied, not fooled by the feigned innocence of his tone. "I am instructed to only release the tea into the hands of Mr Tung, personally."

"Ah, yes of course," said Ling, placing his palms together obsequiously. "Mr Tung does not perceive there should be any difficulty in your following your instructions. And as he is particularly anxious that the tea be released as soon as possible, today even, he has asked me to give you this." He pulled an envelope out of his jacket pocket and handed it to me. "It authorises you to deliver the tea to me."

I took the offered letter, and stared at it with growing annoyance. My orders from Mr Khoo were quite specific. Despite the untrustworthy appearance of his clerk though, if that's what he was, if Mr Tung genuinely was ill then I was faced with a dilemma. Take the cargo back to Hong Kong undelivered, or hand it over to Ling.

"I don't wish to appear rude Mr Ling, but I do have specific instructions from my chairman, Mr Khoo. You say Mr Tung is indisposed, and you present me with a letter which you say is from him. But, and I am sorry to be blunt, I don't know you, or Mr Tung, so how do I know the letter is genuine?"

The flush that spread upwards from Ling's neck, and the narrowing of the eyes, told me he risked losing face, but when it came, the response was ingratiatingly polite.

"My dear Captain Rowden, of course you are right to be cautious, in these ..." he waved his hand in an encompassing gesture "... uncertain times. But I can assure you the letter is quite genuine. Mr Tung is under the weather as you English say, but he dictated the letter personally, and that is his chop at the bottom to verify his signature."

"His chop—"

"His personal mark and seal," interjected Ling, "only he would affix it to a letter."

"I know what a chop is, but—"

"Are you doubting my word, Captain Rowden," snapped Ling unable to control himself any longer.

"No, Mr Ling." He had interrupted me twice, and I met his hostile gaze, reminding myself to keep calm. I wasn't dealing with a Sydney waterfront hoodlum, and it was unusual for a Chinese to openly display anger in front of a foreigner. "But my orders are specific. The best I can do for you today is send a telegram to Mr Khoo informing him of the situation, and asking for his instructions. I've a few matters to attend to this morning,"— I hadn't, I wanted to get my head down and catch up on some sleep, — "but I'll visit the telegraph office this afternoon and we should have an answer by tomorrow. Perhaps you could telephone the agent in the morning and, if Mr Khoo's answer is positive, he'll arrange for the cargo to be released to you."

"Mr Tung will be extremely disappointed at your lack of cooperation, Captain, and when he makes his feelings clear to Mr Khoo ...." He left the sentence unfinished.

"Is that some sort of threat Mr Ling?" He was lightly built, and looked almost effeminate with his smooth skin and the pink carnation in his buttonhole. I was tempted to ignore his Oriental desire to maintain face, grab him by the throat and shake him.

"I am merely the bearer of the message, Captain. You are thwarting the transaction. Mr Tung will be unhappy not to receive his shipment promptly, and Mr Khoo's payment will be delayed. There may be consequences for these actions for which both may hold you accountable."

"I'll take that chance, Mr Ling," I said, through gritted teeth. "I've told you what I'm prepared to do, and it would be a better use of your time, and of mine, if you let me get on with it."

I needed to bring this to an end, before I lost my temper and did something I might later regret. I stood up to signal the interview was over, but Ling raised a hand.

"Perhaps I spoke a little hastily, Captain. Mr Tung has his reasons to swiftly complete the transaction, and he, and I am sure his old friend Mr Khoo also, would not like you put to any trouble. Mr Tung would be quite happy to pay a ... freight bonus, for the release of the cargo today."

I was not surprised by the threat of the stick being followed by the carrot. I had been around the East long enough to expect both. Mr Khoo and Mr Tung were supposed to be old friends, but the tingling in my fingers continued to warn me to be on my guard. There was no point in prolonging the conversation, I picked up Ling's hat and presented it to him.

"Like I said, I'll telegraph my chairman, and will act upon his instructions as soon as I receive them."

Ling rose and snatched his hat. "If that is your final word, Captain then I will relay it to Mr Tung, and we will await your news tomorrow. But it fair to warn you that he is not a patient man, and will not take kindly to your hindering him."

Despite my best intentions I felt the blood rise to my face, and heard it pounding in my ears.

"It would be best if you left now, Mr Ling," I said, quietly, forcing myself to remain calm. "The agent will let you know Mr Khoo's decision tomorrow, if he chooses to make one."

Ling turned to go, no longer attempting to conceal his look of hatred and anger. He raised his right arm, and I wondered if he was going to shake my hand or strike me with it, but instead he yanked the privacy curtain aside and vanished into the corridor without a further word. I listened to his footsteps fading down the stairs, and then sat back in my chair to study Tung's letter. For all the official looking note-paper, polite phrasing and impressive red seal, it could have been written by anyone, perhaps even by Tung himself. But from Ling's manner he, or someone else, clearly wanted to get their hands on the tea in a hurry. Though, why anyone should be that desperate to take delivery of a consignment of Darjeeling Tea was beyond me. But I had my instructions, and the sooner I clarified matters with Mr Khoo, the easier I would sleep. I hoisted my weary limbs out of the chair and reached into the locker for a summer weight jacket, and my worn, but serviceable Panama hat.

Lowther was working at his desk as I tugged the curtain aside and stuck my head inside his tiny office. There was a cup of coffee by his elbow and an open bottle of gin on the desk. I frowned, knowing I really ought to say something. Lowther was too good a man to see destroyed by drink. He needed to find a purpose in life, which he obviously hadn't found serving as mate in a tramp steamer. Perhaps the coming war would solve that for him, if his liver held out long enough.

"I'm going ashore to the Telegraph Office to send a message to Mr Khoo about his damned tea. Seems the man it's intended for can't take delivery, but I don't trust the clerk whose come down to claim it."

"All under control, skipper, how long do you expect to be ashore?"

"Couple of hours, maybe a bit longer. I don't expect to see Ling, the clerk, until tomorrow, but if he does put in an appearance again, just repeat that we're waiting to hear from Mr Khoo."

Lowther nodded, and I let fall the curtain, stepped into the cross alleyway and pushed open the door to the main deck. It was hotter outside, and I felt trickles of sweat start to run down inside my shirt. The sky was a pale hazy blue, and thickly populated by heavy, slow moving banks of cloud, their grey bases promising thunderstorms later in the day. I climbed down the gangway onto the oil stained, timber deck of the pontoon, and walked to the dock gate. I could telephone there for a taxi, but, despite the heat, I felt the need to keep moving, and decided to continue walking the short distance along Taiping Road to Broadway, where I could hail one myself, or take the tram to the Bund. Perhaps the tram was not quite the mode of transport appropriate to my exalted position, and I grinned, remembering earlier days as a junior mate, when I could hardly afford the few coppers for a ticket.

The Sikh policeman at the gate raised his hand to his turban, and I touched the brim of my hat in acknowledgment as I passed through. My fingertips were still tingling, but I put that down to Ling, who had managed to get under my skin with his clumsy attempt to get me to ignore my instructions. Outside, the road stretched about a third of a mile north to Broadway, low godowns and factories crowding right to its edge, so that I had to pick my way among small trucks belching exhaust, and overloaded barrows pushed by sweating, shouting coolies. The air was heavy with dust and grime, and choking with the fumes of badly burned diesel, acrid charcoal smoke, and the stinking mud and refuse in the river.

I was the only European among the throng of Chinese streaming and jostling their way along the narrow road, but years in the seaports of the Far East had accustomed me to its crowded humanity, and I weaved and pushed my way along with the rest, heading towards Broadway. Half way there, the mouth of an alley opened up on the left. It ran between the rear of several small factories, leading towards the muddy bank of Hong Kew Creek. At the end of the road I could see the green trams, with their wooden slatted window blinds, passing along Broadway. I reached into my pocket for some coins for the fare, but as I glanced down to count them, I felt a shove push me sideways into the mouth of the alley.

I looked round, annoyed, expecting to hear a mumbled apology, but all I saw were blank, hostile stares. I tried to push my way back into the moving stream of men, but there seemed to be a closing of ranks, and I could proceed neither forward nor back towards the wharf. Behind me, the alley suddenly appeared dangerously open.

I felt inside my jacket, cursing that, despite my assurance to Major Spencer, I had left the Webley in my desk drawer.

An eddy rippled through the crowd, ejecting two villainous looking Chinese in greasy Tang jackets, who advanced menacingly towards me. I barely had time to register their appearance, one wiry, bareheaded with a thin, skull-like face, and the other thickset with wisps of beard and a skullcap. The expressions on their faces said all I needed to know.

My fighting instincts kicked in, and I raised my fists, transferred my weight onto the balls of my feet, adopting a brawler's stance. But the men were fast. The thickset man charged straight at me, I dodged him, but stumbled over a broken flag-stone, almost falling to the ground. The wiry one reached out, as if to save me from falling, but I felt his hands dart inside my jacket, reaching for my wallet.

Just a straightforward mugging, I thought, almost thankfully, before lunging at the wiry man and grabbing his collar. Only to have my legs kicked out from under me, sending me sprawling onto the road. A quick tap of my pocket confirmed that my wallet had been lifted, and I jumped to my feet, burning with fierce anger.

I glanced around looking for the two assailants. Strangely, they were calmly walking down the alley in the direction of the creek. Skull face glanced back at me and bared his teeth in a threatening grin.

"Think I'm too scared to chase you," I roared, launching myself after them, fists raised, ready to batter their smug faces. They didn't run, but turned to face me, still grinning.

An alarm bell jangled in my head - then there were stars exploding behind my eyes, searing pain, and darkness.

* * *

I opened my eyes, and immediately groaned with the nauseating pain that threatened to split my skull apart.

"Back with us old chap," said a vaguely familiar voice, as I struggled to make sense of the surroundings. I was lying on my back on what felt like a couch, but as my vision cleared I realised was the back seat of a stationary taxi, my feet draped outside the open door.

I tried to sit up, gasped and groaned again. Not only did my head ache like the devil, but my ribs felt as if they were on fire.

"I'm afraid you're going to be a bit sore for a few days, but as far as I can see there's no permanent damage. You must have a pretty thick skull though." A hand approached my face holding a small silver flask. I took it shakily, held the neck to my lips and swallowed, coughing as the fiery spirit hit the back of my throat, but grateful for the steadying warmth spreading out from my stomach. A face swam into focus, and I recognised the sandy hair and moustache.

"Major Spencer," I said, looking up at my rescuer, struggling into a sitting position and gritting my teeth against the pain. "What happened?"

"I was about to climb into a taxi at the end of Taiping Road when I saw a couple of men confront you in the mouth of the alley. A third one sandbagged you from behind. I lost sight of you in the crowd, but managed to push my way through it. They were dragging you into a doorway. Two of them were holding you, and the third was amusing himself kicking you in the ribs. When they saw me coming they dropped you and scarpered."

"Scared of the uniform?" I said, feeling the nasty lump on the back of my skull, but grateful not to see any blood on my fingers.

"The Webley more likely, you're not the only one with a gun, old boy, although it's a shame you seem to have left yours on board. Anyway, I summoned the help of some natives, and we got you into the taxi. I've had a bit of a feel around, if you'll excuse the liberty, and there's nothing broken. You hair covers the worst of the lump. I'd say you got off lightly, although I don't think that was their intention."

"Three of them, eh?" I mused, my memory of the attack starting to return. "I only saw the two who robbed me. I thought it was odd they didn't run when I went for them. The third must have waited his chance to whack me from behind."

"I don't think it was just your wallet they were after. By the look of things, I'd say that at best you'd have woken up extremely sore. At worst, you'd have ended up face down in Hong Kew Creek. Seems like you have some enemies, Captain."

"No more than anyone else who makes a living trading these waters," I said, rubbing the bruises on my ribs. Spencer was right though, nothing appeared broken. "But if I ever see those three again, they'll be sorry. They won't jump me next time."

"What about reporting it to the local bobbies. You won't get your wallet back, but you can give them a description of the goons."

"A seaman mugged in an alley for his wallet? I think the police will say they've better use for their time." I shook my head with resignation, and immediately regretted it as a wave of pain hammered through. "I should have called a taxi, but I felt like a walk, stupid I know."

"Where were you heading? I'd be happy to give you a lift. Or would you rather go back to the ship?"

Go back to the ship! Like a whipped cur with its tail between its legs! It occurred to me that the three goons might have been sent by Ling to dissuade me from contacting Mr Khoo. Perhaps they were watching me even now, from the safety of an upper floor window in one of the godowns. Well, I'd be dammed if I'd give in to a few bruised ribs, and a bump on the head.

"I was on my way to the Telegraph Office to wire my chairman for instructions about one of the cargo shipments." I gingerly rubbed the lump on my skull. "This isn't going to stop me. After that, well I'll see."

"Right you are, old boy," said Spencer, climbing into the back seat beside me and tapping the driver, a smiling, heavily bearded Sikh sporting an orange turban, on the shoulder.

"Telegraph Office."

"*Atcha, sahib*," replied the Sikh, bobbing his head from side to side while engaging the clutch. Blowing the horn to clear a passage, he nosed the taxi the final yards down Taiping Road, and turned left into Broadway.

I leaned back in my seat feeling the pain in my skull subside into a dull ache. My chest felt sore, and I knew I'd have some nasty looking bruises, but I was thankful there were no broken ribs. It seemed that Major Spencer had indeed arrived just in time to save me from a serious kicking, or worse. The more I thought about it, the less it seemed like an opportunistic mugging. The third man waiting, hidden in the crowd until my back was turned, strongly suggested otherwise. And if they were waiting for me, then the finger seemed to point at Ling. Because no one else, apart from Lowther, knew I was going ashore.

As the taxi approached the junction between Broadway, Seward and Tiendong Roads, the heavy traffic became a swirling chaos of cars, buses, rickshaws and bicycles, all vying for position with the trams, as they converged on Garden Bridge. I flinched as the Sikh narrowly missed an oncoming tram, and squeezed the taxi into the tightest of spaces in the merging stream of traffic. To the left the tall, white pyramid of Broadway Mansions slid past the window, as I wondered what was so special about the tea. If Mr Tung was too ill to collect it himself, then surely Mr Khoo would authorise it to be released to his clerk? So why Ling's urgency? Something about it smelled fishy.

Soochow Creek didn't smell much better as we rumbled over Garden Bridge, between its camel humped, steel latticework arches. Beneath the bridge, the creek was so crowded with sampans and lighters that it was almost possible to walk from one side to the other. Crossing onto the northern bank, we passed the Public Garden. On our right was the stately rank of the Bund's neo-classical buildings. The commercial heart of the International Settlement, with its shipping company offices, hotels and banks, bearing the familiar names of Glen Line, Jardine Matheson, the Cathay Hotel, China Merchants and the Hong Kong and Shanghai Bank. On the left were the lines of steamer and ferry wharves, thronging with people.

"So, have you any idea why those men attacked you?" said Spencer, uttering the first words he had spoken since ordering the driver to proceed to the Telegraph Office.

"I've been thinking about that," I replied. "If it wasn't just a random robbery, if their intention really was to thrash me, then there has to be a reason. If they were lying in wait for me, then it means someone knew I would be going ashore. And the only person who knew, apart from the chief mate, was Ling, Mr Tung's clerk."

"Ling, Tung. Who are they?" asked Spencer.

"Tung is a friend of Mr Khoo, the line's chairman. Ling says he's Tung's clerk. Mr Khoo consigned Tung a shipment of tea, which I'm to deliver personally. But Ling tells me Tung's indisposed and can't come to the ship himself, but that he's authorised to accept it in his place. I told him I needed confirmation from Mr Khoo, and that I'd wire for instructions. I was on my way to do that when I was attacked."

"Tea!" said Spencer, chuckling. "To China! Your Mr Khoo has a sense of humour."

"Exactly my reaction when he told me about it. But it's Darjeeling, which, apparently, is hard to come by in Shanghai."

"Quite possibly, I'm no expert on tea. In Australia, we brew it in a billy, a handful of leaves and a big pinch of sugar brewed up over a fire, and stirred with a gum twig. The scent of wood smoke and eucalyptus. Nothing like it, especially with a shot of rum on a cold morning. But you said the tea was consigned to a Mr Tung?"

"Yes, what of it?"

Spencer pointed to a newspaper lying on the seat between us. "Tung's a common enough name in Shanghai, but there's a report in there of a Tung being found shot dead yesterday."

"It might be just a coincidence," I said, although I had learned long ago to be very wary of things that looked like coincidence, "but he'd certainly be indisposed if it wasn't, and that might be a good reason to stop me going ashore. Looks like the sooner I get the cable away to Mr Khoo, the better."

The taxi had just passed Canton Road, with its grimy sugar warehouses, hardware stores and curio bazaar, and was abeam of the ornate facade of the Shanghai Club — baroque I'd heard someone call it — that reminded me of the swanky hotels in London's West End. The Telegraph Office was just around the corner, and, right on cue, the Sikh braked and slewed the taxi across the path of an oncoming truck, which blew a long protest on its horn and received a bellow of abuse in Urdu in reply.

"These coolies cannot drive, sahib," exclaimed the Sikh as he pulled the car into a tight U-turn, and stopped outside the Telegraph Office. I swung open the door. Spencer reached inside his jacket, pulled out a clip of notes, and handed one to the driver.

"I'll tell you what. You send your cable and I'll wait here for you. Then we can walk round the corner to the Shanghai Club for lunch, before you go back to the ship."

I muttered my acceptance, and disappeared into the grand edifice.

Twenty minutes later, we stepped through the imposing entrance to the Shanghai Club, and were intercepted by a liveried concierge who eyed us suspiciously. After a few discreet words from Major Spencer, however, he disappeared into his office to make a telephone call, and a few moments later the Club's duty manager appeared, obsequiously welcoming the major as an honorary member, and myself as an honoured guest.

"I've never set foot in here before," I said, trying not to appear impressed.

"Neither have I. But I have some influential friends," Spencer replied, a wry smile creasing his lips as he lead the way up the white Italian marble staircase to the Long Bar.

"Would these be some of the same friends you mentioned to me before?" I said, wondering just how much pull the major really had.

"Quite possibly."

At the top of the staircase, we encountered a pair of swinging doors, one of which was hauled open by a white jacketed flunky, and I followed Spencer into the room containing the famous Long Bar, over 100 feet long, topped with marble, stretching along the far wall. Its L-shaped section providing a vantage point, from which members could watch over the activities on the Bund through the adjacent window. It was lunchtime, and the bar was crowded. There was a smattering of uniforms, naval officers in tropical white, and army officers in summer weight khaki. The room was buzzing with alcohol-lubricated conversation, and thick with the smell of cigar and pipe tobacco. It was also a European male preserve, a sign behind the bar a reminder that no Chinese or women were allowed within its hallowed sanctum.

Spencer led the way to a less congested part of the counter, about half way down from the L-shaped end.

"I'm told there's a pecking order here. That end," he jerked his thumb at the L-shape, "is for the Taipans. The other end is for the box-wallahs. That places you and me somewhere in the middle. What will you have?"

I had removed my hat and was gingerly rubbing the back of my head. The swelling had started to subside, but it still ached.

"A stiff shot of anaesthetic, if you ask me," continued Spencer, grinning. He turned to the hovering barman and called out, "Two burra-pegs with a dash of iced water."

"Here's mud in your eye, Captain," he said, when the drinks arrived, taking a long, satisfying swallow. "Now, here's a question for you. Why is it called the Long Bar?"

I shook my head, and groaned ruefully, being rewarded with another dull wave of pain.

"Well I'm told that if you lay your cheek at one end, and look along the bar to the other end ... you can see the curvature of the earth." He laughed heartily at the joke and I joined in, despite the heaving of my chest aggravating the bruised ribs.

Spencer drained his glass. "Let's have another, and then head upstairs for tiffin."

An hour later, and we were finishing the last of a splendid curry lunch, served in the third floor dining room. Spencer had asked for a table in a secluded corner, where a potted palm provided some privacy. Despite the pain of my bruises, the two large whiskies had stimulated my appetite, and I ate the hot, peppery curry with relish. Spencer watched me scoop up the final mouthful.

"For a man who was having the stuffing kicked out him a few hours ago, you seem remarkably sanguine, Captain."

"Aye, well I've copped a few beatings in my time ... and handed out as many. A man can live quite happily with a few bruises. But if I get my hands on those goons things might not end quite so happily for them."

As I spoke, I heard a bell tinkle and glanced round to see a waiter weaving his way between the tables holding up a message board, and shaking a small brass hand bell.

"Looks like you've got the answer to your cable," observed Spencer, pointing to the message board, which had my name chalked on it.

I glanced at my wristwatch, made a mental calculation and my brows creased into a frown. "That was quick." I raised my arm to summon the waiter, ripped open the buff envelope, and quickly scanned the single sentence.

Which raised more questions than it answered.

"Perhaps you can explain that," I snapped, angrily flicking the telegram onto the table in front of Spencer.

Who calmly picked it up and read the brief message. "TUNG DEAD STOP RELEASE TEA TO INSTRUCTIONS MAJOR SPENCER STOP KHOO." Not what you expected Captain?"

"You know damned well it isn't. I think I'm being played for a fool, Major and I don't like it. I didn't say anything about Tung being dead, so how could Mr Khoo have known. And he wants me to release the tea to *you*. What would *you* want with a cargo of tea? I'm guessing there's a connection behind all this." I glared at him, restraining myself from smacking the knowing smirk off his face, but stabbing a finger into his chest. "And you know something about it."

Spencer ignored the jabbing finger, pulled his chair closer to the table, and leaned forward lowering his voice. "Sorry for keeping you in the dark, Captain Rowden. Sometimes it's better not to know too much, but circumstances appear to have worked against us." He dropped his voice to a murmur. "I'm afraid it's not tea that you're carrying for Mr Khoo, its opium."

"OPIUM!" I almost choked on the word.

"Keep your voice down," he hissed, "we don't want to attract attention."

"I've just unwittingly smuggled a cargo of — *tea* — into Shanghai, and you knew all about it," I growled. "You owe me an explanation, Major, and it had better be a bloody good one."

The corners of Spencer's mouth creased into an enigmatic smile, and he pressed his palms together and gazed at me, infuriatingly calm, as if assessing the trustworthiness of an inquisitive schoolboy asking to play with the grownups.

"I told you I was travelling to Shanghai to assess the strength of the Chinese opposition to Japan, and the possible reaction from the Japs. Well things are a bit more advanced than that. Our intelligence suggests that the Japs are close to launching an invasion of central China. The question is, how much strength Chiang Kai-shek's Nationalists can muster to resist them. More importantly, as far as Shanghai is concerned, what support can we rely on to prevent the Japs seizing the whole of the city, including the International Settlement?"

I shook my head with frustration, the stab of pain fuelling my anger. "So, things are moving faster than your masters in Whitehall would like. But what the hell's that got to do with me, and a smuggled cargo of ..." I left the sentence unfinished.

"You might not have noticed it, Captain, but our hold out here is pretty precarious. If the Japs wanted the International Settlement, then there's precious little we can do to stop them. Short of hoping the Chinese will defend it. But what's their incentive, love of King George?"

I doubted Chiang Kai-shek, or anyone else in China, gave a tinker's damn for King George and his, so called, Empire. But peddling influence was something the British had excelled at for centuries. "So the opium is a bribe to buy the loyalty of some local warlord, and ensure his troops fight to protect our interests in Shanghai," I said. I'd paid plenty of bribes in my time, so I was in no position to point any fingers, and much as I hated to admit it, Spencer was starting to make sense.

"I wouldn't have put it quite so crudely," he said. "The Nationalists have some good generals, and troops who can give the Japs a run for their money. On the other hand, we don't have anything to stop them with. So it's worth strengthening any potential friendships, wouldn't you say?"

"Your circle of friends seems to be growing," I said, wondering just how close the connection was between Spencer, Khoo and the unfortunate Tung. "So, Tung was the conduit to ensure the ... tea got into the right hands. I'm guessing that someone got wind of it, and killed him in order to get their own hands on it first. With Tung dead, Mr Khoo, or whoever is really behind the shipment, trusts you to do the job instead?"

"Correct, on all counts," replied Spencer, grinning. "For a sailor you catch on real quick."

I let that go, but the look of thunder on my face wiped the grin off his lips, and he continued in a more respectful tone.

"My guess is that whoever this Ling is, he's not working for Tung, but for whoever had Tung killed. You did well to stop him from getting the tea. Perhaps he thought with you out of the way he'd have more luck persuading your chief mate to hand it over. Unlike Tung however, I don't know who the intended recipient was, nor, I suspect, does Mr Khoo. But there are some people I think will be able to help."

"More friends of yours?"

"Not exactly, but there are some Chinese who've done very well out of the International Settlement, and who might be more inclined to see it continue in its current form, than fall under the unpredictable control of the Japanese."

"Better the white devil you know, eh?"

"Something like that," replied Spencer.

I looked at him quizzically, "You were taking a bit of a risk though, using my ship to smuggle opium, and then telling me about it. What's to stop me reporting it to the authorities? Or seizing it and selling it myself?"

"A calculated gamble," replied Spencer, his lips compressed into a thin, hard smile. "You'd make some more enemies. Maybe that wouldn't worry you, but after your experiences in Wewak and Lorengau, you might be in need of a friend at some point in the future."

I was still furious, and not a little disappointed that Mr Khoo hadn't trusted me enough to let me in on the secret. But, as Spencer had said and I knew from bitter experience, sometimes it was better not to know. Even though he'd mislead me, I knew it would be a mistake to make an enemy of Khoo, and apart from that I had a genuine liking for the old man. Which was a lot more than I could say about Spencer. I had the feeling his friendship would extend only as far as he found it, or me, useful. "I can take care of myself," I growled. "I'm not sure I need your kind of friendship."

"You seemed to need it when I found you being used for football practise."

I snorted in annoyance; there was no answer to that. They'd had me cold. But it wouldn't happen again.

Spencer glanced down at his wristwatch. "I think we've done justice to lunch. Now I suggest you get back to your ship, and let someone check out those bruises, while I follow Mr Khoo's instructions and find out who should receive the tea. Do you know the Great World, Captain?"

"The nightclub in the French Concession, yes." I knew it all right. Owned by a bent copper, and home to every vice and gangster in Shanghai. Cramp had accurately described it to McGrath, and for those who could afford it, it offered the most fun you could have in Shanghai, with or without your trousers on.

"Well let's meet there this evening at 10 o'clock. After what happened this morning, I suggest you bring a couple of reliable companions. A few sailors visiting a nightclub looking for some attractive company shouldn't raise too much suspicion."

"Here," he pushed a handful of notes into my hand. "I'll leave you to settle the bill, and there's enough there to pay for the taxi back to the ship. At ten o'clock then, good luck."

He held out his hand and I shook it grudgingly, feeling a bit like Judas must have felt when he'd sold his soul for thirty pieces of silver. For the price of a meal and a taxi back to my ship, I had somehow become one of Major Spencer's pawns in a game where I didn't know most of the other players, and on a board the size of which I could only guess at.

CHAPTER THIRTEEN

I could see that young McGrath was mesmerised by the passing parade of stunningly beautiful women, the Chinese girls wearing brightly coloured, exotically decorated cheongsams that, as Cramp had promised, were slit up the side almost as far as the waist. He was sitting between Cramp and me at a small table on the third floor of the Great World, watching the cabaret of Chinese acrobats and jugglers. The surrounding tables were occupied by a polyglot mixture of European, Chinese and Eurasian men and women, whose attention was half focused on the cabaret, and half on extravagantly and conspicuously enjoying themselves. Quaffing champagne, vodka and scotch, and smoking expensive cigars and exotic looking cigarettes. Weaving in between the tables were the sing-song girls, prepared to sit and flirt for the price of a drink, and the promise of more to those who could afford them. I had ordered beers for us, and three large, frosted, foaming glasses had been delivered by a short-skirted waitress who fussed over me, trying to size up the tip I might be good for, while casting a sly wink at McGrath.

By now, Ling would have realised his first attempt to persuade me to part with Tung's cargo of opium had failed. Knowing the value of it in Shanghai, I had no doubt that he, or whoever was behind him, would not take it lying down. I also wondered at the rashness of Mr Khoo's attempt to smuggle opium into Shanghai, risking his ship, and me, in order to do it. The fact he had kept it secret from me spoke volumes for how dangerous the political situation in China had become. Although the sensitive noses of the customs' service had been suspiciously absent, despite word of the smuggled shipment having leaked into the wrong ears, which suggested, as Spencer had hinted, that the authorities were turning a blind eye. Which still left me with the task of handing it safely over to whomever Spencer decided would direct it to the right quarter.

It also crossed my mind that the notorious night club was an unusual place to transact the transfer, as it was the haunt of a number of well-known gangsters and racketeers who would be keen to get their own hands on it. On the other hand, it was so well known to the authorities, it was not uncommon to see high-ranking officials rubbing shoulders with underworld figures, that there was unlikely to be a repeat of the earlier strong-arm tactics. Nevertheless, I had taken Spencer's advice, and between Cramp, McGrath and myself we packed sufficient punch to deal with several times our number. I had also strapped on the Webley for extra firepower.

I had entrusted McGrath with the briefcase containing the bill of lading, and he sat with it on his lap as the taxi took us through the roar and bustle of the mid-evening traffic along Broadway, over Garden Bridge and south along the Bund towards Avenue Edward VII. Cramp and I had seen it all before, but McGrath was wide eyed at the splendid buildings and bright lights of the Bund. Avenue Edward VII marked the border with the French Concession, and the taxi turned sharply right and followed the sweeping curves of the wide, plane tree lined avenue until it reached the corner with Boulevard de Montigny, facing which was the wedding cake spire atop the baroque facade of the five-storey building that was the Great World.

Once inside, I lead the way upstairs to the third floor, and asked for a table for four to await an expected guest. The room was packed, but a flash of gold into the palm of the gloomy usher bought an insincere smile, and a small but adequate table with a reasonable view of the stage. Cramp was grinning at McGrath's trance like staring, and nudged his arm.

"No need to make it so obvious, Third, you'll be drooling soon."

"Sorry Chippy, it's just that I've never seen anywhere like this place before."

"Yeah, it's different, that's for sure," replied Cramp. "You can get any pleasure known to man in 'ere. Girls, boys, girls and boys, booze, 'ashish, hopium. Whatever you fancy you'll find it 'ere."

"I think I'll stick to beer and just watch the passing parade," replied McGrath, grinning. He raised his glass. "Cheers sir, thanks for the drink." He gestured towards the empty chair. "Who are we expecting, sir?"

"Not expecting any trouble are we, skipper?" said Cramp, before I had time to answer.

"I'm expecting Major Spencer," I replied. "And no, I don't think we're likely to run into any trouble. Bit too public for the likes of those goons who jumped me earlier. But keep your wits about you anyway." Which, for a couple of love-starved sailors, might have proved easier said than done. The crowded cabaret had a thick, intoxicating aroma of cigar and cigarette smoke, expensive perfumes, beer, sweat and the sickly, tantalising smell of hashish. Not to mention the abundance of exotically beautiful women of all colours and sizes. I decided it might be best to take them into my confidence, at least partly, just to keep their minds focussed.

"Look, you two. I'd better explain—"

"Good evening, Captain." The colonial twang confirmed that the voice belonged to Major Spencer, despite the dandified appearance he presented in a white dinner jacket and black bow tie. "Mind if I join you?" He dropped into the vacant seat without waiting for an answer, and raised a hand to attract the attention of a waiter.

"Whisky and water, large one," he ordered. "Any of you fellows ready for another drink?"

I watched McGrath hesitate. "Go on, Third. I think His Majesty's government might be paying for this one."

Clearly impressed by the newcomer's appearance, the waiter bustled off and quickly returned with the drinks, placed them on the table with a flourish, and then slapped down a large plate laden with spring rolls, dim sums and other less easily identifiable delicacies, including some that looked suspiciously like chickens' feet. He almost grovelled as Spencer handed him a large note and told him to keep the change.

"So, what do you think of the Great World?" he continued, nodding his chin in the direction of McGrath.

"Just another brothel, gin palace and music hall if you ask me," I growled, before he had time to reply. "A good place for a sailor to lose his money to a girl, lose his head to drink, and wake up aboard some stinking tub bound for goodness knows where."

"I can't think that's ever happened to you, skipper," chuckled Cramp.

"No, but I've known captains who were quite happy to use the services of the crimps when they were shorthanded. Sometimes a man needs a knock over the head to realise what's good for him. But we didn't have to Shanghai you, did we, Third?"

McGrath swallowed a mouthful of spring roll and shook his head. "But surely the crimps don't operate in a place like this, it looks too—"

"Respectable?" interjected Spencer. "That depends on how you look at it. The owner of this place is Wang Jinrong, one time senior Chinese detective in the French Concession police force. You'll find drug dealers, gangsters, warlords, prostitutes and all manner of shady characters in here, present company excepted of course, but you're unlikely to get rolled or knocked on the head."

"That's reassuring," replied McGrath, spitting tiny chicken bones into a napkin. "But how did a high ranking policeman end up owning a place like this."

"Wang's as sharp as a bag of razor blades and bent as a kangaroo's hind leg," replied Spencer. "And he married a very clever woman called Lin Guisheng who had connections with the local triads, and one in particular, an up and coming hood called Du Yuesheng. The three of them managed to seize control of the local opium trade. At one time they ran a gang that snatched opium straight off the docks, and sneaked it into Wang's home by a back entrance. The profits bought him a variety of nightclubs including the Great World, and enabled Du to become head of the Green Gang, the biggest triad in Shanghai."

"I think I begin to understand why Mr Khoo ordered me to take your advice regarding our cargo of ... tea," I said, impressed with his knowledge of the Shanghai underworld. "So who are we here to meet?"

My question went unanswered as Spencer's gaze turned towards something behind my shoulder. "There's the very lovely Lady Ashworth," he said, "and if I'm not mistaken that burly, Tartar looking gentleman is General Maslennikov, the Soviet military attaché in Shanghai, and her paramour."

I swivelled around in my seat to get a better view. Lady Ashworth was, indeed, standing in the doorway to the cabaret. She looked stunning in a pale, shimmering green silk evening gown that set off her long auburn hair. Mine was not the only head that turned in her direction, like sunflowers attracted by the dazzling light of the sun. Beside her tall and willowy figure, the short, stocky man that Spencer had identified as Maslennikov, made a stark contrast. His hair was cropped short over a head that was almost a square-sided dome. His eyes were narrow and shaded under the overhang of his brow. His cheekbones and nose were wide, and below them a sensuous, thick-lipped mouth was clamped shut, the corners turned down in a permanent scowl.

"Nasty looking customer, isn't he?" said Spencer, echoing my thoughts exactly. "One of Beria's handpicked henchmen."

"Beria?"

"Head of the NKVD, the Soviet internal security service."

Maslennikov was obviously a regular, or a big tipper, as the gloomy usher had transformed into a beaming model of fawning servility, and was leading the pair towards a table with a prime position on the far side of the stage. Their path brought them close to our table. I noticed that Lady Ashworth was gripping Maslennikov's arm, and had her eyes defensively lowered, as if reluctant to meet anyone prepared to greet her. Spencer, however, had no hesitation and rose boldly from his chair as they passed by.

"Lady Ashworth, good evening," he said. "How nice to see you again."

For a moment, I glimpsed the startled look in her eyes, then she regained her composure and broke into a broad smile of recognition.

"Major Spencer, Captain Rowden and Mr McGrath. I'm afraid I don't know the other gentleman."

I introduced Cramp, who gingerly took the offered hand and gently shook it, clearly overawed by the glamorous Lady Ashworth, if not by her lowering, Russian companion.

"Gentlemen, it is so nice to see you. May I introduce you to my good friend and Russian patriot, General Maslennikov?" The general's eyes flashed like daggers, but he extended a stiff bow.

"Ivan, this is Captain Rowden, master of the ship in which I travelled back to Shanghai. Mr McGrath and Mr Cramp are two of the officers, and Major Spencer was a fellow passenger." She paused while we shook the general's hand. Surprisingly, for such a powerful looking man, his handshake was soft and limp, almost effeminate. But I knew better than to mistake it for weakness. The formal smile that creased his lips did not extend to the fish-cold eyes, and I knew he was a man who would delight in making his enemies suffer.

"Well, I see you have found your way to the Great World," continued Lady Ashworth, "our Shanghailanders' answer to the Folies Bergère." Then, noticing the perplexed look on McGrath's face, "Ah, you have not been to Paris, Mr McGrath. Well don't worry. Let me assure you that the Great World is much more amusing."

"A pleasure to meet you all, gentlemen," interrupted Maslennikov, whose menacingly soft voice reinforced the warning of his handshake. "I hear you suffered somet'ing of an unfortunate accident dis morning, Captain Rowden. De streets of Shanghai can be so dangerous. I do hope you ver not hurt?" His English was correct, but heavily accented.

"You are well informed, general," I replied, wondering how he had come by the information, and trying to keep the surprise out of my voice. "Just a clumsy attempt at robbery. Fortunately, Major Spencer was close at hand, and I suffered only the loss of my wallet and a little pride. But I'm keeping my eyes peeled in case there's a chance of a return match."

"I can see dat you are not a man to be, how you say in English, trifled vith, da? But I vish you luck. In dis city such men have plenty of places to disappear. And de police ..." He shrugged his shoulders, "But perhaps some people have nothing to lose but deir chains." He paused, smiling at his own joke, and then said a few quiet words in Russian to Lady Ashworth.

"Of course, my dear," she patted his arm reassuringly. "Captain Rowden, gentlemen, if you will please excuse us, we have guests waiting," she waved an arm in the direction of the far side of the cabaret. "I do hope you enjoy your evening, and please give my regards to Lord Lowther and Mr Griffith."

She reached for Maslennikov's arm. He flicked a hand in a dismissive salute, and led her away between the tables.

"Evil looking brute, don't you think," said Spencer, when they were safely out of earshot. "I hope she knows what she's doing."

"She looked as if she was a bit afraid of him," said McGrath, voicing my own fears. I had noticed some marks on her upper arm that looked as if they were bruises caused by fingers with a very strong grip. And underneath the expertly applied makeup one of her eyes looked a shade darker than the other.

"But what did he mean about people having nothing to lose but their chains?" he continued.

"He was quoting Marx, the man whose ideas inspired the Russian communists," replied Spencer. "I think he was making an unflattering reference to Shanghai. In communist terms the Chinese are the oppressed masses, and the Europeans who run the city are the capitalist oppressors. As a representative of that class he's implying that the captain deserved to have his wallet stolen."

There was an explosion of muffled laughter from Cramp. "I know a few tea leaves back in the big smoke who'd be quite 'appy to say the same." The black look I shot him did nothing to wipe the broad grin off his gypsy face.

Spencer raised his hand to get our attention, and then checked his wristwatch. "It's time we attended to our business, Captain. Do you have the bill of lading?"

I pointed to the briefcase in front of McGrath.

"Right, well we have an appointment to see Mr Wang and Mr Du, the enterprising gentlemen I told you about earlier." We all rose to follow him, but he waved at Cramp and McGrath to sit down, and flicked a large denomination note onto the table. "It'll just be your captain and me, but you can finish the food, and order yourselves some more drinks while waiting for our return."

Cramp flashed me a questioning glance. I patted the bulge under my armpit, and he nodded.

I followed Spencer as he threaded his way between the tables to the rear entrance to the cabaret. We passed close to Maslennikov's table, where some grim looking Europeans in ill-fitting suits had joined him and Lady Ashworth. The men were engaged in deep conversation, all heavily smoking cigarettes that, from the acrid smell, I guessed were Russia's cheapest brand of Belomorkanal. Lady Ashworth's pink Sobranie looked as out of place as she did among that group of unprepossessing men, but she seemed to be listening to them intently, and paid no attention to Spencer and me as we passed.

Then we were out in the corridor, and confronted by a tough looking Chinese thug in a dinner jacket

* * *

I found it hard to believe that Wang's office was contained within the same raucous, roaring building as the Great World. Once the padded, thick wooden door had closed behind us, shutting out the music and laughter, the office was as quiet as Mile End's, Bow Cemetery. There were no windows, the walls were clad with floor to ceiling

Chinese tapestries, and green shaded electric lamps provided pools of light over the huge, ornately carved mahogany desk that dominated the room. Opposite the desk were three leather armchairs for guests, although I imagined less welcome visitors were not invited to use them. Against the wall behind the desk was a fret carved, rosewood bookcase and drinks' cabinet. A leather bound blotter, an antique jade pen and inkstand, and a silver framed photograph were the only ornaments on the mirror-polished surface of the desktop. The photograph showed a younger version of the man sitting behind it, dressed in formal Chinese costume, and standing beside a calmly frowning, and equally formally dressed young woman.

Wang introduced himself as the owner of the Great World, and from Spencer's earlier description, I guessed the woman in the photograph was his spousal partner in crime, Lin Guisheng. A life of crime had certainly paid dividends, thus far at least, because the older version of Wang sitting behind the desk was large, plump and pampered. He was extravagantly dressed in a high-collared robe of dark blue silk, decorated with gold embroidered Chinese lions and dragons, and a blue silk skullcap, from which a golden tassel dangled, topped his moon-shaped, pockmarked face. A gold-foiled, filter-tipped cigarette hung from his scowling lips. Having motioned us to sit down, he reached into a desk drawer and produced an ivory cigarette box, and a cut crystal ashtray that he carefully placed on the desk in front of us.

At a discrete click of his fingers, an exquisitely beautiful young woman emerged from the shadows, lit our cigarettes and poured drinks, before sashaying out of the padded door.

I had met a few well-heeled gangsters in my time, but few who oozed as much richly disguised danger as Wang, and I glanced at Spencer, impressed by the calmly inscrutable way in which he was sipping at the expensive whisky, and discretely trickling exhaled smoke through his nostrils.

"Well gentlemen, I trust everything to your satisfaction?"

The man sitting in the third armchair broke the short silence. If Wang exuded the aura of a gangster, then this man was the physical embodiment of one. His sallow, ugly, angular face was hardly improved by a thick-lipped mouth and large protruding ears, exaggerated by his short-cropped black hair. An expensive double-breasted black dinner suit hung about his cadaverous frame, and bony hairy wrists protruded from starched white shirt cuffs, on which enormous gold cuff links glinted ostentatiously. He was exactly as I imagined an Atlantic City bootlegger might look, even down to the white spats over the gleaming patent leather boots, with the exception of being Chinese. I had noted the body language between the two men when Wang had introduced him, and it was quite clear that, despite Wang being the senior of their criminal partnership, as well as the owner of the office in which we sat, it was Du, as the head of the Green Gang, who was the dominant one.

Even with their reputations and connections to protect them, I was surprised at the ease with which we had been admitted to Wang's sanctum. I still had the Webley tucked reassuringly under my armpit. But even without it I was sure the out of condition Wang, and the perilously thin Du would put up little resistance if we wanted to do them harm. They were obviously satisfied that our intentions were peaceful, or that we knew full well that lifting a finger against either of them would result in a slow and painful death sentence.

"Yes, thank you, Mr Du," replied Spencer, maintaining an air of perfect calm. "And thank you both for sparing some time to meet with Captain Rowden and myself."

"Our time of no consequence," replied Wang, stubbing his cigarette into the ashtray and raising his hands, palms upwards, "if a question of business." He turned towards me. "I understand it a matter of a certain cargo ... of tea, Captain Rowden?"

"That's correct, Mr Wang," I replied, unsure how much, if anything, Spencer had already told him.

"Major Spencer has told us a little," replied Wang, reading my thoughts. "But perhaps you will be kind enough to tell us full story?"

There was the hint of a smile on Wang's face as he listened to me recount my interview with Mr Khoo, and his instructions regarding the consignment to Tung of what he had told me was a cargo of Darjeeling tea. The smile faded when I described the visit by Ling claiming the cargo on Tung's behalf, the thwarted attack by his goons, the news of Tung's death, and Mr Khoo's subsequently telegraphed instructions to accept the advice of Major Spencer.

"Ah yes, an unfortunate business," said Wang, as I finished my tale. "But I assume you know real nature of cargo, Captain Rowden, and intended purpose?"

"I do, now," I said, shooting a glance at Spencer. "And I guess that Mr Tung was killed by those who would prevent it?"

"Just so, Captain," replied Wang. "Our country torn between those loyal to Nationalist government, led by incomparable General Chiang Kai-shek, renegade communists of Mao Tse-tung, and hateful Japanese invaders and their warlord puppets. One of whom is General Han who controls province of Shangtung, north of the Yangtse River. I think he responsible for death of Mr Tung, and attack on your good self."

He paused to light another gold tipped cigarette, the exhaled smoke from which coiled up into the overhanging green lampshade. Then a sly grin appeared on his pockmarked face. "But tell me, Captain Rowden, is it not ironical that British Empire, mightiest the world has ever known, resorts to smuggling opium into China to encourage us to fight against Japanese ... and protect interests in Shanghai?"

There was more than a hint of a sneer in the final sentence, and I wondered if he was trying to provoke a reaction. Personally, I agreed with him, and I could hardly pretend offence, having previously smuggled cargoes equally offensive to moralist sensitivities. Instead, I wondered how Spencer, who directly represented the mighty, but double-dealing Empire, would take the slight. His face had flushed and his pale blue eyes had turned hard, but the lip below the sandy moustache remained phlegmatically stiff as he replied.

"I would prefer to think we are strengthening the bonds of friendship between those with a common interest. A Japanese invasion threatens both China and Britain. Sadly Britain is not in a position, just at the moment, to directly oppose Japan, but it is able to offer assistance to those who can."

"Ah yes, by supplying commodity which, though lucrative, causes degradation and death of thousands," replied Du, the first time he had spoken since inquiring if we were enjoying our drinks. Despite the almost over exaggerated gravity of his words, I could see the devilish twinkle in his eyes, to which the pirate in me felt the urge to respond.

"That seems a bit hypocritical coming from—"

"We're all friends here, Captain," interrupted Spencer, not convinced by the levity of my tone, and forcibly placing a hand on my arm. "Your instructions were to take my advice on the matter of the cargo. Mr Du is both a strong supporter of the Nationalist government, and a *very* good friend of General Chiang, who appointed him head of the Chinese Opium Suppression Board." He paused to let the meaning of his words sink in, and then, seeing my face, quickly continued in case I should burst out laughing and cause Du to lose face. "He's also very well connected in Shanghai, and I'm sure he knows just how to obtain the best advantage out of the proceeds of the cargo. So I strongly advise you to release it to him."

"Hypocrisy something not unknown to you British," continued Du, the glint in his eye betraying his own amusement at the incongruity of the British government offering a fortune in opium to the Shanghai gangster in charge of suppressing opium use in China. Then the glint faded and the corners of his mouth twisted into a pained grimace. "But I remind you that even though we play host to friends in International Settlement, the rest of the city, and majority of population, Chinese. We no need big encouragement to defend ourselves, only are weak compared to Japanese. Fortunately, some among communists and warlords might be persuaded make common cause against even more unwelcome invader. So for that purpose I happy take your cargo, Captain Rowden." He paused, allowing his lips to relax and the glint to return to his eyes. "And then, from one hypocrite to another, I can offer some advice. Japanese troops massing in the north. It wise to complete your business and depart before they interfere with traffic on the rivers. Secondly, General Han not take kindly to his plans being thwarted, he might seek revenge."

I didn't know whether to be offended or flattered by Du's comparison of our motives. There was something in his smug, sneering delivery that grated on me, and

I had seen the misery opium caused the unfortunates addicted to it, chasing oblivion in the dragon of its smoke. But moral judgments were a nicety few of us could afford in the increasingly dangerous world of the Far East. In any case I could hardly refuse to hand over the opium without making an enemy of Mr Khoo, and earning the displeasure of His Majesty's government in the person of Major Spencer. My survival instincts told me I could expect as little sympathy from them as from General Han, and that Du's warning was well intentioned. What it boiled down to was that I didn't really have any other choice.

"My apologies gentlemen, I'm afraid my knowledge of the political situation is limited." I turned to address Du directly. "But if Major Spencer believes you are the right man to assist whatever cause Mr Khoo had in mind, then I am happy to release his cargo to you."

"A wise decision, Captain Rowden, but I think you do yourself injustice," said Du, not for a moment buying my profession of innocence. "Your reputation well known along this coast as one who knows that pearls don't lie on beach, and who deliver what he promise to deliver, without asking too many questions." He glanced at the briefcase in my lap. "I believe you have bill of lading with you. If you happy to sign and release it, I will send my man to collect cases when you ready. I have complete confidence that nothing will happen to them in meantime."

The words could as easily have been a threat, and I felt my cheeks colour, but managed to maintain a smile as I extracted the bill from the briefcase. I spread the paper out on the polished mahogany of his desktop and Wang waggled a finger towards the pen in the jade inkstand. They watched as I carefully dipped the nib, and scrawled my signature across the bottom, before sanding it from the shaker. When the ink was dry, Du reached for the bill, tapped the sand into the ashtray and folded the paper into his pocket. At a nod from him, Wang opened a drawer and extracted a document that he slid across the desk to me. It was a banker's draft for the freight and price of the tea, a paltry sum in comparison with the real value of the opium sealed inside those lead-foil lined tea chests, drawn in favour of Mr Khoo.

"I think you will find all in order Captain, but feel free to wire details to Mr Khoo if you need verification."

"I'm sure that won't be necessary," I replied, folding the draft and placing it securely inside the briefcase.

"Well," said Spencer, rubbing his hands together, "if that's settled, I think we should get out of your hair and re-join our colleagues at the cabaret for a celebratory drink." He rose and stretched out his hand. "Thank you both for your time. My friends in London appreciate it, and won't forget what you've done."

"I hope their friendship prove of value to us in coming days, whose dark shadows already cast before them," replied Du. "But all help in face of common enemy is welcome."

I pushed myself up out of the armchair.

"Before you go, Captain," continued Du, holding up a hand to detain me, "we have some information that may be of use to you. The men who attack you. Would you like to know where to find them?"

"Too bloody right I would," I growled in eager anticipation. "We have some unfinished business, only this time I'm better prepared."

"Ah yes," replied Wang. "I thought your colleagues look capable men, and had seen bulge under armpit, but felt sure nothing here trouble you enough to need it. What happens in street outside, though, other matter entirely. However, if anything should happen, please it happen sufficiently far north of Avenue Edward VII to be inside British Concession. The French Police just a little too nosy." He tapped his own fleshy nose for emphasis. "I speak with experience, as I think you know."

I nodded, and Wang continued.

"There are mahjong tables on first floor. If look there, sure you will find some gentlemen of interest to you. But please," he held up a warning hand, "no trouble on my premises."

"You have my word," I replied.

"And please convey humble respects to Mr Khoo. We not move in same circles now, but when he younger we had several ... mutual interests. He also a great patriot and a loss to his home city." He reached for my hand. "Now, we shake hands to conclude our arrangement. Then you most welcome continue enjoy what pleasures our humble establishment can offer, or make other business, elsewhere."

* * *

I rolled tipsily north along the left hand side of Thibet Road, my gait and slack faced demeanour the obvious result of a very pleasant and entertaining evening spent at the Great World. Puffing on the cigar I had purchased from a smiling, long legged, cigarette girl as I swayed amongst the mahjong tables, I was tunelessly whistling *On the Sunny Side of the Street*, which I remembered hearing Layton and Johnstone sing on the wireless during my last leave. At one point, I stumbled over an uneven paving stone and nearly fell, only saving myself by dropping a hand to the footpath. The awkward, twisting stumble allowing a glimpse of the three men following me, as they slipped sideways into the shadows, thinking to avoid being seen. To my left a line of big, tall trees lined the edge of the Recreation Ground, in the middle of which were the Shanghai racecourse and cricket club. I paused and leaned against a tree for support, apparently taking several deep breaths in an effort to clear my head. Then I stumbled on deeper into the Recreation Ground to be less visible from the road. Weaving my way among the trees, I looked for one that would provide sufficient cover, and stopped, leaning one hand against the tree for support and fumbling at my trouser buttons with the other.

Certain of their quarry now, the three men pushed forward among the trees, I could hear the snap of twigs and the crunch of footsteps on the dry grass. I span around, eyes wide and mouth gaping in feigned surprise, and heard the soft, menacing laughter as they thought they had me cornered. Despite the shadows under the trees, there was enough light to recognise two of them as the goons that had mugged me earlier that day. The third, the largest of the trio, was tall for a Chinese, and had a thin black moustache. Over his left cheek was a livid, fresh looking scar. I'd seen similar men in the Japanese controlled port of Dairen, and guessed he was a Manchu, from the puppet state of Manchuria. A nasty looking brute, he must have been the man who had hit me from behind, and tap danced on my ribs. The fearful pleading look in my eyes concealed the inner grin as the Manchu advanced, overly confident that the drunken looking captain was in little state to fight back.

I remained slumped against the tree, my head lolled to one side, with one hand in my groin where I appeared to be fumbling to do up my trouser buttons. The Manchu's face split into a wicked grin, displaying gold teeth that glinted dully in the reflected light of a street lamp. He reached into his pocket and produced a knife. There was a soft click, and the wicked looking switchblade sprang out of the handle. He waved it threateningly in front of my eyes.

And then froze in surprise to find himself looking down the barrel of the large pistol that had miraculously appeared in the hand that had previously been between my legs.

With his eyes focused on the hypnotic sight of the big calibre barrel raised menacingly at his face, he failed to notice the iron-hard fist that came out of the darkness and ripped into his midriff. As he doubled forward, his mouth opening in a desperate gasp for air, I turned my wrist and smashed the butt of the gun into his face, feeling teeth shatter and a hot spray of blood from mashed lips. The Manchu went down groaning, and I delivered a hard, vicious kick into the kidneys as he fell. It all happened so fast that the other two remained frozen to the spot in shock. But as I raised the pistol in their direction they edged back, looking for a safe place to run.

"I'd stop right there, if I were you," said a calm, but commanding voice. The goons glanced nervously round. They might not have understood the words, but they understood the pistol levelled at their backs by the tall, dinner jacketed man, and his two burly companions that blocked off their escape.

Two pairs of eyes flickered back in my direction as I clicked on the safety catch and tossed the pistol to McGrath. I had no intention of shooting them and drawing unwelcome attention. The Manchu was still groaning on the ground, nursing his shattered mouth, and I could see he wouldn't be game for much more that evening.

Which still left odds of two to one, well in my favour, even without the pistol. I dropped into a crouch, weight on the balls of my feet, and beckoned with my fingers.

"You wanted a piece of me? Well now's your chance," I was sure that both men were carrying knives, but in the foolishly mistaken belief that I was drunk they had left them in their pockets. The burlier one with the wispy beard was the first to find his courage, and jammed his hand into his pocket, fingers scrabbling for his knife. That was his first mistake. A quick jab to his jaw snapped back his head, hard enough to sting but not enough to knock him down. I backed off to let him regain his balance, and pointed towards his pocket, shaking my head. He understood, fists only, and grunted acknowledgment. Then dropped into a crouch and raised his hands, palms flat, the edges towards me, circling them. I had seen Orientals fight this way before. Chinese Hand they called it, a mixture of chops and punches with the fists, and kicks with the feet. He must have felt his confidence returning, as his lips compressed into a vicious grin, and he started to advance towards me.

And made his second mistake.

I was expecting the kick, and it was fast, the leading knee lifting and snapping the foot upwards towards my groin.

Right into the path of my hands.

I believe in fighting with both feet firmly on the ground, you can balance better that way. But a man with one foot in the air is off balance, especially when that foot is in the strong hands of an opponent who likes to fight dirty. I stepped backwards as I caught his foot, allowing it to lift with the momentum of the kick, and then twisted it savagely, feeling the ankle snap, pulling hard on the fractured bones and hearing the agonised scream. I was still holding the foot as he toppled forward, the broken joint sloppy in my hand. I felt the shattered edges of the bones grating, and dropped the leg, leaving the man whimpering and moaning beside the Manchu.

Which left the third man, skull face, the wiry one who had grinned the whole time the three of them had attacked me in Taiping Road, and who now stood like a cobra mesmerised by a mongoose. He raised his open palms in the universal gesture of no resistance, and I could see the sweat breaking out on his forehead, and smell the fear as I stepped forward, my fists clenched and raised.

I wasn't feeling in the mood to be merciful. It was no more than a short arm jab, but it had my weight behind it, and crunched into the goon's body with the sound of an axe splitting a log. There was a tortured grunt as the breath was driven from his lungs, and then his knees buckled. He would have fallen but for McGrath and Cramp catching him under the armpits.

"That one was for me," I said, grabbing the man's chin to lift his lolling head, watching the fear filled eyes, and the mouth gasping for air like a fish out of water.

"Don't you ever come looking for me again," I whispered menacingly into his ear. "Do you understand?" I grabbed his hair and savagely wrenched his head back for emphasis.

There was a flicker of recognition in the eyes, and I felt the head nod.

"Good, now this one's for Mr Tung."

Out of the corner of my eye, I saw Spencer wince at the fury of the blow that crashed into the man's chest with sufficient force to break several ribs. McGrath and Cramp released their hold, and he dropped like a rag doll, flopping down onto the grass gasping and sobbing.

I didn't know if these goons had killed Mr Tung, as well as attacking me. Perhaps if I had known I might have inflicted more serious damage. Or something more permanent. But for all that Shanghai was a rip roaring town, we were in the British Concession where the writ of law, however imperfectly, still ran. Dead men might not tell tales, but there were enough witnesses to us all having been at the Great World, for the police to put enough together to equal at least four. I seriously doubted these three would want to come for me again after tonight, though, and pulled a large, white handkerchief out of my pocket to wipe the Manchu's blood off my knuckles. Then I held out my hand.

"I'll relieve you of that, thank you, Third," I said, taking the Webley from McGrath and slipping it back into the shoulder holster. "I think that's enough excitement for one night, we've accomplished what we came for." I kicked the Manchu's side as he tried to sit up, turned to Spencer and continued. "We'll be free of the cargo the day after tomorrow and I think we should take Du's advice and get clear before General Han finds some more goons to send after us, and before the Japanese make up their minds to invade ... are you coming with us, Major?" I wasn't sure that I wanted him back aboard, but felt it was polite to ask.

"I've some things to attend to first, but I'll let you know before you sail. I must say, Captain, I wouldn't want to find myself on the wrong side of you."

I grinned at him, thinking of the tattoo on my forearm. Cock on the right, never lost a fight. It wasn't strictly true. But I'd given more beatings than I'd taken. "It's amazing what an Industrial School education, followed by several years in the forecastle can teach you," I said, before turning back to McGrath. "Now, Third, if you'd be so kind as to hail a taxi, I think we should return to the ship. Major, can we drop you somewhere?"

"I've taken a room at the Shanghai Club. It's only a short walk down Avenue Edward VII." He grasped my outstretched hand. "Goodnight, Captain, gentlemen."

"Keep safe, Major," I replied, as the soldier's footsteps faded into the darkness. I was glad he'd seen the rougher side of me. Thus far, he'd seemed to be the one holding the cards, but in poker, as in life, it wasn't always the better hand that won. I was still smarting, though, at being dragged into something I would have preferred to steer clear of. It wasn't simply the opium smuggling. I had worse things than that on my conscience and would have been happy to take the risk if Mr Khoo had asked me directly, and perhaps offered me something to sooth the pain of my bent scruples. But I had no desire whatsoever to get mixed up with Spencer's shady world of politics and spying. Smuggling was much simpler when all the parties involved, including those of the authorities that could be persuaded to turn a Nelsonian eye, had some skin in the game. Patriotism and loyalty were misplaced sentiments for a smuggler, after all what had the British Empire ever really done for me and my kind, apart from trying to work us to death for a pittance, and there was an honour among thieves that I doubted Major Spencer would ever have understood.

Hopefully I'd seen the back of him, but with things the way they were I somehow doubted it.

CHAPTER FOURTEEN

Early afternoon and I was standing on the bridge wing in the shade of the canvas awning, massaging my bruised knuckles, enjoying a smoke and watching the crew on the main deck below, working to make the ship ready for sea. The last few hatch boards were being swung into place, before the heavy canvas covers were dragged over them and dogged down with wooden wedges. At those hatches already closed, the derricks were being lowered and lashed into their crutches. McGrath was methodically making his way around the wheelhouse testing that the telegraphs, the wheel and the other bridge equipment was functioning correctly. While in the chartroom, Griffith had pulled out the charts required for the next voyage and was busy laying off the courses.

Stuffed into my pocket was the telegram that had been delivered to the ship mid-morning. It was from Mr Khoo, and read simply, 'AWARE OF SITUATION STOP PROCEED ALL DISPATCH DAVAO FOR FULL LOAD ABACA STOP KHOO ENDS.' I had needed no further encouragement to have all the hands turned to, to make ready for sea.

Up and down the Whangpoo River there was the usual bustle of shipping, among which an ancient, and very dirty Russian steamer was making its way downstream, thick black smoke belching from its tall thin funnel. Reaching for my binoculars I read the name *Admiral Altfater* painted in white Cyrillic letters around the stern, and below it the port of registry, *Leningrad*. Above the old-fashioned counter stern, the blood red ensign of the Soviet Union, with its golden hammer and sickle, provided a flapping splash of colour against the black, salt crusted, rust stained hull. I wondered whether the admiral was some long dead hero of the revolution, and whether such a proletarian looking vessel was an appropriate memorial. I was also interested to see a radio aerial strung between her masts. Tramps of her age rarely carried radio, and there were still miserly British owners who refused to pay for its installation and the wages of the man to operate it. Perhaps the Soviet authorities had a more enlightened view of the usefulness of modern communication methods.

My thoughts were interrupted by the arrival of a Bedford truck that slowly pushed its way through crowded, narrow Taiping Road, and halted at the dock gate. A turbaned Sikh policeman let it through onto the dockside, where the discharged tea chests were stacked ready for collection. The customs' officer, a smartly uniformed Indian, made his way over from the office next to the dock gate. I raised my binoculars for a better view, and watched as a young Chinese in grey slacks and white shirt, presumably Du's agent, climbed down from the cab and presented the cargo clearance papers. The customs' officer examined them, and then walked around the stack of tea chests to compare the markings with the numbers contained in the declaration. I wondered if he would ask for any of the chests to be opened in order to verify their contents. I would certainly have some explaining to do if he did, but the fact that both British Intelligence and the Chinese Opium Suppression Board had an interest in the shipment rendered that unlikely.

My heart skipped a beat though, as he paused his inspection and pointed to one of the chests. I was too far away to hear, nor could I lip read, what he said, but the agent appeared to ask if he could refer to the declaration papers. The officer handed them back and the agent leafed through them. Half way through the performance a brown envelope materialised in the agent's fingers, and disappeared between the papers before they were returned, a sleight of hand that would have earned him membership of the Magic Circle. It was so quick I almost missed it. The eagle-eyed officer clearly hadn't missed a trick though, and I whistled softly in admiration as, with a beaming flourish, he signed the customs' release, and signalled for the waiting coolies to start loading the truck. Twenty minutes later it exited the dock gate, and I breathed a sigh of relief. If General Han still had designs on the opium then it was no longer my concern.

A whistle blast from the engine room voice pipe almost startled me, and I heard Lowther's shouted reply into the mouthpiece.

"Bridge, chief mate." There was a pause while he listened to the message, then, "Right-oh, Chief, I'll let the old man know."

Behind his back, the captain of a ship was always referred to by his crew as "the old man," irrespective of age. In my case I was at least five years younger than Lowther, but there was no offence meant, and none taken as I grinned to show that I'd overheard him, when he walked out onto the bridge wing to report.

"Chief Engineer says we'll be finished topping up the bunkers within the hour."

"Thanks Peter, we'll have the hatches and derricks secured by then. Nothing to stop us leaving, so I suggest you nip down to the dock office and telephone the agent to confirm pilot and tug for 4 p.m." He nodded and turned to go, but I called him back, remembering I had not heard from Spencer since leaving him in Thibet Road.

"Can you also tell the agent to get a message to Major Spencer at the Shanghai Club, telling him our departure time and where we're headed?"

There was no reason I should suddenly have thought about Spencer. My earlier question as to whether he would travel with us from Shanghai had been asked merely out of politeness. I had no idea how long he intended to remain in the city or, even if he were ready to leave, whether passage to Davao would be of any use to him. He would have little difficulty finding an inter-island steamer to take him back to Port Moresby from there, but it was much slower than returning by airplane, and in any case he had, presumably, to report his findings on the military situation, something he was more likely to do in Hong Kong or Singapore.

I should have been more than happy to leave him in Shanghai, doing whatever it was he needed to do for his masters in Whitehall, except that my fingertips had been tingling since I had woken up. Spencer had said he would let me know if he was coming with us, but that had been two days ago, and I'd had no word from him since then. "Keep safe," I'd said as we parted on Avenue Edward VII. I hadn't meant it as a warning, but for some reason I couldn't shake the image of him walking off into the darkness alone. I shook my head, telling myself I was worrying over nothing, and that Major Spencer could surely take care of himself without any help from me.

Twenty minutes later Lowther was back aboard, sitting in my cabin and enjoying a glass of iced water into which I had added a generous splash of gin.

"You look like you needed that Peter, wash the coal dust out of your throat."

Lowther drank gratefully. "Agent confirms all in order for a 4 p.m. departure. No sign of the major though. They've left a message for him at the Shanghai Club. Not much more we can do."

"What's it like ashore Peter, all quiet?" I was sure that General Han was well aware by now who had assaulted his men and why. I had earlier ordered that no one from the crew was to go beyond the dock gate, but even so I was still a bit wary as to whether Han would try something to prevent our departure. If he couldn't get his hands on the opium he might think me a suitable alternative. He probably wouldn't kill me, just keep me painfully alive until someone paid a ransom. If they ever did.

"All seems quiet enough. Bit of a military presence though. Met a young lieutenant in the dockmaster's office. Said there was some sort of flap on, and the army would be sending patrols through the docks from this evening onwards."

"Well that should certainly deter any dacoits. Carry on making ready, and call me as soon as the pilot is on board."

"Aye, skipper," replied Lowther, swallowing the last of his drink before disappearing out of the curtained doorway.

The afternoon wore on. With coaling finished, the crew turned to sweeping the coal dust off the decks, and pouring it into gunny sacks which were carried below to the engine room. Later, the chief engineer would mix it with starch paste to form homemade briquettes for the galley range. Even after a thorough sweeping, though, it would still take a sluice down with clean seawater, once we reached the open sea, to wash the decks clean.

By 3.30 p.m. there was still no word from Spencer and, rather than wait in my stuffy cabin, I pulled my gold laced cap on and climbed up to the bridge. The river seemed to be especially busy just then, with a regular procession of ship's leaving, but fewer than normal arriving. There was also a buzz of activity around the line of warships moored to the midstream buoys. Grey painted launches bustled between them and the Admiralty landing stage, carrying groups of sailors seemingly summoned from shore leave. As the clock ticked its way towards 4 p.m. a flight of biplanes flew high over the city, following the line of the Whangpoo River seawards, towards the mouth of the Yangtze.

At a quarter to four a car swung through the dock gate and the white uniformed pilot emerged, clapping a cap onto his head before climbing up the gangway. At the same time Lowther reported that a tug was alongside with a tow line secured to the bow.

"Ring the engine to standby and send the crew to stations. Single up to two and one," I ordered.

I heard the answering ring from the engine room telegraph, and the ear-splitting blast from Lowther's whistle, ordering the crew to their undocking stations. Then the pilot stepped into the wheelhouse.

"We're singled up and ready to go, Pilot," I said, shaking the offered hand, "but we'll leave at four on the dot, if you don't mind."

"All the same to me, Captain. Just say the word when you're ready."

I didn't know if it was the buzz of activity around the warships, or the steady procession of merchantmen putting to sea, but an air of expectancy hung over the city. As the clock ticked its way through the last few minutes towards 4 p.m., I found myself pacing the bridge wing, wondering why we hadn't heard from Major Spencer. It was silly, I knew. If he chose to return in *Oriental Venture*, or find some other way back to Port Moresby, then it hardly mattered to me. And yet? Something didn't feel quite right.

I checked my watch for the umpteenth time since the pilot had boarded. The hands were approaching 4 p.m., and as I watched the minute hand tick past the hour, I heard the bridge seaman ring eight bells for the change of watch. The pilot was looking at me expectantly. The tug was waiting, snorting impatient sulphury breath from its stack. It was time to go.

I flexed my tingling fingers. "Hoist in the gangway, she's all yours Mister Pilot."

"Look, skipper!"

The urgency in Lowther's voice interrupted the pilot's orders, and we followed his outstretched finger to see the dock gate swing open to admit a speeding car bearing British Government markings. The Sikh policeman barely had time to snap a salute, before jumping out of its way as it flew past, horn blaring, and skidded to a tyre squealing halt beside the gangway, which the crew were about to lift on board.

"Belay that," I roared, craning over the bridge wing.

The front doors of the car flew open simultaneously to disgorge Major Spencer in khaki, and a military driver who stepped smartly to the rear and yanked open the passenger door. I watched in amazement as Spencer leaned in to offer his hand, and out stepped Lady Ashworth. She was clad in cream coloured slacks and blouse, her eyes shaded by dark glasses, and there was a light blue scarf wrapped around her head concealing most of her face. But it was unmistakably her. Major Spencer snapped something at the driver, who ran to the rear of the car and opened the boot to reveal several large trunks.

"Help get those trunks on board," I yelled down to the bemused seamen, who were staring goggle eyed at the vision of Lady Ashworth being assisted up the gangway by Major Spencer.

"Looks like you've got a couple of passengers after all, Captain," said the pilot grinning.

"I'm not sure I wanted any," I replied, wryly. "I've orders for Davao, nothing in them about diverting to drop off a lady passenger." I glanced over the side. "Gangway's aboard, let's get out of here before any more turn up."

"Aye, aye, Captain, let go fore and aft."

The docking telegraphs jangled and the mooring lines went slack. Eager hands ashore lifted the eyes clear of the bollards and the crew heaved them in, chanting in Cantonese as they hauled in unison. The pilot blew a short blast on the ship's whistle and the tug took up the strain, black smoke belching from its funnel. The gap between the ship and the pontoon widened, the bow slanting off at an increasing angle.

"Dead slow ahead!"

"Dead slow ahead," repeated Lowther, ringing the telegraph and watching for the answering ring from below.

Oriental Venture slowly nosed her way into the stream, and then, with gathering speed, began the long, twisting passage down river to the sea.

Looking back at the city all seemed peaceful. The normal afternoon thunderstorm had not developed, and the westering sun was painting the granite and limestone facades of the Bund a honeyed gold. But the unexpected arrival of Lady Ashworth, and the continued tingling in my fingertips suggested there might still be plenty of interest left in the voyage.

* * *

The pilot left us at the mouth of the Whangpoo River, climbing down the ladder and waving a hand to the bridge as soon as he was safely landed on the pilot cutter's deck. I waited until it had dropped safely astern, and then ordered the engine to full ahead.

There was still an hour to go before the change of watch at 8 p.m. "Are you happy to take her down the channel, Peter?" I asked Lowther. "I'll send young McGrath up to assist you, and get Da Silva to bring you both a tray for dinner. I want to have a chat with Major Spencer. I'll come up and relieve you after that."

"No problem, sir. I'm sure he has an interesting explanation for the pierhead jump this afternoon."

"I'm intrigued to hear it," I replied. "I'll be in my cabin, call me if you need me."

"Aye, aye."

I climbed down the stairs to the boat deck, and knocked softly on the door of the starboard passenger cabin. Both Major Spencer and Lady Ashworth were reinstalled in the cabins they had occupied for the voyage to Shanghai. Da Silva undoubtedly fussing over them both and, in the absence of Lady Ashworth's maid, probably offering to unpack, hang up her dresses and stow her other belongings in the drawers and lockers. I wondered whether she had politely declined, rather than have the piratical old Goanese handle her smalls.

Spencer answered the first knock and I jerked my head towards my cabin, raising a cupped hand in the offer of a drink. Spencer returned the nod and we stepped across the passage and into my office. I shut the door, not wanting to be disturbed, waved Spencer to a seat on the couch, and poured two generous glasses of whisky.

"Water's in the jug," I said, placing the thermos beside Spencer's glass, and dropping into the easy chair opposite him.

I waited for him to take a sip of the whisky, before continuing. "Well Major, perhaps you'd care to provide an explanation for your unexpected arrival this afternoon with Lady Ashworth. We're heading for Davao, but by the look of you I don't think it matters where we're headed, as long as it's out of Shanghai."

Spencer poured some more iced water into the whisky, and took a long drink. There were bags under his eyes, and his face was creased and pale. He was silent for a moment, as if waiting for the whisky to revive him. Then a smile started to spread across his face.

"Yes, it's been a busy forty-eight hours," he replied. "And I realise I have some explaining to do. But where to start?" He leaned back on the couch and reached into the pocket of his uniform.

"Mind if I smoke? It helps the grey cells."

I nodded, and Spencer pulled a cigarette out of a sterling silver case, flicked the flint of his lighter, and drew a deep lungful of smoke.

"Helena will probably want to keep to herself for a few days," he said. "That brute Maslennikov has knocked her about a bit."

"That explains the covered face," I replied. "But I'm guessing it's more than just a lover's tiff, if you've chosen my ship as a refuge."

"Afraid so, old boy. You remember I told you that Bobby and Lady Ashworth were part of the Cliveden set, and that she was using her connections there to help the White Russians continue the fight against the Communists, while he was keeping an eye on those promoting the Nazi cause."

I nodded, remembering the discussion in my cabin the day before our arrival in Shanghai.

"Well, when Ashworth died Helena was left almost penniless. A grieving widow still has to eat though, and it seemed to her friends in Whitehall an opportune time to suggest a further exchange of information. The widowed Lady Ashworth still had good connections to official circles, and she was still keen to hinder Soviet endeavours. By becoming Maslennikov's lover, she was able to feed him tidbits she picked up from her sources in Shanghai, bits of gossip she overheard at government house, embassy receptions and so on. And she was also able to pick up interesting snippets of information listening to Maslennikov, and reading any bits of paper that she found lying around."

"So your intelligence friends persuaded her to take up with Maslennikov, and become some sort of double agent, passing information to both sides?"

"Not exactly, no. What she learned from our friends was what they wanted her to pass on. But she suggested Maslennikov. He must have thought he'd hit the jack-pot. A beautiful woman returning his clumsy advances with enthusiasm, who also happens to have friends in high places, and is not entirely discreet. She's a terrific actress, you know. He trusted her completely."

Perhaps I should have been shocked at the idea of an English lady selling herself in exchange for information that would help a cause. But then I recalled that Lady Ashworth, or Helena as Spencer persisted in calling her, was Russian, and that it was Bolsheviks like Maslennikov that had murdered her father. She must have hated him. Yet still had the resolve to repay that hatred by submitting to his caresses in order to betray him. It sounded like a dirty, sordid business. But who was I to judge, I'd done my share of dirty business.

"And in return he was careless enough to let her hear and see things that she shouldn't have?" I said.

"Which she passed on to our friends, and which they paid her for. She played the part to perfection, he thought she was a communist who hated the English aristocracy despite, or perhaps because of, marrying into it."

"So what went wrong?"

"I'm coming to that. On the voyage north I managed to have a few words with her, and explained that I represented some people connected with her friends in Shanghai, who would be interested hearing what the position of the Chinese communists would be in the event of a Japanese invasion. We reasoned that this would be something the Soviets would be keen to know themselves. If the Japs were able to drive a wedge between the communists and the nationalists, and seize more or even the whole of China, then there'd be little in the way of them expanding further. The resources of Siberia would be tempting, and with the Nazi's threatening the Soviets in the west the Japs might have easy pickings. So it would be in Stalin's interest for the Chinese communists to join forces with the Nationalists against the Japs. We wanted confirmation of that, because it's in our interest too. If China falls then our possessions east of Suez, including India, are all at risk."

"And she agreed to find out from Maslennikov?" I replied, wondering how and when Spencer had managed to gain her confidence, after she had sharply brushed off his advances over dinner that first night of the voyage. There was clearly much more to Major Spencer than the bluff solider he outwardly appeared to be. "All sounds a bit like the Great Game."

Spencer nodded. "It seems they also taught you some history at that Industrial School of yours."

I let that pass. About the only thing of value I'd learned there, apart from how to fight, was how to read. I'd put that skill to good use since. Despite all appearances to the contrary, sailors were keen readers, those that could anyway. There being precious little else to do to while away the long, lonely hours. Something about what Spencer had just said bothered me, though. Not the jibe about my schooling, but about Lady Ashworth.

"But how did you know that Lady Ashworth would be travelling to Shanghai in this ship?" I asked.

"Friends of friends, old boy," he replied, tapping his nose. "It was good publicity for Mr Khoo and the shipping line. But remember, there are many Chinese who are just as concerned as we are to keep the Japs from getting their mitts on any more of their country. So a friend suggested to Mr Khoo there could be other advantages in having the famous Lady Ashworth travel in his ship."

"In the company of a certain military attaché," I interjected, beginning to see the picture. Not only had Khoo and British Intelligence duped me into opium smuggling, but they had also pre-arranged the passenger list. Clearly, though, the best-laid schemes had *gang aft agley*. "But you still haven't explained what went wrong."

"Well it seems that the communists have friends too, and they encouraged speculation that my appearance in Shanghai at the same time as Lady Ashworth, was more than just a coincidence."

"You mean someone tipped Maslennikov off to the fact that you might not be just a simple soldier, enjoying a sea voyage for the good of his health."

"Something like that. Whatever it was, his suspicions were aroused enough to keep an eye on Helena, and when he found her taking too keen an interest in certain matters, he confronted her. He has a vicious temper, and tried to beat the truth out of her. Things got a bit noisy, the neighbours complained, and it seems he decided to make arrangements to have her taken somewhere he could conduct a more exhaustive, and private interview. In the meantime he left her locked in his apartment. Fortunately, our friends were watching it, and they managed to break in and get her out. Then we needed somewhere to put her out of harm's way."

"Aboard my ship! But unless you got my message, how would you know where I was going? I could be heading for Vladivostok for all you know," I said.

"I don't think so, old boy," replied Spencer, shaking his head. "As soon as we began to suspect that Maslennikov had doubts about Helena's loyalty, we looked around for a way to get her out of Shanghai. Somewhere well away from China, and the clutches of the NKVD and its goons. Somewhere with connections to Australia so I can get home, and somewhere an actress could take ship for America?"

"America!"

"Helena wants to disappear," replied Spencer. "She's sick of playing roles that barely keep the wolf from the door, while attracting other wolves of a quite unwanted variety. She's still young and very beautiful. What better place than Hollywood for an actress to make a new start with a new name. I did get your message, but I already knew you were heading for Davao, old boy. Helena can catch a steamer there heading for America, and I can pick up a trader heading to Port Moresby or Australia."

I felt like reaching over and smacking the smug smile off his face. How could he possibly have known we were bound for Davao? Unless!

"Did you have something to do with Mr Khoo ordering me to Davao?" I tried to keep the anger out of my voice, but I could feel the blood rising in my face and my knuckles turning white clenched around the whisky glass. It seemed I was still just a puppet jerked about by invisible strings. "Just how influential are these friends of yours?" I snapped.

"Oh, very influential." Spencer's smile started to fade as he realised he'd pushed me too far, and held up a pacifying hand. "But keep your shirt on, old boy. There's nothing underhand about this trip. Davao is one of the main ports in the Philippines for the export of abaca, Manila hemp as you would call it. His Majesty's Navy is a big user of abaca. A call from a certain government department in Hong Kong asking the

Anglo Oriental Steamship Company if it had a ship that could load a cargo of the stuff, with delivery instructions to follow. A handshake on laydays and freight rate, and here you are on your way to Davao. You could even say that I'm the cargo super-numerary, here to keep an eye on the shipper's interests."

"Lady Ashworth's safety must have meant a helluva lot to some people, for you to have gone to all this trouble," I replied, my anger somewhat allayed by the thought of the beaten and threatened woman for whom my ship was now a refuge.

"Indeed. She enjoys the friendship, if I can put it that way, of some very highly placed people. And even the little she knows about our intelligence gathering would be valuable to the Soviets, as well as possibly costing her life. But don't overestimate her importance, Captain. With the threats from Japan and Germany hanging over the Empire, taking advantage of the availability of a vital resource such as abaca at a good price, is also just good business sense."

"And after Davao?"

"To whichever of His Majesty's Navy's suppliers of rope has need of a few thousand tons of hemp. Singapore perhaps or Sydney."

"So I could be stuck with you beyond Davao, then?" I had the sinking feeling that the major was going to keep turning up like a bad penny. I knew I should have been grateful to him for possibly saving my hide in Shanghai, but the last thing I needed was a military intelligence officer looking over my shoulder.

"Needs must I'm afraid old boy. But you have yourself partly to blame. If you hadn't stuck your nose where it wasn't wanted, and snafu'd my operation against Eberhardt, you wouldn't have come to my attention. As it is," he shrugged his shoulders and drained his glass.

He was right of course, but that was little consolation. The best I could hope for was that they'd both get off in Davao. Helen Ashworth, Helena Kovtoun or whatever she chose to call herself, to chase her tinseltown dreams. And Spencer off to bother some other poor bastard.

"Well thanks for taking me into your confidence, at least I know how things stand. Help yourself to another drink if you want. I need to get back up top to relieve the mate. We can talk again in the morning."

I pulled open the door and climbed the stairs back to the wheelhouse, wondering whether Spencer was still holding things back, and rubbing my fingers together to relieve the tingling.

CHAPTER FIFTEEN

awn found us steaming east-southeast into the China Sea, passing the
northerly outliers of the Shengsi Islands fringing the southern approaches to
the Yangtze River. Despite being late summer, it was a cool morning heavily
overcast with thick rain showers, and only a limp breeze to ruffle the oily surface of
the brown water, discoloured by the silt carried down by the mighty river. Visibility
was poor between the showers, and almost totally obscured within them, and
Lowther had called me to the bridge at the same time as posting an extra lookout on
the forecastle, with instructions to ring the bell if he saw anything ahead. There was
a long, low swell from the southeast, and the ship slowly heaved and fell as she
negotiated each crest. To the west, a cluster of junks ghosted along, their crews
trimming the bamboo lateen sails to catch every ounce of the fickle wind.

As we emerged from an especially heavy downpour, I scanned the eastern horizon with my binoculars, thankful to find no inbound ship on a reciprocal course that
had been concealed by the rain. I considered whether I should order a reduction in
speed. But there were only the few junks being left behind astern, and empty brown
sea ahead. The showers were of relatively short duration, so blowing the ship's fog-
horn in the thickest of them was probably sufficient to alert any approaching ships,
provided they did the same in return.

After my chat with Spencer the previous evening, I had relieved Lowther at 9
p.m., and provided him a brief outline of the events that had brought the major and
Lady Ashworth back on board. The passage down river had taken the best part of the
night, and I had remained on the bridge until Lowther returned to relieve Griffith at
4 a.m. I had then gone below to get my head down for a few hours, only to be woken,
seemingly minutes later, by the call of the seaman with the chief mate's compliments, telling me that visibility was seriously reduced.

I was looking forward to a shave and some breakfast, in the hope they would ease the heavy lidded tiredness, which even several cups of Da Silva's strongest coffee had done little to dispel. Otherwise, I felt quite pleased with the ways things had panned out. I had managed to deliver my illicit cargo, and get the ship safely back to sea, with only a bump on the head as a warning of what I could have fallen foul of. By the look of the activity in the port as we left, something unpleasant was obviously brewing between the Chinese and the Japanese. Thankfully, we were out of it, and I only had to see Spencer and Lady Ashworth safely ashore in Davao, before things were back to normal. As normal, that is, for a tramp steamer in the Far East, with a master who seemed to attract trouble.

So to, apparently, did Lady Ashworth, who had narrowly escaped the painful and potentially murderous clutches of Maslennikov. I wondered how successful she would be in making a new life in Hollywood, and whether I would ever watch a film in some smart West End cinema, and see her play a femme fatale, like Marlene Dietrich in *Blue Angel* or *Shanghai Express*. I smiled at the thought of Helena playing a China coaster, a woman living by her wits among the misfits and freebooters who gravitated towards Shanghai, something I reckoned she was especially well equipped for, in both looks and experience.

The bow disappeared behind a heavy curtain of rain that appeared to draw rapidly aft until the whole ship was cloaked in the downpour. For ten minutes we were the centre of a small circle of torrential rain which hissed and smoked as it cascaded onto the flattened surface of the sea. I took shelter in the wheelhouse, and watched the rain sluicing over the decks, and falling in waterfalls over the sides as the scuppers failed to drain quickly enough.

The urgent ringing of the forecastle bell snapped my attention back to the horizon. We were passing out of the shower and ahead the sea was clear for several miles. With the exception of the black outline of what appeared to be an antiquated tramp ship fine on the starboard bow. I studied it through the binoculars. From the lack of bow waves, it appeared to be stationary or making way very slowly. The ship was old and dirty, its black sides streaked with rust. I did a quick mental triangulation, and concluded that if we held our present course it would pass about half a mile away to the south. This was a little too close for comfort, especially if she was having trouble with engine or steering and did something unexpected. I studied her for a few moments more, seeing nothing unusual, and decided to alter course a point to port to gain more sea room. I lowered the binoculars and turned to the helmsman.

"Port the helm, steer—"

"Look, skipper, smoke!"

Lowther interrupted me, and I turned back to see thick black clouds of it billowing from the ship's engine room skylights.

"Belay that, midships the wheel," I snapped, reaching for the engine room telegraph and ringing it back to stand by to alert the chief engineer that we would shortly need to manoeuvre.

"Okay, Peter, I'll take over. Get the third up here and have the rescue boat swung out ready for launching, in case we have to go to their assistance."

I rang the engine telegraph to slow ahead, and as the way began to drop off, I raised the binoculars and studied the other ship. Smoke was still billowing from her engine room skylights, and there was no one visible on the upper decks, although I thought I glimpsed figures, the captain and the officer of the watch maybe, in the wheelhouse. There was no sign of any distress signal, but I noticed the radio aerial strung between the masts, and wondered if I should alert the radio officer, but decided it was unnecessary. Even when he was off watch he left the receiver on, and with the burning ship barely a mile away, any emergency broadcast would be deafening enough to drag him from the deepest sleep. More billows of thick black smoke erupted out of the skylights.

"Poor devils," I muttered. Fire at sea was the seaman's worst nightmare, and I could imagine the hell they would be fighting if a major blaze had broken out in the engine room.

I heard footsteps clattering across the wooden deck, and turned to see McGrath skid to a halt at my side.

"Ship on fire over there, Third. Look up the international signal code, and hoist the flags asking if they require assistance.

"Aye aye, sir," replied McGrath sprinting back into the wheelhouse. Moments later he returned with the flags, scrambled up the stairs to the monkey island and bent them on to the signal halyard. I blew a long blast on the whistle to draw attention to them.

While waiting for a reply, I manoeuvred *Oriental Venture* to a position about half a mile upwind of the burning ship, and stopped the engine, leaving us both drifting in the gentle swell. I didn't want to get too close in case she suffered a boiler explosion. There was still no response to the signal, though. Perhaps they were too busy fighting the fire, or maybe they just didn't understand it. She didn't appear to be British, but that shouldn't have made any difference, the code was supposed to be universally recognised. But at least they seemed to be getting on top of the fire, as the smoke was less intense and the ugly black billows were fading to grey.

There was a sudden flurry of activity on her bridge. Several men emerged from the wheelhouse, one wearing a naval cap, whom I assumed was her captain. Another ran to the signal halyard, and hoisted the flags that, I didn't need the code book to remind me, signified, "Send immediate assistance."

"Hoist the acknowledgment, Third." I looked aft, and shouted down to Lowther on the boat deck. "Looks like they need our help, Peter. Take the chief engineer with you and row over and find out what they want. If necessary we can radio for a tug to tow them into Shanghai."

"Aye aye," he shouted back, as the rescue boat was swung out.

"Keep an eye on her, Third," I said, as soon as he had hoisted the signal, and leaned over the bridge wing to watch the boat being lowered. Lowther, Fraser and the boat's crew were already in it, wearing their clumsy kapok life jackets, and readying the oars.

"Slacken the bowsing tackles and lower away," I heard Lowther yell.

It was a tricky operation, made more difficult by the movement of the ship in the swell. The seamen had to ease the falls at either end of the boat at exactly the same rate; otherwise there was a danger of one end dropping faster than the other, throwing the occupants out. As the boat approached the water, I heard Lowther call to the men to stop lowering. This was the crucial bit. He had to judge exactly the right moment to drop the boat into the water, so that it lifted on the rising swell long enough for the weight to come off the falls for the crew to unhook them. Any mistake could be fatal. I had seen boats upended in bad weather, and men flung out to struggle in a vicious, freezing sea. This time, at least, the swell was regular, and more easily predictable, but I still held my breath until Lowther, judging the moment to perfection, dropped the boat neatly into the trough and she floated free of the falls.

"Ship oars, give way ... together."

Four pairs of oars rose and fell in unison as the oarsmen bent their backs, and slowly the boat gathered way towards the burning ship, looking like an ungainly form of water beetle. Raising my binoculars again, I studied her in more detail. That she was ancient I could tell from the old-fashioned counter stern, the thin straight funnel and the rusty, battered plating of her sides, evidence of long, hard use. Right aft some of her crew were hoisting her ensign, a red flag with a white horizontal stripe through the middle. I didn't recognise it, but we were close enough that I could read her port of registry, *Riga*, the capital and principal seaport of Latvia, a tiny country on the shores of the Baltic. The Lats had declared their independence at the end of the Great War, and had then fought off both the Red Army and the German Freikorps to maintain it. The German Freikorps were Fascist thugs. The same thugs who, like the Eberhardt brothers, were supporting Hitler's aggressive plans to dominate Europe.

Above *Riga* I read the ship's name, *Karlis Ulmanis*. Both were sloppily stencilled onto the hull in clean white paint. I adjusted the focus ring and the image sharpened slightly, to reveal the outline of raised lettering that had been painted over with black, before the white letters had been applied. I wasn't surprised that a ship of her age should have been sold and renamed, it would likely have occurred several times in the length of her obviously long and hard working life. I couldn't make out the original name or port of registry, but the latter was considerably longer than the four letter Riga.

My inspection was interrupted by the rescue boat swimming into view beneath the Latvian ship's stern. Beside the ensign, one of her seamen was waving at Lowther, and pointing to the far side of the ship, where, I imagined, they had rigged their gangway. I watched the boat disappear behind the battered black hull, put down the binoculars, and told McGrath to pull down the flag hoist. The fire appeared to be finally under control as there were only wisps of grey smoke drifting upwards from her engine room skylights. I wondered what damage it had done; whether she was totally disabled or if there was a chance of a temporary repair to get her under-way again. I thought of getting Sayce to send a radio message to the agent in Shanghai to arrange for a tow, but decided it was best to wait until I had Lowther's report on the damage, and then see what assistance we could render. At least the rain showers appeared to have drifted away, and the sky was clearing as the morning warmed up.

I could smell the scent of bacon frying in the galley, and my stomach rumbled, reminding me I had slept little and eaten nothing since the previous afternoon. I wondered whether Major Spencer or Lady Ashworth were up and about. From what Spencer had said the previous evening, Helena was probably feeling the physical and emotional effects of her beating, and would be shy of company, at least until the bruising on her face had gone down. But I was a little surprised that Spencer had not been disturbed by all the activity on the boat deck, and come out to investigate.

I was about to call Da Silva, and get him to fetch me some of that delicious smelling bacon, when a signal lamp flashed on the bridge of the *Karlis Ulmanis*. The lamp flashed four times in quick succession, then a second group of four flashes, then a third. Then nothing. Waiting.

"She wants to communicate by Morse code," I said. "Rig the signal lamp, Third, and call the sparky to help read it." As McGrath darted below, I raised the binoculars to study the Latvian ship's bridge. Both Lowther and Fraser were there, together with a group of seamen and the captain with the naval style cap. As I watched, one of the seamen handed a signal lamp to Lowther. It was too far away to see clearly, but I had the impression that the man was agitated about something, and appeared to be shouting at him. Whatever it was about, Lowther took the signal lamp, raised it, and turned to face *Oriental Venture*.

"I'm ready, sir." I turned to see Sayce pointing our signal lamp towards the *Karlis Ulmanis*.

"Tell him we're ready to communicate and ask him what he wants," I said. "And go slow. Mr Lowther's on the other end. I doubt he reads Morse as fast as you."

Grinning cheerfully, Sayce sent a series of flashes, accompanied by the rhythmi-cal clacking of the shutters as they opened and closed with each letter.

There was a brief pause, and then Lowther's lamp winked out a reply. Sayce called out each letter as he read it, and McGrath jotted it down on a message pad. But rusty as I was, I could read enough of the message to understand it, and felt the blood pound in my ears as my fury increased with each flash. By the time McGrath had finished transcribing the message he and the sparky were ashen faced.

"Tell him the message is received," I snapped, feeling the fury burning to white heat. "And get Major Spencer up here immediately."

For once, my sixth sense had deserted me, the tingling in my fingers having stopped as soon as we cleared the Whangpoo River. I slammed my fist down on the teak rail with frustration. What did the absence of the tingling matter anyway? All the clues were right in front of me. I had just been too preoccupied with thoughts of breakfast and bed, to take notice of them. I banged my fist down hard again.

"Trouble?" Spencer was beside me, a puzzled expression on his face.

I handed him the signal, and watched as his shoulders slumped and his face fell.

"We stopped to offer assistance to that bloody ship over there. She was on fire and called for help. So I sent Lowther and the chief engineer over to see what we could do. But there was no fire, it was just a ruse to get us to stop. She's a bloody Russian, and they're holding our men hostage, until we hand over Lady Ashworth."

"What do you propose to do, Captain?" For once, there was a look of uncertainty in the soldier's eyes.

"Helluva choice don't you think? Hand over Lady Ashworth to an almost certainly painful death, or lose two of my officers and half a dozen seamen." I slammed my fist down again. "She knew she was playing with fire, and so did you." I glared at him with anger-filled eyes. "What choice do I have?"

"It could be a bluff. We could storm them. You've weapons aboard and men who know how to use them."

"It's no bluff, Major," I snapped, handing him the binoculars. "See for yourself, you'll find that several of those men on the bridge are armed, and there are others on the main deck. Without the element of surprise, we wouldn't stand a chance. I've never been shy of a fight as long as there's some hope of winning, but the cards are stacked against us."

"I'll go and break the news to Helena." Spencer turned away grim-faced, and went below.

* * *

The oars rose and fell in a ragged stroke, as the doubled-ended lifeboat crawled its way across the half mile of gently heaving sea towards the *Admiral Alfater*. The blood red Soviet flag had replaced the red and white Latvian one, and some of her crew were already perched on a stage hanging over the stern, painting out the name of Karlis Ulmanis, whoever he was. I gripped the tiller, steering for the gangway. The third mate sat on one side of the stern sheets, and Lady Ashworth on the other, the blue headscarf, the same one she had worn coming aboard, wrapped tightly round her hair and the lower half of her face. I expected to see fear or anger in her eyes, but instead there was a look of resigned sadness, and dark streaks showed where mascara stained tears had slid down her cheeks. Piled into the bottom of the boat were the trunks containing the possessions she had fled Shanghai with. Cramp sat in the bow, half-heartedly calling out the timing of the oar strokes.

I nudged the boat clumsily against the gangway, avoiding the rescue boat that already trailed at the end of its painter, and Soviet seamen secured it while I assisted Helena climb up to the deck. Behind us, the boat's crew followed, carrying her possessions. It seemed miserably little for a woman once married to an English aristocrat. Gaining the deck, we were confronted by a ferocious looking Tarter in a greasy cap and stained blue shirt, armed with what looked like a flintlock pistol. Another man with an antiquated rifle was covering the rescue boat's crew, huddled dejectedly on a hatch cover. They lifted their heads in anticipation when they saw me step onto the deck, but dropped them again when the Tartar jerked the muzzle of his pistol towards the stairs, indicating we should climb up to the bridge.

Up close, the aged ship was as unprepossessing as she appeared at a distance. Dirty, salt-stained, paint peeling and rust-streaked; her crew had clearly given up the battle to keep her presentable. She also stank of boiled cabbage, coal dust, sweaty bodies and despair. I had sailed in some miserly, ill-maintained ships in my time, but none as bad as this.

The man who confronted me as I stepped up onto the bridge looked even older than the ship he commanded. Grizzled curls pushed their way down his neck from under the brim of the naval cap that, together with an old-fashioned brass buttoned pea jacket, suggested he had seen service in the Imperial Russian Navy. His eyes were the faded blue of a Siberian winter sky, and were set in deep sockets surrounded by rugged creases, the result of countless years of watch keeping in all weathers. He was unarmed, and raised two fingers to the peak of his cap in a gesture of respect to my rank. I nodded in return, and stepped forward to allow Helena, and the rest of my party, room on the bridge wing. The crew none too gently dumped her trunks onto the stained, worn deck planking, and lounged behind them.

Clustered around the old Soviet captain was a small body of his men. Officers or seamen it was impossible to tell, as they were all scruffily dressed in greasy, worn serge shirts and trousers, patched in a quilt-work of faded colours. Several were armed with ancient, bolt action rifles, which they held across their chests, dirty fingers curled around the trigger guards. Behind them stood Lowther and Fraser, both stony faced. Fraser was sporting the beginnings of a black eye, and I guessed the hotheaded Scot had lashed out once he realised the fire was a ruse. Lowther was also no coward, but he would have seen that resistance was pointless against the armed Russians. He caught my eye and shook his head as if apologising. Heaven knows, but if anyone had to apologise it should have been me, for falling right into the trap.

Beside the old captain, one man stood out. Small and wiry, with dark, thin features and a shock of thick, black greasy hair, he was dressed the same as the others in blue dungarees and shirt, but looking at his young, clean shaven face, clean hands and neatly trimmed nails I could tell he was no seaman. There was an ugly Nagant pistol in his fist, menacingly aimed towards me.

When he spoke the Soviet captain's English was understandable, and his voice was calm, with quiet authority.

"I apologise for ruse de guerre. But was necessary. Helena Kovtoun is traitor to Soviet Union, and my orders are seize her and take her back there, where she will be investigated and tried."

"Ruse de guerre be dammed." I began as I meant to go on, in outraged, injured innocence. "We are not at war, and Lady Ashworth, if that is who you mean, is a British citizen, the widow of a highly respected peer of the realm, and well connected with members of the British government." It was pretentious and long-winded, but I was determined to seize the moral high ground. "She is travelling lawfully in a British ship, and you have no right to detain us, or to interfere with her. I demand that you—"

The small dark man spat on the deck at my feet, interrupting my eloquence and shouting something in Russian. The Soviet captain held up his hand, motioning him to be silent.

"Our commissar not very fond of reactionary, self-styled aristocrats. He has devoted life to rooting them out of beloved motherland. He understand a little English, but have trouble speaking it, especially when angry. Whatever right or wrong, my order is to take Helena Kovtoun to Vladivostok. If you hand her over, you and your men can return to ship. If you resist, my men are armed, and we will take by force —"

His words were drowned by another flood of angry Russian from the commissar. The men with the rifles stiffened and levelled their weapons threateningly towards us. I glanced at Helena, realising she understood everything the man had said. The resignation had disappeared. Her eyes blazed with anger, and the scarf had fallen open to reveal her jaw clenched with determination. I owed it to her, and to myself, to make one last try, even if the situation appeared hopeless.

"I protest in the strongest possible terms, Captain," I said, trying deliberately to ignore the commissar. "This is an outrage for which you will be held responsible. To seize a British citizen on the high seas, I am—"

The commissar's Nagant jabbed into my chest and I could see from the cold fury in his eyes that I was pushing my luck.

"It seems you leave me little choice, Captain," I continued, holding up my arms, "but I can assure you I will be informing the authorities of this act of piracy."

"Call it what you will, my orders—"

"I care nothing for your orders." The vehemence in Helena's voice was shocking. "And I care even less about your protestations, Captain Rowden. I will not go back to Russia and let men like that," she almost spat the word at the commissar, "question me or touch me. If you have no choice, Captain Rowden, then I do."

As she uttered the final words, she reached into her clutch bag, pulled out a small revolver, pressed it firmly into her breast, and pulled the trigger.

There was a sharp crack from the gun, Helena staggered under the impact of the bullet, and crumpled towards the deck.

The third mate was the first to react, darting forward to catch her as she fell, and gently laying her down onto the worn teak planking, before starting to check for signs of life. But the blood bubbling out of the smoke blackened hole in her sweater, spreading a dark red stain over the material, and dripping onto the rough, dirty teak, was the unmistakable sign of her life ebbing rapidly away.

The shot, and Helena's dropping to the deck, took the Russians by surprise. Their eyes followed her as she slumped, and the momentary distraction was sufficient. The shot was still ringing in our ears as Cramp and the boat crew dropped to their knees, unlatched the lid of one of Helena's trunks, and whipped out what was inside it. At the same instant, I slid a hand inside my jacket. By the time the Soviet captain and his men looked up, the situation had changed. They were starting down the barrel of my Webley, and the Bergmann machine pistols that had, almost miraculously, appeared in the hands of Cramp and my men.

The third officer continued to kneel beside the lifeless body of Helena. "There's no pulse, Captain and she's not breathing," he said, in his pronounced nasal twang.

I nodded in acknowledgment, and then turned my attention to the Soviet captain. I needed to seize the initiative, before the shock wore off and one or other of them, the weaselley commissar looking the likeliest, decided to act like a Hero of the Soviet Union.

"It looks like we have a standoff here, Captain," I said, fixing him with the steeliest glare I could muster. "My men are also armed, and I think a shootout would lead to unnecessary loss of life. I suggest you let us withdraw to our boats." I paused, and then added as an afterthought. "And with Lady Ashworth dead, I think we can forget the attempted—"

A stream of vitriolic Russian cut me off again. The commissar, apparently enraged by Helena's suicide, no doubt depriving him of the kudos of delivering her to his NKVD masters in Vladivostok, raised the Nagant and pointed it directly at my head.

"He is telling you to drop weapons," said the Soviet captain, warily. "He very angry and unpredictable young man, and advisable you do as he say."

Advisable, yes! A firefight would almost certainly cause deaths on both sides, but perhaps the Soviet captain thought that a small price to pay to corroborate a story that British sailors had attacked his ship, and killed Helena Kovtoun in the crossfire.

The commissar's eyes blazed hatred, and I could see his finger whiten on the trigger, which, on the Nagant, had a heavy pull. Even if it were the double action version, he would only get one shot off before Cramp killed him. But by then I'd be dead. I had to think of something fast, or I wouldn't be the only one.

"NO!" I heard Lowther's desperate shout. "If you're going to shoot anyone, shoot me."

The Commissar's hand wavered as he glanced round to see Lowther struggling with one of the Russian sailors for possession of a rifle. Another raised the butt of his own and clubbed it viciously into Lowther's back.

It was all the opportunity the third mate needed.

From his crouching position next to Helena's body, he launched himself at the commissar's knees, bringing him down in a rugby tackle. The pistol fired involuntarily, and a bullet zinged past my ear. There was a short scuffle as the Nagant was twisted out of the commissar's grip, then he was pinned on his back, the burlier third mate astride his chest, fists balled and threatening to pound the man's face.

"Let him up, Third," I said "and secure that weapon," pointing to the Nagant lying on the deck where it had fallen. He reached for the pistol, clicked on the safety catch, and pocketed it. Then he lifted his weight off the commissar's chest, dragged the man to his feet, and shoved him into the restraining arms of Cramp.

I turned my attention to the Soviet captain, who was eying the scene with what looked very much like the beginnings of an ironical smile.

"I don't want to, but if we have to fight our way off this ship we'll give a very good account of ourselves." I said. Our machine pistols would make short work of his men, but we wouldn't all get away. And there were more Russians with rifles guarding the rescue boat's crew. "My suggestion still holds, captain. No shooting and we'll be on our way. Oh, and we'll take Lady Ashworth's body with us. She deserves a better funeral than she'd get in Russia."

The Soviet captain glanced at the commissar who had ceased struggling against Cramp's iron grip, and then at the machine pistols in the hands of my crew. With their antiquated weapons, his men were no match for my band of cutthroat Chinese pirates and Somali tribesmen, and he knew it. It occurred to me that he had probably not accepted this task with relish. A radio signal from his superiors in Moscow, ordering him to intercept a British ship, armed with only a handful of old rifles and a wild-eyed boy of a commissar wielding a pistol. He had done well to convince me that his ship really was on fire. But we'd got the drop on him and now it was over. He nodded, barked a few words in Russian and his sailors lowered their rifle muzzles.

"And the men on the main deck?"

"*Da!*" he leaned over the rail and shouted to the men below.

"Go and check please, Peter."

Lowther grabbed a machine pistol from a Chinese seaman and disappeared down the ladder.

"Thank you, Captain," I said, feeling a sudden wave of relief. "We'll return to our boats."

"Just one moment, if you please," he replied. "I must satisfy myself that Kovtoun dead."

I would have asked the same in his shoes. It was one thing to have failed to bring her back alive. But at least he could confirm to the NKVD that she was dead, and would cause them no further trouble.

I nodded, and we knelt together beside the body. The Soviet captain reached towards the blood soaked sweater, obviously intending to tear it open and examine the wound below.

"For pity's sake, Captain," I said, gently pushing his hand aside, "please leave the lady with some modesty. She's not breathing, there is no pulse, she's no longer with us."

He bent his ear to Helena's face and listened, then reached for her wrist, feeling for the pulse.

"*Da*, I am satisfied," he said, climbing back to his feet. "I shall report her death to authorities."

"Very well, Captain, then we'll be on our way. But just so there's no further interference, we'll take your friendly commissar with us and return him when we're safely aboard our own ship." I could have sworn that the hint of a grin flashed across the Soviet captain's face. "Do the honours, Chippy."

Cramp gleefully grabbed the commissar by the scruff of the neck and propelled him towards the ladder. He raised a large, heavy fist and shook it in the struggling man's face. "You can come the easy way or the hard way, mate. It's up to you."

The third mate and one of the Chinese seamen gently picked up the lifeless body of Lady Ashworth and followed Cramp down the ladder to the boats. The sombre procession brought up by the remaining seamen carrying her luggage. I covered the withdrawal with the Webley.

"A word please?" requested the Soviet captain, as I turned to leave the bridge.

"Aye, if you're quick."

"We will not trouble you leaving and, as I have said, I shall report Helena Kovtoun's death in Vladivostok. But I'm afraid that news not save that man's neck." He angled his chin in the direction of the commissar, who was now seated beside Cramp in the bow of the lifeboat, his hands tied with the end of the painter. "In his service, failure not an option."

"And will it go hard for you too?" I didn't care what happened to the commissar, but I would be sorry if the old captain suffered the same fate.

"Perhaps, but I am a seaman. Maybe I will lose my command, perhaps even my rank, but the sea is still the sea." He shook his head wistfully. "I will not shake your hand with that man watching." His creased eyes sparkled. "And if anything were to happen to him, well we would not miss him. But perhaps two deaths would be hard to explain. *Radzia bora*, for God's sake be careful!"

I jerked my head around in time to see the third mate stumble as he stepped into the boat, losing his grip on Helena's body, which tumbled onto the bottom boards with a sickening thud.

"Thank you, Captain. Send a boat to pick your man up once we reach our ship." I raised two fingers to the peak of my cap and then, without waiting to see if the salute was returned, ran down the stairs to the main deck and climbed into the boat.

"Cast off!"

The crews bent their backs and the two boats set off for the half-mile pull back to *Oriental Venture*. The day had brightened considerably since the early morning showers had cleared. The silt-stained sea had taken on a greenish hue under the bright blue arc of the sky, and a gentle southerly breeze was creating small waves across the backs of the long, rolling swell. It was a harder pull back, and the men were sweating profusely by the time we nosed alongside the gangway.

I tossed a lifejacket into the bow and jerked a thumb towards the commissar.

"Put this on him, Chippy, and then chuck him over the side. He won't drown, and if he's lucky the sharks will leave him alone long enough for his comrades to pick him up."

* * *

"Take Lady Ashworth's body to her cabin," I instructed the third mate, once we were all safely back aboard. Then, turning to Lowther, "See the boats are safely stowed and secured, Peter, and meet me in the passenger suite."

Without waiting for an answer, I bounded up the stairs to the bridge, where a pale, grim faced Griffith awaited me.

"Lady Ashworth?" he said.

"She's been shot," I replied. There was no time for further explanation. "Get the ship underway. Set a course for the Formosa Strait. Make them think we're heading back to Hong Kong. After a couple of hours, we'll head back east and resume our original course. And post a man in the crow's nest to see if we're being followed."

"Aye aye, sir," said the sombre faced Griffith, whose hopes at seeing the boats return safely would have evaporated with the sight of the lifeless body of Lady Ashworth being carried back on board. He turned back into the wheelhouse, where I heard him ring full speed on the engine telegraph, and order the helmsman to steer south-west. As the throb of the engine increased, and we picked up speed, I glanced astern at the Soviet ship's lifeboat. It had reached the commissar in the water and the crew were pulling him aboard.

"Pity the Nobby Clarks didn't get him," I muttered.

In the passenger suite, the body of Lady Ashworth lay on the bed, the third mate and I looking over her like grim faced mourners keeping vigil. Then the door opened and Lowther entered with a gloomy expression on his face. I caught a whiff of gin, and guessed he had made a swift detour to his cabin for a reviving drink.

"Come to pay your respects, Peter?" I observed, darkly.

Lowther looked down at the lifeless body. Despite the blood soaked sweater clinging to the breast, with its dark, smoke ringed bullet hole above the heart, Lady Ashworth's face looked peaceful and composed.

"That was pretty rash of you back there," I continued. "But I'm glad you did it. I'd run out of ideas myself. If that nasty little shit of a commissar had pulled the trigger, things might have got sticky."

A pained grimace creased Lowther's face as he massaged the small of his back where the rifle butt had slammed into it. "When I saw you come aboard with Major Spencer dressed as the third mate I thought something was afoot. But I never expected her to shoot herself. At the very least I thought you'd be able to force them to hand her over, if you could manage to get some of the weapons on board. That part worked at least."

Major Spencer grinned ruefully as he removed McGrath's cap. He had shaved off his moustache, but even wearing the uniform, he bore little resemblance to McGrath. "Whatever happened over there I didn't want them to know that an Australian Army major had anything to do with it. They might report the presence of an Australian third mate, if they noticed the accent, and if the Soviets check the crew list in Shanghai, they'll find confirmation in the name of McGrath."

"That was quick thinking, tackling the commissar like that," I said. "I don't think he knew what hit him, and thank God the shot went wide. But I'm still kicking myself over falling for it. That ship left Shanghai just before we did, I saw her go. Flying the Latvian flag, though, I just didn't make the connection. What did they use for a fire, anyway?"

"Couple of buckets filled with waste oil, damp rags and paraffin," replied Lowther.

"Very effective. Well at least we're out of it now, with not much harm done."

"You bloody, hard hearted, bastard," exploded Lowther. "When there's a dead woman lying there."

"Easy, Peter," I said, prepared to overlook the outburst. "There's precious little we can do about it now."

He stared at me with a mixture of fury and contempt. Then the professional mask clamped down.

"I suppose we'll have to prepare her for burial at sea," he said, stiffly. "Although I'm not sure how we're going to explain it." He paused, shaking his head, the lifeless body of the beautiful woman on the bed almost certainly reminding him of another time and place, and the woman he had lost. For a moment I saw behind the mask, and thought I saw his lip tremble. Then he pulled himself together "I'll tell the boatswain to cut a length of canvas and get her sewn into it."

"Not so fast, Mr Lowther," said Spencer, the hint of a smile playing across his lips. "You might want to check her pulse again."

"What for? It's clear she's—"

"Dead?" croaked a shaky female voice. "I am so sorry to disappoint you, Peter." Lady Ashworth raised a trembling hand to her forehead. "Oh my God, I feel dreadful."

Lowther jumped like a startled rabbit when he heard Helena's voice, and then grabbed for her sweater. "But you've got a bullet in you. We need to—"

"It's okay, Peter," I said, seizing his hand before he could rip open the blood soaked sweater. "There's no bullet."

Lowther's jaw dropped and Spencer laughed heartily. "You should see your face, Lowther. A tribute to Lady Ashworth's acting skills, wouldn't you say. And some good old fashioned smoke and mirrors."

On the bed, Helena was smiling weakly, and making an attempt to sit up.

"I think you should remain lying down for a while longer," said Spencer, gently lifting her head and placing a second pillow under it to make her more comfortable. "It'll take some time for the effect of the neurotoxin to wear off."

"A disappearing bullet, neurotoxin. What the hell is all this about, Major?" asked Lowther, removing his cap and scratching his scalp.

"There was no way the Soviets, and in particular that nasty looking commissar, were ever going to let Lady Ashworth get away. They would have had their orders from the top. Seize her by any means. Our only chance was to convince them she'd committed suicide. The gun is a stage pistol that fires blanks, but holding it close to the clothing the muzzle flash is enough to burn a hole and puncture the bladder underneath, which was filled with the blood of one of the crew's goats."

"And the neurotoxin?"

"Something I picked up from the Dyaks, the head hunters of Borneo. They tip their blow pipe darts with a poison, that in small enough doses can paralyse a person, and slow their breathing and heartbeat so they appear dead."

"Sounds risky, if you miscalculate."

"It is, but some friends of mine in London have made something of a study of the effect of such poisons."

"And that stopped the pulse so the Soviet captain couldn't feel it?" said Lowther.

"No, the poison only slows it down. That's where this came in." Spencer pulled a small rubber ball from his pocket. "If you trap this in the armpit it cuts off the circulation to the wrist so the pulse can't be felt. It was taped into Lady Ashworth's armpit. I squeezed her arm against her body when she fell, and retrieved the ball when we dropped her into the bottom of the boat."

"You mean dropping her was deliberate?" Lowther looked almost offended, as if he had been the one dropped into the boat.

"Afraid so. People see what they want to see. What better way to maintain the illusion than to clumsily drop a corpse. I'm sorry Lady Ashworth, the poison stopped you feeling it, but you'll have some nasty bruising on your ribs."

Helena groaned theatrically. "I can feel them already."

"So there you are, Peter," I said. "With luck they'll have fallen for the trick, and report that Lady Ashworth killed herself. If they start to have doubts, they might try to follow us, and make another attempt to snatch her. But I've ordered Griffith to head south-west, as if we were returning to Hong Kong. We'll alter course later and head east to pick up the original track. There's no reason they should know we're headed for Davao, so we've hopefully seen the last of them."

"Well you certainly had me fooled," grinned Lowther. "All that stiff upper lip stuff, about no harm being done. That was just to wind me up. And it worked. I apologise for my outburst, I should have said you were a bastard ... sir!"

"I deserved that," I said, returning the grin. It was good to see Lowther smile, even if it was at my expense. "Well gentlemen," I continued. "Now that Lady Ashworth is safely restored to life, I suggest we let her rest." I reached for a spare blanket and covered her with it. "Please stay here until you feel better. I'll come back in an hour to check on you."

Helena raised a hand and took hold of my arm.

"You've risked your lives for me, Captain. Thank you, and please thank the rest of your men."

There were tears in her eyes, real ones this time, not the theatrical type she had shed in the boat. They moved even my hard, cynical old heart.

"It's good to have you safely back aboard. But we're not clear of the reefs yet. We've still got to get you to Davao, and you're going to have to stay out of sight until we get there. So I can't thank the crew, they need to go on thinking you're dead."

"Perhaps I am," she replied dreamily, relaxing back on the pillow and closing her eyes.

When I returned she had changed her blouse, repaired her tear stained makeup, and was sitting in an armchair contentedly smoking one of her colourful Sobranies. Da Silva had brought me a pot of tea and I laid the tray down on the table, reaching into the drinks' cabinet for an extra cup.

"Ah you English and your obsession with tea. After a near death experience, something stronger is called for. If you look again in that cabinet you'll find a bottle of Wyborowa vodka. It's Polish, not Russian, but it's better than the lighter fuel turned out in the Soviet Union these days. Fill two glasses and let's drink a toast to freedom."

"Freedom?" I said. "I suppose you're free of that thug Maslennikov."

"I'm free of a lot more than him," she replied, as I pulled the bottle out of the cabinet and poured two glasses of the clear, oily vodka, and handed one to her.

"It should be ice cold, but scroungers can't be choosy." She raised her glass and chinked it against mine.

"To freedom and a new life in Hollywood." She tipped her head back and downed the vodka. "I should smash the glass against the fireplace, but there isn't one, and it would only make a mess for someone to clean up." She grinned. "Oh well, now we can have that tea you so thoughtfully brought. Won't you sit down?"

I took the other armchair, intrigued by her mood. It's not every day you see a beautiful woman brought back from the dead, knocking back hard liquor.

"So how does it feel, being dead?"

She sipped her tea while pondering the question. "It feels very liberating," she finally replied, laughing, showing her fine white teeth, and shaking her auburn hair. "I'm free of Lady Helen Ashworth, pretending to be an English lady. And I'm free of Helena Kovtoun the dancer and actress with the shady past. I shot them both, there were British and Russian witnesses who will swear to it. You brought the body back aboard, and will make an entry in the log after you bury it at sea somewhere off the coast of Formosa. I am so looking forward to attending my own funeral."

I joined in her laughter; it was an amusing thought, but dangerous.

"I think it would be better for everyone if you didn't," I replied. Apart from Major Spencer, Lowther and myself, no one knows you're still alive. I might have to swear a couple more into the secret. But it's best if the rest of crew go on thinking you're dead. That way there will be no lips loosened by drink to give you away."

She nodded pensively. Then her mouth split into a wide grin, and more peals of laughter filled the cabin. "Even better, I get to miss my own funeral."

I put a finger to my lips. "I'm serious, no one must know you're still alive. You'll have to remain in this cabin until we get to Davao, and I'll have your meals brought in by Da Silva. His lips are as tight as a duck's backside, but you'll be amazed what he can conjure up over a spirit stove in the pantry."

"And will you visit to entertain me, or shall I resort to the vodka bottle, and whatever penny dreadful novels I managed to throw into the trunk before Major Spencer bundled me into his car." Her grin had turned teasingly flirtatious, but I decided it was best to play the delivery with a straight bat.

"I've got quite a good selection of books in my cabin. But you could use the time to consider what you'll do when you get to Davao."

"I've already worked that out," she said, with a dismissive toss of her head. "I'm free remember. You have no idea how liberating it is to be dead. All of my past, all of my mistakes, all those awful men like Maslennikov, gone, all gone to the devil. The papers will report my death. A few lines in the obituary column, wife of the late Lord Ashworth, friend of the Astors, exotic background. After a few days I'll be forgotten, and good riddance. Then a fresh new face arrives in Hollywood, part of the flotsam of Shanghai fleeing the chaos of China for a new life in America. A girl with a pretty face who can act and speaks several languages. A new name, perhaps a little cosmetic surgery to hide some of the wrinkles. Makeup, costume, I don't think anyone will recognise the former Lady Ashworth, and I think I'll do very well on the silver screen." Her eyes were gazing into the distance, as if she could already see her name in lights on Times Square. Then they flicked back towards me. "What do you think?"

"I don't want to rain on your ticker tape parade," I said, "but how will you get to America without papers. You'll need a new identity, a new passport, everything?"

"Major Spencer owes me a favour or two, don't you think? And I'm sure a man with his connections can find the necessary paperwork to admit one more refugee."

I nodded. She was right. I had no doubt that Spencer, or at least his friends in Whitehall, had the ability to produce a set of documents that would fool even the most eagle eyed immigration official, if they chose to do so. Would they do it for Helena, though, or was saving her life payback enough for whatever services she had provided. I had a feeling that nothing would turn out quite as simply as she imagined. But she was a survivor and I hoped she'd make it.

She leaned forward, stubbed the Sobranie into the ashtray and stood up to walk to the bathroom. I heard the squealing of the old brass taps, and the gush of water into the bath.

"I need to wash the blood and filth from that Russian ship off," she called through the open doorway. "But there's no need to leave. Help yourself to one of my Sobranies, and another vodka if you want one."

I'm no prude, but keeping a beautiful woman company while she bathed was not exactly something that happened to the average tramp ship master every day. It fleetingly crossed my mind that as she didn't, legally speaking, exist, I had a fairly free hand to pursue any dishonourable intentions I might have harboured. And she had asked me to stay, so I pulled a pastel pink, gold tipped Sobranie from the box, lit it and inhaled a lungful of smoke. It was milder than my normal Senior Service, with a spicy flavour that could have been the exotic blend of Balkan tobaccos, or just my imagination.

I was in the act of pouring myself another tot of vodka when I heard a girlish giggle, and turned to see Helena framed in the bathroom door, wearing a full-length bathrobe.

"I think next time I'll offer you a Black Russian, that pink Cocktail does not suit you at all."

I was pleased at the possibility there might be a next time, but the sight of her face reminded me of what Maslennikov had done to her. Without makeup the battering she had taken was obvious. There were livid knuckle marks on both cheekbones, one eye was ringed by a purple bruise, and her lower lip had a deep split in it.

She saw me staring, and one end of her mouth curled upwards, painfully I imagined. "Now you know what theatrical makeup and lipstick can hide," she said. "But, that's not the worst of it." She swivelled and dropped the robe to her waist. I glimpsed the swell of her breasts, but that's not what grabbed my attention. Her naked back was a criss-cross of dark, livid welts and bruises.

"My God, the bastard."

"He beat me with the buckle end of his belt."

"If I ever get my hands on him."

"Pray you never get close enough. He tears men apart."

She hitched the robe back up, and turned to face me. Her eyes were dry, but burning fiercely. "I really would have shot myself, rather than go back to that. I've another pistol in my bag, which fires more than blanks."

I'd seen men beaten bloody, but the sight of what Maslennikov had done to her sickened me.

"Even more reason we get you to Davao unseen." I stubbed out the pink cigarette. "Enjoy your bath, and let me know if you need anything." It sounded pathetic, but I couldn't think of anything better to say. So I let myself out and left her to it.

CHAPTER SIXTEEN

"**W**e therefore commit her body to the deep, to be turned into corruption, looking for the resurrection of the body ..." I stood, bareheaded, beside the bier on which the red ensign shrouded parcel lay, reading the words of the service for burial at sea. I was not religious, and there was no corpse being committed to the embrace of the ocean, but I still felt moved by the simple words of the Prayer Book. It was ten o'clock in the morning on the day after our encounter with the *Admiral Alfater,* and *Oriental Venture* lay hove to, gently heaving and rolling in the long ocean swell. The mourning party consisted of Lowther, Cramp, who had rolled up an old straw mattress, weighted it with some scrap iron donated by the chief engineer and stitched heavy canvas around it, the Chinese boatswain and six of his men, who were holding the bier against the starboard side rail, waiting for the signal to raise the inboard end.

"... When the sea shall give up her dead, and the life of the world to come, through our Lord Jesus Christ. Amen." I completed the prayer and nodded to the boatswain. The bier rose and the canvas parcel, containing what the log would record as the mortal remains of Lady Helen Ashworth, scraped down the rough wooden planks, slid over the side and splashed into the western Pacific Ocean. I stepped forward to the rail and glanced down into the crystal clear water, watching the canvas parcel slide deeper and deeper, until it disappeared into the blue depths.

"Carry on, McGrath," I called up to the third mate, who was watching respectfully from the bridge wing.

The burial party dispersed as the ship slowly gathered way. Cramp unclipped the ensign from the bier, rolled it up and handed it to Lowther.

"Thanks Chippy," he said. "Make sure the word gets passed around among the hands that Lady Ashworth was buried at sea this morning."

"Aye aye," replied Cramp. "There's no daht some of us'll raise a glass to 'er memory when we reaches Davao, if you takes my meaning, sir."

"Well don't overdo it. And keep your eyes peeled. I think most of the lads are pretty trustworthy, but let me know if you see anyone snooping about the passenger quarters."

"Don't worry, Mister Mate, I'll keep a weather eye cocked."

"I didn't see the point in it myself," Lowther said later, as we sat in my cabin enjoying a drink before lunch. "Surely just making an entry in the log would have been sufficient."

"You're probably right, Peter," I replied. "I doubt the British authorities will raise any questions, after I report the death to the consul in Davao. An unfortunate case of suicide, probably brought on by lingering grief at the death of her husband. No, it's the Russians I'm worried about, when they hear from the *Admiral Alfater*. If they smell a rat and start asking questions around the waterfront, well, if any of our crowd are asked they'll confirm that the ship was stopped for a burial at sea, that's the truth."

"But we can't keep Helena's presence on board a secret all the way to Davao. Most of the officers already know she's alive, and some of the crew are bound to suspect."

"We'll just have to do the best we can, Peter. Da Silva will look after her, and bring her meals, and she'll just have to stay confined to her cabin. It's only a week to Davao."

"But she'll have clothes to wash, and she can't remain cooped up all the time."

"Look, Peter, it's up to her," I replied, firmly. "The crew have all been officially told she's dead and buried. If Helena wants Lady Ashworth gone for good, then she needs to keep out of sight until we can land her in Davao. We can rely on the officers, but who knows what some slack jawed engineer will say after a skinful. Okay, eventually someone's bound to blab, the best we can hope is that by then Helena is safely hidden under a new identity somewhere. And the least anyone on board knows about it the better."

I thought of Helena alone in the passenger suite, no doubt smiling as she waited for her own burial service to be completed. It was only a matter of a few days before we arrived in Davao, but it was one thing keeping Helena out of sight on board, it would be quite another getting her ashore in the Philippines without any papers. I had been giving that some thought, though, and a possible solution had occurred to me that I wanted to bounce off Major Spencer. If it worked, there might be no need for her to set foot in the Philippines. She would still have to land in the U.S. though. The immigration authorities didn't take kindly to undocumented arrivals. But Helena was a resourceful woman, and perhaps Spencer would do as she believed, and provide her with papers. How he could do that while we were at sea, though, I couldn't imagine.

I had just about finished my glass of rum, and was on the point of suggesting we head down to the saloon for the noontime curry, when there was a polite knock on the door and Sayce, the radio officer, appeared around the privacy curtain.

"Sorry to disturb you, sir, but there's a telegram from Mr Khoo. I thought you should read it straight away."

He handed me the buff coloured form. It took only seconds to read, but the implications were alarming.

"JAPANESE INVADED CHINA STOP HEAVY FIGHTING AROUND SHANGHAI STOP NATIONALISTS AND COMMUNISTS AGREE COOPERATE STOP. PROCEED DAVAO AS PLANNED STOP KHOO ENDS."

I handed it to Lowther, watching his eyes narrow and his mouth twist into a frown. I turned to Sayce. "Ask Major Spencer to join us, and then send an acknowledgment to Mr Khoo."

Spencer arrived moments later, and I handed him the message.

"Just what we were expecting," he said, after a quick glance at its contents. "But not quite so soon. Sounds like Shanghai's being defended though, and the alliance with the Communists will give the Japs something to think about."

"Looks like your efforts might have paid some dividends, Major," I said.

"As I recall it was your cargo, Captain," Spencer replied. "I just helped you deliver it."

"Well it sounds like a right mess, and we're well out of it."

"I wouldn't be so sure," said Spencer. "The Japs won't be content with China. Once they swallow it, they'll set their sights on French Indo-China, the Dutch Indies and the Philippines. Maybe even India and Australia. I think we've heard the first shots in the next big war. The one you fought to avoid, Commander Lowther."

The privacy curtain whisked aside again, and the radio operator's head appeared.

"I've tuned the shortwave receiver to the BBC Empire Service, sir, you might want to hear this."

We squeezed into the radio room to listen to a crackly, disembodied voice, fading in and out as the signal bounced off the ether, reading the news of the invasion. Japanese aircraft were blamed for dropping bombs on Shanghai, some of which had fallen inside the International Settlement. There was heavy fighting all around the city, including along Soochow Creek on the border of the British Concession. But Chiang Kai-shek had sent his best troops to defend the city, while also agreeing to form a united front with the communists.

"Mr Khoo seemed to know the fighting was imminent, when he sent the message telling us to get out," I said.

"It wouldn't be the first time my masters in Whitehall have read the runes incorrectly," replied Spencer, unabashed by the implied criticism. "But perhaps you should tell Helena. It was her home town."

She greeted the news with a muffled sob. Large, bright tears welled up in her eyes and slid slowly down her cheeks.

"I'm sorry Helena, there's no doubt friends of yours caught up in that mess," I said, wondering if I should risk offering to comfort her.

She dabbed at the tears with a handkerchief, and then blew her nose. "I loved Bobby Ashworth," she said. "He drank more than was good for him and he gambled, but he was always good to me. Shanghai was an escape from the bills and worries of England, but we were happy there. And then ..." a solitary tear formed and dropped, "... he died and left me. But that's not what the tears are for. They're for the city, for the Shanghai I loved, and all those people who call it home. Whatever happens life will never be the same for them again. You British might not realise it yet, but your empire's finished in China. The Japanese and the Chinese will fight it out between them. God knows who'll win, but whoever does won't want the British back running parts of it. In the meantime it's going to be a bloody business."

I wondered whether Maslennikov was caught up in the fighting. Nothing would have given me greater pleasure than to hear he had been killed by one of the bombs that hit the International Settlement. But somehow I doubted it. I also didn't doubt that taking Helena in my arms and comforting her would give me some pleasure. But I'd learned to my cost that making love to a woman when she was vulnerable, invariably came back to bite you where it hurt. In any case, she was on her way to Hollywood, and I would still only be master of a battered old tramp. There was no point whistling for the moon.

* * *

Oriental Venture rolled lazily in the long Pacific swell marching steadily in from the east, her foremast slowly tracing a giant arc against the background of the bright blue, cloudless sky, and the deeper, azure of the ocean. A moderate breeze was icing the tops of the waves with small crests of foam. I stood on the bridge wing clutching a mug of freshly brewed coffee, filling my lungs with the clean air blowing out of the vast reaches of the western Pacific, and enjoying its cool, salty fingers ruffling my hair. At the end of the bridge wing, Major Spencer was also enjoying the fresh, sunny morning, and puffing contentedly on a cigarette. We were alone at the centre of a vast circle of blue water, underneath a dome of endless blue sky.

"Easy to imagine we're the only ones left in creation," mused Spencer, pushing the stub of his cigarette into the sandbox hooked to the rail. "Out here, away from all the fighting and troubles ashore."

"Aye, this life does have its attractions on days like this," I agreed. "But the respite's only temporary. The perils of the sea are never far away and then, just when you think you've made it to safe haven, you face another set of perils ashore. What do you think, Third?"

McGrath had emerged from the wheelhouse holding his sextant, in readiness for a morning sun sight. "As we used to say in the old *Garthpool*, sir. Don't worry, worse things happen at sea. So I didn't worry and worse things did happen."

Spencer laughed heartily while McGrath finished observing the sun through the sextant, using the mirrored sight to measure its altitude above the horizon. Clicking his stopwatch, he read the angle on the scale, and went back into the chartroom to make his calculations.

"Seems we're all a bit philosophical this morning," continued Spencer. "But have you considered what to do with Helena once we reach Davao. It shouldn't be too hard to find a ship heading to the States that will give her passage, but how do we find one that won't ask too many questions?"

So much then, for Helena's faith in the major's benevolence, I thought, wondering whether I should enlighten him as to her expectations.

"I've been thinking about that," I replied, instead. "And I may have a possible solution. Have you heard of Jim Coffin?"

"Jim Coffin?" echoed Spencer. "No I don't think I have. Is he a friend of yours?"

"Not exactly a friend. He's an American captain, been master on all kinds of ships trading mostly around the Pacific. When he was younger he spent time in the whaling fleet, where he earned something of a reputation, and the nickname of 'Grim Jim'."

"Grim Jim," repeated Spencer, chortling like a ruddy faced parrot. "Funny sort of nickname."

"You'd be a brave man to laugh at it in front of him," I replied. "Only his friends call him Grim Jim."

"And don't tell me, he hasn't many friends." Spencer chuckled at his joke.

"He's a big New Englander with a hot temper and a short fuse. But he's been around the traps. He's a good seaman, knows these waters like the back of his hand, can sniff out a good deal when there's one on offer, and knows when to keep his mouth shut."

"High praise coming from you," replied Spencer.

"Aye, he's a good man as long as you don't cross him. Anyway, last I heard he'd bought his own ship, an Australian tramp called the *Nimrod*, and was trading her around the west Pacific. Interesting thing about her is that she's a bit of a sister ship to *Oriental Venture*." I patted the wooden railing with proprietorial pride.

"You mean she's identical to this one?" asked Spencer.

"More or less," I replied. "During the war, so many ships were sunk by U-boats that the government created an emergency shipbuilding programme to replace the losses with standard designs that could be built at several allied shipyards. *Oriental Venture* and *Nimrod* were a type of G-Class design offered by Thompsons in Sunderland, the largest type they built. The government usually paid for them, but a speculator with an eye for the main chance ordered these two. He thought he'd be able to sell them at a good price once the war ended. He even got Thompsons to include some passenger accommodation in the design, knowing it would make the ships more attractive for charter by the liner companies. Missed his chance though, and Mr Khoo bought this one cheap during the freight slump. She's 20 years old now, but Thompsons built a fine ship, and she's still up to the job, even if she's not quite the picture she was when she first slid into the Wear." I paused, chuckling at the thought of Mr Khoo taking the slightest notice of whether a ship looked attractive or not. "Although I doubt she was much of a picture even then," I continued. "It takes a rare breed of men to see anything pretty in ships like this."

Of which, I supposed, I must have been one, as I did find the old girl attractive. But perhaps, as her master, I was expected to be biased. I let my gaze wander over the extent of my command. On the foredeck, a gang of seamen was busy renewing the lashings securing the derrick booms, while others were armed with wire brushes and pots of paint, engaged in the continual battle against rust. I turned to look aft expecting a similar scene, but my eye was arrested by the thick plume of smoke streaming from the funnel and stretching away over the horizon, like a big black pointer to our position.

"Third Mate, why are we making so much smoke?"

McGrath almost jumped out of the wheelhouse, summoned by the harsh edge on my voice. He stared up at the billows of greasy, black smoke. "I don't know sir. I'll send word below to the chief engineer."

"That smoke will be visible for miles," I snapped. "I don't expect the Russians will have worked out where we are heading, but we don't want to take unnecessary chances."

McGrath hurried away and I turned back to Spencer. "Anyway, what was I saying? Ah yes, Jim Coffin. Well if anyone knows how to get a woman on board a ship bound for America, without anyone noticing, then he will. I'm going to get sparks to send a ship to ship radio message to him, and with a bit of luck he'll pick it up and we can arrange a rendezvous somewhere... Third Mate!"

"Sir," replied McGrath, appearing at my elbow, an exasperated expression on his face at the second summons, which I chose to ignore. "Chief Engineer's sent word that some of the coal we picked up in Shanghai seems a bit dodgy," he reported. "He's inspecting the bunkers with the second engineer to see what can be done about it, and will report to you when he's finished, sir."

"Dodgy!" I snorted, enjoying playing the irascible old man. "The owners will have paid for the best steaming coal. They'll have someone's guts if we've allowed the supplier to pull oakum over our eyes, and supply us with some soft rubbish suitable only for the Indian railways." I grinned at him. "Thank your stars it's not you. Now, ask sparks to come and see me in my day cabin, and send my compliments to the chief mate and ask him to join us."

"I want you to try and make radio contact with Captain Jim Coffin on the *Nimrod*," I said, once we had gathered in my day cabin. "You can look her up in the register of ships. I don't know if Coffin will have changed her port of registry and call sign, but use the one in the register. I'm sure his radio operator will recognise it. If you make contact pass him this message." I handed Sayce the hand written telegram form.

"Right you are, sir. There's a silence period coming up, but I'll give it a go right after that. Have you any idea where he is? If he's over 500 miles away we probably won't reach him until tonight, when reception improves."

"Sorry, Sparks, he could be anywhere, but I'm hoping he's still trading around the islands. Just do your best." Sayce turned to leave, but a thought occurred to me.

"Incidentally, Sparks, have you heard any more of those coded transmissions we picked up after leaving Manus Island. We passed on what you received to Major Spencer here, and I'm sure he'd be keen to know if you've heard any more."

"I heard nothing on the way to Shanghai, sir, but if they were transmitting from the Bismarck Sea we might have been a bit too far away. We'll stand a better chance as we get further south, off the Philippines."

"What do you think, Major?" I said. "If those messages did originate from the *Dortmund*, is she still likely to be skulking around New Guinea?"

Spencer's knitted brows indicated that he was mulling over the question, and I took the opportunity to glance across at Lowther seated on the settee opposite. His face was drawn and pale, and his hand gripped a tumbler half full of iced water which I suspected also held a stiff measure of gin, as he had arrived already clutching the full glass. It was late morning, lunch was not far away, but Lowther looked as if he had started early. Normally he kept his drinking, and his demons, under control. But something appeared to have changed, perhaps the stress of being taken hostage aboard the *Admiral Alfater,* and the shock of seeing Helena covered in blood, apparently dead, had triggered memories that he was struggling to forget. It wasn't in my nature to play confessor or therapist to my crew. A man did his job, or I got rid of him, sometimes assisted by a kick down the gangway. But Lowther was more than just another man. He was the closest thing I had to a friend, and it was my failure to spot the Russian trap that had nearly got some of us killed. I wondered if I should offer him a spell of leave next time we reached Hong Kong; give him a chance to blow off some steam in the bars and bath houses of Wan Chai.

"I relayed your intercepted messages to London," replied Spencer. "The boffins are studying them now, but they appear to be in some sort of randomly generated code. Very hard to break. But my guess is she's still in the area. Probably waiting for another shipment of weapons, to replace the one you deprived her of."

"That could make sense," said Lowther, the colour returning to his face after another swig of gin, "if the Nazi's are positioning her in advance of hostilities."

"But what about the damage?" said Spencer. "You said the *Dortmund* ran aground on a reef as she tried to cut you off."

"Hard to say," I replied. "She was steaming at full speed when she touched, and if she struck coral she could have ripped her bottom open. But my recollection is that the patch she grounded on was mostly sand. We cleared it, just, but the *Dortmund* draws more water. She might have sprung a plate or two, but if it was close to the bow the damage might be confined to one tank."

"Meaning?" said Spencer.

"Meaning they could have a tank full of seawater but still be afloat. What do you think, Peter?"

"Modern German ship like that, probably has some ice strengthening around the bow," said Lowther. "If she only slid up on hard sand there would be some buckling, perhaps some sheered rivets, but if it was a small enough area they could ballast her by the stern to lift the bow out of the water, and fill the bottom of the tank with quick drying concrete. That would suffice until they could find a drydock. The nearest ones are in Batavia or Brisbane. It shouldn't be hard to find out if she went to one of them."

"We can check with the Lloyd's agent when we reach Davao," I said, before turning back to Sayce. "Okay, Sparks, you can start trying to get hold of the *Nimrod*, and keep me informed how you get on."

"Right-oh sir," he replied, pushing his way past the curtain, and disappearing down the stairway to the radio shack.

"What do you think are our chances of contacting your, Jim Coffin?" asked Spencer.

"If he's within range of our transmission, if he's listening, if he hasn't got better things to do. Lot of ifs, but Grim Jim loves a mystery, especially if there's a woman involved."

"Heavens above, Captain, are you sure the gentle Lady Ashworth will be safe with your Captain Coffin."

"I'm sure that Helena Kovtoun is more than a match for Grim Jim, even if he is a bit of a pirate," I said, wondering just how Helena would take to the barrel chested, lantern jawed, hard drinking New Englander, and his crew of cutthroat misfits, whose reputation was even worse than my own. I had a feeling *Oriental Venture* would appear genteel by comparison. But we would take that ferry when we got there. "We'll just have to wait and see what luck sparks has in raising him," I continued. "Then if we can get her over to him without raising any attention, and the crew spread the word about the burial at sea ... and those who know the truth keep their traps shut. Lady Ashworth should disappear without trace. Unless the American authorities ask too many questions."

"There'll be a rush of stateless people fleeing Shanghai now the Japs have invaded," replied Spencer. "A pretty young widow, whose missionary husband was tragically killed in China, while spreading the word to the heathen celestials, is sure to tug the heartstrings of the most hardened American official. A good story like that, and the temporary passport I can arrange should see her right. Plus I've one or two friends in America who might see the advantage of a beautiful actress who speaks fluent Russian."

I raised an eyebrow. "More friends in high places?" The type who charged a price for their friendship, apparently. It seemed that Helena was not easily going to break her attachment to the major and his friends. Which made me wonder whether I too would see the last of him after he got off in Davao.

"And low ones, Captain. You can never have too many friends."

* * *

The start of the evening watch, and *Oriental Venture* was steaming steadily south by east into a gentle swell, which her bows languorously rose to meet. It had been a glorious sunset, the last rays of the sun setting the base of the clouds on fire, the colours rapidly turning from gold to red, to a fading ember shade of pink as the sun disappeared behind the distant hills of Mindanao.

I stepped onto the bridge at 8 p.m., just as McGrath relieved Lowther, to witness the moon rising out of the sea, a huge, shimmering ball that appeared low enough to touch, and whose rays silvered the rippled surface of the water, and bathed the ship in a cool, eerie light. Over towards the land a sprinkling of lights glimmered, fishermen hoping for a good catch under the moon, otherwise the horizon was empty.

Leaving the two of them to get on with their handover, I strolled into the chartroom to check the chart. Noting the position that Lowther had plotted after taking his evening star sights, I traced my finger along our intended course, parallel to the coast of Mindanao, tracking south and then west as it curved away towards the tip of Cape San Augustin. From there we would turn north, across the gulf to Davao City, where we were due to arrive the following afternoon.

His watch over, Lowther, joined me in the chartroom for a few minutes while we discussed the arrangements for loading our cargo of Manila hemp. Then he wished me a good evening and headed below.

But not for long. I was in the middle of writing my night orders, when the chartroom door was flung open, and Lowther burst in bearing the buff form of a telegram.

"Third Mate!" he yelled for McGrath, who immediately popped his head into the chartroom hearing the urgency in the voice.

"Nip down below and ask Major Spencer to join us. Sparks has picked up a message."

He was back in under a minute closely followed by the major. Meanwhile Lowther handed me the form and I held it under the red chartroom lamp to read, but could only see meaningless groupings of letters.

"Is this my answer from the *Nimrod?* Is it some kind of joke?" I said, annoyed that Jim Coffin should think we had time to waste trying to understand it.

"Yes, and no," said Lowther, and then, seeing the look of thunder on my face, rapidly continuing. "Sparks has been calling the *Nimrod* again this evening, trying to raise her as instructed. With the same result. There was no reply, just like on the previous couple of nights."

"Well, what's this then," I interrupted, shaking the telegram under his nose.

Lowther ignored my impatience. "Not long after he sent the last call, he picked that up."

"So! Is it from the *Nimrod* or isn't it?"

"He thinks it is, but no, it's not the answer to your telegram"

"That doesn't make any sense. Why would Coffin ignore my message, and then send something like that." I spread the message out on the chart table. "It's just a series of letters and numbers."

We stared down at the paper, as if expecting sudden inspiration.

"SSS, SSS, SSS, GVTQ, GVTQ, GVTQ, SSS, SSS, SSS, 0720N 13," read Lowther. "Sparks says the transmission was clear and the signal strong, so it was sent from not far away. It was also cut short, the signal stopped right after the thirteen, as if it had been interrupted. I've told him to keep listening."

"Why do you think it's from the *Nimrod?*" asked Spencer, voicing the obvious question. The one I should have asked if I'd been more alert and less prickly.

"By the call sign, here," Lowther pointed. "After the three groups of S's you see the letters GVTQ repeated three times. That's the call sign of the *Nimrod*, or at least that's the one listed for her in the shipping register."

I had not thought to check myself. But it was a startling revelation, or one hell of a coincidence. And as I read the message again I began to see the sense in the numbers.

"That's a British call sign," I said. "So unless it's been reassigned, Coffin either retained it when he bought the ship, or hasn't got round to changing it."

"I thought you said she was previously owned by an Australian company," said Spencer. "So why the British call sign?"

"Mercantile colonialism," I replied. "Australian ships are regarded as British. But assuming it is from the *Nimrod*, what does the rest of it mean? My guess is that 0720N is the start of a position, latitude seven degrees twenty minutes north."

"And thirteen?" asked Spencer.

"Is the longitude," I said. "It could be thirteen east or west, but that would be on the other side of the world. It's more likely the start of 130, 130 degrees east or west. If it was west it would put the ship in the middle of the Pacific Ocean." I examined the chart. "Seven degrees twenty minutes north is very close to our own latitude here," I stabbed the chart with a finger close to our position off Mindanao. "If you follow the meridian east," I slid my finger across the chart, "then that signal could have come from somewhere east of here," stabbing the chart again. "One hundred and thirty degrees east, she could be as close as two hundred miles away."

"But why send out a position like that, unless it was meant for you?" said Spencer, "Perhaps he's letting you know where he is, or suggesting a rendezvous."

"If it was meant for us, the message would have started with our call sign," I said. "But it doesn't, which means it was more likely a call to anyone who was listening."

"Like a distress call?" said Spencer. "But I thought the signal for that was SOS."

"It is," I replied. "And it's an easy signal to remember, three dots, three dashes and three dots, repeated. So I don't think it's meant to be SOS. I also don't recall any mercantile signal that's just made up of three letter S's, though. Does sparks have any idea what it means?"

"No, he's never heard of it before," replied Lowther, his brows knotted in thought. "But there is another possibility, though it's an odd one," he continued. "There was an emergency naval signal that ships used during the war, if they were under attack by U-boat. That signal was SSS, for 'I am under attack by submarine.' But it was only used during the war."

"But we're not at war now," I said. "So why should someone send such a signal? Unless ..." the answer occurred to me even as I voiced the question "... unless they were under attack by a submarine, and whoever sent it realised he had very little time, remembered the old naval signal, and decided to take a chance and use it."

"I seem to recall that Coffin's second mate, Flynn, was a signalman in the *Barham* during the war. Perhaps he remembered the signal for submarine attack," said Lowther.

"But why not just send the distress signal, SOS, at least anyone who heard that would recognise it as a call for help?" said Spencer.

"Perhaps, but SSS is also a warning to other ships," said Lowther. "Anyone hearing that signal in wartime would know if they went to help they might also be attacked. But as you said, skipper, we're not at war."

"Not that we've heard," I replied. "But if your ship was under attack by a submarine you might be forgiven for jumping to that conclusion. And that means that somewhere out there," I waved a hand in the direction of east, almost reluctant to express the inevitable conclusion to our thoughts, "there is a submarine that has just attacked a merchantman going about her normal business. That's an act of war ... or piracy." I paused and turned to Spencer. "Major, you seem to attract trouble. Have you got any theories?"

"I'm as in the dark as you are," he replied. "There have been sightings of Japanese and Nazi submarines around some of the Pacific islands, hardly surprising given that the Japs, at least, seem bent on further conquests in the East. But there's no law against a submarine cruising in international waters if it leaves shipping alone. I suppose it's possible that a Japanese submarine might attack a Chinese ship now that they are, since the invasion, at war."

"Ships sailing from the East Indies and Australia would pass this way if they were heading for China," I said. "But it's not a Chinese ship that's sent that signal. As I recall there are supposed to be rules governing the actions of naval ships that intercept freighters — assuming that it's not just blatant piracy."

"Normally a submarine is not supposed to attack a merchant ship without first identifying that it belongs to an enemy, and then giving the crew the opportunity to surrender and escape in the boats," explained Lowther. "The Germans followed those rules at the start of the war, but then abandoned them, and just attacked on sight any ship heading to or from Britain."

That brought back some unwelcome memories, and I felt a burning flush of anger colour my face. My father had been killed by a U-boat. Fed up with the way the German submarines attacked coastal shipping with near impunity, and before there were enough naval escorts available, the Admiralty had turned to using decoy ships, harmless looking merchantmen, that packed a hidden punch. Any unwary U-boat that ventured too close on the surface was likely to find itself outgunned when the decoy — Q-ships as they were known — dropped its disguise and opened fire at short range. My father had been posted to such a ship, but had been killed, along with the rest of the crew. Machine-gunned in the water after the German, smelling a rat, had torpedoed them without warning. If Lowther was right, then a submarine had just attacked a British ship without warning, either deliberately or by mistake. The tingling in my fingertips confirmed my decision.

"If it had been an SOS distress call then, under the law of the sea, I'm obliged to render assistance. The SSS signal could be a warning, but it could also mean there are men adrift in boats, or in the water. I think we have a duty to investigate.

Normally I'd send a telegram to the owners telling them of my intention, but if that is a submarine out there attacking ships, then I don't want to warn it of our presence, so I'll tell sparks to maintain radio silence. But as you represent the charterers, Major, I should tell you that we'll be late for our arrival in Davao. But then, under the circumstances, I don't think you'll object."

"If there's a Jap sub attacking British ships, then the authorities need to know, but we need to be certain, so I agree we should take a look," replied Spencer.

Listening to our deliberations Lowther had busied himself at the chart.

"I've plotted a course to seven degrees twenty minutes north and one hundred and thirty degrees east, skipper, and extended it east along the meridian. I think you should take a look."

I bent over the chart and followed Lowther's finger as he traced a pencil line due east into the Pacific. The line came to rest on a group of tiny islands.

"What are they?"

"We know them as the Pelew Islands, sir? The natives refer to them as Palau, which probably just means islands."

"Are they inhabited?"

"Oh yes. And here's the interesting part. Up to the end of the war they were German, now the Japanese own them. Run east along the meridian to one hundred and thirty five east and you come to Koror, the main settlement. It will take us just over 36 hours to get there, less if the attack was further west."

Probably too late for any poor bastards in the water. If they didn't drown or die of exposure, then the sharks would get them. I hoped they'd been given time to get away in the boats.

"Right, Peter, confirm the course to the third mate and let the chief engineer know what we are about. Post extra lookouts from first light, and make the ship ready to receive survivors. And break out the arms again. We can't fight a submarine, but we might as well have some means to defend ourselves against boarders if piracy is what it's about. I'll tell Helena. I doubt she'll be pleased with the diversion, but it can't be helped."

CHAPTER SEVENTEEN

Sunrise was not far off as I conned *Oriental Venture* inshore towards the reef. We had steamed east for two days sighting nothing. Not even any wreckage that might have floated to the surface from a sinking ship. There had also been no further transmissions from the *Nimrod*, although sparks had picked up another message that appeared to be in a code we could make no sense of. Having come this far east, though, I had decided to have a look into the anchorages close to Koror, to see if they offered any clue as to the origin of the radio messages, or the fate of the *Nimrod*.

Together with Lowther, I had pored over the largest chart we carried that covered the Pelew Islands, and had studied the Admiralty sailing directions. Koror was in the centre of the island chain, protected by an almost unbroken line of reefs that enclosed a large sheltered lagoon. There were several entrances, but all were too shallow for ships as large as *Oriental Venture*, which were directed to anchor in Koror Roads, sheltered behind an outlying section of reef.

If a submarine had sunk the *Nimrod* it was unlikely she was still in the area. In which case, having found no wreckage, we were on a wild goose chase. But the absence of wreckage could also mean that she had been seized, perhaps in the belief that her cargo was destined for China. Which was entirely possible, although why a Japanese submarine should have cause to suspect a British ship this far out in the Pacific, I found hard to imagine. Perhaps the submarine had decided to escort the *Nimrod* to the nearest Japanese territory to carry out a more thorough inspection. The Pelew Islands were Japanese, so Koror was a logical choice. But would the submarine's captain be so blatant as to anchor her in the roads? Japan was not at war with Britain, and someone would be sure to notice if a British ship arrived as the prize of a Japanese submarine. No, if the *Nimrod* and her captor were anywhere nearby, I thought they were more likely to be tucked away out of sight in some secluded anchorage.

And a close examination of the chart suggested that such an anchorage might, indeed, exist.

A few miles south-west of Koror was an indentation in the island chain forming the main part of the reef. At the northern end of the indentation, the sickle shaped island of Urukthapel curved away west and south. Its north-eastern tip sprouting its own section of reef that extended south, forming the handle of the sickle. The southern end of the indentation was bordered by a roughly circular shaped island called Mecherchar, whose south-eastern edge was fringed by another section of reef pointing north. The water bounded by those two islands and their reef extensions, formed a large, semi-enclosed bay, in the middle of the entrance to which were two reef outcrops. Between the southerly outcrop and the Mecherchar reef the water was too shallow to admit a large ship. But between the northern outcrop and the reef-handle of Urukthapel's sickle, the depth appeared sufficient to admit a ship the size of *Oriental Venture,* which could then quite happily lie at anchor in the sheltered southern end of the bay.

I could have taken the ship directly into the bay, sounding my way in through the northern channel, but that would have betrayed our presence to anyone already anchored there. A further inspection of the chart suggested a better alternative, however. West of Mecherchar on the outlying reef, I noticed two islets, between which the reef took a sudden bend north-east, before curving sharply west again, creating a narrow inlet. There looked to be just enough water depth and space between the islets to allow *Oriental Venture* to swing safely around her anchor. Better still, at the apex of the inlet was a shallow passage that would admit a boat into the lagoon, across which it was only a short row to Mecherchar, from where we would be able to see into the bay on the other side, without being seen ourselves. Perhaps I was being overly cautious, and should have steamed boldly into the Koror roadstead. But the tingling in my fingertips had returned, and after the near debacle with the *Admiral Alfater*, I was in no mood to take chances.

Approaching in the pre-dawn twilight, I was confident I would have *Oriental Venture* hidden away in the pocket between the two islets before the sun rose, but I had warned Fraser to make as little smoke as possible. Now, against the paling light of dawn, as we slowly nosed towards the reef, I could clearly make out the two islets fine on either bow, while I hoped our own dark shape was still masked by the dark-ness in the west. With McGrath and Cramp on the forecastle, and the anchors ready for letting go, I cautiously conned the ship towards the centre of the gap between the islets, listening for the calls of the boatswain as he cast the hand lead to sound the water depth. No bottom at twenty fathoms was still the call as the bow approached the gap, the water still too dark in the pre-dawn light to provide any visible clues as to depth. I wondered whether the seabed between the two islets would shelve too steeply to provide a holding ground. More worryingly, it might shelve very suddenly, giving me no time to stop or turn before the coral tore the bottom open. Investigating the source of a possible distress call was one thing. Putting my own ship into danger was quite another, and I hardly dared consider what Mr Khoo would say if I wrecked his ship on a remote Pacific reef.

"By the mark twenty."

The boatswain's call indicated he had found bottom with about ninety feet of water beneath the keel. I could see the palm trees and shrubs taking on colour in the strengthening light, and the waves breaking over the sandy fringes of the islets.

"By the deep sixteen."

Shelving then, but it was too late now to turn. I had stopped the engine and we were coasting slowly into the gap.

"By the mark ten."

My hands tightened on the handrail. There was only thirty feet under the keel and the water was shallowing rapidly, but we were almost exactly in between the two islets, a cable more and we would be tucked out of sight inshore of them.

"By the mark seven."

Only thirteen feet under the keel! I could feel the sweat break out on my brow and barely registered the tops of the palms flecked with gold as the rim of the sun cleared the horizon.

"Slow astern."

I peered down at the crystal clear water, through which the brightening yellow sand appeared frighteningly close in the rapidly strengthening light, watching for the first sign of gathering stern way.

"By the mark seven."

Levelling off, I breathed easier.

"Drop anchor. Stop engine. Three shackles in the water." That meant an anchor cable length of nearly three hundred feet, seven times the water depth, more than enough to hold us as long as the weather remained good, but short enough, I hoped, to keep us out of the shallows.

There was a grumbling, clanking rattle from the foredeck, followed by a loud splash as the anchor hit the water, and a cloud of dust rose over the windlass as the ship's stern way dragged the rusty chain out of the chain locker.

I heard three strokes on the forecastle bell, immediately followed by Lowther's report. "Three shackles in the water."

"Screw up."

I could see Cramp screwing the windlass brake on as hard as he could, while McGrath leaned over the bow watching the angle of the cable. As the ship's weight came on it would tighten, dragging the anchor until its flukes bit into the seabed.

The docking telegraph jangled.

"Brought up, sir."

The anchor was holding and the ship was positioned mid-way between the islets in the centre of the small inlet. It had looked easy, but a stray current could easily have swung the bow onto the reef, or it might have been too deep to anchor, in which case I would now be sweating on turning the ship in her own length in order to get out again. It was still not plain sailing though. The last of the land breeze was holding the ship's bow towards the reef. Later in the day, the sea breeze would swing her round the other way.

"Thanks, Peter. You can ring finished with engine but tell the chief to keep sufficient steam up that we can slip and run for it if we have to. Set a double anchor watch, and put a man in the crow's nest so we aren't taken by surprise. And get McGrath to take the rescue boat away and sound all around the ship. We don't want to bump into any nasty shallow patches, when we swing. And when you're ready come down to my cabin and we'll run over the plans for tonight."

I went below, able to relax now that we were concealed in the centre of what appeared to be a pretty snug anchorage. Sheltered by the islets to north and south, and by the reef to the east, we only had to worry if the weather blew up from the west. Fortunately, there was no sign of that. A mile and a half away across the lagoon the thickly wooded island of Mecherchar looked deserted. Little more than a cluster of low sand hills covered by dense tropical forest and mangroves, and interspersed by shallow lakes, it looked difficult to cross. On the other side was the large sheltered bay that looked like an ideal anchorage, if a piratically inclined submarine commander wanted to conduct a thorough and undisturbed search of his prize, safely away from prying eyes.

I rubbed my fingertips together to ease the tingling. I was keen to find out what was in that bay. If I could believe the radio message, a submarine had attacked the *Nimrod*, either sending Jim Coffin and his crew to the bottom with their ship, or seizing and holding her somewhere. But for what purpose? And if she was being held was I looking in the right place? Or was it all some crazy wild goose chase.

I hoped some of the answers lay on the other side of the island, but I was going to wait for dark to find out, to make doubly sure that no one was expecting us.

* * *

The rest of the day passed quietly. The ship swung to her anchor in the sea breeze that sprang up during the afternoon, bringing some relief from the sun beating down onto the exposed steel decks. There was still no sign of life on either of the two islets, which were little more than sand hills covering the top of the coral beneath.

Each was forested with dense stands of tall palm trees, against which *Oriental Venture* would have been hard to spot. Even so, we sighted no other ships passing to seaward, and no native craft fishing in the lagoon. If the islands were inhabited, there was little evidence of it on this side. Which suited me fine.

During the afternoon, I ordered McGrath to take the rescue boat and investigate the narrow channel that appeared to lead from the head of the inlet into the lagoon. With a seaman on the hand lead, he sounded his way up the narrowing head of the inlet, and discovered that at its apex there was indeed a channel, just sufficiently wide and deep enough to admit a boat. Once through the channel the bottom dropped away into deep blue water, across a mile of which lay Mecherchar, and McGrath recorded the compass bearings and soundings that would enable us to retrace his course after dark.

Back on board he reported to me with his findings, and between us we sketched the inlet, and the channel through to the lagoon, marking on it the soundings and bearings he had taken.

It was now approaching midnight, and the ship lay quietly at anchor, all lights doused or hidden, and the crew forbidden to smoke on deck or to make any noise. A partial moon rode high in the clear, star-studded sky, providing just enough light, I hoped, to find our way across Mecherchar, have a look at what was on the other side, and make our way back again. I ordered McGrath back into the rescue boat. It was going to be a long night for him, but he had youth on his side. Plus I trusted his small boat handling skills. As, apparently, did the Chinese crew at the oars, most of whom were grinning excitedly at the prospect of a midnight excursion. There was nothing to plunder, but I imagined it appealed to the latent streak of piracy that still inhabited their oriental souls. Cramp, Spencer and I made up the rest of the party. If the *Nimrod* or a submarine were anchored in the lagoon, then I wanted to see for myself. Few had more experience of sneaking around in dark places than Cramp, and I suspected the major was equally at home with nighttime jungle patrols. That left Lowther and Griffith in charge of the ship. I didn't expect anything to go wrong, but left instructions that if we got into serious trouble we would fire a red flare. Which was their signal to get the ship underway and report the situation by radio.

"Give way, together," said McGrath, quietly, as we shoved off. The order followed by the creaking and splashing of oars as the Chinese seamen, their grinning teeth visible in the moonlight, pulled energetically away from the ship's side.

"Row easy, dammit," hissed McGrath. "Don't you know that sound travels more easily at night?"

In their attempt to make less splashing one of the men caught a crab, and was sent sprawling off the thwart onto the bottom boards.

"Just row normally," I said, once the muffled laughter had died down, and an orderly stroke resumed. "I doubt there's anyone within hearing range."

Using a shaded torch, McGrath kept a check on the compass heading as he steered the boat towards the channel at the head of the inlet. I could hear the soft booming of the low swell breaking over the exposed coral heads, and there was just enough moonlight to see the white water on either side as the boat nosed into the channel, McGrath steering carefully to keep her to the middle. I didn't fancy having to climb into the dark water, and scrabble about over the sharp edged coral if he ran the boat aground, but he steered us safely through and the seamen settled to their task, the oars rising and falling steadily as the boat hissed softly through the calm water of the lagoon. It was a warm night, but I shivered as a splash from an oar wet my face.

"It seems further than it did this afternoon," said McGrath, softly.

"Your senses play tricks on you at night," I replied. "Just trust the compass and we'll get there soon enough."

Ahead of the boat, Mecherchar loomed as a low dark mass against the horizon, seeming to float away as we rowed towards it. Until, half an hour later, the keel kissed the sand, the crew unshipped their oars, jumped into the water and ran the boat up onto the gently shelving beach. I gathered them together.

"You stay here with the men, Third, and guard the boat. Keep a sharp lookout, and if you see a red flare, or we're not back by sunrise, head back to the ship as quick as you can and tell Mr Lowther."

I heard his whispered, aye aye, and then, motioning Spencer and Cramp to follow me, I headed towards the dark shadows beneath the trees.

We had about five hours to daylight. More than enough to cover the mile or so across the island to the other side, from where we would be able to see what, if anything, was anchored in the bay beyond. But the absence of habitation meant there were no trails. We would have to force our own path through the forest, and once through the line of palms fringing the beach the going quickly proved tougher than I expected. Dense bushes grew thickly beneath the rain forest canopy. And although there was just enough moonlight filtering down through the foliage to allow me to pick a way through the vegetation, I still needed frequent stops to shine a torch onto my pocket compass to check we were not going around in circles in the darkness.

It was slow going. I couldn't see where my feet were landing and often had to carefully feel my way over or around rocks and tree stumps. And we seemed to be making an awful lot of noise as we floundered and pushed our way through bushes that only grudgingly ceded our passage. Behind me I could hear Spencer's laboured breathing, and his curses as he lost his footing or blundered into a thorny bush that raked his arms and face. I had clearly overestimated his jungle warfare capabilities.

I couldn't hear anything of Cramp, which was not surprising as he was a good man to bring up the rear. As a boy, living in the mean, poverty stricken lanes of Wapping, he'd been used to finding his way about in the dark. Slinking down alleys, and over the fences and walls of the docks where he had pilfered whatever he could sell or trade to put food on the table and clothes on his back. The night held few terrors for him, the danger of boots and knives flashing in the darkness were greater threats than the rush of bats or the scrabbling of rats. So I didn't think that thorny bushes, or the possibility of snakes and tropical spiders, held much terror for him. Which was cold comfort, because I couldn't say the same of myself. The jungle was surprisingly quiet, though. Eerily quiet. No frogs croaking, crickets buzzing or bats screeching. The only noises I could hear were those we were making ourselves, as we forced our way through the undergrowth towards the far side of the island.

Yet my senses were crawling. We hadn't see a sign of another human being on any of the surrounding islands. Not a wisp of cooking smoke, not the distant glimpse of a fishing canoe, nor a brown-skinned figure slipping between the trees. Nothing. But I could feel that we were not alone. I couldn't hear it, let alone see it in the darkness, but I could feel it. Someone, or something, was in the jungle with us. Watching us? Or hunting us? Or perhaps it was just my overactive imagination.

But, almost without being aware of it, my movements became stealthy. Easing my feet down with each step, and sliding gently through the bushes, I tried to minimise the noise I was making. Behind me I could hear Spencer cursing again as he stumbled over a rock. He seemed to have dropped back some distance, so I stopped to wait for him, concealing myself in the black shadows of a fallen tree. Standing motionless and silent, breathing softly and turning my head slowly from side to side, listening intently for the slightest sound. There was nothing. Nothing but the gentle rush of blood pulsing in my ears. Nothing but Spencer's muttered curse as another creeper scraped his face. Nothing ... but, the softest rustle, the merest whisper of disturbed leaves. My hand dropped to my belt, and I reached for the sheath knife.

As a powerful hand closed over my mouth, and the needle sharp point of a blade jabbed into the side of my throat.

"Easy now," a voice whispered in my ear. "Don't struggle and I won't cut yer throat."

I could feel the brute strength in the arms holding me, and knew that the knife would sever my windpipe before I could wrestle free. I relaxed and dropped my arms to my side.

"Good, that's sensible. Now I'm goin' to take me hand off your mouth and you're goin' to tell me who ye'are and what you're doing here. If yer shouts ..."

The point of the knife dug deeper into my neck for emphasis, persuading me there was no particular reason for secrecy. The man wielding the knife wasn't Japanese, that much I could tell by his accent, and Cramp was still gliding silently through the bush towards me and would make short work of him when he found us. Provided I didn't get skewered in the meantime.

"We're from a ship anchored beside the lagoon."

"You British?"

"Yeah."

"Is your ship the *Oriental Venture*?"

Despite the knife at my throat, I stiffened in surprise, and had to force myself to relax.

"Yes."

I was even more surprised when the knife left my throat, and the arms relaxed their grip. I span around expecting to see the man who had grabbed me, but met only the darkness, and a low throaty chuckle. Whoever it was had faded back into the shadows.

"It's not that easy man, but I'm still here. You need to call your friends. If you're looking for the *Nimrod,* I can help you find her."

I called to Spencer and Cramp, who came crashing through the undergrowth towards the sound of my voice, from which I managed to eliminate the startled edge. They found me crouched in a tiny clearing, staring into the bushes.

"There was a man here a few seconds ago, who said he could help us find the *Nimrod*." It sounded ridiculous, and I saw Cramp's face in the moonlight creasing into the disbelieving smile of a man thinking his captain was suffering from the collywobbles.

Which froze on his lips at the sight of a huge, Pacific islander materialising out of the bushes.

"Who the hell are you?" I snapped, rubbing my neck where I could still feel the needlepoint of his blade.

"Easy, sir," he replied. "I'm Ratu, quartermaster of the *Nimrod*. If you gentlemen is lookin' for us, then I'm mighty glad to see you. If not," the knife blade flashed wickedly in the moonlight, "you probably won't make it back to the beach."

It was three against one, but something told me that Ratu, if that was his name, was very much more at home in the jungle darkness than we were. And if he was from the *Nimrod*, then he probably knew what had happened to her. Unless it was a trap, and whoever had seized her had been expecting us. But how would they know we were coming?

"You talk politely to the Captain, and put that knife away," snarled Cramp, drawing his own sheath knife and crouching, ready to spring at the looming figure, which seemed to merge into the background even as we watched him.

"Hold on, Chippy," I said, grabbing his arm, "I think he's on the level." I turned back towards Ratu, the whites of whose panther like eyes glinted fiercely in the moonlight. "I'm Rowden, captain of the *Oriental Venture*," I explained. "We picked up a radio signal from the *Nimrod* three days ago. I know your captain, Jim Coffin, and decided to investigate. The message suggested you had been attacked by a submarine."

"Submarine! Yeah that's right. But they was not lookin' for us, they was lookin' for you. But seein' as they attacked us thinkin' we was you, then I guess we both on the same side. If you want to know what's happened, then follow me, and I'll take you to where you can see the *Nimrod*, and the submarine."

I decided that further questions, and I had plenty of them, could wait until we had seen what Ratu had promised to show us. So we followed him as he lead us through the jungle, unhesitatingly finding his way in the near total darkness along what appeared to be the barest of a trail, that sloped gently upwards to what I guessed was the summit of one of the island's low hills. It could have been a trap, but there was no tingling in my fingertips now, and my senses told me I could trust him. Still, it was hard to keep pace, Ratu seemed to glide through the bushes, and over rocks and trees, as if his feet knew exactly what was in their path, and I was sweating profusely by the time we reached a bald patch of sand at the top of the hill. I glanced up at the sky to get my bearings, and then looked east towards where the bay was clearly visible between the trees that thinned towards the summit. The setting moon cast a silvery rippled path over the inky water, and I followed Ratu's outstretched arm. It was too far to make out the hull shapes, but the anchor lights of two vessels hung suspended against the black backdrop. The nearer showing only a single light, but the further showing the two lights of a larger vessel, and below them a dim cluster of deck lights.

Spencer handed me the night glasses he had carried in a rucksack, and the hulls swam into focus, their dark silhouettes edged with reflected moonlight. The larger ship certainly had the appearance of a traditional three-island tramp, similar to *Oriental Venture*. But it was the smaller vessel that seized my attention. With its long low hull, and squat central conning tower, it was unmistakably a submarine.

"Take a look, Major," I said, handing him the glasses. "We've found what we came looking for."

Which raised the very interesting question as to what we were going to do about it. But first we needed some answers, and I sat down on the cool sand and motioned to the others to do the same.

"Council of war," I said, grinning inwardly at the dim vision of four men crouched melodramatically in the darkness, three of us with pale serious faces, painted into piratical skulls by the silvery moonlight. The fourth, coiled as a spring, like a huge cat. "You need to answer some questions for us, Ratu."

He glided across the sand and squatted on his haunches, close enough now for me to see the worn dungaree trousers and shirt, and the thick curly hair and strong, determined features of an islander, Fijian by the size of him. Instinctively I held out my hand, and felt the warm, dry, muscular grip of his handshake.

"Glad to Captain. Guess you know now I'm telling the truth." His teeth flashed in the moonlight. "Sorry for stickin' you in the neck. But I had to be sure who you was."

"No harm done. Now tell me what happened when that sub attacked you?"

"We was heading from Bougainville to Manila. We was just past the islands when we spotted the sub in the moonlight, on the surface. It was steering a course to intercept us. When it got close it fired a shot without warnin'. It landed just ahead of us."

"A shot across your bows, a warning to stop," suggested Spencer.

"Yessir, that's what Cap'n Coffin said. And then he said he weren't heavin' too for no lousy, unidentified submarine, and he called the chief and told him to clap on more steam."

"That sounds like Jim Coffin all right," I said, grinning invisibly in the darkness.

"Yessir, well we tries to run but they fires again. Cap'n Coffin tells the radio man to call for help, but the submarine shoots at us, hits the mast and cuts the antenna."

"They heard the start of the signal and fired at the mast to stop it," observed Spencer. "Good shooting in the dark. Perhaps her captain knew what the SSS meant, or maybe he didn't care."

"What happened then, did they board you?"

"Yessir. Officer come aboard demandin' to see the ship's papers. Cap'n Coffin furious, never seen him so angry. But he fetches the papers and the officer read 'em, and then say that he don't believe we the *Nimrod*. He say we really *Oriental Venture*. Then big row with Cap'n Coffin, and they bring us here."

I could easily fill in the details Ratu had left out. Jim Coffin, with his blood up, was a frightening sight. It must have been a brave submarine commander, or a very confident, well-armed one, to seize his ship and force it into a remote anchorage in the Pelew Islands. But, more importantly, why was a Japanese submarine hunting us. Had the Soviets asked for their help in tracking us down? But if so, how did they know where to look?

"Did the Japanese captain give any idea why he was looking for us?" I said, hoping Ratu might have overheard something.

"Japanese?" exclaimed Ratu. "No, sir. That submarine ain't be no Jap, she's German."

"German!" It was my turn to be surprised.

Then the truth started to dawn.

"The ships look alike, so they thought you were *Oriental Venture?*"

"That's right, sir. Cap'n Coffin try to explain, but they don't believe him. They think we *Oriental Venture* sailing in disguise. They searchin' now, lookin' for something."

"And I think I know what for, don't you, Major?" I said. "They're trying to get Eberhardt's weapons back. God knows how they stumbled across the *Nimrod*. But they've got her now, and I wonder how long it will take them to work out that the guns aren't on board."

"And what they'll do to Coffin in the meantime," said Spencer. "They'll think he's lying about the guns, like they think he's lying about the identity of his ship."

Whatever they were doing to him, Jim Coffin was hot tempered and stubborn as a mule. Which was hardly likely to endear him to any Nazi interrogators. He wasn't the only man aboard, though.

"What have they done with the rest of the crew?" I asked Ratu.

"Cap'n Coffin and the officers, still on board. Locked up in the forecastle. Rest of the men ashore. Couple of abandoned native huts, close to the beach. They's guarded by some men off the submarine."

"And I'm guessing you managed to escape?" I said.

"Yessir. Was easy," replied the big man, grinning. "When the Germans come on board I hide myself. Plenty of places to hide in *Nimrod*. They threaten to sink her unless Cap'n Coffin sail here. Then, when we arrive, they take the crew ashore but they not find me. They not know about me. I listen when they question Cap'n Coffin. They beat 'im bad, many times. Feel sorry for them when he get free. Too many men with guns on board, so I slip over the side and swim ashore, see if maybe can set the crew free. Then I see you comin' in, sistership to *Nimrod*. I guessed you'd be comin' ashore lookin' for her."

"Some meeting," interjected Cramp. "With a knife at the captain's throat."

"I'm sorry mister, but had to be sure you was friendly."

"It seems like your past is catching up with you, Captain Rowden," said Major Spencer. "If that Nazi submarine attacked the *Nimrod* thinking she was *Oriental Venture* — well the ships look nearly identical — they put two and two together and ... well poor Captain Coffin seems to be suffering for your sins. Question is, now we are here, how do we get the Nazis off the *Nimrod*, and both of us get away?"

"Good question, Major." I was pondering that myself. If it was me the Nazi's were after, then it was hardly fair that I abandon Jim Coffin to their tender mercies to beat the truth out of. "I wonder whether they have any idea what Coffin was trying to signal when they attacked, or whether someone might have heard it," I continued, the germ of an idea forming.

"Perhaps the Nazi captain thinks he's safe, especially in Japanese controlled territory. He probably thinks no one would dream of attacking him here, let alone a band of ruffians from another tramp ship."

"Ruffians, we'll see about that," I snorted, pleased that the major had grasped my train of thought. "But even with the element of surprise, we'll still need a decent plan to put a U-boat out of action, and re-take the *Nimrod*. There's bound to be some shooting. And what if the Japs hear it. Have they got troops here, or warships?"

"From what we know in London, Captain, the Japs don't have much of a presence in these islands. They were awarded them by mandate from the League of Nations as a prize for being on the winning side. But there's not much here for them, and there's probably only some pensioned off administrator banished to Koror for upsetting the Emperor. I doubt there's much of a military presence. Anyway Koror is a good ten miles away, they won't hear any shooting from there."

"That's all very reassuring, Major, but we still have several dozen Nazis and a submarine to deal with. I suggest we get back to the ship, and you and Commander Lowther put your military experience together, and come up with a plan. You don't have long. The Nazis might feel themselves safe, but eventually they'll work out that Coffin is telling the truth, and then? Are they likely to just let him go, and admit they committed an act of piracy in peacetime?"

I stood up and glanced east across the bay. The horizon was starting to lighten. It was time to move, before McGrath followed orders and marooned us.

"Come on then," I said, urging them to their feet. "We've got work to do."

* * *

Sunset found *Oriental Venture* steaming slowly west, away from her anchorage between the islets. Anyone watching us during the day might have imagined we had pulled in for temporary repairs, although they might also have been intrigued to watch the crew practise their rowing skills in the ship's boats. Another had been launched, in addition to the rescue boat, and both had been enthusiastically rowed around the ship for several hours, before their perspiring crews were allowed to cool themselves by jumping into the water and skylarking about, splashing and shouting until the distant sight of a cruising fin had them scrambling back aboard. Then, in the late afternoon, the boats were hoisted back inboard, the anchor was heaved in, and I conned the ship out of the inlet, and set course due west towards the setting sun.

We had seen no signs of human activity on shore throughout the day, and I was reasonably certain that no one had seen us arrive or depart, but I was taking no chances and continued steaming west until the islets disappeared into the darkness, before I turned the ship about. Heading south and then east, following the direction of the reef, I kept well offshore to avoid running into any rogue outcrops. Needing to remain invisible in the darkness, I also ordered the ship blackened out. The navigation lights and the deck lamps were switched off, and Lowther checked all the deadlights were in place, so that not a chink of light was visible anywhere.

Getting the ship prepared was the easy part, though. The officers and crew caused me greater concern. Apart from Lowther and Major Spencer, they were all civilians, while what I was asking them to do, cut the *Nimrod* out from under the guns of a U-boat whose crew was bound to resist, was more like a military operation. Most of the men had taken part in some pretty hairy actions before though, some of them even under my command. Piracy on the China coast, or fighting the British in Somalia, had their own share of dangers. But this was different. We were up against a ruthless enemy, and there was little to be gained. There were no prizes for success, no riches or glory. Just the certainty of wounds or death if we failed.

I intended to lead the cutting out attempt myself, and I needed Lowther and Spencer, with their military backgrounds, to take charge of the arms and explosives. Cramp insisted on coming, and I knew that he would always have my back if things got really sticky. I saw the disappointment in Griffith and McGrath's eyes, though, when I told them they had to remain on board. I had obviously not sufficiently outgrown my youthful lack of self-preserving sense, and was feeling the same excitement their envious eyes revealed I had deprived them of. The ship still had needs though, and if everything went pear shaped they would have to get her away, navigate to the nearest friendly port, and explain what had happened. Chief Engineer Fraser and his team were also needed to keep the boilers fired and the engine turning. Which left the crew and the stokers. I needed men who could row the two boats, and shoot a rifle if they had to. I left it to the boatswain and the chief stoker to select enough volunteers. Of which there was no shortage. Privately, though, I hoped, if we could free them, Nimrod's crew would be able to retake their own ship, if Lowther and Spencer could distract the submarine. The exploits of Grim Jim Coffin and his cutthroat crew were legendary in the South China Sea. So if anyone could outfight a group of Nazi sailors I hoped they could. Still, it was a risky thing to attempt, and there would be recriminations if we failed and men died.

The plan that Spencer and Lowther put together seemed to have a reasonable chance of success, provided we could free Jim Coffin's crew and maintain the element of surprise. It was those few moments of uncertainty on the part of the Nazi sailors, most of whom would be sleeping soundly in their bunks, which would make the difference between success and failure. Now, as the first part of that plan unfolded, the ship was blacked out and making her way towards a position close to the southern tip of Mecherchar Island.

The outer edge of the reef came close to the island at this point, and the water in between was a tangled mass of reef heads and sand bars. Ratu had put his time ashore to good use, though, and had observed a tiny gap in the reef leading to a narrow twisting passage that would allow the boats to skirt the southern shore of Mecherchar, and enter the bay close to the anchored submarine. He pointed it out to me on the chart. It was a much shorter distance to row than from our original anchorage in the inlet. But first we had to find the correct dropping off point in the darkness, with little more than dead reckoning and intuition to guide us. As I conned the ship away from the anchorage, Ratu offered to take the wheel. As the *Nimrod's* quartermaster, he quickly found the feel of her sistership's rudder and I was impressed by the way she responded to his touch. Listening to him during the day, it was clear he had deep-rooted respect and affection for Captain Coffin, and that he was an exceptional seaman. I asked him where he had acquired his skills, and was unsurprised by his answer. The Fijian islanders were living descendants of the great Polynesian navigators who had guided their druas, double-hulled sailing canoes, over vast distances across the Pacific, using knowledge of the stars, trade winds, currents, wave patterns and migrating birds, passed down from generation to generation. Ratu had been taught by his grandfather, and claimed to be able to find his way to any destination in the Pacific. Whether or not that was true, he had immediately grasped the problem of how to find the drop off point and assured me he could steer us there.

Watching him at the wheel, using the stars for direction and time keeping, and feeling the wind on his face through the opened bridge windows, sniffing the air as if gauging the proximity of the reef by the strength of the seashore-scented land breeze, I felt unashamed admiration. There was a sense of power and nobility that I rarely, if ever, experienced among seamen of my own kind. I wasn't even sure if I could lay any kind of claim to it myself. Or perhaps it was just the recollection of having a knife held to my throat by frighteningly powerful arms.

There was no time for personal reflection though, I had McGrath take frequent log readings and plotted our progress by dead reckoning, hoping that my calculations had left no room for error. I was strangely relieved therefore, when Ratu announced we had arrived at the required spot on the black featureless ocean, at precisely the same time as I reached the same conclusion.

It was close to midnight, and I was satisfied that we were as close as could be dared to the tiny passage through the reef. Turning the ship so that she was shouldering the easterly swell to minimise the rolling, and keeping just enough way on to maintain steering, I ordered the boats away and handed responsibility over to Griffith. All he had to do was keep her far enough offshore to be safely clear of the reef, but close enough to see our signal flares. Then either run for it, or, if we signalled success, take the ship into the bay at dawn and anchor her. It sounded simple enough, but until there was sufficient daylight he had precious little to help establish his position, and he would have to sound his way into the bay. He was a good navigator, though, and he and McGrath were both good seamen, so I felt easier about trusting them. But if he did put the ship aground, and I couldn't get her off, then, assuming we survived, we'd be sailing out aboard the *Nimrod,* and I would have some explaining to do.

Before quitting the bridge, I took a compass bearing of the small gap in the surf that marked the entrance to the passage through the reef. After the calm of the previous two days, a long swell had set in from the east, evidence, perhaps, of a storm far out in the Pacific. While not large enough to cause any serious difficulty in launching the boats, I could hear the booming as the swells, slowed by their entry into shallow water, reared their crests and thundered onto the reef. It made the gap easier to see, but it would require careful steering and timing to get safely through. Any misjudgment would send a boat crashing onto the jagged, sharp corals, tearing it, and men, to pieces.

I put myself in command of the rescue boat, with Ratu as pilot to lead the way through the gap in the reef and into the lagoon. Lowther and Major Spencer would follow in the second boat, carrying the bulk of the weapons and explosives. Once we were into the lagoon, assuming we got there, we could not let any sound betray our presence. Which was why McGrath had earlier exercised the seamen in the art of silent rowing. First oiling the rowlocks and wrapping them in old rags to muffle the creaking, then demonstrating how to feather the oars between strokes to avoid splashing.

With the boats safely in the water, I waved a hand in salute and saw Griffith's dark silhouette on the bridge wing raise a hand in reply. Water thrashed at *Oriental Venture's* stern as she forged ahead, turning due east away from the dangers of the reef, only the white capped water churned up in her wake visible as she slipped away into the darkness. Then the crew were pulling hard toward the line of breakers, Cramp at the helm, Lowther's boat following closely behind, as I watched the ranks of the swell approaching out of the eastern darkness. The moon was still up, but banks of high cloud obscured its light. Nevertheless, the line of white, breaking swell-crests were clearly visible to the west where the inky darkness of the island blended into the sky behind the reef. From the boat, low in the water, the gap in those breakers was invisible, but Cramp was steering the compass bearing I had noted before leaving the bridge.

According to the pilot book, the current should have been setting north-easterly at a rate of about a knot, which meant that in the twenty minutes it would take us to reach the reef, we could be swept up to 300 yards in that direction. I had allowed for this when I heaved the ship to and launched the boats, but I wanted to be sure we weren't swept past the gap, and ordered Cramp to alter course a point further west. Glancing astern, I was glad to see Lowther had altered course to follow. Both boats were double-ended whalers, with sturdy clinker built hulls, designed for working in open waters. In experienced hands they rowed well, but McGrath's coaching was soon forgotten as the men struggled with the swell and abandoned any attempt to row quietly. It hardly mattered; the swell crashing onto the reef would drown any noise. Once inside the calm of the lagoon, though, it would be a different story.

Ratu, the huge Fijian, was crouched in the bow. With eyes and ears as keen as a jungle cat, he seemed able to sense the lull in the waves that marked the narrow opening in the reef, and I instructed Cramp to follow the line of his outstretched arm and alter course half a point to starboard. If I'd had any doubts that Ratu could safely lead us through the passage into the lagoon, watching him steer the ship to the dropping off point, using only his arcane but finely honed navigational instincts, had dispelled them. More surprisingly, though, Ratu had also proved a capable assistant to Spencer and Lowther as they drilled the crew in the use of the rifles and the potato masher hand grenades. I asked him where he had picked up such knowledge. He grinned and shrugged his shoulders, admitting only that he had served for a short while in the Fijian army, before working on a tobacco plantation in the Philippines. There he had pulled a younger Jim Coffin out of a fight with an American tobacco planter in Manila, and the two had sailed together ever since.

We still had to get both boats safely through the reef though, and a hail from the bow, and Ratu's waving arm indicated we were approaching the gap. Stretching away into the darkness on either side was a line of white, broken water where the swell was bursting against the coral with a deep booming. Right ahead was the dark gap that lead through to the calm of the lagoon. It looked frighteningly narrow, with the surf breaking dangerously on either side

"Easy on the oars." I twisted my head and saw Lowther still following close astern, and raised an arm in the agreed signal for him to hold off, while we made our attempt to run through the gap.

It was going to take careful judgment, timing our final pull with an incoming swell, and riding it through the narrow gap, with sufficient speed to maintain steering, so that we did not broach sideways onto the razor sharp coral heads that lined the sides.

I looked over my shoulder, watching the large, smooth crests heave up out of the darkness, counting the seconds between them, feeling for the pattern. I had spent many hours in small boats as a young seaman, and Cramp had practically grown up in them, but my mouth was dry, and my hand was painfully gripped tight over the gunwhale as I waited for the right moment.

The crest of a swell passed under the boat, lifting it and enabling me a final check that we were pointing directly into the gap.

"Pull hard now boys," I yelled as we fell back into the trough in front of the oncoming wave. "Put your backs into it."

The boat surged forward, propelled by the straining backs and bending oars. I said a quick prayer to Saint Woolos that I had timed it right, feeling the stern lift as the swell overhauled us.

"Pull, pull," I yelled.

The boat gathered speed as the wave lifted it, carrying it bodily forward towards the dangerous line of breakers. I felt the stern slide sideways, but saw Cramp yank savagely at the tiller to correct it. We were riding the wave now, surfing ahead of the crest, the crew struggling to keep their stroke. Then we were shooting into the gap, breakers on either side, wicked coral heads inches below the boiling surface, barely sufficient clearance for the oars. But it was enough, and we were shot through, like a cork out of a bottle, into the calm of the lagoon beyond.

"Easy on the oars, take a breather," I called, as the boat continued to glide forward on the ebbing momentum of the wave. Then I turned to look back at the gap, expecting to see Lowther's boat gliding gently towards me. But the calm water inside the reef was empty, and it was too dark to see beyond the line of breakers.

My heart sank as I wondered whether Lowther had misjudged his approach, and driven his boat onto the wave beaten coral, where it and his men were even now being pounded to death on the razor sharp heads. We couldn't row back through the gap against the swell, and there were too few of us in my boat to take on a submarine load of Nazis. All I could do was hope that he was out there still, waiting for the right moment to run the gap. I could see nothing beyond the line of the breakers, and I realised I was holding my breath, counting the seconds between one breaking swell and the next ... and still no sign of Lowther's boat.

Ratu must have had better eyesight than me, because he was suddenly pointing at the gap, and calling in terror.

And then I saw it. The darker shape of the boat, angled across the face of a large swell, bows pointing directly at the breakers, oars flailing like the legs of an upturned crab.

"Turn, turn," I yelled, as if will power alone would do it, knowing that it was hopeless and that Lowther couldn't hear above the booming of the breakers.

The swell broke onto the reef, the water smashing its energy against the unyielding coral in an explosion of noise and spray. But not all of it. Like a ball bouncing back from a wall, some of the water rebounded from the coral, the backwash catching the bow moments before the point of impact, and slewing it away from the reef. Just far enough for the boat's momentum to carry it the rest of the way through, and into the safety of the lagoon beyond.

Lowther brought the boat gliding alongside. His face pale in the moonlight, but he was grinning with relief.

"That was a close one."

"Aye, Peter, I thought you were a goner there, and we'd be pulling your bodies off the reef."

"Well, there's no time for gossiping," he replied, his voice unnaturally loud in the relative quiet of the lagoon. "Lead on, skipper, and let's trust that Ratu can find his way in the dark."

* * *

The passage through the coral head strewn shallows of the lagoon proved surprisingly easy. Ratu seemed to have a sixth sense as he softly called for course alterations to port or to starboard, and guided us through the channel he had observed during his exploration of Mecherchar Island. Occasionally I felt the hull bump and grind against a shallower patch, but the crew was rowing easy to minimise the noise, and there was no harm done, other than to the paintwork. Finally, we worked our way around the southern tip of the island, and into the deep water of the bay in which were anchored the *Nimrod* and the Nazi U-boat holding her captive. About three quarters of a mile offshore I could see the pale, yellow glow of the U-boat's single anchor light, and a short distance beyond the anchor lights and deck lamps of her prize. There was not much moon left, and our boats would be hard to spot in the darkness, but I hoped that the remoteness of the anchorage, and the lack of response to Coffin's radioed alarm, had lulled the Nazis into a sense of security from which they would not awake until it was too late.

I heard Ratu softly hissing from the bow to gain my attention, and saw his arm waving in the direction of the shore. I thought I could make out a pale streak where the sand divided the darkness of the water from the land, but there were no landmarks to provide any guidance, so Ratu must still have been relying on the heightened senses that had brought us safely this far. I told Cramp to steer in the direction he pointed, and glanced astern to check that Lowther was still following. Away from the reef edge, and the booming of the surf, a profound silence had settled over the lagoon, broken only by the occasional splash of a leaping fish, or the soft creak of wood against a muffled rowlock.

"Easy oars," called Cramp, as the silvery-pale line of the beach materialised out of the darkness, and moments later the keel slid up onto the sand with a reassuring hiss. The men stowed their oars and jumped out to drag the boat up the sand, as Lowther's boat grounded softly behind us. I crossed the beach to the deep shadows of the bushes, and flashed a shaded torch onto my watch to check the time. It was an hour and a half since we had left *Oriental Venture*, but seemed longer. I called softly for the others to join me.

"We've made good time," I said, "thanks to Ratu leading us through the passage. But we need to press on." I turned to the boatswain who had accompanied us in Lowther's boat.

"Take charge here, boatswain. Have the men drag the boats in amongst the mangroves and hide them. Keep out of sight if anyone comes. We'll leave most of the weapons and the grenades in the boats. But there's to be no shooting, unless there's no alternative. If anyone comes snooping, then use a quieter way to silence them."

The boatswain's eyes narrowed and his lips curved upwards in a piratical grin, revealing a row of broken, stained teeth. I knew that Mr Khoo and the boatswain were clan related, although the contrast between the urbane, westernised Khoo and the rough, villainous looking seaman could not have been greater. But I was pretty sure that the boatswain had lead one of the pirate gangs that had operated out of Bias Bay in the 'twenties. He had an easy air of authority over his men, no doubt a combination of trust and fear, and I didn't doubt he was willing to stick a knife into anyone who challenged him. He nodded in acknowledgment, and there was a flurry of whispered Cantonese as the seamen dragged the boats under cover, and melted into the shadows.

Which left Lowther, Cramp, Spencer, Ratu and me crouching among the bushes at the head of the beach. I had the big Webley snuggled reassuringly under my arm-pit, and Lowther and the major both carried Bergmann machine pistols. Cramp had a wicked looking sheath knife strapped to his belt. But of all of us it was Ratu who would have struck the fear of God into anyone unfortunate enough to challenge him. He had found a big machete among the boatswain's stores, and had painstakingly honed it to razor sharpness. The long, curved blade glinted dully in the last of the moonlight. In his huge muscular hands it would chop a man's head off as easily as pruning a dead flower off a stalk.

"Right, Ratu, let's go and find the rest of your crew. Lead on."

According to his report, the Nazis had found a couple of abandoned native huts in a clearing beside a small fresh water lake, a short distance from the beach. The Nimrod's crew were imprisoned there, chained hand and foot, and guarded by three Nazi seamen who were relieved at sunrise and sunset. One man normally patrolled outside the hut and the other two watched the men inside. Having already experienced Ratu's ability to disappear and hide in the jungle darkness, I was not surprised he had been able to observe the Nazi routine without being spotted. I hoped his skills would not fail him now, as we needed to overpower those guards without giving away our presence.

Ratu struck out from the beach with the unerring sense of direction of one born to find his way through the deepest jungle. The rest of us followed in single file behind him. Ratu had said that a path lead from the beach several hundred yards inland to the small clearing. If there was a path I couldn't distinguish it from the surrounding jungle, and my feet were invisible in the darkness, so I just focused on maintaining sight of Ratu's back as he confidently weaved his way around bushes and trees, hoping the others were able to keep up.

After about ten minutes he held up a hand to signal a halt. Then he dropped onto hands and knees, and beckoned us to do likewise and follow him. I pushed the thought of spiders and snakes to the back of my mind and dropped down behind him. Slowly we crawled and pushed our way through thorn-thick bushes until we sighted the clearing in the centre of which I could just make out the dark, boxy shapes of the native huts. Chinks of light around the door of the larger one showed that men were inside it. I pointed towards it and Ratu nodded.

"Where's the sentry?" I whispered into his ear.

Ratu raised an arm and pointed. I followed his outstretched finger. At first I could see nothing, just the hut's outline against the darkness of the jungle. Then, in the deepest of the shadows, the slightly paler form of a man swam into focus. He was leaning against the wall and, as I watched, a match flared, illuminating a ghostly face. The flame faded, replaced by the firefly glow of a cigarette end, and I could smell the smoke as it drifted across the clearing in the humid night air.

"They're very sure of themselves," whispered Spencer, who had crawled up beside me. "And I'll bet their captain would have their guts if he caught them smoking on duty like that."

I was about to reply when I felt a gentle touch on my arm, and turned to see Ratu holding a finger to his lips. The big Fijian pointed towards the sentry, and jerked his thumb across his throat.

"Wait here," he mouthed, before disappearing silently into the bushes, as if the darkness had simply absorbed him, leaving me to marvel at how such a large man could move through the jungle with the stealth of a cat.

I watched the red firefly with grim fascination as the Nazi seaman moved the cigarette up to his lips. The tip glowed brightly as he dragged in a lungful of smoke, bathing his face a pink disk of reflected light.

Then it vanished.

I heard nothing and saw nothing, but where there had been a man standing in the shadow of the hut, enjoying a peaceful smoke, there was only dark, brooding silence.

I felt, rather than heard, the slight rustling of the leaves at my ear, and then Ratu was back, his face creased into a broad grin.

"How do we get into the hut?" I whispered, wondering whether both of the remaining guards were inside, or if the Nazi captain had increased their number.

"Easy. They not expectin' us," replied Ratu, his white teeth flashing a devilish smile. "I just open the door and we walk in. Move quick, and they won't have time to do nuthin'."

It sounded too simple, but surprise was everything. Even if the men inside the hut heard us approach, they would assume it was their mate. Why should they think otherwise? It made sense, but I hoped I was right. It would be a very different story if the guards were ready, weapons loaded, pointing at the door. Any shooting would alert the crew on the U-boat, and that would spell disaster. Could we get back to the boats and find our way back through the reef before the Nazis found us? And even if we could, how would we find the ship? I swallowed grimly. This was no time for doubts.

"Okay."

I gestured to the others to come closer and quickly whispered the plan.

"Ratu's taken care of the man outside. Now we're going straight in. Ratu first, then me, then you three. We jump them as quick as we can. No noise. Only shoot if you have to."

Heads nodded in acknowledgment.

Ratu rose and stepped out from the bushes. On the soft, grass covered earth of the clearing his feet made no sound. He beckoned us to follow. The silence was as intense as the darkness. Even the frogs and crickets seemed to have fallen quiet; there was only the hammering of my heartbeat in my ears.

It was only a few short steps to the hut and then we were pressed against the wall, Ratu and I either side of the rough timbered door, with Spencer, Lowther and Cramp behind us. Ratu placed a massive hand on the door.

"On three," he mouthed, holding up his fist. Then, silently, watching him raise one finger at a time, I counted softly, "One ... two... three."

He shoved hard against the door, which swung easily open. I caught a glimpse of two startled faces as the Germans realised that the man in the doorway was not the one they were expecting.

But by then Ratu had pounced.

The Germans were sitting on stools either side of a low table. Ratu grabbed the nearest one before he had time to react. His huge fists striking hammer blows to the head that felled him like a poleaxed ox.

I was fractionally slower. The second man had time to jump up and reach for the machine pistol lying on the table. Grunting something in German his fingers scrabbled for the gun, but I kicked the table away, and it clattered across the wooden floorboards. The man lunged at me, grabbing me by the shirt, shouting with fury and tumbling us both to the floor.

A knife appeared in his hand, thrusting down towards my chest. I grabbed the wrist, and for a second we were locked in a deadly arm wrestle.

Then Ratu struck. The stool looked tiny in his massive hand as he smashed it down on the back of the German's head. There was a sickening thud and he went limp like a rag doll, a trickle of blood starting to flow from behind one ear. I heaved the body off me, and stood up.

There was a single hurricane lamp hanging from a hook on the wall. By its light I could see a huddle of men, handcuffed and chained together. Some had broken bloodied noses, others burst, bruised lips. They were as odd an assortment of men as I had seen in a long time. Afridis from Afghanistan in dirty pantaloons and white, knee length disdashes, their heads covered by traditional turban wrapped kullahs.

Malays in loose blue tunics and trousers with songkok hats. Somali stokers in sweat stained singlets and sarongs with embroidered caps or turbans. But to a man they were all grinning.

"Hey, Ratu," one of the Afridis called. "What took you so long?"

"Melek, you old pirate. Where the keys to them cuffs."

"In the pocket of the big one you bashed with the stool. Man, will he have a headache when he wakes up."

"If he wakes up," Ratu replied, rifling through the man's pockets, and triumphantly holding up a bunch of keys.

Moments later the men were free, rubbing their bruised, bloodied wrists and stretching their cramped muscles. Their eager eyes followed us as we checked our machine pistols, and added the two belonging to the German seamen.

"Okay, you men," I said to the circle of grinning faces. "We don't have much time for explanations. My name is Rowden, captain of the *Oriental Venture*. We've two boats and more weapons down at the beach. We're going to take back the *Nimrod*, free your Captain Coffin, and do as much damage as we can to that Nazi U-boat. Are you with us?"

One of the Afridis stepped forward. "I'm Melek, boatswain of the *Nimrod*. That's my brother Hakim," he pointed to another of the Afridis. "We are with you Captain Rowden and, *Insh Allah*, we will soon take *Nimrod* back from the infidels."

"Right then, gag and shackle those Germans, then follow us back to the beach and we'll get to work. Ratu, lead on."

CHAPTER EIGHTEEN

"**S**top rowing ... boat your oars." At the soft-spoken command, the men ceased rowing, lifted their oars out of the water, and quietly laid them in the boat.

I rested my arm on the tiller as the boat drifted to a stop. Ahead of us the low, threatening shape of the U-boat loomed as a dark shadow against the horizon. At the head of a stubby mast atop the conning tower, or sail as I knew English submariners called it, a single anchor light glowed a dull yellow. Although the light was visible for several miles it was not designed to illuminate the area around the submarine, nevertheless I knew that any object on the surface within 100 yards of it might reflect enough light to catch the attention of a keen lookout. Outside that circle, however, blending against the inky black shadows of the island from which it had emerged, the boat would be almost invisible.

It had taken us half an hour to row quietly out to the submarine, the men taking extra care not to splash the oar blades, and wetting the rags wrapped around the rowlocks to prevent creaking as the oars levered against the jaws. Noise was our biggest enemy. If the U-boat's lookouts couldn't see us, they would certainly hear us if we creaked and splashed our way towards them. And while I was pretty sure that my crew had mastered the art of silent rowing, I wasn't certain I could say the same of Coffin's crowd of ruffians. They were in the other boat, commanded by Cramp and Melek. I'd ordered them to give the U-boat a wide berth on their way to the *Nimrod*, which lay a little further offshore, her lights a homing beacon to her crew eager for revenge. I hoped they were there by now. Lying invisible in the darkness, waiting for the moment when the few Nazis aboard her would be distracted enough for them to swarm up the side unnoticed and retake her.

Before they had quit the hut, Melek and Hakim had questioned the first of the Nazi seamen to recover his senses. I hardly dared think what they had threatened him with, but he had eagerly revealed that the U-boat's captain was arrogantly confident no one had missed the *Nimrod*, or was looking for her. Most of his crew slept aboard the submarine at night. Apart from the trio guarding the prisoners ashore, only the captain and a handful of men remained aboard the *Nimrod*, and I hoped they were as relaxed about keeping a lookout as the three at the hut had been. Two of them had been left gagged and trussed like chickens. The third didn't need securing. He had been enjoying his cigarette when Ratu's machete slit his throat, and would never have known what was coming for him.

Now, Ratu sat in the bow, a large dark, brooding figure. Beside him was a small wiry Iban, or Sea Dyak, whom Ratu had introduced as Bema. Headhunters from Borneo, the Sea Dyaks lived in long-houses along the river banks, and waged ferocious raids on their enemies. They were fearless of the sea, sailing long distances in their bandongs, large slender canoes driven by a sail of woven leaves and rattan. It was Ratu and Bema whom I was trusting to deal with the U-boat's lookouts, so that we could board her.

Because the only way to seize the U-boat and disable it, was by stealth. Frontal assault was out of the question against trained sailors armed with machine guns, and an 88mm deck gun capable of shooting 20 shells a minute. No, the only way we were going to get on board was quietly and unseen. Ratu, as stealthy and deadly as a Jaguar, was an obvious choice, and had quickly volunteered. He had suggested Bema, who flashed a savage grin at me, displaying a row of teeth each filed to a sharp point. The man was now crouched beside Ratu wearing only a brown loincloth, a scrap of rag twisted round his head, and grasping his razor sharp mandau, a short machete, that in his practised hands was deadly against man or beast. They made an odd couple; the huge, muscular Fijian and the wiry Sea Dyak, but they were cheerfully confident of their ability to silently clear the deck of the U-boat, so that Spencer and Lowther could get aboard.

In the middle of the boat sat Major Spencer, re-checking the equipment he had assembled and personally loaded into it. In a wooden crate lay a row of stick grenades, the type known to both German soldiers and British Tommies as 'potato mashers,' with a fat, cylindrical head packed with high explosive secured to a wooden handle. At the base of the handle a cap unscrewed to reveal a cord with a ball at the end. A gentle tug on the cord was all it took to ignite the five-second fuse, time enough for a man to throw the grenade and take cover. Spencer had carefully packed several grenades into two haversacks. In addition, he had made up a number of baled charges, taping the heads of four grenades around the head of a fifth. These were too heavy to throw, but were a deadly weapon dropped into a confined space. Spencer packed three of these improvised bombs into each haversack, and raised a hand to indicate he was ready.

As well as the grenades, Lowther and Spencer each had a Bergmann machine pistol slung around their necks, and several more were stowed in the boat. There was bound to be some shooting. I didn't have much confidence that my untrained seamen would be able to distinguish friend from foe in the darkness, but we would just have to make do with what we had.

I raised my night glasses and studied the U-boat's deck, searching for the lookouts, waiting for the movements that would betray their presence. My eye caught something, a patch of darkness moving past the outline of the 88mm gun. A man on deck then, probably making a periodical check to the bow and stern. The shadow continued forward, and finally stopped beside the jagged edged profile of the net cutter. I swung the glasses to the aft deck. It was flush, with nothing on it that could hide a man. Aft of the conning tower I could see an escape hatch, opened to provide some additional ventilation to the hot and stuffy interior. If there was a light in the compartment below, it was not visible through the open hatch. I leaned forward, hissed softly to gain Spencer's attention, and pointed it out to him.

I expected to spot another lookout in the conning tower and raised the night glasses, tucking my elbows into my chest to steady them, and focused my attention on the sail. There! The familiar shape of an officer's cap caught my eye. As I watched, the man emerged from the shadow of the sail and stepped onto the open railed gun platform aft of it. Two lookouts then, both probably armed. I whispered the information to Spencer, who relayed it to Ratu in the bow. The big man raised a fist with thumb upwards. Then he stripped off his seaman's shirt, and, lithe and silent, slid over the side of the boat, followed immediately by Bema, the latter with his mandau clamped between his teeth. I watched the bobbing heads as they swam towards the U-boat, but quickly lost sight of them in the darkness, guessing they were swimming underwater as much as possible to avoid detection.

The minutes ticked by, seeming to take an eternity, and I anxiously scanned the U-boat's deck through my night glasses, searching for any sign that Ratu and Bema had made it undetected. The man at the bow was still there, taking advantage of the solitude to have a quiet smoke, the unshielded red firefly tip, a tellingly insubordinate confirmation that his guard was down.

Which was a deadly mistake. I never saw Bema arrive, but one moment the sailor was there, a dark silhouette against the star-gemmed sky. The next he was gone. No call of alarm, no splash of a body falling over the side. Nothing. Silence.

I swung the night glasses aft to examine the sail. The officer with the cap was still slouched over the gun platform rail, no doubt looking forward to his relief, and the prospect of a few hours in his bunk. There was no sign of Ratu, and I wondered if he was still in the water. Then, part of the deeper shadow of the hull seemed to detach itself and slide slowly up the ladder to the gun platform. I froze on my seat in the stern sheets, my knuckles clamped on the night glasses, hardly daring to breathe, as if the slightest sound would make the German turn round. Surely he must hear something, even if it was only Ratu dripping sea water onto the deck. But if he did turn it was too late.

The shadow pounced silently, absorbing the slouched figure of the lookout, enveloping it and dragging it down. To oblivion.

I relaxed, and took a long slow breath as the unmistakable profile of Ratu on the gun platform waved his arm with the all clear.

"Out oars, pull hard," I hissed to the waiting seamen. The boat quickly gathered way and I steered it towards the U-boat's side.

"Boat your oars," I whispered as we glided alongside, careful not to bump against the hull. But there was Ratu ready to fend off and hold us, while Lowther and Spencer grabbed Bergmanns and haversacks, and scrambled up onto the U-boat's timber sheathed deck. Two more Bergmanns were passed up into the eagerly outstretched hands of Ratu and Bema. Lowther had shown both men how to change the magazine and operate the firing bolt, and I hoped they'd remember if, or more likely when, the shooting started. Once they were clear, I allowed the boat to drift a short distance off the U-boat's side, our task being to provide fire-support if any of the U-boat's crew appeared on deck. I felt the weight of the Bergmann. It was surprisingly heavy. I was more used to the familiar Webley, but this was no work for a revolver.

On the U-boat's deck, I saw Spencer signal to Lowther to take the escape hatch, before he softly climbed the steps of the conning tower. Lowther returned a thumbs up and tiptoed quickly aft, the haversack hung over one shoulder and the machine pistol over the other, Bema padding silently behind him. I could imagine the rancid smell of diesel fumes, sweat and cooking fat that must have greeted them as they knelt beside the open hatch. I watched Lowther reach into the haversack and pull out a baled charge, then swung the glasses towards the sail. Spencer was out of sight, presumably bent over the access trunk to the control room, but the bulky, reassuring silhouette of Ratu was visible.

Lowther raised a thumb to show he was ready, and I saw Ratu turn to relay the message to Spencer.

The big man straightened. "Okay ... now," he hissed, the need for quiet having passed.

I watched Lowther fiddling with the base of the grenade's handle, exposing the detonator cord and tugging on it. I heard myself counting the seconds, "One ... two ... three." Then he dropped the charge down the hatch, slammed it shut and span the securing wheel.

"Four ... Five."

I felt rather than heard the simultaneous explosions, the shock wave transmitted through the water and hammering against the boat. I grabbed at the gunwale to steady myself, and by the time I looked up Lowther had pulled a second charge from the haversack and was spinning the hatch wheel to open it. There was a momentary pause as he wrenched open the hatch and dropped the charge, then a third explosion, followed a split second later by a fourth as Spencer's second charge detonated in the control room. It must have been hell for the men down below in those confined spaces.

"*Aufgeben, Aufgeben*," I could hear Spencer shouting down the conning tower for the Germans to surrender. The answer came in a stream of hot lead flying up the hatch, raising sparks as bullets ricocheted and whined off the coaming. Spencer was ready, and I heard the hatch clang shut and grimly counted to five before another explosion wracked the bowels of the U-boat. As the noise died away, there was a banging from below Lowther's feet. Slowly, the wheel began to turn from the inside. Lowther stepped back, aiming his Bergmann at the hatch as it swung open. The pale, frightened face of a young sailor, little more than a boy, appeared over the coaming.

"*Kamerad*," he sobbed. "*Kamerad*."

And then, from the darkness, further out in the bay I heard the sound of more explosions and shooting. It was far from over.

* * *

"Pull, pull," I yelled as the crew bent their backs and the boat surged forward. There was no need for secrecy now, explosions and gunfire were lighting up the foredeck of the *Nimrod*, and I guessed Cramp had laid his boat alongside the bow, where Melek and his men would be fighting to gain a foothold.

Leaving Lowther and Spencer to take the surrender of the U-boat's crew, I steered the boat towards the *Nimrod's* stern, praying to St Woolos that we would not be too late. It was only a couple of hundred yards, but, from the volume of fire directed towards the forecastle, the Nazis were making a fight of it. Under normal circumstances the U-boat's trained seamen would have been more than a match for Melek's cutthroats, even though outnumbered and probably outgunned. But the last thing they would have been expecting was the *Nimrod's* crew, armed with machine pistols and chucking hand grenades, swarming up makeshift rope ladders, desperate to seize their ship back. Even so, the Nazis had reacted quickly, and the firefight was intense. So we had to get there fast. If Melek's men wavered, and the Nazi captain re-gained the initiative, we could expect little mercy for what we had done to his men, and his precious U-boat.

The boat's crew needed little encouragement and pulled for all they were worth, rapidly closing the distance until the stern of the *Nimrod* loomed overhead. Despite the gunfire from the bow, this end of the ship was still quiet, and we were out of sight under the overhang of her counter. The Nazis would not remain ignorant of our presence for long, though. We had only moments in which to get on board; otherwise we would be sitting ducks for anyone who spotted us while still in the boat. The boatswain stood up, spreading his legs against the sides to counter the rocking, and raised a bamboo pole lashed to the top of which was a grappling hook attached to a rope ladder. He swung the pole up towards the stern rail, and hooked the flukes over it. The rope ladder dangled back into the boat. I gave it a good hard tug, slung the Bergmann over my shoulder and started to climb.

Behind me I heard the boatswain calling to the crew in a mixture of Cantonese, English and Somali. I glanced over my shoulder to see a cluster of grinning Chinese and African faces, watching their captain shin up a rope ladder in the dark, like a 17th century pirate. For a moment I had a flash of doubt they were going to follow me. Then eager hands reached for the ladder, and moments later we were crouched on the poop, readying our weapons. I left the Bergmann hanging over my shoulder, and drew the Webley. The walnut stock felt more comfortable in my hand than the machine pistol, and I clicked off the safety catch.

There was another intense bust of firing forward. We had made it to the deck undetected, but we had to move fast, and take the Nazis from behind, while they were still distracted by Melek and his crew.

"Take your men and go forward on the starboard side. Head for the foredeck."

The boatswain nodded, muttered a few words in Cantonese, and half the boat's crew sprang after him as he sprinted forward along the deck.

I turned to the small group of Somali stokers that remained. Hard, lean bodied men, their muscles honed by hours of shovelling coal in the hellish conditions of the boiler room. Now, in their patched and faded dungarees with coloured rags knotted round their brows, devilish grins splitting their dark faces, and with machine pistols or Mauser rifles clasped in their rough, work hardened hands, they looked enough to frighten me, let alone anyone brave enough to stand in their way.

I raised the Webley. "The rest of you follow me."

Then we were up, and running forward along the main deck.

We reached the aft end of the accommodation unseen, the attention of the Nazis still focussed on the explosions and firing from the forecastle. How much longer, I wondered, before they realised the threat from aft. And where were they holding Jim Coffin and his officers? I took a chance.

"Boat deck!"

I sprang up the stairs and sprinted forward, the Somalis close at my heels. Ahead of me the forward accommodation door burst open, and a Nazi sailor stepped onto the deck, framed in the light beaming from inside the doorway. He thrust a machine pistol forward over the rail and pulled the trigger, spraying a stream of lead towards the forecastle where, judging by the intensity of the firing, Melek's men had established themselves and were working their way aft. I aimed the Webley, squeezing against the heavy pull of the trigger, but hesitated, suddenly reluctant to shoot a man in the back. There was no hesitation by the Somali beside me, his Bergmann spat death, and the Nazi slumped to the deck.

"Captain's cabin," I yelled, hoping that my intuition was correct, and sprinted forward again. Reaching the accommodation door I kicked the dead Nazi aside, and yanked it open, forgetting in my haste there could be men behind it ready to shoot. But the passage was empty. The door to the captain's cabin was open. I paused, holding the Webley in front of me, and stepped into the doorway, conscious that at any moment a bullet could tear into my chest. There was more firing from the deck below. I took a deep breath, and darted into the cabin.

Two grim faced Nazi officers looked round in surprise. One, in the tropical white uniform of a U-boat captain, was holding a Luger to the head of a man bound to a chair. A big man, bare-chested, his face almost unrecognizable under a mess of blood and bruises, one eye swollen shut. The other was aiming a machine gun at three men lying on the floor, their hands cuffed behind their backs and their legs bound.

I felt a twinge of regret at the likely fate of the Nazi captain, when the *Nimrod's* crew caught sight of Jim Coffin being used as a punching bag.

"Halt!" the Nazi captain snarled, recovering his poise, his voice loaded with arrogant authority. "If anyone moves I shall pull ze trigger and kill your precious Captain Coffin." He looked me directly in the eye. "If you are in charge of zese men, zen I suggest you tell zem to lay down zeir veapons before anyone else gets hurt. Schnell!"

"Go ahead, shoot the Nazi bastard," croaked Coffin, his voice defiant, despite the beating he had taken.

The U-boat captain's eyes were hard and cruel, and I knew he would shoot Coffin out of hand, given the chance. Perhaps it would be the last action of a desperate man once he realised the game was up. Or perhaps Melek had failed, the bodies of his men, and mine, bleeding out their lives on the foredeck, overpowered by the better-disciplined Nazis. Because, outside, the shooting had stopped, and all I could hear was the clatter of boots climbing the stairs from the main deck.

I steeled myself for the moment of truth. If we had failed then the men who appeared through the doorway would be Nazis. I could take a chance and pull the trigger on their captain, but he would almost certainly kill Coffin once he saw my intention. The Somali's and the rest of the Nazis would open fire and we would all perish in the crossfire. Perhaps the U-boat captain had come to the same conclusion. A wicked grin spread across his arrogant features, and he pressed the muzzle of his pistol to Coffin's head.

"Last chance, before I shoot him."

But it was Cramp who pushed through the doorway, with Melek and Hakim behind him, their excited faces turning black with anger when they saw what the Nazis had done to Coffin and the others.

A relieved grin spread across my face.

"I wouldn't do that if I were you, Captain. Your men have surrendered, the *Nimrod* is ours. If you so much as hurt another hair on Jim Coffin's head I won't answer for what his men will do to you. But it will be long, slow and infinitely painful."

Melek drew a wicked looking curved knife from his belt, and thumbed the blade.

Arrogant to the last the Nazi captain eyed me calmly. "I think you are forgetting. I also have a submarine. If you harm me, then it vill sink zis ship, and kill you all."

"Blue flare." I heard the boatswain's voice calling from the boat deck.

I smiled, the sweet flush of victory infusing my grin. "I don't think so, Captain, we have your submarine too."

* * *

"Bluey," Grim Jim Coffin yelled down the voice pipe to the engine room. "Get steam up, I want to be ready to sail as soon as possible after sunrise."

Dawn was not far off, the eastern sky already paling, but over the islands to the west the night was still dark. I stood on the bridge wing of the *Nimrod*, a Verey pistol in my hand preparing to fire a flare. I raised the pistol, pulled the trigger and a bright green flare soared into the lightening sky. I opened the breech, ejected the cartridge and loaded another. Moments later a second green flare burst high over the bay, the signal for Griffith to bring *Oriental Venture* in to join us.

With his purple, swollen shut eye, livid bruises, and wounds dabbed with iodine, Coffin looked a sight to frighten horses, never mind small children. But I knew he had copped worse beatings, and his face wore a lopsided grin as he set Melek and his crew to work clearing up the mess left behind by the firefight. Two dead German sailors were laid out on the boat deck, their corpses respectfully covered in lengths of canvas. Two others were in the sick bay where Lowther was doing his best to save them from permanent disablement. One had taken a shot right through the shoulder, smashing bones on the way. Lowther had given him a shot of morphine, manipulated the bones back into place as best he could, and bound the shoulder to his chest. He would need a hospital to reset the shattered bones. The other had taken a bullet in the thigh, which Lowther had extracted with a pair of long nosed pliers, filling the wound with sulphur powder and bandaging it. Despite the amount of shooting, I was relieved to find that none of my own crew, or that of the *Nimrod*, had suffered more than superficial cuts from flying splinters. The U-boat captain, his first lieutenant, and the rest of the surviving Germans were now locked in the forecastle, with a couple of cutthroat Malay seamen to guard them.

On the U-boat itself, in addition to the two lookouts, one of whom had been the second lieutenant, several men had been killed, and a larger number injured in the internal explosions that had destroyed the galley, and seriously damaged the control room. The engines, however, were unharmed and the boat was safe to motor on the surface, but would not be able to dive without repairs. To be on the safe side, however, Spencer disabled the 88mm deck gun, removing the breech and dropping it overboard.

After the final grenade had been dropped into the control room, the U-boat's crew had streamed up out of the hull, many holding their heads, dazed, deafened and bleeding from the ears, their eardrums fractured by the blast. Spencer had made them sit on the deck, with Ratu and Bema stationed on the gun platform, covering them with their Bergmanns, while he and Lowther made a thorough search of the boat. Making certain it was secure, he had fired the blue flare to confirm its capture. They had then ordered the German sailors below with orders to wait there for the return of their captain. Ratu and three of the *Nimrod's* seamen were standing guard, with orders to shoot anyone who as much as showed a hair above the deck.

As soon as they heard the first grenade explode inside the submarine, Melek and his men had swarmed aboard *Nimrod's* forecastle, almost catching the Nazi seamen completely by surprise. They had fought back though, keeping Melek's men pinned down on the foredeck, until the arrival of the boatswain, and his ragtag band of Chinese pirates turned the tide. Caught in the crossfire between Melek's men and mine, the Nazi sailors had decided the old tramp was not worth more of their lives, and had laid down their weapons.

I was thankful it was over. I had no idea how the U-boat's captain would explain his losses, and the damage to his boat. But frankly I didn't care. He had committed an act of piracy in international waters, and had suffered the consequences. In any case, Spencer assured me his report to the military authorities would exonerate me from any accusations the Nazi government might level. So all I had left to do was get my ship back, and persuade Coffin to carry a passenger.

"So Bill Rowden," he drawled, interrupting my train of thought. "Lucky for me you heard my radio signal. I was beginning to wonder whether I could deal with that Nazi bastard on my own."

"Jim Coffin, you know you're a sight to frighten the very devil."

"Yeah, well perhaps if you'd got here more quickly. But then I don't expect that old *Oriental Vagabond* of yours can make more than eight knots downwind." He laughed, his chest heaving, and winced at the stabbing pain of the bruises and cracked ribs. "Don't make me laugh, it hurts. But like I said, I'm dammed grateful to you. Those Nazis were playing hardball."

"I think your man Ratu would have eventually figured a way to free your crew, and get back on board," I replied, grinning. "Odd looking bunch of pirates you have there, but obviously some good men amongst them."

"Pirates!" snorted Coffin. "Just good, honest sailor men trying to make a living."

"Ratu's a fine navigator too, we wouldn't have got through the reef without him. Told me his grandfather taught him."

"His grandfather used to eat people," said Coffin, his bloodied lips curling into a painful looking grin. "But he can sure navigate, better than both my mates, even with their sextants." He dabbed a non-too clean handkerchief at his lip. "But what gets me," he continued, "is why those Nazi bastards were looking for you in the first place. They damn near tore my ship apart looking for something. They were convinced she was the *Oriental Venture*. Thought I was some stand in skipper trying to take them for a ride." He shook his head, wincing at the pain of the beating. "I've a mind to go forward and have a private chat with that Kraut skipper. Find out if he can take it as well as he can dish it out."

"Some Nazis tried to pull spun yarn over my eyes, and use *Oriental Venture* to run guns into New Guinea," I replied. "I found them, and ... confiscated them. Seems they were meant for some sort of supply base among the islands, for the replenishment of U-boats and surface raiders. The Nazis realised I'd taken them and wanted them back. They tried once before, a German ship called the *Dortmund* tracked us to Manus, and attacked us there, but we fought them off."

"Jeez, and you call us pirates. Sounds like you ain't no different. But tell me Bill, what's this about some business you wants my help with?"

"You received that message then?"

"Sparks picked it up right before we sighted that Nazi bastard. With him trailing us I was a bit preoccupied."

I grinned. "It's something I think you'll rather enjoy." I was about to tell him, when a blast on a ship's horn grabbed our attention and we raised our eyes to see *Oriental Venture* slowly nosing her way into the bay.

A surprised whistle escaped Coffin's lips. "Jeez, she really is identical to the *Nimrod*. I couldn't tell them apart, no wonder those Krauts had trouble. But tell me something, if you and your chief mate are here, whose driving that old tub."

He whistled again when I told him the second mate was in charge, and Coffin watched with admiration, as Griffith manoeuvred the ship to a position about a quarter of a mile away. The anchor splashed into the water, and I could imagine his relief.

"Seems like a good man you got there. Not sure I'd trust my second mate, Joe Flynn, to do anything so pretty. But here's another question, who's that army guy you're carrying, Major Spencer. Seems a handy man to know when the lead's flying."

I considered the question carefully, wondering how much I should tell him.

"He's the Australian military attaché in Port Moresby. Travelling with us as a passenger to Davao, and hoping to catch an onward passage home from there."

"You don't say? The stories Ratu and Bema are telling about him and your chief mate bombing that submarine. Don't sound like no desk bound, cocktail swilling, attaché to me."

There was a discrete cough at his elbow, and Coffin turned to see Major Spencer frowning at him.

"What's that about being a desk bound cocktail swiller?"

"No offence meant, Major, but where I come from a military attaché is usually some passed over bird colonel that the Pentagon needs to keep out of trouble."

Spencer broke into a broad grin. "None taken, Captain Coffin. But you chaps don't have an Empire to run, and only a handful of troops to do it. Makes the job of keeping a tab on what your neighbours are up to quite important I'd say."

"Thought your Royal Navy was what kept your tea drinking, perpetual sun shining Empire afloat."

"They're good for scaring pirates, old boy. But when there's any real fighting to be done."

Coffin looked like he was about to laugh, remembered his cracked ribs and thought better of it.

"Well I'd say when it comes to fighting, judging by how your boys and my boys fared last night, the odds are about even. Whadya say?" He held out his hand, and Spencer shook it.

"I wouldn't argue with that."

Coffin turned back to me.

"Now, Bill, about this business I can help you with. As I said, I did get your radio message, but I was a bit tied up trying to shake off a U-boat at the time."

"Before I answer that Jim, can you tell me where you're heading?"

"Sure, it ain't no secret. I was on my way from Bougainville to Manila when the sub started chasing us. I've got a cargo of canned pineapples, palm oil and copra waiting there, bound for San Francisco."

"Okay. How do you feel about carrying a passenger?"

"A passenger. Since when did you start carrying passengers?" replied Coffin, laughing, despite the ribs.

"It's a long story. But this one's a refugee from the fighting in China. Came aboard in Shanghai, looking for a way to get to America," I said.

"Don't they all. What's he like? Can he pay the passage?"

Spencer glanced at me, his face split into a wide grin.

"Come on," said Coffin. "What gives?"

"This passenger is a lady, and yes, she can afford to pay the passage."

"A dame, you want me to carry a godammed dame. Hell, we're hardly fit to carry passengers, let alone dames."

"Calm down, Jim," I replied. "She won't be any trouble to you. If you're calling at Manila you can lay in anything she needs there, and she'll pay you for it. Truth is she's escaping some bad things in her past. She needs to make a new start somewhere, and needs someone who can get her there discretely, without asking too many questions."

"And you think I'm the guy on the white horse?" Coffin stopped, and his battered face twisted into a rueful smile. I knew there was plenty in his past he was not proud of. But, despite his denial, a woman looking for a way to escape and start over, was surely bound to appeal to the sense of chivalry I knew still lurked in his red-blooded American breast. Even if he did try damned hard to hide it.

He shrugged his shoulders and the lopsided grin widened. "Okay, let me meet the dame, and we can talk it over."

* * *

"Good morning to you too, Captain Rowden. No I couldn't sleep thinking about Mr Lowther and Major Spencer, and all of you. Was it really so necessary to risk your lives. Surely once the Germans realised their mistake they would have let the *Nimrod* go?"

I was back aboard *Oriental Venture,* and had knocked on Helena's door, to find her fully dressed and pacing the suite like a dangerously beautiful wildcat.

"Perhaps, but their colleagues were quite prepared to kill us when they attacked us at Lorengau. And if Jim Coffin couldn't convince them of his innocence, God knows what they would have done to him and his men. But surely, from what I've heard about you, you must know there's something bigger at play here. If the Nazis are bent on war then we can't let them control the trade routes. Britain depends on its ships for its food, fuel and raw materials. The Germans nearly strangled us last time with their U-boats, and it looks as if they're preparing to try the same again." I paused, suddenly conscious that I was sounding ridiculously pontifical.

"Yes, yes, I've heard all that before, from that funny little Winston Churchill." She paused, her face creasing into a frown, her fingers twisting the diamond ring and the plain gold band on her finger. "But that's all in the past." The frown faded, replaced by a smile that lit up her face, as if she had passed from darkness into light. "So tell me, what is he like ... this Captain Coffin?"

"He's a New Englander from Boston," I replied, happy to change the subject. "Big hearted, but with a big temper to match. A good friend but a bad enemy. Most people who cross him live to regret it."

"You make him sound positively dangerous. Should I be afraid of him?" There was a touch of coquetry in her voice.

"He's a bit rough around the edges but I don't think you ... I don't think you'll have much trouble with him. He doesn't have much experience with English ladies. The bar girls in Manila and Nagasaki are more his style."

"But, is he to be trusted?"

"I'm sure your ... reputation, will be safe enough."

Helena erupted into peals of laughter. "I didn't mean that. I'm not worried about arriving in the United States with my honour intact. I just want to get there without arousing any suspicion. Lady Ashworth and Helena Kovtoun are dead, and need to stay that way."

I thought I was too old and grizzled for blushing, but I still felt the flush of blood to my cheeks. If I was going to start worrying about the moral welfare of a woman who had risen from Russian dancer to aristocrat, then perhaps I really ought to also confine my attentions to bar girls in future.

"No better man than Jim Coffin to keep a secret. But don't take my word for it, you'll be able to decide for yourself shortly."

"And what about you Bill Rowden. Now that you can finally get me off your hands. Are you happy to see the back of me?"

"It's been a pleasure having you on board." I regretted the pompously silly words as soon as I uttered them, and was not surprised to hear Helena chuckle.

"Oh, so bourgeois. But you were not at all pleased when Mr Khoo made you carry me to Shanghai."

"Was it so obvious?" She was right, but I'd thought we'd made a fair fist of it, for a battered old tramp.

"Oh yes, but you did try to be a gentleman."

It was my turn to laugh. "One thing I'll never be is a gentleman. Haven't you heard your friend Lady Astor's suggestion that merchant seamen should wear a yellow armband, to warn good girls of the diseases they might catch from them?"

"Lady Astor was a friend of Lady Ashworth, she's no friend of mine. But that does sound the sort of thing she would say." Helena paused, smiling, then continued. "I heard someone once say that no man is a gentleman to his tailor. Please don't think me immodest, but I can tell you that without their clothes, you can't tell a gentleman from a lout."

I could have as equally well replied that without their clothes, ladies and bar girls were also indistinguishable. But since she had raised the subject I decided to push my luck. "I would have thought you capable of working out the difference before they got to that condition."

"Captain Rowden!" she protested, pretending to fan her face. "I think I mis-judged you. I took you for the strong, silent type, wedded to his profession and without much experience of the niceties of polite conversation with ladies."

"I haven't had the pleasure of spending much time in the company of ladies. And my relations with women have usually been more mercenary than affectionate."

"Well perhaps we have something in common there," she replied, smiling ruefully. "I've had my share of mercenary relationships."

Then she stepped forward and placed a hand on my arm. "In another time and in another place, perhaps." Her voice was wistful. "But the world is about to be torn apart and our lives with it. And who knows what will happen before it is over. You have your ship and I will have my new life in Hollywood. If I make it maybe you will see me on the screen. Who knows, perhaps you will visit Los Angeles, if so it cannot be that hard to find a famous actress. And if I don't make it? Well, you will still have your ship." She withdrew the hand and turned away. "Thank you for saving me Captain Rowden. Now I must go and finish packing my things. Think of me some-times."

Two hours later, we rowed Helena and her trunks over to the *Nimrod*, and made our way up to Coffin's day cabin, aft of the chartroom, the identical position to my own aboard *Oriental Venture*. She was dressed in comfortable slacks and a loose fitting blouse, but had taken care with her makeup, and her face showed no traces of the beating she had taken from Maslennikov. Coffin rose from his chair and greeted her open mouthed, gingerly taking her hand, and mumbling a self-conscious welcome.

"My goodness, Captain Coffin, I do believe you're staring," she said, returning his gaze just as intently, obviously intrigued by the big, fiery looking man whose bruised and swollen face with its large crooked nose could easily have intimidated her.

"I'm sorry ma'am," Coffin replied. "I'm afraid we don't get too many lady pas-sengers in this old tub." Then, apparently recovering his composure, and tipping me a sly wink. "Not like the luxury that I'm sure you've been accustomed to over there with Captain Rowden."

"But the ships are identical ..." Helena began, before seeing the twinkle in Coffin's eye, and realised he was teasing her.

Coffin gestured that we should find a seat. I took the battered armchair, and Major Spencer and Lowther the settee, with Helena perched between them. There was a large coffee pot on the desk, and Coffin poured us each a cup of the strong, fortifying liquid.

"Bill tells me you need passage to the United States," he said, as soon as we were settled. "With someone who don't ask too many questions. I can offer you that, lady. But despite the ships being sisters, you won't find my men quite as gentleman-ly as Captain Rowden and his officers."

"A gentleman is just a man who buys two of the same morning paper from the doorman of his favourite nightclub, when he leaves with his girl," Helena replied coolly. "All I ask is for privacy."

"As a fare paying passenger you call the shots, lady. Anyone bothers you, you tell me and he'll regret the day he was born."

Helena smiled serenely at him. If anyone could take care of herself she could, and I grinned, knowing she had already sized up Grim Jim, and knew exactly how to deal with the big American.

"I'm sure we'll all get along just fine Captain Coffin. Why don't you introduce me to your officers?"

Coffin sent his steward scurrying off to fetch them, and introduced them as they arrived. Pug Murphy, the first mate, an Irish American. Short and thickset with pow-erful shoulders, heavy jawed with a thick black beard. Joe Flynn, British, formerly a Royal Navy signalman who had served in the *Barham*. Bluey Case, the Australian chief engineer, his luxuriant red hair now streaked with grey. Helena shook each of their hands and confidently returned their inquisitive glances. It was going to be an interesting trip for all of them I thought, remembering something Mae West had said, "A dame that knows the ropes ain't likely to get tied up." Helena knew the ropes, well enough at least to tie any love hungry sailors in knots, and I could see that she and Coffin would get along fine. It was time we returned to *Oriental Venture* and got underway. I swallowed the final mouthful of my coffee and stood up.

"Just a moment," said Helena. "Before you go, there's an old Russian custom I should like to observe. Captain Coffin, do you have any glasses?"

He crossed to the sideboard, opened the door, and lifted eight glass tumblers onto the desk.

Helena raised herself from the settee and looked at each of us in turn.

"Thank you all for everything you have done. I will always remember you... all of you ... and you're ship." Her voice faltered, and she blinked back a tear. When she continued her voice had recovered its strength. "In Russia, whenever people part to go on a journey, it is the custom to drink a glass of vodka together. Captain Coffin has kindly provided the glasses." She reached down to the capacious handbag at her feet and pulled a full bottle of vodka from it. She handed it to Coffin who produced a corkscrew from his desk drawer, and deftly extracted the cork. Handed the bottle back, Helena divided it equally among the eight glasses. She picked one up and we gathered round and took one each.

"In Russia we do not say good bye. We say, *dasvedanya*, until we meet." She raised her glass. "*Dasvedanya*."

"*Dasvedanya*," we echoed."

Helena threw her head back, drained the glass in one gulp, and slammed it onto the table with bang.

"Lady!" exclaimed Coffin in admiration. "Looks like it's gonna be a swell voyage."

* * *

The farewell blast from *Nimrod's* whistle shattered the calm of the bay causing a flock of sea birds to take fright.

I watched from the bridge wing as Jim Coffin conned his ship out of the anchorage. Slipping past us, and then, with gathering speed, ploughing forcefully through the opening in the reef and out into the Pacific. The slender figure of Helena, her auburn hair streaming in the breeze, waved at us from the boat deck and I watched until I could no longer distinguish her.

I turned and looked astern. The rescue boat had returned from the U-boat, having delivered her captain and his crew, plus two corpses sewn into canvas. Lowther and Major Spencer had accompanied them; their Bergmanns trained onto the Germans in case they had any further thought of resistance. Fortunately, the fight seemed to have gone out of them, nonetheless I breathed a sigh of relief when all the boats were safely hoisted in board. I caught sight of Spencer clambering out of the boat with what looked like a big typewriter in his arms, but then forgot about it in the flurry of orders for departure.

"Hoist away," I yelled to McGrath on the forecastle, and heard the clanking of the windlass as it began to haul the anchor from the seabed.

The docking telegraph rang, followed by Lowther's confirmatory, "Anchor's aweigh."

"Slow ahead ... starboard ten ... midships ... steady as she goes."

Oriental Venture gathered way, her bows rising to meet the easterly swell as she forged through the gap in the reef, the water changing colour from turquoise to the deep, cobalt of the ocean.

"Full away. Set course for Davao, Mr Lowther. You have the ship."

"Aye aye, sir."

Printed in Great Britain
by Amazon